Edward Bellasis

Memorials of Mr. Serjeant Bellasis, 1800-1873

Edward Bellasis

Memorials of Mr. Serjeant Bellasis, 1800-1873

ISBN/EAN: 9783337092634

Printed in Europe, USA, Canada, Australia, Japan

Cover: Foto ©Raphael Reischuk / pixelio.de

More available books at **www.hansebooks.com**

MEMORIALS

OF

MR. SERJEANT BELLASIS

(1800-1873)

BY EDWARD BELLASIS,

LANCASTER HERALD.

Author of "Cherubini: Memorials illustrative of his Life.

"Quærite ergo primum regnum Dei et justitiam ejus, et hæc omnia adjicientur vobis."—S. MATT. vi. 33.

PREFACE.

In the religious revival within the English Protestant Establishment some sixty years ago, Catholic principles received a testimony to their genuineness in successfully appealing, amongst other classes, to the lawyers; to the trained intellects of "a grave profession that is especially employed in rubbing off the gloss with which imagination and sentiment invest every-day life, and in reducing statements of fact to their legitimate dimensions."[1] Such an advocate as Hope-Scott, whom Mr. Gladstone regarded as "distinctly at the head of all his contemporaries in the brightness and beauty of his gifts,"[2] may be said to have embodied the best that the profession of Blessed Thomas More could contribute in later days to the ranks of faithful seekers for the one Eternal Truth.

Revolving, too, so to speak, round that brilliant forensic luminary, readers of Hope-Scott's *Memoirs* will not fail to note two other lights in Edward Badeley and Edward Bellasis. The three were fast friends. The ties between Hope-Scott and Badeley are sufficiently indicated in Mr. Ornsby's narrative; while, in illustration of the intimacy between Badeley and Bellasis, it may be mentioned that no Christmas-tide passed but the Serjeant took his children to see

[1] Dedicatory Letter to Badeley, p. v. in Cardinal Newman's *Verses on Various Occasions*, Ed. 1888.

[2] Ornsby's *Memoirs of James Robert Hope-Scott of Abbotsford, D.C.L., Q.C.*, vol. ii. p. 274, 1st Ed.

Badeley at Paper Buildings; they saw him yearly,
too, at their Christmas Day feast, and knew who had
supplied the turkey. The connection between Hope-
Scott and Bellasis has been less clearly shown. "God
bless you, my dear friend," wrote the former to the
Serjeant in 1868, "for you are very dear to me, and
to many more besides." Then, when J. G. Lockhart
died, Bellasis wrote to Hope-Scott, "God rest his
soul. . . . Your friendship makes it impossible that
anything can happen to you that is indifferent to me."
Brought together in 1840, they quitted the Anglican
communion within six months of one another in the
beginning of the 'fifties, and more especially after that
event, they became as brothers in their mutual con-
fidences. As co-trustees of the Shrewsbury estates,
they were fellow-labourers in the ten years' conduct
of a *cause célèbre;* they alike argued before Lords
and Commons Committees, occupied identical law-
chambers (at first in Parliament Street, and then in
Victoria Street, Westminster), wintered abroad for
years on adjoining properties at Hyères, and finally
died in 1873, about the same time. "There was a
great deal in common in the dear Serjeant and Hope-
Scott," wrote Dr. Newman when these survivors of
Badeley were gone. "This similarity," he continues,
"is what made them such great friends; and, therefore, in mercy, we may say, they were taken away
so nearly together, that one might not lose the other.
One thinks of the words of Scripture—'They were
lovely in their lives and in their deaths were not
divided.'"

Hope-Scott, Badeley, and Bellasis afford examples
of clever men of business, always industrious, but
never too occupied to attend to the affair of their
own souls and of the souls of others in any way

dependent upon them. Albeit in the world they were not worldly men. They were men of strong and balanced character. They were looked up to by many, and for their attractive qualities they were widely and affectionately esteemed. "To inspire love was their special characteristic. They were so honest and so true."[1] Moreover, they were prosperous, and attained to eminence in their professional careers, so that these words of Divine assurance might fitly come at the head of any notice of them: "Seek ye first the kingdom of God and His justice, and all other things shall be added unto you." Mourners, indeed, around the bier of Hope-Scott at Farm Street Church were reminded in poignant words how much in his case had been likewise "taken away": "through much tribulation," he entered "the kingdom of God," whereas the Serjeant's life, taken as a whole, would not be inaptly summed up as "equable and sunny."

It has been deemed that some notice of Mr. Serjeant Bellasis, beyond the two or three columns in the *National Dictionary of Biography*, would not be out of place among the Memoirs of the time; for the late Serjeant, although not one of the more conspicuous public men of his day, nevertheless played some part in the Tractarian Movement of 1833, in connection wherewith he has left papers of interest. He was also an able, and, for nearly a quarter of a century, a notable member of the Catholic body.

[1] Letter of Dr. Newman, May 10, 1873.

TABLE OF CONTENTS.

—

CHAPTER I

CHAPTER III.

LIST OF ILLUSTRATIONS.

CHAPTER I.

BIRTH AND PARENTAGE.   SCHOOL-DAYS.   EARLY PATRONS.
POLITICS.   PROFESSIONAL CAREER.

EDWARD BELLASIS was born the day after St. Edward's day in
the year 1800 at Basilden Vicarage, a pretty spot on the
Thames, situate to the right of the Great Western main line,
going from Pangbourne to Goring, on the Berkshire side of
the river.   He was baptized on the 20th of November following.
Before he was two years of age he lost his father, a clergyman,
according to his friend Edmund Lodge, Norroy, "of remarkable
talents and acquirements."

George Bellasis, the Serjeant's father, was very tall in stature,
and old inhabitants of Kendal forty years ago could still recall
his imposing appearance as he came along Stricklandgate, with
periwig and bob-tail, and a gold knobbed cane.   Among
several fine portraits of him by Abbott, Fothergill, and others,
he is depicted in wig and gown as a Doctor of Divinity, and
in one case holding a roll of music in his hand, since besides
possessing a ready pencil, he was skilful on the violin, violoncello, and organ.   Thus the *Cumberland Pacquet* of June 3,
1789, in recording an occasion when the Mayor and Corporation
of Kendal attended in state a service at the parish church, adds
that the organist being ill, Dr. Bellasis "took upon him the
additional condescension of playing the organ, after which he
preached with great energy and persuasion a sermon suitable for
the occasion."   Dr. Bellasis, a native of Westmoreland, was born
in 1730, educated at Appleby School, and Queen's College,
Oxford, and at length, in those good old days for pluralists, he
held simultaneously for several decades of years three Berkshire
livings, Yattendon, Basilden, and Ashampstead.   By his first
wife, Margaret Harvey, daughter of an incumbent of Pangbourne, allied to the Lybbes of Hardwick, he had two sons and
a daughter, who all lived and died childless in India, where their
uncle, General John Bellasis, Commander of the Forces at
Bombay, had preceded them in 1763. The elder son, Joseph, one

B

of the Indian military adventurers,[1] of whom Avitabile, Allard, Court, Ventura, and de Boigne were the most celebrated, was killed while storming a fort near Lahar, in the Mahratta States in 1799, and the younger, George, received in the same year a gold medal for gallantry as Commandant of Horse Brigade at the celebrated siege and battle of Seringapatam. Dr. Bellasis had married a second time, June 9, 1796, Leah Cooper Viall, only surviving child of Emery Viall, and on his death-bed he lamented that his two children by his second wife would not recollect him. He desired, accordingly, that the elder of the two might follow him to his grave as chief mourner, holding a black ribbon tied to the handle of the coffin. This the Serjeant's sister did, being four years old at the time, and thus remembered something about her father. Their mother, a lady of singular beauty, was born in 1763, at Walsingham, in Norfolk. Her son tells us that she had "an extraordinary talent for learning, and an indefatigable determination in the pursuit of it." "Calm and composed," she had "forethought and method" too, and "was an excellent accountant," and "initiated me in mathematics and astronomy as well as in French." "During her whole life," he adds, "I never heard her speak ill of any one, and never heard her use an angry word."[2] In General Bellasis' opinion, she was "a wonderful, excellent, and accomplished woman."

In June, 1802, she writes of her son, the future Serjeant: "I have a hundred pretty things to tell of my Edward." In September: "Edward is one of the stoutest and strongest boys I have seen of his age, and most engaging; he attempts to talk everything, and makes himself understood;" and in November: "Edward is so fine a boy that I am scarcely believed when I tell his age, two years and one month." In 1804 Mrs. Bellasis married as her second husband the Rev. Joseph Maude, and lived till 1808 within the precincts of Reading Abbey ruins. From Abbey House she writes in October, 1804, "Edward is a lovely boy, and of a very affectionate temper, though high-spirited. He is just

---

[1] See Major Lewis Ferdinand Smith's *Sketch of the Rise, Progress, and Termination of the Regular Corps formed and commanded by Europeans in the service of the native Princes of India;* also the *Calcutta Review,* July, 1880, No. cxli. art. 3, "Indian Military Adventurers of the Last Century"; and Sir Henry Lawrence's *Some Passages in the life of an Adventurer in the Punjaub* (Delhi, 1842), in which Bellasis is made the hero of a fiction founded on fact.

[2] MS. Autobiography of Mr. Serjeant Bellasis. Where no other document is cited, any words of the Serjeant quoted must be taken as coming from this manuscript.

come in from school. His first inquiry is always whether mamma is at home, and then he comes with his fine, intelligent blue eyes to relate all the wonders he has seen. He has now brought me his new spelling-book to let me hear how well he can read part of the 118th Psalm." In 1808 young Bellasis was sent to Christ's Hospital, where he remained seven years and a half, "a long dull time," he calls it, "thrice only during the whole time had I any holiday away from school," and his occasional "leaves," for a day or so, he spent with two Wesleyan Methodist families, the only people he knew about London outside the Hospital. "Whether it was that the qualities I afterwards exhibited did not come to maturity while I was at school," he continues, "or whether the paucity of masters made it difficult for a boy to get on, or whether a certain slowness of apprehension retarded my progress amongst others quicker than myself, I cannot say, but I think the two latter combined to obtain for me the character of being idle. My mother, who came to see me in 1814 when I was thirteen years of age, was told by the head-master, Dr. Trollope : 'Madam, he is a bad boy.' I thought this unjust and was not conscious of deserving it at the time, though I admit I frequently did not know my lessons and must have seemed to him to be idle. However, I never exhibited this quality afterwards, when I left school, but became in after-life as industrious and persevering as it was possible to be." On leaving school he went to a solicitor's office, but at the advice of Sir Alan Chambre, one of the Judges, and a friend of his mother's, he ultimately entered as a student at the Inner Temple in 1819, and on July 2, 1824, was called to the Bar, and put on wig and gown for the first time in the Court of Chancery, Lord Eldon being then Chancellor.

Among his early friends were Lewis Hayes Petit, a barrister, who filled his shelves with law-books, and Edmund Lodge, the herald and author. How he got to know Petit, he can relate himself: "In the year 1816, whilst living with my mother at Stafford, on occasion of the Assizes, I had wandered as a boy into the County Hall to see if I could get to hear some of the proceedings, and was standing tip-toeing at the outskirts of the crowd, when I felt a hand on each shoulder pushing me on towards a green table, above which the Judges were sitting. On turning round I perceived it was a barrister in a wig. He asked me who I was and whether I would like to stay and

hear some of the trials, and I did in fact stay all that day, and
met him by appointment in court the next day. He asked me
to come and call on him in London; this I did. He took me
by the hand, gave me my first Blackstone, had me frequently
to dine with him, and introduced me to his friends." A curious
but comfortable high-backed chair with Petit's initials painted
thereon, was his gift to Mr. Bellasis, and remained a feature
in the latter's study for nearly fifty years. His intimacy
with Lodge was owing to an equally accidental circumstance.
"Among my father's papers," he writes, "were some letters
from him, showing him to have been an intimate friend;
but my father had been dead twenty years and my mother
had never known him. I had been rowing on the Thames,
and had landed at the stairs at the bottom of Bennett's Hill,
and walking up towards St. Paul's, I saw a brass plate on
the door, 'Mr. Lodge, Lancaster Herald,' so I knocked at the
door, and, on making myself known to my father's friend,
was received with open arms. . . . He was a scholar, and
a very elegant writer, and was the author of *Lodge's Portraits
of Illustrious Personages*, and of *Illustrations of British History*.
His society was also of advantage to me, as I met there
literary men, among others Mr. John Gage (afterwards Gage-
Rokewode, a Catholic gentleman) and Theodore Hook. . . .
Another friend I had at this time (1818) was the Rev. John
Maude, Fellow of Queen's College, Oxford, a younger brother
of my step-father, and I used to get an annual invitation
from him to spend a week there at the time of Founder's
day, where I met agreeable society." The painters, Sir George
Hayter and Daniel Maclise, became also acquainted with Mr.
Bellasis, and about 1831, Maclise, then an unknown man, took
excellent portraits of him and his first wife, his mother and sister,
General Edward Bellasis, Edmund Lodge, and other friends.
He also got to know Professor Faraday, and Dr. Neils Arnott,[1]
author of the *Elements of Physics*, and became one of the
"managers" of the Royal Institution. This scientific connection
developed his innate love for science which later on became
of great assistance to him in his profession.

At first he practised exclusively in the Court of Chancery,
save in the case of two election petitions in 1838, *i.e.*, those of
Shaftesbury and Salford. His father-in-law, Mr. Garnett, as

---

[1] The Serjeant saw him exercise successfully mesmeric power. This, though of
great professional assistance to him, brought the doctor into a little disrepute with
some.

Edward Ballatis

Tory candidate for Salford in 1837, lost the seat by only one vote. In a subsequent contest there in 1841 the Serjeant says : " I had no notion that bribery was going on, nor do I believe that Mr. Garnett knew it, but towards the end of the day, when it was plain we were not to succeed, ... one of the committee asked me to take two bags to a place of safety. They were bags of gold. I put one into each of my coat-pockets, and passed through the mob with them, but they were so heavy, that I was afraid they would tear my coat-tails off." "The construction of the then Election Petitions Committees," he remarks, " as well as their decisions, were so unsatisfactory, the latter depending entirely upon the party majority in the Committee, that I determined that I would take no more political cases." " I had always been a Tory in politics," he elsewhere says, "but at this time (1835) I had become very political, and was one of the most active members of the Constitutional Association, established to counteract the effect of the Reform Bill; there were constant meetings in various parts of London, the object being to obtain a knowledge of the real extent of the Conservative party, as it then began to be called." A visit, however, to the House of Commons in December, 1837, must have convinced him, had he ever thought of entering Parliament, that his sensitive nature could never have put up with politics as a career. The questions he heard debated in a very full House were a proposal to compensate the late Speaker, Lord Canterbury, for losses sustained by the burning of the Houses of Parliament, and the propriety of dismissing Colonel Verner for drinking at his own table to the toast of " The Battle of the Diamond." One was not, and the other was, a party question, yet both were decided on strictly party lines. " I paid great attention," he writes, " to the whole proceedings and came away disgusted in the highest degree. I expected, of course, some sharpness of argument and expression in a discussion carried on *vivâ voce*, on topics of interest, but I was not prepared for the acerbity of manner and language, the disingenuousness of statement, the want of courtesy and the general animosity which was obvious at once to a person unaccustomed to the scene ; the cheers of exultation when anything was said calculated to wound the feelings of one of the opposite party, the shouts of triumph at the utterance of any ill-natured retort, the snarling tone of almost all, mingled with the roars of laughter at any casual mistake or slip of language, made the assembly appear

like a meeting of childish demons rather than Christian men."
In later years, he would complain that, although holding Conservative principles, yet as a Catholic in a Protestant country
he was compelled to *vote* only for that party, whether Conservative or Liberal, which might chance at the time to be the
more favourable in his opinion to the interests of his own
religion.

As a good adviser to others in important matters he seems
to have inspired confidence at an early age, and to have been
at times consulted by men much older than himself. A curious
illustration of this was his friend, Mr. Willoughby, coming to
ask his assistance in 1826 over a love affair. It seemed
that Mr. Willoughby had become attached to a cousin of
Mr. Bellasis, a daughter of Dr. Lawrence Gwynne, Sheriff of
London. Not knowing the lady's father, he asked Mr. Bellasis
to pen a letter for him to the Doctor, explaining his position
and prospects, with a view to becoming in due course, if
acceptable, a son-in-law. It was a difficult note to write, but
Mr. Bellasis wrote it and Mr. Willoughby signed it, and it went
off to Dr. Gwynne, who on receiving the letter showed it to
Mr. Bellasis, asked him what he thought of it, and since it was
not an easy one to answer—would he frame for him a reply
thereto? So Mr. Bellasis answered his own letter, the sequel
being a happy union between the parties immediately concerned.

In the same year, too, the Rev. Mr. Newcome, on being presented to Tottenham Vicarage, had been offered £200 a year
or so, in lieu of tithes, by the London merchants and traders
forming his parishioners, and on his objecting to its inadequacy,
and threatening proceedings, they formed a committee with a
common purse to defend any one who might be attacked.
Alarmed at the combination, Mr. Newcome was advised to
consult a young barrister of twenty-five, one Mr. Bellasis, who
had said there was no difficulty in the matter ; and this was
the advice young Bellasis gave : " If you go to law in face
of the common purse, you will be in litigation for years, and
the subscribers will hardly feel it, but if you will take a bold
course with them, they will be alarmed in their turn, and you
will have them at your feet." " Well, what do you recommend ? "
said his client. " Commence a separate suit in Chancery
against each of the committee ; some of them will give in, and
the rest will not act with diminished numbers and they will
give in, and the committee being broken up, all the parish will

come in." "This," says the Serjeant, "was done. We filed a Bill in Chancery against each of the twelve members of the committee; within a fortnight they had all given in; and the rest of the parish followed like a flock of sheep, and the income so produced was upwards of £1,000 a year."

An accidental circumstance led Mr. Bellasis before the Parliamentary Committees. The great era of railways was just commencing when, in 1835, he was engaged by his friend Mr. Wood, of Hanger Hill, near Ealing, to defend the latter's interests against the then projected Great Western Railway. "The first thing I had to do," he writes, "was to cross-examine the engineer, Mr. Brunel. . . . At that time no one knew anything of mechanics, and the simplest questions having relation to dynamics were discussed, and I became familiar with all the points relating to the motion and power of engines, their friction and gravity." The Christmas following his father-in-law was waited upon at his place, Lark Hill (now Peel Park), Salford, by George Stephenson with a deputation, come to ask Mr. Garnett to be chairman of a proposed company for making a railway from Manchester to Birmingham, to be called the South Union, in opposition to the Cheshire Junction Railway. Mr. Garnett consented, and Mr. Bellasis was retained as junior counsel. "I set myself," states the latter, "to master the subject with all my might. . . . We were ultimately successful, and as the whole of the work from day to day had in fact fallen upon me, so I succeeded in obtaining a certain reputation for a knowledge of such subjects, which never afterwards left me. . . . In its progress every possible dynamical question in relation to the working of railways was discussed and contested, as well as a vast variety of points, mathematical and mechanical, relating to their construction. Engineering talents of the highest order were enlisted on both sides, in fact the whole subject was exhausted." Thus he was thrown constantly with George Stephenson, his son Robert, Mr. Bidder, and other great civil engineers.

One of his most elaborately scientific cases came on in 1852, when the River Dee Company engaged the Serjeant to attend an inquiry instituted by Mr. Rennie, the engineer, on behalf of the Admiralty, prior to erecting what was called a Standard on the banks of that river, the purpose of which was to determine from time to time whether the Dee was kept by the Company at the statutory depth of sixteen feet below the high water mark

of "a moderate spring tide." The old Standard had been swept
away in a flood, and had not been replaced for sixty years, and
then, owing to the complaints of the merchants trading to
Chester, it had been replaced by a new one and after the lapse
of sixty years more, a doubt had now arisen as to whether this
second Standard truly represented the first. There was nothing
better to determine this properly, owing to the vague language
of the Act as to "a moderate spring tide" and other disturbing
causes, save a calculation based upon the seventy and sixty
years' observations of the respective Standards. The Astronomer
Royal, Professor Airy, was thereupon called in, and he termed
his mode of calculation the principle of "minimum squares,"
which came time after time before the committees and created
much interest and no little amusement owing to the difficulty of
explaining to non-scientific minds deep mathematical questions.
Nevertheless an attempt was made to cross-examine Mr. Airy.
Q. Well, Mr. Professor, you seem very confident in your conclusions. A. Yes, I am, very. Q. Could you oblige us ignorant
people with some explanation level with our capacities? A. I
will endeavour to do so, but it will be rather complicated.
Q. We will try to follow you as well as we can; please begin.
The Professor then entered upon a long A B C demonstration,
which so puzzled his questioner that there was a general laugh.
At length examining counsel gravely said: "I think, since you
have got so far as X, we will stop," on which Henry Merewether
said out loud, amid much merriment, "Don't stop at X, but
apply your Y Z (wise head) to it." The Serjeant, thinking
that people would comprehend this case better by seeing a
model of the Dee Standard, had taken great pains in con-
structing one. It was by no means a small apparatus, with a
glass tube and worked by a handle, and on being brought
into the committee-room by two men, Serjeant Merewether,
the opposing counsel, exclaimed: "Goodness, gracious, what
on earth is this? It must be a musical instrument." Then
with a rapid change of tone and facial expression, he added,
amid general laughter: "I see, it is my learned friend's
fiddle-de-Dee," an unexpected sally, which threw ridicule on
the machine, and rendered it useless for any serious explanatory
purpose.

Another amusing incident the Serjeant was wont to relate
in connection with a Scotch Bill before the Committee, in which
an uncle and a nephew took opposing sides, Hope-Scott being

counsel for the uncle, and Bellasis for the nephew. The Serjeant as a rule always refused to attend to business on a Sunday, but one Sunday morning this nephew sent in his card at breakfast time. With great reluctance the Serjeant admitted the young man to his study, heard all that he had to say, and then they parted. The nephew had not left the room a second or two, before he re-opened the door and said in a half-whisper: "You'll be so kind as not to tell my uncle you've seen me this Sabbath-day." The following morning the Serjeant was relating the incident to Hope-Scott, when the latter exclaimed: "Is it possible? why the uncle came to me yesterday for his talk, and on going out, entreated me on no account to mention to the nephew that he had been to see me on the Sabbath-day."

In 1836 Mr. Bellasis was occupied with a dispute between Lord Petre and the Eastern Counties Railway. The Directors proposed to intersect the former's property for seven miles, for the most part in deep cutting. Lord Petre kept hounds, and on objecting to such a route the Company agreed to bring in a Bill to vary it next year if he would now withdraw his opposition. The only legal method of doing this was by an agreement that if they took the objectionable route they would give him a sum, purposely put at so large a figure as to make it worth their while to keep their promise with him. The Company after-wards refused to vary their route, alleging that their agreement with Lord Petre was illegal, with the result that they had to pay the money. "This has ever since been quoted," writes the Serjeant, "as an instance of a landlord's rapacity, but this is unjust. Lord Petre only wished to avoid a seven mile ditch through his property, and it was I who inserted the penalty of £100,000. . . . When they tried to evade their contract, they were very properly made to pay."

The Parliamentary business at this time, he complains, "was conducted before both Houses by tribunals wholly unsatisfactory. The Committees were more or less open to all members, and although ordinarily ten or a dozen members might be present whilst the evidence was proceeding, if any decision was likely to take place, members were sent for, and came crowding into the committee-rooms to join in the vote. . . . I have known a committee . . . suddenly swell to sixty upon the approach of a division. Things were not quite so bad in the House of Lords, . . . but I remember that on one occasion after an argument on the South Union Railway Case when, as we believed, the members were equally divided, the Marquis of Londonderry, just as the division was about to take place, walked into the committee-room, . . . we were indignant at the interposition of a noble Lord, who had not heard a word of the evidence, and we said that this canvassing for votes was abominable. The decision was in our favour, and we afterwards discovered that the abominable canvassing had been ours, as the Marquis voted for us."

It was in 1844 that Bellasis received the degree of the coif, Mr. Badeley being his "colt," or attendant, in the quaint formalities, proceedings, and ceremonies attending the creation of a Serjeant-at-Law. Apropos of this event, he explains his case for promotion in a letter of Feb. 17, 1844, to Mr. Justice Coleridge, who had kindly interested himself in his behalf. "I have arrived at the position of being senior amongst the juniors habitually practising before Committees of the Houses of Parliament; there is in this present Session an unusually large amount of private business, so much in fact, as to be far more than can be done by those who usually practise before such Committees, and consequently there must and will be an influx of the Bar, both seniors and juniors from the other Courts to do it; if I am not able to take any position as a leader this Session, I probably lose the opportunity altogether, as persons my juniors in years though seniors in rank will be brought into our committee-rooms, and of them many will probably obtain a permanent footing and thus keep me out. You mention that I might probably get advancement by means of a silk gown; that is not probable, as having been so many years disconnected with the ordinary Courts, I have been lost sight of by the Judges, and could not obtain it without having recourse to making as it were lay interest for it, and I confess I am very averse to seeking professional advancement through interest, or through channels unconnected with my profession. . . . I see no other mode of taking my fair position (than by) applying for the degree of the coif."

"We, the three new Serjeants," he writes July 12, 1844, "were directed to be at the House of Lords at half-past nine in the morning in our silk gowns and long wigs, and after the Queen's Counsel had been sworn in, we were summoned before the Chancellor, each of us accompanied by an attendant, who is called 'the Colt,' whose business it is to present the rings, and be the new Serjeant's Esquire upon the occasion. The ceremony was as follows: 1st, having the Queen's writ in my hand, I advanced to the Lord Chancellor, seated in his chair in his full robes, and requested that it might be opened and read, which was done accordingly, and was a command from Her Majesty that her trusty and well-beloved E. B. do, forthwith, taken upon him the dignity of a Serjeant-at-Law, under a penalty of £1,000; then various oaths were administered, including one of very ancient date; after this the Lord Chancellor rose from his seat and came and shook hands with us, calling us 'brother.' Then my colt, Mr. Badeley, presented the Chancellor with the royal ring, requesting him to present it to Her Majesty, and also with a ring for himself; we then retired, and my colt went into the House of Lords, where all the Judges were assembled, and delivered rings for me to the Lord Chief Justice Tindal, Mr. Justice Coleridge, and Mr. Justice Patteson, who thereupon desired me to be brought into the Bar of the House, where I received the congratulations of my learned brethren. And thus the matter ended." He wrote to Mrs. Maude on the occasion: "I thank you much, my dearest mother, for your affectionate congratulations and Mr. Maude for his. I knew it would gratify you, and I think I desired the rank more to please you than for any other reason; you may well look back with gratification to the time when you were left with two little children to struggle for, when you have lived to see your son, through your unwearied kindness and anxious care, and by the help of the friends you found him, raised to rank and station in his profession. I send you a Serjeant's ring, which, though usually only sent to gentlemen, I cannot refrain from sending to my dear mother, to wear for my sake. I have had it made small and light, and I hope it will fit. The Queen's ring was very large, and massive enough to cover two joints of the finger, the rest were of various sizes, according to the dignity of the person they were presented to." "I cannot express to you," the Serjeant's mother says to him, " how much joy it gives me that my dear fatherless son should, by the blessing of God upon his talents and industry, have attained so honourable a situation in his profession."

At the Spring Assizes in Buckinghamshire in 1852, the Serjeant was consulted by Mr. Scott-Murray, who was High Sheriff, and had, as usual, to meet the Judge of Assize, on this occasion the Lord Chief Justice, Lord Campbell. It is usual for the High Sheriff to be accompanied by his chaplain, who on this account took his Catholic chaplain (Father John Morris) in the carriage with himself and the Judge. "The Chief Justice took umbrage at this," writes the Serjeant. . . . "Mr. Hope-Scott and I were consulted by Mr. Scott-Murray, and the letter to the Lord Chief Justice was prepared by us—chiefly, indeed, by Hope-Scott—and it was generally thought that the Sheriff had the best of it. . . . There is no doubt that Lord Campbell was in the wrong. He set out by assuming that the Sheriff's chaplain was provided by him for the service of the Judges, but it appeared that the Judges had formerly their own chaplains, and that they had been discontinued by them from economy, and that the Sheriff's chaplain was in no sense chaplain to the Judges. Moreover, none of the other Judges came in aid of the Chief Justice, and since that time no objection has been made to the attendance of Catholic chaplains, when the High Sheriff is a Catholic."

On the 22nd of November, 1852, Serjeant Bellasis accompanied Dr. Newman to the Court of Queen's Bench, when Sir Alexander Cockburn moved for a new trial in the Achilli trial." "Newman," he says, "was averse to a new trial, but allowed himself to be persuaded at the last moment, . . . and it was a fine scene to witness the vexation of the Chief Justice (Lord Campbell) as instance after instance was produced of his partiality upon the trial. The rule *nisi* was granted for a new trial. On the 31st of January (1853), I was again present by the side of Dr. Newman when he received his sentence of a fine of £100 for the alleged libel upon Dr. Achilli. The judgment of the court was pronounced by Mr. Justice Coleridge in a bitter manner."[1]

Few other legal events in the Serjeant's life call for notice. In 1838 he had been appointed a magistrate both for Middlesex and Westminster, and it should be mentioned that in conjunction with Mr. Swift as magistrate for Middlesex, he was indefatigable in securing for Catholic prisoners in London proper religious ministration, and he had to contend with much bigotry and prejudice at the hands of his brother magistrates

---

[1] "You will do me a great favour in taking me into Court on Monday morning," writes Dr. Newman to the Serjeant, Jan. 28, 1853. "The Judges paid him (Newman) great respect, and though Coleridge preached him an immensely long Puseyite sermon, much of which he might as well have spared, full credit was given for Newman's belief of the truth of his charges, and for proper motives" (Badeley to Hope-Scott, Feb. 1853. *Memoirs*, v. ii. p. 201).

in this matter of simple justice. He used to say that their
opposition to a proper compliance with the discretionary proviso
on the point in the Middlesex Prison Ministers Act for 1863
had no other reason in it than the remark of one of their
body to this effect, that "When we says what we says, that's
what we always says." The Government took the matter up,
and an instructive correspondence between the Serjeant, the
Home Office, and the Visiting Justices appeared as a Parliamentary paper in 1864. In 1863, the Duke of Norfolk made
the Serjeant steward of his Norfolk and Suffolk manors, and in
1869 a Commissioner to inquire into the College of Arms.

In all some three hundred and forty-two cases comprised
Mr. Serjeant Bellasis' professional work before the Committees
between 1835 and 1866, the year previous to his retirement.
It was business, as he says, "of the most varied kind, chiefly,
however, relating to railways from one end of the kingdom to
the other, and to a very great extent in Scotland ; it included
also important navigation Bills relating to the Clyde, the
Forth, and the Tay, . . . the reconstruction of the laws on the
Salmon Fisheries ; also Acts for regulating the supply of water
to various great cities and towns, Manchester, Liverpool, Edin-
burgh, Glasgow, and London." And as counsel he took quite a
paternal interest in the London Watermen and their Company's
rights. In 1867 "business was again offered me," he says,
"but . . . on mature consideration I declined it. I had been
following my profession for forty-two years, and I had gone
through a great deal of mental labour . . . and I thought it
best to discontinue my professional business before it began
to discontinue me. I consulted my dear friend Edward
Badeley, and he answered me by the lines—

> Solve senescentem, mature sanus equum, ne
> Peccet ad extremum ridendus et ilia ducat.
>
> Horace, *Ep. ad Maecenatem.*

It may be added that Serjeant Bellasis, in speaking, had
a beautifully clear delivery, an index, as was his uniformly
neat handwriting, to a clear and methodical intellect.
"Throughout his whole legal career," writes a friend of
him, "he was highly esteemed by all with whom he had
any official relations ; by his brother barristers and the solicitors
who were employed on his own side for the indefatigable
industry, combined with a humility which led him frequently

to underrate his own abilities; by his opponents for his unruffled temper, frankness, and almost chivalrous courtesy; and by his clients for the anxious zeal, punctuality, and painstaking exactness with which he served their interests." "During the Committee season," writes Mrs. Bellasis, "he was often to be found in his study at four o'clock in the morning, digesting a heavy brief and a mass of papers, which had frequently only been delivered at his private house so late as eleven o'clock the previous evening, and which were to provide material for a speech in Committee before luncheon." Writing to his father-in-law, Mr. Garnett, Feb. 3, 1844, he says: "It is my nature to be eager in whatever I take up, whether it is meteorology, or geology, or theology, or business. . . . I have never let any matter of recreation interfere with my business; it is not for me to speak of myself, but I feel confident that I never had anything entrusted to my charge in the way of business into which I did not throw my whole mind, and all the energy I was possessed of; all amusement, all recreation, everything has given way to business; it is never out of my mind day or night." Scotch clients soon got to know the Serjeant's worth and were devoted to him, and a pleasant incident may here be recalled of Sir Alexander Anderson, Provost of Aberdeen, agreeing to give five guineas to a Catholic charity in which one of the Serjeant's daughters was interested, on condition of her being photographed in her father's wig and gown. The portrait was taken and the Provost kept his word. "One of his practical maxims," continues the friend already cited, "was never to undertake any cause which might possibly be unsuited to his own particular capacity, or to which he did not feel that he could devote his undivided attention. Upon this point he was amenable to no persuasion, and this conscientiousness, amounting, as his friends frequently thought, to scrupulosity, led him to decline many lucrative fees." Thus in a letter of June, 1844, to the late Mr. Charles Few, he says: "You know what my wish is, to do justice to those clients who may intrust me with their business, by confining myself, as far as it is practicable, to one Committee at a time; it was this and this only which compelled me to return your brief in the House of Commons. At present I know of no Committee which will be sitting at the time you mention, but it may happen that Bills, in which I have been engaged in the Commons, may come on at that time in the House of Lords, in which case I should be

unable to give you that undivided attention I could wish."
Without violating the etiquette of the Bar, or even a severe
morality, he could have taken more business, relying upon
juniors, and confining himself to general superintendance and
direction, but this he would never willingly do. It was, perhaps, a
rare example, but one inspiring great confidence in all with whom
he had any business relations at Westminster. A like high-
minded conscientiousness is seen in matters connected with the
Shrewsbury Case. The last Catholic Earl had made Mr. Hope-
Scott and the Serjeant his residuary legatees, and also left them
material parts of his landed estates (in Worcestershire, Berks,
Salop, and Oxfordshire). On hearing of this they declined to
take any benefit here. A new will was accordingly prepared,
the devises to Hope-Scott and Bellasis were omitted, and the
whole of the estates, instead of a portion, stood devised to Lord
Edmund Howard, with a subsequent codicil making the then
Duke of Norfolk, instead of themselves, residuary legatee, in case
there might be any residue, they remaining as before executors,
receivers, and trustees.   "Nothing," wrote Cardinal Wiseman to
the Serjeant, in February, 1857, "could have exceeded the
honourable, generous, and disinterested manner in which both
you and Hope-Scott have acted throughout, in the performance
of the duty accepted by you, towards the lamented Earl; and
the Earl likewise in March, 1856, thus expressed himself about
their course as to his will: "The extreme disinterestedness that
you and Mr. Hope-Scott have invariably shown in all matters
connected with myself makes me value your friendship the more,
and leads me to appreciate such splendid marks of noble and
honourable minds."

On Earl Bertram's death, it may be added, proceedings
ensued on the part of Lord Talbot of Ingestre, who claimed the
title of Earl of Shrewsbury, as well as the estates attached
thereto by Act of Parliament, but in August the Committee for
Privileges adjourned *sine die*, his lordship having so far failed to
prove his case. Early in the spring of 1858 the case came on
again, and in July a report was made in his favour. The recovery
of the title did not necessarily involve that of the estates, and
the second act of the litigation commenced by an action of eject-
ment in the Common Pleas for the recovery of Alton Towers,
which succeeded. Whereupon the trustees appealed to the
Exchequer Chamber, where in February, 1860, the matter was
again decided against them, leaving, however, various other

matters for future decision. Finally in July, 1867, judgment was given by the Lord Chancellor (Lord Chelmsford), who had sat with Lords Justices Cairns and Turner, in favour of the trustees (Mr. Hope-Scott and Serjeant Bellasis), in the suit of Howard *v.* Shrewsbury, which gave a very considerable property to their *œstuique trust*, Lord Edmund Howard, viz., a portion of the unentailed estates of the Earls of Shrewsbury, recovered from the trustees in the first instance by Lord Shrewsbury and Talbot. This was the trustees' one success.

In May, 1834. and when still young in his profession, the Serjeant had occasion to write to some friends in answer to an ill-considered attack that had been made by a certain Doctor, upon lawyers in general, and we cannot, perhaps, better conclude this brief sketch of his own legal career than by quoting from it, as an expression of his own views as to some of the duties, difficulties, and dangers that beset the barrister's path. " I would premise," he writes, "that there is no profession or trade, however exalted, or however humble, that has not its own peculiar temptations ; and I admit at once that a barrister's is not exempt from this rule, but he is subject in the course of his career to many and great temptations, and I must admit also that there are many individuals who have not principle enough to escape their influence. But I am not concerned with the faults of individuals, although they may deserve all that your author says of them and more, I only wish to defend my profession from the gross abuse contained in the first line of your quotation.

" It is a common, stale, hackneyed charge, that 'barristers will take any side for a fee, and make no scruple to argue against their conviction,' and this I take to be the material part of the charge made by the Doctor, so far as it relates to the profession in general. Perhaps you are not aware that a barrister is compellable to take a brief in the court in which he practises, however degraded or vexatious he may suspect his cause to be, and the blackest murderer has a right to command the first talent within his reach, to take care that if he be condemned, he be condemned according to law.

" So much for a barrister taking any side for a fee ; he must take it, and it frequently happens that a barrister is obliged to decline a brief on the side to which his feelings or opinions would incline him because his services have been demanded by the other party. Then as to a barrister arguing against his convictions, I plead guilty, he often does, but the result of the cause frequently shows him that his conviction was wrong, and that if he had acted upon what he thought his conviction, he would have done a great injustice to his client. Who makes him the judge? His client's cause (say) is referred to an upright and learned man, whose duty it is to decide it, and to help him to a proper conclusion, the counsel on one side says all that is to be said on that side, and the counsel on the other side all that can be produced on the other side, and the judge alone is the person to decide. But here is the point of temptation, his desire of victory may sometimes tempt a counsel to mis-state his case to the judge, he may try to mislead him by misquoting authorities, he may lend himself to unworthy subterfuges, and make himself a party to the malice or fraud or vindictiveness of his client. I say, he may do this, but it forms no part of his duty, nor any part of the practice of an honourable barrister; that there are some who do this I cannot deny, but they are well known in their profession and appreciated accordingly. It is often asked by a barrister of his client, 'Who is on the other side?' If the answer is 'Mr. A.,' oh, then, every care must be taken to avoid even verbal inaccuracies, as every advantage will be taken; if it is 'Mr. B.,' ah, he is an honourable man and never takes an unfair advantage.

"Suppose a person proved guilty of any of the worst of crimes by the evidence of an accomplice, his counsel need not justify the deed, he need not attempt to palliate it, he need not represent his client as an innocent and persecuted man, if he does not think him so, but he is bound to defend him, and he may honourably do so, by showing the little dependence to be placed upon the evidence of an accomplice, the probabilities of the latter having strong motives for exaggeration, and he may demand that such evidence be corroborated by testimony unimpeachable, and all this although he may know his client to be guilty from an actual confidential confession; were it otherwise, see the result, one man is convicted upon the testimony of an accomplice only, there is a precedent established, and numbers of innocent persons may suffer from that transgression of a salutary rule.

"As to bruising the broken reed in roughly cross-examining, this may sometimes be brutally done by inconsiderate men, but every honourable man contents himself with asking such

c

questions as he thinks necessary, as kindly as circumstances will admit ; if he does otherwise, he is a brute, and is thought so by his brethren of the Bar ; and, moreover, when any disgraceful scene of this kind occurs, it is sure to be blazoned forth by the thousand tongues of the press, while the quiet, judicious, temperate conduct of a gentleman on such an occasion has no charm for the public ear, and therefore is not mentioned, . . . and this leads to the belief that the casual exhibitions of this sort of feeling are common and frequent, which is far from being true. . . .

"In fine, therefore, I admit that a barrister is soon taught that considerations of right and wrong have nothing to do with his brief, for they have nothing to do with it, and ought to have nothing to do with it in the sense in which I have explained it ; and also that his business is to do the best for his client, however bad his case, but he must do it, and may do it, like a gentleman, like a man of honour and a Christian. I do not pretend to say but that there are many individuals to whom some of the epithets of your quotation may be applied with truth. My own profession is open to the world, and must partake of the common weaknesses and vices of our nature, but when these things are charged against the whole profession, I repudiate them. . . . Is our profession altogether barren ? All rascals ? no gentlemen ? not one ? No, says the Doctor, not one. *Credat Judæus.*"

Edward Bellasis.

CHAPTER II.

SERJEANT BELLASIS used to think, from all he had heard, that
his own father must have been of the old High Church school,
but his step-father was a Low Churchman, whose intimates
included members of the Society of Friends; he employed a
Quaker doctor, and held in honour the respected names of
Marsh, Ryder, Simeon, Wilberforce, and Wilson, all Evangelicals.
He was thoroughly sincere, honest and earnest," writes his step-
son, his wife (the Serjeant's mother), "adopting his views, and
never opposing what he thought right." A prayer in use by
them so late as 1849 is significant. "Confound, we beseech
Thee, O Lord, everywhere heresy and error, frustrate the
machinations of Popery, whether within or without the Church.
May all the devices of the Bishop of Rome against Thy sacred
truth be confounded. Lord, may Popery soon receive its final
overthrow, and Babylon long foredoomed, cease to oppress the
earth."

Strict notions, we are told, prevailed in the household
against card-playing and theatre-going. One day, however,
young Bellasis slipped off to Drury Lane, only to meet
there in the pit his step-father's own brother, the Rev. John
Maude. Said the latter, "If you tell of me, I'll tell of you."
Another visit to Drury Lane Theatre is recorded in a diary
entry of November 5, 1822. A friend had obtained an *entrée*
"to see the stage and all the paraphernalia, . . . the complication
of the machinery is wonderful; after viewing the whole of that
immense building, the wardrobes, including dragons and devils,
thunder, lightning, and rain, I returned to the Temple."

Mr. and Mrs. Maude were devoted to the Bible Society, while
their son's chief religious text-book was Doyly and Mant. And
here on Mr. Bellasis reading, when still an Anglican, in the old
Bible translation Preface, how the former rulers of these English
realms were greeted as, "most dread Sovereign," "bright occi-

dental Star," "the Sun in his strength," "Wonder of the world,"
"most tender and loving nursing Father," and "that sanctified
person who, under God, is the immediate author of our true
happiness," candour compelled him to observe that "if these
expressions had been used towards the Blessed Virgin, they
would have shocked Protestants, but they do not strike them
as unsuitable when applied to such earthly monarchs as Queen
Elizabeth and James I." And in 1830 he had to take to task
this very Bible Society for issuing a *Negro* (pigeon) *English
Version* of the inspired Word. "The translation," he writes to
a friend, "professes to be into the language spoken by the
English negroes in our West India islands (which is, of course,
a sort of broken English), and has been made by a Dutchman.
. . . Just imagine a Dutchman endeavouring to spell in his own
way the broken English of a negro, and you will not wonder at
the confusion which follows. . . . Negroes who can read . . .
are accustomed to the English mode of spelling. . . . What
negro. . . would recognize the words 'run away' in 'ronneweh,'
or 'by and by' in 'bambai,' or 'close by' in 'klossibei,' or 'on
the first day of the week' in 'en na fossi deh va wieki'? . . .
and 'the cup of the New Testament' is translated 'de glasi
wieni va da Njoe Testament.' . . . The book is not now to be
got, and it is understood from authority that it will shortly be
sold with a new title-page calling it the 'Surinamic Version.'"
On this question of Bible-reading he observes in a letter of
December 11, 1843 : "I quite believe that there is many a poor
man, who, in default of any specific teaching on the part of the
Church, finds a kind of sacrament in the mere reading of the
Bible, and that many untaught persons do, when they read in a
religious and obedient spirit, extract from it more of the real
truth than might be anticipated, but I cannot think that it is a
safe rule for any, and certainly not for the indifferent or self-
willed to say, 'there is the Holy Book, thou hast only to open
and read.'"

Mr. Justice Allan Park, in a testimonial about 1829 for Mr.
Bellasis, says that he "is of the soundest principles in Church
and State," but there is little in the Serjeant's own early diaries
and memoranda to indicate precisely what were his own religious
opinions, although there is sufficient to show that he was religiously minded. On Sunday, August 18, 1822, he writes : "In
the morning at St. Botolph's, Mr. Geary preached, he has a very
good delivery, but is not sound in his doctrine, I think." Again,

on Sunday, 8th September, following: "We all went in the
evening to the Gravel pit Meeting House, I heard a good slice
of heresy. . . . We sang a few Psalms at Dr. Petts', among the
rest the Evening Hymn, but to my great annoyance they all
declined singing the last verse, 'Praise God from Whom all
blessings flow,'" and on Sunday, 29th September, "In the
morning went to the Caledonian Church in Cross Street, Hatton
Garden, and after climbing into the chapel through a window,
heard a most beautiful sermon from Dr. Chalmers." A visit
on November 26, 1820, to "St. Mary's Roman Catholic Chapel,
Moorfields," however, only "astonishes" him, and "impresses"
him with "the superiority of the reformed Protestant religion."
In the same month he has a talk with a friend on Liberty and
Necessity, and on Self-Love being the sole motive of action and
guide to the will, and observes, "I took part against both
doctrines, and am firmly convinced of their fallacy, . . . for it
does appear to me that these doctrines eventually tend to the
destruction of all moral rectitude of conduct and to the sub-
version of all our hopes of happiness hereafter. It is a subject,
however, that I must read something more about, as I find
myself very deficient in answering objections and arguments of
this description. I do most earnestly hope that the Almighty
will preserve me from the wide-spreading and ensnaring doctrines
of infidelity which seem almost to threaten the whole moral
principle of the country." In February, 1823, he notes having
read twenty-six pages of Dr. Wardlaw's book, *Unitarianism
incapable of Vindication*, and that his opponent, Mr. Yates, says,
"No human voice can say, Halt to the march of intellect," the
Doctor retorting. "This, alas, is true of its retrograde, as well as
of its advancing march." Mr. Bellasis, when twenty-two years
of age, is very severe upon a certain Mr. Palmer's *Principles of
Nature*. "I have no hesitation," he writes March 8, 1823, "in
pronouncing this work to be the most ridiculous and absurd
attempt ever made to throw discredit upon the Christian
Theology; it has neither common sense nor common honesty;
it is an unintelligible jargon of nonsense that would not impose
upon the understanding of a child of seven years old."

"The friend," he says, "who exercised most influence over
me at that time (1823) was Louis Hayes Petit, with whom I
frequently dined; he was an old-fashioned High Churchman,
very regular in his religious duties, and he lent me many books,
particularly those of Bishop Horne, and Mr. Jones of Nayland,

a class of writers I much preferred to those my dissenting
associates took interest in." But whatever the precise texture
of Mr. Bellasis' religious beliefs, on one point there was "sense
amidst confusion." His mind, as he tells us, had been imbued
with an absolute hatred of Popery, with a belief that Luther
and Calvin were holy men raised up by God to reform the
Church, and that Cranmer, Ridley, and Latimer were martyrs
for the faith under "Bloody Mary," so that long afterwards
he could recall how it had come upon him as a surprise to
read in his friend Mr. Lodge's *Portraits*, about "good Queen
Bess," that "her prudence saved her from the disgrace of
open profligacy." His patron Petit, too, of Huguenot extrac-
tion, rather fanned his anti-Catholic prejudices. Once Petit at
a banquet had said to the Duke of Sussex (then in favour of
Catholic Emancipation), "Your Royal Highness will forgive me
for differing, when you remember that my family have already
been driven out of one country by the Catholics, and we don't
want to be driven out of another." It was Mr. Petit, however,
who introduced the young barrister, who had been so put out
with the Bible's Society "Surinamic version," to the two other
great Church of England Societies, for Promoting Christian
Knowledge, and for the Propagation of the Gospel in Foreign
Parts, at that time both anti-Evangelical. Mr. Bellasis also got
some High Church notions from his friend Mr. Jebb's uncle, the
Protestant Bishop of Limerick. One day he asked Dr. Jebb
why the rules of the English Prayer Book were not obeyed.
"In what respect?" inquired the Bishop. "It is provided,"
replied the lawyer, "that 'every priest shall say daily morning
and evening prayer, either privately or openly,' and yet who
does it?" Luckily his lordship could answer for himself, "I do."

In this somewhat serious frame of mind, during the summer
of 1833, Mr. Bellasis determined upon a foreign tour, such as in
the case of Faber, Hope-Scott, and Mr. Allies, had effected so
much towards disarming anti-Catholic prejudices. Accompanied
by Mr. Jebb, the Bishop's nephew, he reached Paris in June,
but the friends did not stay there long. Louis Phillippe
had just seized the Bourbon crown, the very tricolor flag that
had waved over the guillotine at his own father's execution,
was now floating above the Tuileries, where the new monarch
resided : workmen were everywhere effacing the *fleur-de-lis*,
while the mob after pulling down the Archbishop's house, had
set about destroying every cross and crucifix that they could

lay their hands upon : and the Conservative lawyer with High Church tendencies, vented his feelings in verse that truly prophesied the downfall of the revolutionary King :

Let's order the horses, let's hasten away,
    One sees nothing here but the tricolor flag,
And now I have nam'd it I may as well say,
    I scorn and abhor that contemptible rag,
On peep-shows and cabinet doors let it flare,
    On omnibus tops where it flutters so cheap.
But not on the palace, to see it float there,
    Makes me really feel shame for thee, Louis Phillippe.

Let's order the horses, let's hasten away,
    In vain I look round for the gay *fleur-de-lis*,
It has vanish'd, not moulder'd by time's slow decay,
    But struck by rude hands from each scutcheon I see.
No wonder the lily of France should be fear'd
    By a Jacobin crew sunk in cruelty deep,
But when thine as the hand of the spoiler appear'd,
    'Twas contempt that I felt for thee, Louis Phillippe.

Let's order the horses, let's hasten away,
    See, see, all around us what fragments are strewn,
Frail mortal, dost wage with thy Maker the fray?
    Is the Cross, too, an object of enmity grown?
On, on in thy course, in thy heartless career,
    Tho' thy deeds for a time may make piety weep,
Retribution will come, nor will one shed a tear
    For a base-hearted ingrate like Louis Phillippe.

The travellers crossed south-eastern France in a barouche and pair, making for the Swiss frontier, and passing over the Simplon into Italy, visited Milan, Verona, Padua, Venice, Florence, Perugia, Rome, and Naples. "There were no Murray's Handbooks in those days," the Serjeant writes, "and we missed much. However, I visited the churches, . . . and very soon had many of my ideas corrected about the Catholic religion. I was surprised at the earnestness of the people at their prayers, and wrote to my mother that though I might, indeed, have got into the land of superstition, it certainly was not the country of irreligion." The friends arrived in Rome by the Porta del Popolo, on the 17th of August, 1833, devoted themselves chiefly to the Roman antiquities during a three weeks' stay, and only saw the chief churches, including the ruins of St. Paul's outside the walls, destroyed by fire in the previous year, 1832. "I had been so much accustomed to whitewash in our churches at home," the Serjeant writes, "that the polished

marble and gold of St. Peter's were something new to me, and
I observed upon the suitableness of decorating the house of
God, implying, as I thought it did, earnestness and sincerity."
They came in, too, for Pope Gregory XVI.'s blessing from his
gallery in the Court of the Quirinal, and were "much struck
with the kneeling multitude," but, as he tells us, "we saw
nothing of the religious side of Rome. We had no letters,
nor was the season favourable, since every one was absent
at his *villegiatura*, . . . my religious inclinations had undergone
no material change, I had seen nothing but the exterior of
things, but I had come to the conclusion that Roman Catholics
were devout people, and that in many things they were misrepresented, and I found myself not infrequently defending
them, when I thought them unfairly attacked."[1]

This tour was followed by others that deepened his first
favourable impressions of Catholics. On 20th of July, 1841,
he writes from Brussels to his mother : "I can scarcely tell
you which place we have liked best, but we have hitherto
remained longest at Louvain ; it is a university, and we made
acquaintance with two of the professors, Monsieur Verhoeven,
and Monsieur Malou [afterwards Bishop of Bruges], who made
our stay very agreeable." After mentioning a visit to a convent
of nuns called "Sœurs de Marie," he continues, "This is a
Catholic country, and we have been taking pains to see all
the services of their Church, and to that end have been to
a great many churches, and have seen a great deal that pleases
us, as well as some things which offend and distress us ; of
the earnestness and sincerity of the people and priests I have
not the slightest doubt ; their manner is most reverential, and
there is not a day in the week in which the churches are not
frequented by hundreds either for public service or for their
own private prayers ; rich and poor, all classes down to the
poorest beggar in rags, are to be seen at their devotions at
all hours of the day, and the services themselves are most
impressive. . . . I am quite satisfied that this is a far more
religious country than England, as well as a more moral one.
We have been among the lowest of the low, and in some of
the largest cities, and we have never seen a drunken man,

---

[1] In the same spirit when visiting Thorndon three years later, in 1836, he
notes, "Lady Petre showed me the chapel, and I was much struck with its beauty
and at the reverence with which everything sacred was treated. I think this visit
made me less than ever disposed to listen to disparaging observations about Catholics."

we have never heard an oath, nor have we ever seen a person male or female, who had the slightest appearance of vice of any kind, and those to whom we have talked upon religious subjects, have conversed in the most serious manner ; as to their habits, my wife was sketching in the Cathedral of Louvain yesterday, and she saw not only the mistress of the hotel, but the waiters come in to say their prayers, one after another, as they could be spared." On August 16, 1841, he writes from the Moselle : "We visited in succession the baths or watering-places of Ems, Schwalbach, Schlangenbad, and Wiesbaden, all full of German company, . . . gambling was constantly going on in public every day, and three times as much on Sunday as on other days, additional tables and additional rooms being prepared to accommodate the public ; it was rather a new sight to us to see gaming at all, but to see ladies gaming was very new. . . . we were yesterday at the baths of Bertrich (in a Catholic country), and nothing of the kind is attempted or permitted, . . . nearly the whole population go to Matins and Vespers every day. . . ."

In August, 1844, he writes to various friends from Bavaria and Austria : "We have met on the roads for the last 200 miles, large parties of pilgrims, men and women, young and old, dressed in the most picturesque colours, sometimes as many as 100 or 200 in number, some singing hymns in full chorus as they walk in a kind of procession, the noise of their voices being wafted across the country as they go, others repeating litanies in response to one man who walks first, book in hand, as a kind of leader These seem to be very common, as there has not been a day when we have not met some, and on some days half a dozen different parties. The loud chorus of voices on the otherwise quiet roads has a very solemn effect ; they are all very sober and quiet in their demeanour, and proceed in a very solemn way, and as Mr. Murray coolly says in his Handbook, 'It is difficult to think they are not sincere.' . . . Nuremberg is a very curious place. . . . Although it is entirely Protestant, yet the churches have remained untouched and unaltered since the last Mass was said some hundreds of years ago, the altars all remain, with the candles and crucifixes and the lace coverings, just the same as they used to be, but unused. St. Laurence's Church gives one the idea of a petrified system only waiting the touch of some magician to bring all to life again. . . . I think, so far, Wurzburg has pleased us most,

Nuremberg is indeed very picturesque, but they are a Protestant
set, and we do not take much pleasure in seeing churches which
preserve all the outward appearance of being Catholic, retaining
the whole of the images and ornaments of Catholic times, and
having even all the side altars, as well as the high altar, covered
with antependiums and altar-cloths, but the service being
merely the Lutheran preaching and singing in which there is no
use for the things they are inconsistent enough to retain. . . .
The churches at Salzburg yesterday evening at the *Salve* were
crowded in the extreme, the people most devout. . . . At
Berchtesgaden, where we stayed two days, we found twice a day
the whole town deserted, even the stalls in the market-place left
apparently to take care of themselves, the whole population
being in church. We hear a very high character of the present
Archbishop of Salzburg, the Primate of Germany, he is only
thirty-four, Prince Schwarzenberg by birth, and a Cardinal, but
living, as we were told, a saintly life, popular in the highest
degree, giving his whole income to charity, and accessible at all
times to the poorest. . . . We rather liked the Bavarians, and
the Austrians still better, and every step we take in the Tyrol
interests us more and more in the people. It is perfectly
obvious that the ordinary habit of the population here is to be
at church every day, men and woman, and greater decorum
and reverence I never witnessed, and the wayside chapels are
constant, and not unfrequently tenanted. I miss, however, the
priests here ; they do not wear any dress by which they can be
readily distinguished, which I think is a disadvantage. . . . Mass
is going on at the church opposite, and the custom here is that
the church bell is rung . . . at the Consecration and Elevation ;
the stage coach has just arrived, and as the church bell is
ringing, the driver, passengers, and all are standing in the road
with their hats off saying a prayer. . . . We found last night
a crucifix and cup of holy water in our bed-rooms, and we
find in the churchyards every monument is furnished with a
china or metal pan containing holy water, which the relatives
fill from time to time, . . . and they sprinkle water . . . upon
the grave as they pass. . . . The whole population go to church
twice a day, and for that purpose there are services at all hours
to suit all classes ; the first Mass is usually at five o'clock, and
the towns and villages are all alive at that hour (go where you
will), and the churches are occupied by a succession of people
from that time till nine ; in fact, they are a thoroughly religious

people of which we have continual instances. A few days since we passed through a village in the Tyrol, where there was a triumphal arch at the entrance, and the houses and church were ornamented with evergreens and flowers ; we found the Bishop had come to a Confirmation, and his coming was hailed as a time of rejoicing as if for some great event. The arch was inscribed with the word *Wilkommen* (welcome) in large letters done in flowers, and the Bishop did not, as with us, make a flying visit of a few hours, but, though it was only a small village, he stayed there three days and was accessible to all. And the day after this we were delayed near half an hour in starting because the postilion and stable boy were both at church, and we have seen passengers by the stage coach, coach-men and all, on arriving in a town, all of them go to church to say their prayers."

We cannot better conclude this account of Serjeant Bellasis' religious impressions abroad than by citing the letter he wrote to Dr. W. G. Ward at the latter's request, January 26, 1844 : "On first going abroad," he says, "in 1833, I went with those impressions respecting the Roman Catholics and their system with which I had been brought up, and which were current amongst those with whom I associated ; I expected to find all classes irreligious or indifferent, the poorer classes ignorant, and the priests purposely keeping them so, and I went prepared to look at their religion and their religious services with distaste.

"At first, I confess, every thing that I saw seemed to confirm the impressions with which I started ; if I saw people diverting themselves on Sundays, I concluded it was a wilful and deliberate desecration of the day ; if I saw priests walking amongst them, I concluded they were winking at it ; if I saw a poor person by the roadside on his knees before a cross, I concluded he had placed himself there for us to see, and I thought all meanly-clad monks were lazy beggars ; the very constancy of the people at church I attributed to formalism, and I thoroughly believed they worshipped images, for I saw them kneeling before them, and I thought that proved it.

"The notion that I should find the foreign Catholics indifferent was very soon dispelled ; the very manner in which I saw a French steersman at the helm of his vessel take off his cap on passing the large crucifix on the pier at Dieppe surprised me, and the earnestness and devotion I saw in the churches was something quite new to me, but then I fell back upon the idea

that it was all superstition and idolatry, fraud in the priests, and
ignorance in the people.

"Of the higher classes of laity in the countries in which I
have travelled, I have seen nothing,[1] but I have seen a good
deal of the priests, of the poor, and of the schools for the
children of the poor; and the more I saw, the more and more I
became convinced how utterly groundless my impressions were.
Of the priests (I speak now of Belgium and Prussia, where I
saw them most) I have a very pleasing recollection; here and
there I met with a mere argumentative theologian, but as a
body I was struck by their kindness of manner and simplicity
of life; although in the conversations I had with them I might
not agree with them, yet the very idea that they were not
honest and sincere quite shocks and distresses me. I feel and
still feel convinced that they were religious men.

"That the poor are ignorant is, I believe, an entire misap-
prehension; I never talked to any who were so; I should say
they are far, very far better instructed in religious knowledge
than our own people of the same class, and their attention to
their religious duties is, to my mind, quite affecting. I have
seen in large manufacturing towns, hundreds upon hundreds of
workpeople in their working dress at Mass at five o'clock in the
morning before going into the factories, with their books, and
joining heartily in the service, and I need scarcely say what a
contrast this forms to the habits of the same class of persons in
this country.

"I have visited also many Catholic schools abroad, chiefly
those under the superintendence of the Christian Brothers, and
my opinion is that we have nothing to compare with them,
either as to the regularity and order of the schools, the extent
of the secular education, the carefulness with which religious
instruction is conveyed, or the number and character of the
masters.

[1] In August, 1846, however, he writes from Prague of a visit to Count Thun
"at a fine castle, standing on a rock 160 feet high overlooking the Elbe: we found the
family most interesting," he continues, "and spent two or three days there most
agreeably, and this gave us an insight into the mode of living of a first-rate Bohemian
family. The house is immense: when I tell you that the corridor was 340 feet in
length, and that from our bed-room to the drawing-room was a walk of 140 yards,
you may guess its size. There is a chapel in the house and service every morning at
eight o'clock, and with the family, and servants, and visitors, and gardeners, and
persons employed about the premises, they mustered about 100 persons at chapel.
Their kindness to us was unbounded, and they gave us letters onwards, first to
Toplitz, where we were most kindly received by the Prince and Princess Clary, and
where Count Francis Thun has been dedicating the whole day to us."

" Upon the whole, my last impression on returning from a foreign country (Belgium) to our own was, that I was coming out of a religious country into one of indifference; the open churches of the former, the frequent services, the constant worshippers, the solemn ceremonial, the collected air of the clergy in their ministrations, the indubitable devotion and reverence of the people, their unhesitating confidence in their Church, has nothing approaching to a counterpart with us; I know nothing more disheartening (I speak of the effect produced upon myself), than a return to England after some time spent in Catholic countries; every thing seems so careless, so irreverent, so dead; with all my heart I wish, and especially for my children's sake, that I could see in this country some approximation to the solemnity, reverence, devotion, and earnestness which I have witnessed abroad.

" All this may seem harsh towards my own country and my own Church, but they are nevertheless the impressions which I have derived from what I have seen; I am of course liable to be swayed by prejudice as well as others, but so far as I know myself, my prejudices, both those of education and family connection, were all the other way, and I feel they have been overcome by facts which are irresistible. I have now given you what you asked for: my impressions of the Church on the Continent, and you are quite at liberty to make what use of it you please."

His impressions of Catholicism abroad contrast strangely with those of Protestantism at home given in a letter of August 9, 1843:

" I cannot say, in our assumed character of lay rural deans, we saw much to gratify us; we lamented over the miserable state of Tewkesbury Abbey Church, a place once splendid, now wretched; we admired the Cathedral of Worcester, though it is all yellow-washed in the inside, but we did not admire the congregation or the services, or the cool way in which the clergy present marched out of the church without any pretence of celebrating the Holy Communion, although the altar was prepared and 'all things ready,' and guests willing to partake; in fact we saw the wine poured out of the chalice back into the black bottle, and the former wiped out with a dirty duster, and finally the said chalice and the paten wrapped up in the said duster on the altar and then carried away. At Wolverhampton, a town full of Dissenters, . . . we saw a fine collegiate church, the clerical

staff of which consists of a Dean, eight prebends, and a perpetual
curate, but neither the Dean, nor any of the eight prebends, nor
the perpetual curate, are or ever were resident, the 'duty being
done' by two curates who are remunerated by the fees; in such
a town as Wolverhampton, such a staff, if resident, would be
invaluable, but the Cathedral Bill has reformed Wolverhampton,
not by causing the clergy to reside, but by abolishing their
offices; double the number of clergy would be but a sorry
supply for such a place."

His impressions of Catholicism, too, at home, were much
the same as those abroad. In a letter of August 18, 1843, from
Bleasdale, North Lancashire, he says: "I am fast coming to the
conclusion, as a matter of fact, that the morals and general
conduct of the Catholic population in these parts are superior,
not to say very superior to that of our own people, whatever
may be the cause; it may be that their system is being
carried out consistently, whilst ours is neglected. The Catholic
schools here are conducted by Sisters of Charity and Christian
Brothers, men and women who have dedicated themselves
for life to the task, looking for no return; at Preston, our
neighbouring town, there is an establishment of the latter;
twelve or more persons,[1] one being a superior, live together;
they have their little apartments, hall, library, chapel, and
go out every day to the boys' schools in the town, whilst our
schools are conducted by some expensive master, £60 per
annum being barely sufficient to obtain even one moderately
qualified. It remains to be seen whether a system of education
conducted entirely by masters, who are stipendaries merely, can
compete with a system where the instructors labour for the love
of God."

And on September 9, 1843, he writes to the Rev. W. Upton
Richards: "As we think your coming here would do good in
many respects, and as we are planning a visit to Stonyhurst
College (having commendatory letters from Sir Thomas Gage-
Rokewode to Mr. Barrow, the President of the College), and are
fearful of trusting ourselves without a safe escort, and for divers
and sundry other good and weighty reasons are desiring your
presence, can you come down here on Friday the 15th? . . .

---

[1] Writing to Rev. E. E. Estcourt, on SS. Simon and Jude's day, 1843, he says:
"Last year they were ten, they have now increased to seventeen, and they are
preparing their house for forty. . . . They are educated men far superior to our
schoolmasters."

If you can, bring a sermon or two in your portmanteau, and your Oxford hood, and select the former so as not to have more Popery in them than will go down in these parts." And to the Rev. E. E. Estcourt, on SS. Simon and Jude's day, 1843, he notes : " Richards of Margaret Chapel is staying with us, and he and I and Garnett paid a visit the other day to Stonyhurst College, a Jesuit establishment in this neighbourhood (Bleasdale), including, besides a college for priests, a school for about two hundred boys of the better class of Roman Catholics. The discipline is perfect ; strict, but not in the sense of severe."[1]

He lived with his family many months at a time during the autumn recess at Bleasdale Tower, belonging to his father-in-law, Mr. Garnett. "Only think," he writes to Mr. Richard Twining, August 18, 1843, "of my dining yesterday at a large party of whom more than two-thirds were Roman Catholic ladies and gentlemen, and amongst them a priest of the Roman Catholic Church, and another of our own, a strong Evangelical. I found them very nice people indeed ; they are our nearest neighbours here—Mr. Brockholes and the Fitzherberts."

It will now be understood that after the Serjeant's enlarged personal experiences of Catholicism abroad and at home, he came to view with impatience his old prejudices about it. He had come back from the Continent, indeed, as he says, "still a thorough Anglican," but he could neither abuse, nor listen to abuse of, either Catholics or Catholicism. So when at a public meeting, in the course of a single speech, a respectable clergyman of the Church of England spoke of both one and the other in these vituperative terms, as reported on September 12, 1840, in the *Manchester and Salford Standard,* he was roused to a remonstrance. "Soul-enslaving, mind-paralyzing nonsense," said the parson, "absurdity and folly," "lying, anti-Christian apostacy," "a proverb, astonishment and a by-word," "masterpiece of Satan," "tyrannizing, abominable, apostate Popery," "idolatry, abomination, and a curse," "Popish priests are wolves and special instruments of the devil,"

---

[1] The Rev. W. F. Wingfield, on announcing his conversion to the Serjeant, November 2, 1845, from Stonyhurst, thus conveyed his impressions : " Mrs. Wingfield and myself have spent a *most truly happy week* here, where we have been made partakers of the unspeakable benefit of communion with the Catholic Church. I feel myself quite unequal to do justice to the kindness and hospitality with which we have been received by the Rector and the Society in general, whose habits and sentiments we have found most edifying."

"Popish services are witchcraft and necromancy," "a pious
Papist is a creature divested of every liberal sentiment," "a
mass of darkness and ignorance," "gross absurdities," "curse
of God upon him," "atrocious system of abomination and
falsehood," "a Papist who arrives at infidelity is promoted by
the change." This clergyman was followed a month later, on
October 14, 1840, by another clergyman of the Church of
England, who was reported as informing his hearers that the
more sincere Roman Catholics are, "the more they will practise
falsehood and deceit;" that the Roman Catholic religion is
"Antichrist," "a diabolical system," "a rascal," that it has
"a brow of brass that shrinks not from shame and infamy;"
and finally, "that infidelity is better than Popery," the speaker
affirming that he made this last assertion "calmly and
deliberately," and he affirmed it, too, after a solemn prayer had
been offered up to Almighty God that grace might be vouch-
safed from on high to shed a *softening* and *hallowing* influence
over the proceedings. "If," said Mr. Bellasis in the course of
a temperate letter addressed to "Members of the Church of
England who attend Protestant Meetings," "the Roman Catholic
communion is worse than infidelity, then Voltaire was a better
man than either Pascal or Fénelon; Robespierre, Marat, Anar-
charsis Clootz, and the wretched heathens of the French
Revolution, who set up the goddess of reason, and abolished
the Christian State, were in a safer condition than the oppressed
and persecuted clergy of France; the opinions of Tom Paine
should be preferred to those of Thomas à Becket; and Robert
Owen and his socialists are nearer salvation than the best of
Roman Catholics in this country." "Again," he says, "if the
Roman Catholic communion have utterly lost the Holy Spirit,
and are governed by the spirit of the devil (awful words to
put in such proximity), and if their ministers are his ministers
and not the ministers of Christ, then our Bishops and clergy,
prior to the Reformation, were all ministers of the devil, too;
from whence then do we trace our Orders? Cranmer (if this
be true) had no other title to the office of a Bishop than that
which was conveyed to him by the consecration of Antichrist.
. . . How unspeakably awful to hear *all* attributed to the devil,
not errors only, but all! the ministers his, the holy services
witchcraft and necromancy! Can any danger be like this? If
you who speak, or you who countenance such things, are wrong,
if His Spirit is still there, and if you call it the spirit of the

devil, read once more our Saviour's words, and think, I entreat you, how fearful is the risk you run (*i.e.*, Whosoever speaketh against the Holy Ghost, it shall never be forgiven him "). All this is on the supposition that you are only *possibly* wrong, but when I show you that your own Church holds no such doctrine, that she holds Roman Catholic Orders to be true Orders, a Roman Catholic priest to be a true priest, . . . you will see that in the judgment of your own Church you *are* wrong. . . . The Romish communion, as a body, is a Christian Church, and we have towards it Christian duties." So much in answer to mere abuse delivered ten years before any " Papal Aggression," " but so far as my observation has extended," he says in a note elsewhere, " I think I perceive that there is a constant and almost universal habit of misrepresenting and exaggerating the doctrines and practices of Catholics by Protestants, when they set themselves to refute or find fault with them. I do not, however, perceive that there is any such habit in misrepresenting the doctrines of Protestants on the part of Catholics." In later years, as his wife writes, the Serjeant, no longer agitated and perplexed about his religious belief, " had a most happy way of dealing with bigotry, and of disarming dislike by his great urbanity ; and having during sixteen years studied the tenets of the Catholic Church in order to meet my ultra-Protestant objections, there was no one point that he was not prepared to meet effectually." When opportunities came, then, of helping wayfarers along the road to truth he had traversed himself, his attitude was well delineated by a familiar illustration (one found carefully written out among his private papers) : ".A stranger is traversing my garden, I see him trampling under foot my choicest and most favourite flowers ; my first feeling is anger, and I hasten towards him with words of remonstrance on my lips ; but, as I approach, I perceive that his trespass is not wilful, he is blind ; at once my anger vanishes away, and its place is supplied by sympathy and kindness, and a desire gently to direct his steps." The excessive and protracted pains, however, that the Serjeant took during his travels, from dawn to "dewy eve," to ascertain the truth about Catholics and Catholicism abroad, gave Dr. Schöll of Treves the notion that this too brief span of mortal existence would never see the conversion of so cautious a man. " Ah, ce pauvre Monsieur Bellasis," he was heard to exclaim, " il a tant de scrupules ; il n'entrera jamais dans l'Église."

D

CHAPTER III.

DURING the period of his first marriage (1829—1832) with
Frances, only child and heir of William Lycett, of Stafford,[1]
Mr. Bellasis had been a regular Sunday attendant at the Found-
ling Hospital Chapel. On his second marriage with Eliza Jane,
only daughter of William Garnett, of Lark Hill (now Peel
Park, Salford), he came to reside at 17, Bedford Square,
Bloomsbury, his home for nearly fifteen years,[2] and in 1838
he occasionally visited Mr. Dodsworth's church in Albany
Street, and during a time of sorrow at the loss of his second
wife's second child, Eliza, in 1839, he was attracted to a small
chapel in Margaret Street, because of a daily eight o'clock
morning service there; an exceptional thing at that time.[3]
During the Lent of 1839 he alternated his religious attendance
between Margaret Street and Lincoln's Inn Chapel; indeed,
throughout the whole year he "persisted in attending the daily
service, and in obeying scrupulously the rules of the church."

On the death of Mr. Charles Thornton, in the spring of
1839, Mr. Frederick Oakeley succeeded him at Margaret Street,
and "it was at once plain," the Serjeant writes, "that he did
not mean to content himself with the squalid condition of the

[1] This union was but short-lived. Their only child, Charlotte, after a convulsive
attack, though getting to look well again, never smiled, and Maclise was so struck
by her appearance that, unknown to her father, he came and made a beautiful
drawing of her. She died in her second year, to be soon followed by her mother,
who was in a decline, and was attended by Mr. Julius, a surgeon of eminence, and
Sir Henry Halford, but her strength failed her from day to day. She passed away
on the 27th of December, 1832, and was buried by her infant daughter's side near
the east end of Carisbrooke Church.

[2] By this marriage, on October 21, 1835, at the Collegiate Church (now
Cathedral), Manchester, Mr. Bellasis had a numerous family of four sons and nine
daughters, of whom ten have survived, the eldest being Margaret Jane (Mrs. Edward
Charlton), born in 1837, the youngest Henry Lewis, born in 1839, now a priest
(1893).

[3] On Candlemas day, 1844, he writes from Reading that a friend had gone out
there "in quest of a Church service, but in this town of twenty thousand inhabitants
there was no service to be found save in the Catholic chapel."

My dear Clara,

In the first place I would not have you for a Godmother, if I thought you looked upon the matter as a mere form. I, like you, think it a responsible office but that is no reason for your avoiding it, do you think you are going to pass thro' life without responsibilities? Every period of life brings with it responsibilities and duties, you have already the duties of a daughter and the duties of a sister to perform, beside many other in various relations of life including the duties of a friend, and amongst the latter you may reckon that of becoming a Godmother when a suitable occasion presents itself. You say that if our object in asking you is to please you, you would decline it, we thought it perhaps might please you, but our object was to please ourselves, and to provide our baby with a God mother from amongst those of our friends upon whose sympathy and affection we place the strongest reliance, and need I say it? you are of that number. Their dear has selected one Godmother from amongst her own early friends, she wishes to select another from amongst those to whom I have introduced her, if therefore you can show me any one of my friends who occupies a more prominent place in the affectionate regard of myself and my wife than you do, just name the person and we will relieve you from the responsibility. In the mean time and until you have finished your painful search after such a person, will you [to please us] become God mother to Miss Margaret Jane Butler and conjointly with Miss Mary Garnett of Liverpool.

Your affectionate friend
Edw. Rutledge

chapel ; the altar was raised, the pulpit removed from its central position, and suitable decoration added, including a cross at the back of the altar. All this I entirely approved of, and assisted him in."[1]

Some disapproved, and we learn that Mr. Carus Wilson for one was "deprecating the proceedings at Margaret Street Chapel ; the chief things he objected to were the cross, which he said was 'obviously made a religious use of,' and what he called the Pope's banner in the window, viz., the Lamb and flag."[2] The Serjeant of course deemed the services "very nice, and Oakeley," he adds, " has commenced intoning parts of the service more after Cathedral fashion."[3] At Bleasdale Tower, too, Mr. Bellasis tells us, " we have recommenced our choir, and are making all the children musical, and have got the Church services into something like order again ; for in our absence everything falls back again into the old careless system."[4]

He did not stop here, but proceeded, as he puts it, to " commit some Popery." He had already set about improving the " miserable barn " of a church, by erecting a proper communion-table and a stained glass window, and in the

---

[1] "The doubt now seems to be," writes Mr. Oakeley to Mr. Bellasis, from Oxford, on the vigil of St. Matthew's day, 1839, "whether the cross is to be immediately over the altar, or some way above it. . . . Does it strike you it would look strange as a single object on the wall ? I am decided in favour of having it in relief, and of the same colour with the wall. At Littlemore you remember it is, as it were, on the altar. . . . I am puzzled for something very simple in the way of lights for the pulpit and desks. . . . The designs I hear of do not seem to me Catholic. I shall be very glad of hints. . . . I am glad to hear the altar is approved."

[2] Mr. Bellasis to his brother-in-law, W. J. Garnett, March 4, 1843.

[3] To the same, January 8, 1844.

[4] A pleasing account of zeal and good work for religion by a family in the north, but meeting with little encouragement from their clergyman, is given by the Serjeant in a letter of December 13, 1843, to Mr. R. Twining : " Last week we went to pay our promised visit to Mr. and Mrs. Greene, at Whittington, and spent three days there very agreeably ; we were more pleased than ever with our young friends, and saw their school of sixty girls, of which you have heard us speak, with great interest ; these young ladies have managed by kindness and attention to attach these girls to them in a manner quite surprising, and their knowledge of true Catholic doctrine is quite refreshing ; they are, however, sadly hampered by their clergyman, who objects to everything, and is continually making complaints to their father ; his last inroad upon their plans was the forbidding the observing of festivals. Of course there is no service at the Church on those days, and so our young friends have been in the habit of taking the children a walk on saints' days, and allowing them to decorate their school-room with flowers. I should have thought nothing could be more innocent or proper, but Dr. Roberts insists that it should be discontinued, and says it may be the way to bring the children up heathens, or Papists, but not Christians."

autumn of 1840 he had "ventured to put up a stone cross on the gable." Later on he erected a new font, and consulted the Rev. John Brande Morris about an inscription for it to "a good little man who was curate of the chapelry." "Can you give us a hint?" he writes on September 5, 1843. "We think, *Orate pro anima,* &c., would be perhaps too astonishing to the Protestants, if they found out what it meant, but perhaps they would not be so much offended at *Cujus animæ propitietur Deus.*" At length the inscription ran : *O vos qui huic fonti jam adsistentes adoratis, mementote inter precandum animæ Gulielmi Fenton olim in hoc sacrario suo suasu relintegrato, ministrantis ;* "as far as we durst go," he adds, "and which, indeed, we covered over with a matting when the Bishop came to consecrate the church."

In 1839, he had been consulted about a monument erected to a Catholic in Carisbrooke Church, where his step-father ministered, and which bore the inscription : "Pray for the soul of Thomas Woolfrey : it is a good and holy thought to pray for the dead." "There was a universal outcry about it," writes the Serjeant, "the whole Anglican Hierarchy being opposed to its legality. This gave me occasion to inquire into it, and I could not find that it was expressly condemned by the Protestant Church ; and more, I came to the conclusion that it was a commendable practice ; but I was much puzzled that all the Bishops condemned it, my then feeling being that we were to look to them for guidance. However, the case came before the Ecclesiastical Court in the cause of Breeks *v.* Woolfrey, and it was decided that prayers for the dead were not forbidden. This seemed to show that the Bishops were not always right."

The only letter to his mother to be found touching on controversy, and dated August 3, 1843, refers to the same subject. He had happened to advert therein to "the fact that our Saviour Himself represents even the rich man in a state of punishment praying for his relatives left behind him." She answered, that "the rich man was so wrong in his views on various points, that we cannot well take a lesson from him !"[1] When she died in 1849, her son's own earnest prayer for her soul was carefully written out all the same, while in Catholic

---

[1] "Respecting prayers for the dead," she likewise observed, "we think them unscriptural and unavailing, consequently useless. . . . Our own Church deliberately discarded them at the Reformation. . . . Thankful may we be in . . . having Moses and the Prophets," &c.

days the Serjeant would from time to time make a pilgrimage
to her grave, and sprinkle it with holy water, nor was his
father's grave at Basilden forgotten, for it received similar treatment. The duty, too, of praying for the dead was early inculcated upon his children. "Walter Twining," he says, "died
this morning without a sigh. . . . He was no common child. . . .
Margaret and Katharine shed their first tears at death. I do
not quite understand how they came to cry, for I told them
that God had sent to fetch little Walter, and that the angels
had carried him away to Heaven, but this mode of telling them
did not hinder it. . . . Eliza tells me that Katharine went
upstairs, and made Susan (the nurse) go out of the room, and
then she went into the corner and knelt down, no doubt to pray
that God would make little Walter very happy, as we have taught
her to do for little Eliza, and as, indeed, she told her mamma
she should do. I hope this is a proof that we have made a
lodgment in even such young minds as our children's, of the
notion that the departed are still to be objects of interest, and
to be remembered in our prayers, and that we may and do help
them by praying to God for them."

It will be gathered from much of the foregoing that
Mr. Bellasis must have already "read and appropriated" the
Tracts for the Times. This was so, thanks to the Rev. W.
Gresley's recommendation of them at Stowe House, Lichfield,
in 1836. They had at that time swelled to a volume, which
Mr. Bellasis had purchased, and begun to read. "The very
first tract," he writes, "engrossed me; they gave a system to
my High Church proclivities; I thought the reasoning conclusive. They did not, however, at first give me any leaning
toward the Catholic Church. . . . They gave me the idea
of acting consistently and upon a principle, and also of submission to Church authority." And in 1838, he says: "I
began to read the *British Critic* and some of Newman's
Sermons, and we were so taken with the latter that Eliza
and I, having been to the Isle of Wight, returned by way of
Oxford, to get sight of the author, and on the 22nd of
April we went to the afternoon service at St. Mary's, when
Mr. Newman officiated and preached; his sermon was on
Korah's rebellion, which he compared to modern dissent. . . .
I began to think that as religion had to do with supernatural
matters, we must get it from some authority, and not from our
own fancies and reasonings. At this time I did not imagine

any other authority than the Church of England, and was dissatisfied to find that her authority was not obeyed; at all events, I was determined to obey her myself, so far as I could, and I began the observance of fasts and festivals, which was particularly enjoined but not in practice carried out. . . . It was a satisfaction to me to think that, at all events, I was obeying the authority I acknowledged."[1]

It was this question of authority and of obedience thereto that began seriously to exercise the legal mind in 1841. "We denied the right of Dissenters to have separated themselves from the Church of England, and yet we claimed that it had the right to disunite herself from the Catholic Church. How was this?"

In a letter (amongst others of the same purport to divers friends) of October 23, 1843, to Brande Morris, author of *Nature, a Parable,* &c., he asks:

"1. What was the theory of Church authority on which the Reformation in England took place; was it that each national Church, or each Archiepiscopate, or any number of Bishops acting together, or each particular Bishop, had the right to determine matters of faith without reference to the rest of the Christian world?

"2. Are we prepared to allow to all other similar bodies the same right we then assumed ourselves?

"3. What is the nature of the obedience due from us to the decisions of our national Church?

4. "Is the same obedience due from persons within the sphere of other national Churches, as we hold to be due from us to our own?

"These questions," he continues, "Gresley is trying to answer upon Anglican principles, so you may suppose it is no easy job for him."

"He has given Mr. Gresley some nuts to crack," writes

[1] Every Lent, from 1832 to 1850, he would draw up some six to fourteen rules of observance submitting them to the clergyman of his district for approval. Having declined once or twice a relative of his wife's, Mr. Entwisle's invitation in Lent, he at length explained the reason, March 1, 1844: "We never dine out, if we can help it, on Fridays, and by way of making some trifling distinction, during Lent, we extend the rule to Wednesdays as well as Fridays. The difficulty I have in telling you this is, first, that it looks like display, as if we thought ourselves stricter than other people, and secondly, it has the appearance of criticizing what others may think fit to do; I feel confident, however, that you will acquit me of either of these intentions—in fact we look upon it as a mere private fancy of our own. . . . And now pray put this letter in the fire."

Mrs. Bellasis to a friend, "which will appear, I dare say, in his next book."

"I told him," wrote the Serjeant to the Rev. Upton Richards, "that it was highly desirable that he, or some having the ear of the public, should state plainly what the Anglican theory of Church authority was, for it was there that the shoe pinched."

An elaborate correspondance ensued on this subject between himself and Gresley, "the writing of which," he says, "necessitated more careful inquiry, and tended to give me a still greater leaning towards the Catholic Church."

"You know my opinion about the Pope," he writes to a friend, March 31, 1843. "I think he is the Head of the Christian Church, and that Henry VIII. committed a great sin in throwing off the Pope's authority and assuming it himself, and I wish that authority were restored." In another letter to the Rev. Mr. Blew, of February 26, 1844, he says the present position "is an irregular state of things, brought about by unfavourable circumstances, untenable logically, but justifiable as things are, and it was this view that I wished Gresley to take, but he preferred adopting our present condition as the true and proper one, with which I cannot agree."

In 1843, business happening to be slack at Westminster, Mr. Bellasis' leisure was "employed in researches upon the validity of the consecration of Archbishop Parker, upon which depended the claim that the Anglican Church made to have the Apostolic Succession." He writes to Brande Morris, April 29, 1843: "I had no particular object in examining into the case of Barlow, but I was so struck by the contrariety of statement on the subject that, as a matter of curiosity, I determined to ransack that one point to see where the truth lay." "I occupied myself with this subject," he continues, "both at the British Museum and at the Archbishop's library at Lambeth Palace. In particular I made a careful search into Cranmer's Register; indeed, I made an index of it. My confidence was much shaken." The result of his inquiries, placed at the disposal of Seager and Haddan (engaged on a new edition of Courayer), were communicated in letters to Mr. C. Blandy at Reading, several times printed.[1]

To their "conclusive and momentous force," Cardinal Newman bore witness in October, 1882, and when told by some

---

[1] *Was Barlow a Bishop?* Third issue. Catholic Truth Society.

one of his having had a mind to send a copy of the letters to
a certain Anglican prelate, His Eminence observed to him:
"Had you done so, one would have looked to the newspaper
placards for an announcement, 'Attempted assassination of the
Dean.'"

In a letter also to Dr. Pusey, October 30, 1843, the Serjeant
discussed a curious point about Barlow's assistants at Archbishop Parker's consecration, *i.e.* Scory and Coverdale, and their
own consecrations. These, it seems, took place on the same
day at Croydon and Lambeth respectively, according to the
Lambeth Register, a fact that needed explanation. "It certainly
is not probable," Mr. Bellasis says, "that three Bishops should,
with the proper offices and notaries present, consecrate one
Bishop at Croydon; that they should all receive the Holy
Communion, and then adjourn to Lambeth, and taking the
officials with them, consecrate another Bishop; that the Bishop
of London should preach his sermon over again, and that they
should all again receive Holy Communion."

In 1843, Dr. Blomfield, Bishop of London, as is well known,
"becoming alarmed," to quote the Serjeant, "at the supposed
tendency to Catholicism evinced by Oakeley . . . commenced
proceedings against him in the Ecclesiastical Court, Hope,
Badeley, Roundell Palmer, myself, and others, subscribing to
defend him, . . . but the Rev. Upton Richards took his place,
entertaining, however, the same opinions."

Lively incidents in the Tractarian war appear in the
Serjeant's correspondence at this time. In a note to Oakeley
of September 16, 1843, he says: "We hear from some friends
in this quarter that you and your chapel are under consideration
by the Bishop, and that he says openly at his dinner-table that
he will either have your book of Devotions for the Holy
Communion or the chapel." The Bishop also proceeded against
Richards' Catechism, and "the suppression of it," the Serjeant
thinks, addressing its compiler, August 30, 1843, "will do great
harm to the cause of the Church of England, even on Anglican
principles; of course if I cannot get yours, I shall get the
Dean's, and if I thought that the Church of England, as such,
really did reject the doctrines of yours, I should swallow the
Dean's whole rather than lose what yours contains. 'There
now!' 'as we say in these parts)." And to Mrs. Bellasis,
November 20, 1843, he writes: "Richards assured the Bishop
some time since that he was no party to the publication of the

second little Catechism which came out as a substitute for his own, and that he was not even aware that such a thing was intended till he saw it; and yet the Bishop told Oakeley the other day that he had no doubt that there was a good understanding between Ward (the author of the second) and Richards, and so Richards has written to the Bishop to ask an interview, and means to give it him well." And to C. Blandy, February 28, 1845, he writes: "We have had a very hard fight; on Wednesday in last week, Oakeley (having seen the Bishop the day before) received a letter from 'Charles James' requesting him to resign his licence. Oakeley had entreated him the day before not to be in a hurry on so important a matter, and almost wrote his fingers off, writing all Tuesday night, to get some kind of defence before the eyes of the Bishop before he took any step; and the pamphlet you have read was actually written and printed within twenty-four hours, but not in time to reach the Bishop, before he had written to Oakeley to the above effect; Oakeley replied by saying, that he begged till Monday to consider, offering not to officiate in the meantime; the Bishop replied giving him till Tuesday. In the interim between Wednesday and Tuesday, Oakeley made up his mind that if he was to go, it must be at the Bishop's own responsibility, and his friends in London beset the Bishop on all sides. Gladstone wrote to him; Coleridge and Patteson (the Judges), Barge, Q.C., Twining, and others, did so also. Robert Williams and I called upon him, but all to no purpose; the only thing that frightened him was that Coleridge told him plainly, that although he did not agree with Oakeley, yet that an interference even with an extreme person on the one side without interfering with extreme persons on the other, was a position he could not support; that if Oakeley went, Baptist Noel, Villiers, and others, must go likewise; further, that many High Churchmen continued to support the Church societies, although disapproving their proceedings, because upon the whole their views were treated with impartiality, but that so soon as any partial interference took place, that instant such persons would fall off; that they remained for peace, and if the peace was broken, their reason for remaining was gone. This shook him, and he then took the opinion of Dr. Lushington whether Oakeley's letter to the Vice-Chancellor was inconsistent with his subscription, and he replied that it was a very difficult question, depending in great measure upon historical considerations, and in fact was

so doubtful that he advised him not to act against Oakeley.
So then, it is now admitted that it is a doubtful question
whether 'all Roman doctrine' is or is not consistent with the
Thirty-nine Articles! Nothing was more unexpected, and
Oakeley recommenced his ministrations to the great joy of his
friends." [1]

As trustee and treasurer for the fund towards re-building
Margaret Street Chapel, the Serjeant had no easy task in its
disposal, and this of course primarily owing to Oakeley's
leaving the Church of England before the re-building had
begun. "The original proposal from Oakeley to receive contributions for the purpose," he writes, October 24, 1845, to
Canon J. B. Mozley, "specified that the fund was to be placed
'unconditionally' at his disposal. . . . Oakeley . . . has transferred the whole fund into my name. . . . In the meantime
I have received various applications from persons, . . . they
desire to have their contributions returned to them, or to be
allowed to give them a new destination. The Dean of
Chichester (Dr. Chandler), on the other hand, is understood
to object to the return of any part of the fund;" *i.e.*, the fund
was for a church, not for Mr. Oakeley; an "offertory" once
given, could not be recalled, &c. Dr. Pusey and Mr. Gladstone
inclined to a similar view, the latter, however, allowing that
there was room for legitimate difference of opinion, and in a
letter to the treasurer, December 17, 1845, taking "the
opportunity of bearing testimony to the very judicious manner
in which you appear to have executed a task of delicacy." [2]

A passage of arms between Dr. Blomfield and Mr. Wingfield
is narrated in a letter of November 23, 1843, to Mrs. Bellasis.

[1] What the ultimate loss of Oakeley was to Margaret Street, may be gathered
from a very interesting letter of Ward to Dr. Pusey. See *W. G. Ward and
the Oxford Movement*, p. 354. "He (Oakeley) claimed the right to *hold*, as distinct
from *teaching*, all the peculiar doctrines of the Church of Rome, while remaining a
clergyman of the Church of England. Bishop Blomfield felt it his duty not to pass
over this extraordinary claim. He might have summarily revoked the licence of
Mr. Oakeley, but he thought it better, with the advice of his Archdeacons, to give
him the same benefits which he would have enjoyed as an incumbent." (*Blomfield's
Memoir.*) "Work your will, gentlemen," was Oakeley's attitude before the Court
of Arches that condemned him, "but I will neither seek your aid, nor deprecate
your conclusions."

[2] He writes to Dr. Pusey, February 9, 1846: "I did not see how I could hold
subscribers' money against their will." On November 22, 1845, the fund amounted
to £1,483 4s. 11d. (Three per Cent. Reduced), and £879 8s. 5d. (Three per Cent.
Consols), and the amount out of the latter then reclaimed was £521. The fund
was at length transferred into the names of Dean Chandler and Mr. Beresford Hope,
and the present building proceeded with.

The Bishop, on the point of discipline, was probably right ; on the other hand, the Rev. William Wingfield, brother of Mrs. W. G. Ward, had Mr. Bellasis' sympathies, and is referred to as "a very quiet, cool, and exemplary person." "The case is this," the Serjeant continues. "Wingfield is curate to Mr. Cooper at a West End chapel. Cooper desired Wingfield to read the Fifth of November service. Wingfield said he could not, Cooper said he should, Wingfield said he would not, so Cooper read it himself. The next day Cooper told him he must leave the curacy. Wingfield said, 'You will, of course, give the usual six months' notice.' 'No,' said Cooper, 'you must go at once, or else I shall apply to the Bishop.' 'Well then, apply to the Bishop, but I cannot by leaving at once, as you propose, admit myself in the wrong.' Cooper applied to the Bishop, and the Bishop sent for Wingfield. 'How is this, Mr. Wingfield, that you would not read the Fifth of November service ?' 'My lord, it is not a Church service, but a State service, and I could not conscientiously read it. Bishop : 'But Mr. Cooper desired you to read it.' Wingfield : 'He did, my lord, but that did not make it right to read it.' Bishop : 'But putting aside this point, as you do not agree, you must resign your curacy.' Wingfield : 'My lord, I cannot resign my curacy. If I have done wrong let me be dismissed, but I cannot admit myself wrong by resigning.' Bishop : 'If you do not resign I shall deprive you.' Wingfield : 'I am in your lordship's hands, but resign I will not.' Bishop : 'But you differ with your Rector.' Wingfield : 'I differed in declining to use this service, which I do not understand your lordship commands.' Bishop : 'That is not now the point ; you differ.' Wingfield : 'We do, my lord, but my predecessor refused to read the Athanasian Creed, and Mr. Cooper did not think that a cause of dismissal.' Bishop : 'It does not signify ; you must go.' Wingfield : 'Very well, my lord, you can withdraw my licence, or Mr. Cooper can give me six months' notice, but under the circumstances I cannot go voluntarily.' Bishop : 'I will give you three days to consider.' Wingfield : 'It is unnecessary, my lord, I have made up my mind.' Bishop : 'If you will not resign, you shall never hold a cure in my diocese again, and I will not countersign your testimonials, so that you can get no employment in any other.' Wingfield : 'In that case I can retire into lay communion.' Bishop : 'You had better

consider about it.' Wingfield : ' I have considered and determined, and I will not resign.' Bishop : 'You have all the
arrogance of a certain party in the Church, to which, no doubt,
you belong.' And so they parted, and it remains to be seen
whether the Bishop will drive another real hard-working man
into lay communion."[1]

The Serjeant's own view of the service to which Mr. Wingfield objected is given in a letter to Mrs. Bellasis, Nov. 6, 1843 :
" It had not occurred to me that I should fall in with the Fifth
of November service at Carisbrooke, but sure enough we had it
in full, and with all its proper emphasis ; if it had not been that
I wished to receive the Holy Communion with my mother, I
think I should have gone to Newport and avoided it, but
I submitted to it on that account. It is really a shocking
service. There is throughout a bitterness in the prayers which,
unsuitable at all times, is particularly so in addresses to God
Almighty. Mr. Maude, moreover, read the prayer which is
directed to be read on that day in lieu of the prayer, 'In time
of war and tumults,' wherein we pray God to 'cut off' our
bloodthirsty enemies, and those who turn faith into faction, &c.
The sermon . . . ended by saying we were to learn three
things from that day's service—love for our Protestant faith,
loyalty to the Queen, and *brotherly love and kindness* to all.
I hoped it was all over when the Communion began, but no,
even that was desecrated with expressions about 'hellish
malice,' &c."[2]

Mr. Bellasis' letters to H. Tritton, Mr. R. Twining, and others,
refer to a case of greater interest. The Rev. N. Woodard,
"an earnest and right-minded person," was a poor clergyman,
with a wife and family dependent upon his very small clerical
stipend. He had ministered for over two years in what was
one of the worst East End districts in 1843, St. Bartholomew's,
Bethnal Green, and after three years' unremitting labour in
establishing schools and daily services, he had succeeded in

---

[1] " In his intercourse with his clergy, his natural quickness and occasional
abruptness of manner might at times have worn the appearance of harshness, but it
was chiefly on the surface " (*Memoir of C. J. Blomfield, D.D.*, &c. vol. ii. p. 211,
a work which gives an interesting account of an able and many-sided character).

[2] He writes in his journal for November 5, 1822 : "Our garden was a complete
scene of the re-acting of the Powder Plot. Guns, cannons, squibs, crackers, and the
whole of the usual accompaniments of the celebration of that worthy individual Guy
Fawkes, were brought to commemorate his disappointment, as if, because Guy did
not make an explosion on that day, there is to be one made by every one else
whenever the day comes round. *Lucus a non lucendo.*"

implanting a "Church spirit among people heretofore wholly
Dissenters or heathen." Woodard's "self-denying habits" and
"specific Catholic teaching" (none other, as he thought, being
of any avail)[1] had reached and attracted his congregation, and
they had been plainly recommended, on the authority, amongst
others, of Cranmer, whose *Catechism* is very explicit upon the
point, to make their minister "acquainted with their state of
mind;" for "on being convinced of their true repentance he
had power to absolve them." The Bishop got to hear of this
thorough-going discourse by means of an anonymous letter, and
Woodard was brought to book. "Your doctrine is erroneous,"[2]
his lordship said, in answer to Woodard, "and your being
so excellent a person makes you more dangerous." When
Woodard brought forward Bishop Bull as an authority for the
language employed, the Bishop replied that Bishop Bull was
not Woodard's Bishop; that while it might not be difficult to
produce some authority for certain isolated expressions, yet the
tone and spirit of the sermon appeared to him to be highly
objectionable. He begged that the correspondence might
terminate. Subsequently, after a vain entreaty that the
doctrine of the sermon might be examined by a proper
tribunal, Woodard was compelled to retire. The Serjeant's
note of December 9, 1843, describes an interview his lordship
had with Woodard; how he summoned the Rev. C. B. Dalton
in "to sit in a corner and hear what passed, and then asked
Woodard whether he was prepared to recant his opinion that
'a priest had power to convey God's pardon to penitent sinners.'
This Woodard positively refused to do. He was willing, he
said, to put himself under the Bishop's guidance as to the
propriety of putting that doctrine forward in this or that place,
or at this or that time, but the doctrine itself he could not deny.
The Bishop then told him that that made it impossible for him
to help him, were he ever so much disposed. "But I do not see,"

---

[1] A similar opinion came from an unexpected quarter. "Met Mr. Danby at
Lancaster," the Serjeant writes. "In former conversations I have had with him he
had appeared to be a very Low Churchman. To-day he said it was quite plain that
the poor had lost all respect for the clergy as a body; that in his opinion nothing
would restore the proper sympathy between them but impressing the people with a
sense of the *priestly office*. He said, further, that the majority of the clergy did not
hesitate to speak of the Church of England as doomed, but that it would last their
time" (28 Aug. 1842).

[2] The Bishop's views against auricular confession are fully given, apparently in
reference to this very case, in a letter dating from Fulham Palace, July 6, 1843
(*Blomfield's Memoir*, vol. ii. pp. 83, 84).

writes the Serjeant to Woodard at an early stage of the case, "on what principle it is that he takes so serious a step as that of actually dismissing a clergyman from his cure for saying what you have said, whilst undoubted heresy is preached in other quarters of his diocese, week after week, with impunity."

Then there was a Unitarian lady's case for re-baptism that much interested Oakeley and others, and the Serjeant wrote to Dr. Pusey about it on St. Luke's day, 1843 : "Your opinion was conveyed to the lady on whose behalf it was asked, and she applied to the clergyman of her parish, and he to his Bishop, the Archbishop of Canterbury. The case was plainly stated to him, and that she had been baptized in the name of God only, without any mention of the Holy Trinity. The Archbishop said he was clearly of opinion that Confirmation supplied the defects of Baptism." Dean Church writes of Dr. Howley and three other Bishops that they "might be considered theologians,"[1] but it may be safely affirmed that had this Primate really been a legitimate successor of St. Dunstan, St. Thomas, and St. Edmund, as maintained by "the cuckoo continuity"[2] theory, His Grace could never have propounded here the view that he did, and still have remained till death an undisturbed occupant of the see of Canterbury. "It would be presumptuous in me," writes the bewildered Serjeant, October 23, 1843, to Mr. W. Ford, "to pass any judgment upon the Archbishop's decision, but my opinion is a very strong one, that if the original baptism was not in the name of the Holy Trinity, it is null *ab initio*, and cannot be remedied but by *un*conditional baptism, and (even if it were only doubtful), that conditional baptism is absolutely necessary for safety." The sequel to this strange affair, exhibiting the Primate as heretical in the judgment of East and West, is given in a letter from the Serjeant to Dr. Pusey on St. Andrew's day, 1843 : "I enclose you an extract from the lady on whose behalf I applied to you respecting re-baptism ; you will see that she thinks it her duty to submit to what her parish priest (Mr. Bowdler) and the Archbishop have determined for her. I do not myself see how to find fault with this determination on her part; it is surely acting on a true principle

[1] *Oxford Movement*, First Edit. p. 217. It will be remembered that Dr. Howley's successor, Sumner, and his brother of York sitting as assessors, concurred in the Gorham decision of March, 1850, Bishop Blomfield dissenting.

[2] See Sermon, by the Rev. W. Humphrey, S.J., entitled, *The Unity and Continuity of the Church*, Third Edit. 1892, p. 11. (Burns and Oates.)

Wyresdale Tower, Garstang
St Andrews Day 1843

My dear Dr Pusey,

I enclose you an extract from a letter from the lady on whose behalf I applied to you respecting re baptism, you will see that she thinks it her duty to sub mit to what her Parish priest, (Mr Rowden,) and the Abp: have determined for her. I do not myself see how to find fault with this determination on her part, she is surely acting on a true principle however unprepared our authorities may be the doctrine on

Dr Ashworth joins me in sending our best re spects and regards believe me dear Dr Pusey

Yours most sincerely
Edw Pallodes —

however unprepared our authorities may be to be relied on." . . .
Extract: "I feel more and more that it is my duty to obey;
the case was put fairly and fully to the Archbishop, even to the
expression of my earnest desire for re-baptism, and what was
his decision? 'After going well into the case, and giving it all
due consideration,' as Mr. Bowdler has since written me, 'that
he saw neither the necessity nor the propriety of it.' . . .
I confess I have not courage wilfully and deliberately to
disobey him whom God has set over me. As I regard the
matter settled by the Archbishop, settled beyond my power to
revoke, it will be wisest not to harass myself with opinions
which only make duty the more difficult."

We may, however, trust that the lady's "earnest desire" to
carry out our Blessed Lord's express commands may have
saved her from the consequences of her edifying submission
to Archbishop Howley.

It was the Serjeant's connection with Margaret Street Chapel
from 1839 that naturally led to his knowing some of the Oxford
leaders as he did. He had of course become very intimate, as
an influential and active parishioner, with Oakeley, the incumbent, and it was Oakeley who, in the autumn of the above year,
had given him letters of introduction to Mr. Newman, W. G.
Ward, of Balliol, and Brande Morris, of Exeter. "I spent,"
he says, "three days at Oxford, breakfasted with one, and
dined with another, and went over to Littlemore."[1] "How
very nice Littlemore is," writes Oakeley to the Serjeant, in
1839, *à propos* of this visit. "I had not before seen the altar
and its accompaniments. I hear you were much pleased, and
was very glad to find from your kind note that all had passed
off so well. You will be a welcome visitor at Oxford whenever
you can come. Monday is the 'feast of the dedication' of
Littlemore, when Newman's friends go out, and it is kept,
together with the ensuing days, as a festival. The poor seem to

[1] Mr. Bellasis' first letter to Mr. Newman appears to have been written March 7,
1840, from Bloomsbury, and runs as follows: "My dear sir, — I received yesterday
from Messrs. Rivington a newly-published book, *The Church of the Fathers*, as a
present from the author; and I am told I am indebted to you for it; pray allow me to
thank you for your kind recollection of me, and at the same time for your friendly
reception of me during my visit to Oxford last month. May I also take the occasion
which your kindness affords me of expressing my deep sense of the benefits which I
have derived from the study of your writings. It would not be becoming in me to
praise them, but a sincere expression of personal gratitude, may not, I hope, be
considered impertinent on the part of your obliged friend and obedient servant,
EDWARD BELLASIS."

take great interest in adorning the church, and it seems altogether the most perfect specimen of a village festival one can imagine." In 1840, Mr. Bellasis' visit to Oxford was several times repeated. He was generally the guest there either of Morris, of Exeter, or Oakeley and Ward, of Balliol; and Hope-Scott, Badeley, Pusey, and Roundell Palmer, got to know him, while Mr. Newman, happening to be in London during this year, came to dine at Bedford Square. Then again, in the spring of 1841, Mr. Bellasis tells us that he visited the Yonges "at Otterbourne, an outlying chapel of Hursley, on occasion of the opening of Mr. Keble's church at Amfield. Here I enlarged my acquaintance amongst the friends of Mr. Newman, especially Keble himself, Mr. Henry Wilberforce, Mr. Ryder, and Mr. Leigh. Mr. Newman himself was also there, and I spent two days in their company." And in the same year he became acquainted at Oxford with Dr. Todd, Johnson the observer, Albany Christie, David Lewis, of Jesus, Palmer, of Magdalen, Dalgairns, and Sir George Bowyer; and in 1842, with F. W. Faber, Robert A. Coffin, and William Dodsworth.

"We have had a rather pleasant, interesting man visiting us," writes Canon James Mozley to his sister, in January, 1840, "a Mr. Bellasis, a barrister from London, very High Church, a friend of Ward, of Balliol, who happens to be away just now. Newman and others have entertained him. It is amusing to see the variety of a Londoner in Oxford. Of the London element he retains enough to make a change from what one commonly sees here; though with none of the disagreeable features of it; for example, he is so much more fluent, and can give regular narrations with spirit, showing a person who has been accustomed to argue and make speeches." And again, in May, 1842, he says: "Mr. Bellasis, from London, came for a day on purpose to see Tom, and he and Harriet had some pleasant talk. He describes the body of lawyers in town as changing rapidly; and really holds out a prospect of the old union between the legal and ecclesiastical bodies being revived."[1] Although not, like his father and brothers, an Oxford man, the Serjeant seems to have become acceptable there, and by his honest zeal and active sympathy in the cause, to have won the regard and confidence of many of the Tractarians in those days of trial for the assertion of Catholic principles. In 1842, upon occasion of Archbishop Howley's receiving an

[1] *Letters of Canon Mozley.* pp. 66. 135.

address from Cheltenham directed against the Tracts, and
replying thereto that the matter would have his "grave consideration," a proposed counter-address from "members of the
profession of the law" was submitted by Mr. Bellasis to
Dr. Pusey and Mr. Newman. Both wrote very cordially to him
on the subject, while making comments and suggestions.[1]

"The Archbishop's answer has grown more and more
ominous in my mind since I read it," wrote Mr. Newman to
him. "First, an answer to such an address is a very unusual
thing. Then he makes it just at this time, increasing the
existing excitement, and suggesting hope to the very party that
is violent. There is no trimming of the balance. And then it
argues a change of policy. Last March he put down all
addresses from the clergy *for* the Tracts, on the ground that
otherwise he could not put down addresses against them. Now
he almost takes the initiative, and braves the discord which is
likely to be the consequence of it. . . . The words, 'grave
consideration,' unless used in the light mocking way of the
hustings, must imply a great deal. I have no view at all what
they mean. . . . My difficulty is, how he can do anything
without interfering with our divines, except, indeed, express
hatred of Rome."[2] At length a postponement of any legal
address was determined upon. "I am more than disposed to
think that you are right in delaying it," wrote Mr. Newman,

[1] See Appendix B for text of the address: "It would certainly seem better to
leave out any opinion about the Tracts," wrote Mr. Newman from Oriel, January 5,
1842, "the *end* would be quite the same without it. . . . There is something
awkward, perhaps, in the *form* of the address, though I cannot quite describe what
I mean. The clause about doing nothing in this time of excitement, though very
much to the purpose, seems rather free." Dr. Pusey wrote, January 3, 1842: "I
was against any address of sympathy to us last year, as feeling that we did not want
it, and I was afraid lest it shd. call forth a counter-declaration, and commit people
before they considered what they were doing. I had not heard of ye Cheltenham
address, or ye ABp's reply. But if they have begun the attack, I quite agree
with you that it is desirable that there should be counter-addresses; else ye Bps
will be misled. I very much fear that they do not in the least realize the state of
feeling in ye Ch.; and will consequently make mistakes wh. may be very
injurious; it is natural to judge of things by ye sensation they make; they have no
idea of strong, deep, quiet feeling. I hope that ye poetry el. (election) will, amid all
its evils, have some effect this way; but I should think that such addresses as you
speak of will also do good, both as expressing sympathy, putting ye Bps more in
possession of ye real state of things, and inclining them in ye end, perhaps, to wish
all such addresses at an end on both sides, wh. will tend to give us what we so
much want—peace. I like the topics you have mentioned, and agree with yr
reasons why ye barristers shd. begin."

[2] Compare J. H. N. to Keble (Mozley, *Corr.* ii. 381, 382). Also: "They talk
(but this is a secret) of an address of lawyers to him (the Archbishop) for the Tracts."

E

from Littlemore, February 10, 1842. "It is true that the want
of sympathy is the trial of various persons up and down the
country, and is in a certain sense preying on their minds and
doing them harm, but it calls for nothing *immediate*, nor would
be removed by one manifestation. You lawyers are far too
powerful a gun not to be reserved for some great occasion, and
with much gratitude for the personal feeling which in the case
of yourself and others is united to an interest in the principles
in jeopardy, still I sincerely hope you may not have occasion
to come forward. Meanwhile, both parties, ultra Protestants
and R. Catholics, consider that the Government is leaguing
with the Bishops to exterminate us. . . . I do not see how it is
possible."

But although nothing came of the addresses to Howley or
Blomfield,[1] Mr. Newman again expressed himself grateful for
that sympathy the want of which he particularly felt at
this very time. "I am very much obliged by the kind
consideration you show towards myself," he writes on the
16th, "and assure you I feel it much. I do not know that
it makes me unhappy at all, because it somehow seems to
be my lot, but certainly hardly anything is said to me, or
comes to me, even from friends, of a sympathetic character.
The truth is, I suppose, it is difficult for them to put themselves
into my place. This only makes me more grateful to those
who do. . . . However habituated one may be to bear ice
and snow as one's climate, I don't suppose it ceases to be
the nature of things that sunshine and zephyrs are the more
pleasant of the two, and I thank you for the friendly words
which have been wafted from Bedford Square." And on the
23rd of March he wrote: "The storm from Lambeth seems
blowing off, but I am out of the way of hearing news here, and
perhaps am flattering myself unwarrantably. Or perhaps it is
merely 'hushed in grim repose.'" To which the Serjeant
replied: "The storm has apparently passed away, as you say,
but some think that if the pilots who were some time since
placed under hatches for endeavouring to change the moorings
of the vessel, are not again allowed to look out and touch the
helm, there is great danger that she will go ashore, or at least
that more of the crew will lose confidence, and try to make
their escape."

[1] Of any address to Blomfield Newman says: "*Omne ignotum pro magnifico*
will tell more with the Bishop of London than signatures on paper."

"I do fear," wrote Dr. Pusey to the Serjeant, January 3, 1842, "that we are suffering very much from want of courage. Truths are deprecated, and things allowed to go by default when, if persons were to speak out boldly, they would carry others with them, *e.g.*, what a torrent ag^st. Tract 80,[1] and feeble defences, instead of saying boldly that people were all sick, and are but like ill-trained children, who are clamoring that the medicine is unpalatable."

When Mr. Newman retired into lay communion in 1843 Mr. Bellasis made a point of being present at the last Littlemore festival commemorating the dedication of the church, and he heard the last Protestant sermon preached by the celebrated Vicar of St. Mary's, on "The Parting of Friends," and has given us an account of the proceedings.

To Mrs. Bellasis, September 24, 1843. Exeter College, Oxford: "I came off by the Great Western . . . on to Steventon, and got to Oxford at half-past eight, and took up my quarters at Exeter College with Morris. This morning we were at early Communion at St. Mary's at seven, and at the Cathedral at Christ Church to service at eight. Dr. Pusey was at St. Mary's, and he and I and Morris went to the Cathedral together. We also went to his house with him, and had a good deal of very agreeable talk, he is quite recovered, and I never saw him looking better; proceedings are being taken by him to compel the Vice-Chancellor to state his charge against him, and hear him.[2] . . . At present I have seen no one else except Ward, Christie, and Lewis, of Jesus, but there is a large assembly from all quarters. Newman, I am told, is very much out of spirits, he gave up his living on Monday last, and went up to London with a friend to a notary for that purpose; as soon as he mentioned that he was come to resign a living and that his name was Newman,

---

[1] *On Reserve*, &c. By Isaac Williams.

[2] The Serjeant writes to a friend in 1843: "You mention the Vice-Chancellor and his unheard-of conduct towards Dr. Pusey, that in itself is surprising, but that a man of known character should be openly condemned before the world for preaching a Catholic verity, and that the whole of the bench of Bishops should remain silent, leaving it to be supposed that they acquiesce in the justice of the condemnation is very strange. Could there be a more obvious duty in a Bishop than to stand forth to defend those who are suffering for the truth?" When Dr. Pusey's tongue, so long silenced by authority, was untied again, the Rev. J. B. Mozley wrote to the Serjeant, February 12, 1846: "Pusey's sermon has gone off quietly, the thing said about it in high quarters is, that it is much to be lamented, but not to be complained of."

the notary said: 'May I ask whether you are the Mr. Newman from whose sermons I have derived so much pleasure?'"

To Mrs. Bellasis, September 25, 1843: "After writing to you yesterday I remained chatting with Morris till noon, and then as he was going out to afternoon service at Water-Eaton, three miles off, Ward and I walked out with him about half-way. Ward and I then returned, and I called on Dr. Pusey to talk to him about Ford's question relating to the re-baptism of Unitarians, respecting which he gave me a most satisfactory answer. We, that is, every one in Oxford, went to St. Mary's to afternoon service, as it was supposed that Newman would preach there for the last time; he did preach, but made no allusion to his retirement, his text, 'The just shall live by faith,' striking, as usual, both in matter and manner, and very solemn.[1] After church, a small party dined with Morris in Exeter College, the influx of Newman's friends having filled the Observer's table, where we were to have dined; our party were Morris and I, Mr. Macmullen, Goldsmith, and Mr. and Mrs. Tritton, and we sat talking till near midnight. . . . We are just going to start for Littlemore. Dr. Pusey and I walk out there together, and I am now going to call upon him at Christ Church for that purpose."

To Mrs. Bellasis, September 26, 1843: "I cannot delay giving you an account of the proceedings of yesterday till I come, so, though I have but little time to write, I shall try to do it. I called on Dr. Pusey at quarter before ten, and you may suppose he is very well when I tell you that he walked me out to Littlemore, three miles, at such a pace as almost to knock me up. The service was at eleven, and, as usual, the chapel was decorated, with flowers upon the altar, in the windows above, over Mrs. Newman's tomb, and on every seat on both sides of the middle aisle, chiefly dahlias, Passion flowers, and fuchsias, and they were most beautiful as well as elegantly arranged, the service commenced with a procession of the clergy

---

[1] He writes to Richards, October 1, 1843: "I heard Newman preach at St. Mary's on the Sunday, and in the course of his sermon he said: 'If people see others more careful and more strict than themselves, they generally avoid following their example by saying 'their principles are good, but they carry them too far,' *as if such a thing were possible*. The next day I received a letter from Gresley . . . his letter ends with these words: 'At any rate, I trust you will not take any step without carefully endeavouring to divest your mind of the notion that it is necessary to carry out principles to their full length, when it is obvious that *the full lengths of even the best principles are sinful extremes*. How curious that I should hear two such contrary propositions so nearly simultaneously,—which is the true one?'"

and school-children from the schools to the chapel, chanting
a psalm as they walked; the officiating clergy were Newman
(for the last time), Pusey, Copeland, and Bowles. There was a
Communion, and Newman preached his farewell sermon. It is
easy enough to tell you these simple facts, but it would be no
easy thing to convey to you any adequate impression of the whole
scene, the crowd of friends from all parts, the half-mournful
greetings, the extreme silence of the chapel, though crowded till
chairs were obliged to be set in the churchyard, the children
with their new frocks and bonnets (Newman's parting gift).
I did not see Newman himself speak to any one before service,
the offertory was stated to be intended to be applied to completing the re-seating of the chapel, and the communicants were
one hundred and forty in number. But the sermon I can never
forget,[1] the faltering voice, the long pauses, the perceptible and
hardly successful efforts at restraining himself, together with
the deep interest of the subject, were almost overpowering;
Newman's voice was low, but distinct and clear, and his subject
was a half-veiled complaint and remonstrance at the treatment
which drove him away. We had a contrast drawn between the
conduct of Ruth and Orpah towards their mother-in-law, Orpah
kissed and left her, but Ruth clave unto her, and the conduct
of Ruth recommended to our imitation.[2] Then we had the
story of David and Jonathan, the scene of their separation,
when David quitted the Court of Saul, leaving his friend behind
him, with an address almost personal to Dr. Pusey who sat by,
and an application of the story to themselves. Then fancy
such a passage as the following, addressed to the English
Church: 'O my Mother! my Mother! how is it that those
who would have died for thee fall neglected from thy bosom?
how is it that whatever is keen in intellect, or patient in
investigation, or energetic in action, or ardent in devotion, or

---

[1] To W. Ford, September 30, 1843: "Newman's sermon at Littlemore was
affecting in the extreme, on the occasion of his retiring into lay communion, last
Monday. . . . His sermon hinted at the cause, and alluded also to the many persons
who are now refused Orders because they partake of his opinions; his apostrophe to
the Church of England was singularly beautiful." To Rev. Upton Richards,
October 1, 1843: "You would probably hear of Newman's farewell sermon; it was
very striking, and very affecting and most masterly. There was not a dry eye in the
church. I trust it will be printed, but could not ascertain that it would be so."
(See the last of the *Sermons on Subjects of the Day*.) The Serjeant used to say
afterwards that there was not a dry eye in the church except Newman's own. His
self-control communicated in a subtle way to his listeners his own intense feeling.

[2] W. Lockhart (it was playfully said at the time) was the Orpah referred to.

enthusiastic in affection, remains unused by thee? why are they
forced to stand idle in the market-place, whilst with ready
hands and eager hearts they are eager to toil for thee? How
is it thou hast no words of kindness, no sign of encouragement
for them, but that thou suspectest, or slightest, or scornest, or
fearest them, or at best dost but endure them?' Or fancy
his allusion to his own mother's laying the first stone of the
building, and to the many happy anniversaries of the consecration, of which that was probably the last. 'these have been
happy days, we met with cheerful hearts, and kept festival
after our fashion, now we eat our feast with our staff in our
hands, sorrowing most of all that thus at least we shall meet no
more.' And then his conclusion: 'And now, my friends, my
dear friends *(here a long pause)*, if you should be acquainted with
any one who by his teaching, or by his writings, or by his
sympathy has helped you, or has seemed to understand you, or
feel with you, &c. Oh! my friends *(here a long pause)*, remember
such a one and pray for him.' After the sermon, Newman
received the Communion, but took no further part in officiating.
Dr. Pusey consecrated the elements in tears, and once or twice
became entirely overcome and stopped altogether. However,
nothing I can say to you can give you the remotest idea of the
sorrowfulness or solemnity of the scene. It is understood that
Newman's successor will be Mr. Eden, Fellow of Oriel, a good
man, but one who, as an Evangelical, will think it a sacred duty
to change everything, and lift up his voice against all that has
been done.[1] And thus the services of the greatest man of our
times, the acutest and most laborious, and most energetic of
the sons of the English Church is lost to us, he retires into lay
communion. At the same time a new head has been elected
to Corpus Christi College who keeps hunters. . . . Visiting
Oxford does not loosen but tighten the ties that hold me;
what loosens them is the want of sympathy from those with
whom we ordinarily live and associate: the unexpressed
suspicion, the want of an encouragement to persist in what I

[1] To C. Blandy he writes, October 23, 1843: "Only think of the Provost of
Oriel College refusing testimonials to Mr. Eden in order to his entering upon
St. Mary's, because he would not distinctly repudiate No. 90!" Dr. Hawkins
thought it wiser, on second thoughts, to give way here, since his action, or inaction,
would only have tended to create a precedent for doing without any testimonials.
See *J. H. N. Corr.* Edit. Morley, ii. 426, 427. Writing to R. Twining from
Bleasdale, December 13, 1843, the Serjeant writes: "Our curate, Ashworth, has
just returned from being ordained priest at Chester, the Bishop allowed his examination to pass, although he was told that his answers were entirely Popish."

believe the true and right course. Every man has his times
of flagging, however earnest he may be; to live with those who
think and feel with you, is like swimming with the tide; if you
flag, you go with the stream and are carried on by those about
you; but to live amongst those who cannot sympathize with
you is swimming against the stream, if you flag, there is nothing
to help you on. If anything ever carries me towards Rome,
it will be want of sympathy from our own brethren in the
English Church; I don't think people see this at all, and so
they go on calling names, and saying, 'Get out, we don't want
you,' and then they are surprised that people go."[1]

And in another place, he dwells upon the evil of these
divided beliefs. "Where faith is one, and those who profess it
are united, they not only carry with them the assent of the
good, but their moral force rouses and carries forward the
indifferent and careless, as pebbles are moved by a rapid torrent.
When faith is divided, or when those who profess it contend as
antagonists, their moral momentum is destroyed, and the
indifferent fall away like sand in a slackened stream." And
he puts his thought into verse—

> As in a current with a rapid stream,
> The waters, as they flow, loosen and lift
> The sand and stones which in their channel lie,
> And in their own direction waft them on,
> Tho' in their nature heavy and inert;
> So, amongst men, the action of the just,
> Rouses and raises dull and careless souls,
> Awakes them from their listless apathy,
> And onward urges them to nobler ends;
> And the more rapidly the waters flow,
> Larger and larger are the stones which rise,
> And less and less resisting follow on,
> So the increase of earnestness in faith,
> Shakes from their torpor souls more sluggish still,
> And gives fresh life to those that lie as dead.
> And as the current, slackening its speed,
> Lets fall the heavier grains, which stop and sink,
> Their weight prevailing o'er momentum lost,
> Thus, too, the souls late wakened into life,
> If the example which aroused them fail,
> First hesitate, then stop in virtue's course,
> Then fall, and slumbering sleep a second death.

[1] On Feb. 12, 1846, the Rev. J. B. Mozley wrote to the Serjeant: "It is,
indeed, a sad thing to have friends going in this way. And you especially must feel
t deeply, and the last loss as much as any. I mean J. B. Morris."

CHAPTER IV.

ADVANCE TOWARDS CONVERSION. DIFFICULTIES AND PERPLEXITIES. ULTIMATE RECEPTION INTO THE CHURCH.

LOOKING back in November, 1845, upon the influences exercised by the Tractarian movement upon himself and his wife, the Serjeant wrote to her: "Certain subjects of unbounded importance have during the last few years agitated the world, subjects to which none can be indifferent; they sprang up nobody knows how, and interested all *pro* or *con* in a manner quite inexplicable, amongst others ourselves; and a certain view instilled itself into our minds, or was impressed upon them quite irrespective of any previous opinions we might have entertained, and indeed contrary to what might have been anticipated from our previous prepossessions; the illness of our child took us first in the hour of distress to Margaret Street Chapel, the rest seems to have followed step by step without any seeking on our part; the views which impressed us we have discoursed upon and interested ourselves about for years, each of us disclosed to the other every thought with the most unbounded confidence, and thus each, no doubt, acted upon the other as a regulator; I cannot doubt, on the one hand, that your opinions have been swayed by me, as, on the other hand, mine must have been modified by you."

"We had many careful conversations," he says elsewhere, "upon various matters (difficulties at that time) in the Catholic system. These conversations I put to paper in the form of dialogues between 'Philotheus and Eugenia,' and they exist among my memoranda. Some years after, my daughter Mary selected some of them, and had them printed under the title of *Preliminary Dialogues*, some copies of which still remain.[1] The

---

[1] *Philotheus and Eugenia: Dialogues between two Anglicans on Anglican Difficulties.* Their subjects are: The Incarnation; the Rosary, and doing acts with an invention; Social Prayer; Prayer and Worship, the Mass; Latin Prayers; Intercession and Invocation of Saints and the Office of the Blessed Virgin; Supernaturals and Miracles; Supposed abandonment of our Reasoning powers; Reading the Bible; Paid Agents of Charity; Purgatory; the Jesuits; Is the Church of England our Mother? Imitation of Catholic Practices. By Mr. Serjeant Bellasis. Second Edition. London: St. Anselm's Society, Agar Street, London, W., 1892.

necessity of qualifying myself to explain to her all the conclusions at which I had been long arriving, compelled me to a
degree of precision which I should hardly have reached if I
had had no one to convince but myself, so that her hesitation at
adopting my views was of the greatest possible service to me."

The sense of disillusion and distrust on the other hand, felt
as to the Church of England, viewed in its teaching capacity,
receives definite expression in a memorandum of March, 1848 :
"When our Lord ascended into Heaven He left behind Him
His Church to point out to man the way to holiness, and to
help him on his path. To save man from the futile attempt of
groping his own way, the Church is to teach him God's holy
truths, to instruct him in holy practices, to encourage him, and,
if necessary, to restrain him. If a man flags, it is the Church
which is to urge him on ; if he strays, it is the same Church
which is to bring him back ; if he doubts, she is to certify him ;
now, all this implies that the Church itself is to assume a
position of superiority, so as to direct and rule.

"But the Church of England does not direct and rule,
neither does she assume an attitude of authority ; she is for
the most part silent, and when she breaks her silence, it is
with uncertain and hesitating sounds ; instead of forming and
moulding individuals or the State, she submits herself to be
formed and moulded, now by the secular power, now by individuals for themselves ; all find fault with her, all talk of her as
defective, all assume a patronizing air, and instead of submitting
themselves to be mended by the Church, every one is for
mending it, and takes credit for countenancing and supporting
it. And the Church is willingly acquiescent and subservient,
and is content to be an humble dependent.

"As an ecclesiastical police she is useful, as a Christian
Church she has ceased to perform her duty ; there is neither
counsel for the doubtful, support for the weak, medicine for the
sick, rest for the weary, nor restraint for the unruly. ' The
diseased have ye not strengthened, neither have ye healed that
which was sick, neither have ye bound up that which was
broken, neither have ye brought again that which was driven
away, neither have ye sought that which was lost.' "

"We must improve the Church," said Mr. Richards to the
Serjeant one day, who replied, "No, I want the Church to
improve me." "I had very many conversations with my
Protestant friends and relatives," he writes, "as well as with

friends who more or less partook of my conclusions. I found
the former inconclusive in the highest degree, and I think
their views repelled me quite as much as the Catholic
system attracted me." What they meant, too, by certain
theological terms was no longer his own meaning of them.
"Scriptural," in their mouths, signified Scripture, in accordance
with their own understanding of Holy Writ ; " self-denial "
meant denying that they could do any good; "confession,"
admitting themselves in general terms to be sinners ; " repentance," leaving off a sin ; "Catholic," latitudinarian ; and "faith,"
their own opinion.

As early as January, 1840, too, a clergyman of the Church
of England had made these statements in conversation, much to
the Serjeant's perplexity : (1) Early Christianity was not to be
relied upon, and religion was in a better state now than in the
fourth century. (2) The canons were not binding on the laity,
if not made the law of the land by Act of Parliament. (3) The
grace of God did not pass to the persons ordained, or consecrated by the laying on of hands by the Bishop. The laying
on of hands in ordination was not an outward visible sign of
any inward spiritual grace, and in no sense any sacrament.
(4) Preaching was a means of grace in the same sense as the
sacraments, and had been productive of more holiness. (5) Our
salvation did not depend in any degree upon the work of the
Holy Spirit in our own hearts and conduct, but solely upon
the imputation of Christ's righteousness to us. (6) Our Saviour
was not present at the celebration of the Holy Communion in
any other sense than that He is present everywhere. (7) The
communion-table was not more sacred than anything else in
the church, and was in no sense an altar. (8) The Holy
Communion was in no sense a Sacrifice. (9) It was not certain
that none but Bishops could ordain ministers. (10) Faith
without proof was in no degree superior to faith with proof, and
the case of St. Thomas did not prove that it was. (11) A
person having once had a true and lively faith, and having
taken hold of Christ, could never fall away. (12) "Work out
your own salvation," meant work out the degree of happiness
you are to have in Heaven ; your salvation was worked for you.
(13) A bad man could not be a minister of God, and if he
administered the sacraments no inward grace could be expected
to accompany them. (14) The baptism of an infant unaccom-
panied by sincere prayer by those present did not convey any

inward grace. (15) The infant child of unbelieving parents could not receive the spiritual grace of Baptism ; there was no promise of it to the children of unbelieving parents.[1]

The Rev. Joseph Maude, too, a clergyman of the Church of England, on a visit to his brother the Serjeant, in December, 1849, expressed the following views : " No decision of the Privy Council, or the Bishops, or the Convocation, or any other body, is binding on the conscience of an individual. The authority of the Church in matters of faith, mentioned in the Thirty-nine Articles, means that the Church has authority to declare what her own rules and doctrines are ; it does not mean that you are bound to acquiesce in her decisions, and if you do not agree therewith you ought not to stay in the Church.[2] The formularies of the Church of England were intended to include both opinions on the subject of baptism ; those who hold baptismal regeneration, and those who deny it, may both continue in the Church. The differences between the Church of England and the chief dissenting bodies are merely differences of ecclesiastical government ; they agree in essentials, and a person may be saved in any of them. Even a Papist may be saved, although he (the speaker) believed the Romish Church to be Antichrist.[3] The

---

[1] The Serjeant does not give the name of this clergyman, but styles him a "respectable Evangelical." He adds, " I think it very possible that the time may come when it will appear very strange that some of the above opinions should ever have been current in the Church, and so I make this memorandum of them."

[2] " Although the Roman Catholic Church," he writes in March, 1848, "will put out heretical members, and excommunicate them, it never supposes that it can be the duty of any one to quit it voluntarily ; and therefore urging a person to quit the Catholic Church and go into some sect, is unknown and impossible. In the Anglican Church it is not uncommon to hear it said, even by Bishops, and high authorities of the Church, that such and such persons 'ought to go,' that it is a kind of intrusion in them to stay ; this is said by High Churchmen against Evangelicals, and by Evangelicals against High Churchmen, which shows that neither party consider it a duty to stay, only an advantage, because if it be a duty to stay, it cannot be right voluntarily to go." It may be added here that writing to his brother (on his way to Oxford, in February, 1845, to vote against Mr. Ward), the Serjeant, after saying, " I do not conceal from any one that I hold what you would call *ultra* opinions ; that, in fact, I coincide, so far as I know them, with the opinions entertained by Mr. Ward," goes on to say, " it has never, however, occurred to me that it is the duty of persons holding such opinions to quit the Church of England . . . it is our wish and desire to remain . . . but we shall consider any decision that may be come to by the University affirming the first intended proposition as a solemn intimation . . . that . . . we ought not to stay, *Liberavi animam meam*," whereas if it had merely "been proposed to censure Mr. Ward for intemperate language, or to declare that the University did not concur in his views," he is careful to say, " I should have thought such propositions quite unimportant as regards others."

[3] Referring to this favourite and fairly intelligible, if not strictly charitable, Protestant view of the major part of Christendom, the Serjeant wrote to Mr. Maude,

unity which our Saviour desired, and which the Apostles inculcated, merely shows that we should try to agree, not that it is a
duty to give up our opinion in order to do so. There will be no
real unity till the millenium."

On the other hand, the foregoing speaker's father, the
Rev. Joseph Maude, admitted to his step-son, the Serjeant, in
January, 1843, that there was something wrong in the present
state of the Church, that it ought to be at unity, every one
speaking the same thing. Our Saviour, he thought, evidently
intended that there should be some body or other to which an
appeal might be made, setting at rest all disputed questions ;
as in early times, when the decisions of the Apostolic body
were final and conclusive. Hence came the opinion of the
Irvingites that there ought to be still such a body. Mr. Maude
did not say that he acquiesced in this solution of the difficulty,
but he fully admitted the want of an infallible judge of controversies—a remarkable admission, coming as it did from so
honest and sincere an Evangelical. The chaos of opinion as to
practice, doctrine, and authority within the pale of the Established Church extended itself no less to its views about the
Catholic Church.

Thus the Evangelicals told the Serjeant that the whole of
the Roman Catholic system was the work of the devil himself,
that the Roman Catholic Church was Antichrist, the Pope the
man of sin, &c.

The Old High Churchmen informed him that the Church
of Rome was grievously corrupt, and that at the time of the
Reformation the Anglican Church separated from it, and
purified itself from the prevailing errors and superstitions, and
was now the most perfect Church on earth.

The New High Churchmen maintained that the Roman
Catholic Church was a true Church, that the Anglican Church
was unfortunately separated from it ; yet, that although the
latter had neglected or abolished many undoubtedly true
doctrines, and given countenance to many erroneous ones, it
still retained its vitality, and so claimed the submission of all
who had been brought up in it.

Lastly, the Extreme High Churchmen declared that the

sen., in October, 1850 : "The chapters in the Revelations to which you refer
contain very awful matters, which it would ill become the Church of England in
her present miserable state to pretend to fix upon any other body of Christians ;
still less can it be prudent for individuals to assume the office of expounding them
when we are expressly told that no prophecy is of private interpretation."

Roman Catholic Church was the only true Church; that the Anglican Church had unjustifiably separated from it, and was thus schismatical. Moreover, it encouraged, if it did not propound, heretical doctrine; so that private individuals who became convinced of this were quite right in quitting the Anglican Church.

The Serjeant himself had painfully gone through all stages from Low Evangelicalism to Extreme High Churchmanship, until at length the time came when he found little of real difficulty in any Catholic doctrine. This is sufficiently illustrated, some time before his actual conversion, by a little paper of September, 1847, referring to "Confession," perhaps a greater stumbling-block to Protestants inclined to Catholicism than anything else, after Papal Supremacy.

"It is plain," he says, "that I have committed sins, in deed, in word, and in thought, all my life long up to this time. Suppose I was about to die, on what ground should I rest my hope that God would pardon them all, and take me to Heaven?

"'On the merits of our Saviour.' True: these are sufficient to atone for the sins of the whole world; but, as all will not have the benefit of them, what reason have I to hope that I shall be of the number of those who will? 'God is merciful.' True: He is merciful; but it will not be enough to plead that God is merciful in order to obtain pardon; He is just also, and will not pardon impenitent sinners.

"Am I an impenitent sinner? An important question. Can I plead sincere sorrow and penitence? that is, is the remembrance of my sins really grievous and the burthen of them intolerable to me? Do I look upon my past sins with abhorrence? Can I honestly say that I do this? And if I do not, is it not plain that I cannot look for pardon on that ground?

"But, perhaps, when I come to die I shall be more penitent than I am now. I shall then abhor my sins, and grieve and sorrow and be really penitent. Is it not rather more probable that I shall be too ill and weak to think at all, or that I may wander in mind, or die suddenly? Well, then: 'What do you propose to yourself?' To try to be more sorry; to grieve more; but how?

"Is it not possible that submitting oneself to confession may be the true way to become really penitent? Is it not also possible that the imperfection of my repentance may be supplied by the sacramental grace of confession? If I were to die this minute, being, as I feel I am, without real contrition, how could I expect entire pardon?

"If not *entirely* pardoned, whither, upon Church of England principles, must I go?"[1]

The end of all doubt and hesitation about the truth of Catholicism was nearing, and the Serjeant's thoughts on religion in 1850 show how he had then become a Catholic all but in name.

"I find myself living in the world," he says, "amidst a vast variety of beings.

"I perceive that the class of beings to which I belong has certain qualities of a higher order than the rest, and peculiar to itself, viz. :

"1. Freedom of action or will, exemplified in this, that man does not follow an unvarying habit or instinct like all other animals, but is inquiring and inventive.

"2. A sense of right and wrong, in other words, a conscience.

"3. A capacity for reflecting on his origin and probable future.

"Some one must have made and endowed all these beings, and he must have had some reason for giving them those distinctive powers ;—that one is God.

"Some animals are savage, others cruel, others cunning ; they are made so, follow their nature, and are obviously not responsible, but freedom of action in man, involving a power to do or to abstain ; and again, the sense of right and wrong, probably given to guide him, both tend to the conclusion that man is responsible.

"The capacity for contemplating a future state of existence would be a futile gift if there were no such thing.

"As God and a future state could not be discovered by our natural senses, they belong to the order of 'supernaturals.'

"The existence of supernaturals is probable on other grounds. Our senses are obviously limited. There are some things which

---

[1] Four years before he had thus written to Mr. Richards on Confession in the English Church : "To confess your sins to a human creature because it is your *duty* to do so is one thing, to confess because your *feelings prompt you* to do it is another thing, and I think a person may well hesitate at adopting a practice so solemn as this as a duty, when he is not certain that his own confessor may not be dismissed for inculcating it. I once heard it said by a person not indisposed to confession, that if he did confess it should be to a priest and in a Church which claimed it as a bounden duty, and not in a Church or to a clergyman who allowed it to those who fancied it."

must exist, and which, nevertheless, we cannot grasp, even with our imagination, for instance, infinity of time and infinity of space.

".Again, there are some animals whose senses are more acute than ours.

" It would be as absurd for man to suppose that there are no beings in existence beyond those which his senses can show him, as it would be for a limpet on the rock to conceive the world confined to the interior of his shell, or for a blind man to disbelieve colours, or a deaf man harmonies.

"It may, therefore, be concluded that there is a God, that man is responsible, and that there is a future state of existence.

"A further proof consists in this, that there never was a nation, ancient or modern, savage or civilized, which had not a distinct belief in all these.

" This belief in subjects of so high a character, so clear, so uniform, and so universal, must have had some common origin.

" This the Catholic Church affirms to have been an original Revelation from God, handed down in all nations, but obscured and corrupted in the lapse of ages in all but one ;—that one the Jewish nation.

"The most ancient writings in the world are those of the Jewish nation ; Moses, the chief writer of the oldest portion, lived five hundred years before Orpheus, Homer, and Herodotus, the oldest of the heathen writers, and these were contemporary with King Solomon.

"These writings contain a high morality, an account of the creation of man, prophetic indications of the future.

" It is notorious that at the time of the coming of Christ, the religion, as well as the morals, of the whole world had degenerated into the basest and most brutish superstition and practice, except amongst the Jews.

" It is also well known that at that time there was an universal expectation amongst the Jews, founded on their ancient prophecies, of the coming of the Messiah, who was to restore all things. Not only Jewish but heathen traditions tended to the expectation of a great kingdom to be established by some mysterious conqueror.

" At the summit of the Roman power, all the world being at peace, Christ came, but in so humble a sphere that His real character was not recognized except by a few poor fishermen.

"These, however, received **the new Revelation from His**

mouth, and He established them as the nucleus of a great society, which was to teach and transmit His doctrine, and that humble society overcame the existing philosophies of the world.

"That society, the Catholic Church, consisted at first, and has ever since consisted, of all nations without distinction, and was intended to be, and was, independent of the petty distinctions of States and civil governments. All were to be *one*, without divisions, governed by one graduated hierarchy, from the Chief Bishop or Pope, of whom St. Peter was the first, through Patriarchs, Archbishops, Bishops, Priests, &c.

"To this society our Lord promised His continuing presence, preserving it from error. It is this society which in after-times collected the Sacred Books, then existing among Christians, into one volume, the New Testament. It is this society which has from time to time made and enlarged the Creeds, as growing heresies or the prevalence of false opinions made it necessary.

"That society to this day has but one voice, and from one end of the world to the other, from Japan to South America, the same answer would be given by its Bishops and priests to any question relating to articles of faith or morals.

"That society has existed, and still does exist, in nations where the governing powers are heathen, and it always was, and always must be, wholly distinct from the civil power, whose duties relate to this world, and to the preservation of life and property.

"If this were not so, the Christian religion would always be subject to be changed at the will of the civil power, as has happened in various countries where it has claimed authority over the Church.

"It has been so changed in England, and the Established Church there has become a mere civil society dressed up in vestments of religion, with the adoption of such portion of the Catholic system as pleased the civil rulers at the time.

"There is no nation in which this system of independent Churches exists where it was not commenced by notoriously wicked men, and from selfish motives, as, for instance, in England by Henry VIII.

"The key-note of the Catholic Church is obedience to authority.

"The key-note of the Protestant Church is independence, and the right of private (individual) judgment.

" The former suits and is possible for all, rich, poor, learned, ignorant, young, old. The latter does not suit and is not possible for those who are incapable of judging, that is, for those who cannot read or reason ; and it cannot be a practicable rule even for those who can, as is evidenced by the variety of conclusions at which such persons, acting independently, arrive,—in this country, for example.

" A Catholic takes his religion from the society appointed by our Lord to teach it, and occupies himself, if he is a good Catholic, in acting up to it, so as to save his soul.

" A Protestant, if he acts upon his principles, must occupy himself in finding out his religion, a task he never completes, but spends his time, which should be dedicated to obeying and acting out a known law, in endless endeavours to find out that law for himself.

" The doctrines and practices of the Catholic Church, as they are really held and taught by her (not as they are represented by Protestants), will bear the strictest examination, and will be found to be, all of them, conducive to the preservation of the true knowledge and worship of God, to be in accordance with Holy Scripture, and to tend to holiness of life.

" Many of her doctrines are mysteries, the Christian religion itself is a mystery ; indeed, anything relating to supernaturals must be so ; but the Catholic takes his religion from the Catholic Church, and does not occupy himself in criticizing it, or in imagining that he could have made it better.

" Assuming that there is a Church to which it is our duty to belong, the great question is—which is it ?

" The Roman Catholic holds that the Church founded by Jesus Christ was intended to unite in one body all peoples and nations, irrespective of their races, language, or civil government, which latter may or may not be from time to time favourable to the true religion.

" The Established Church of England holds that each national Church is separate, distinct, and independent, possessing all that is requisite within itself, and under the dominion of the State or Sovereign.

" Can this latter theory be consistent with Christian unity, and with all Christians speaking the same thing ? "

" I am quite aware," he writes to Mr. E. Le Mesurier in Italy, January 22, 1846, " of the abuses which exist in the Catholic Church as well as in our own, and which must be expected

F

wherever the purposes of the Almighty are to be carried out by the instrumentality of frail men, and I fully concur that great abuses did exist at the time of the Reformation, but I cannot, and do not, think that the proper mode of dealing with such abuses was to set up an independent national Church and form new Articles of Faith for ourselves without reference to the rest of the Christian world.[1] It is plain if we had the right to do this in England, every other nation, great and small, has a right to do the same, which could never produce that unity which clearly ought to exist in the Church. . . . An evil day is coming upon us, no one can help seeing the power and progress of absolute infidelity in this country and in Germany, and we are ill-prepared for the encounter, split up into a hundred sects, and fighting and devouring one another instead of making one bold phalanx against the enemy. In the event of such a conflict, it is plain we must, like a demoralized army, be cut up in detail." And he refers to a little book published by Dolman, Smith's *Short History of the Protestant Reformation,* "consisting solely of quotations from Protestant writers, which gives a curious insight into the admissions made by our own writers as to the origin and progress of the Reformation." "What presses upon us here," he also says to the same, on the 31st, "is the utter state of division and estrangement which exists everywhere in this country, and which gets worse and worse, the utter powerlessness of the Church as regards the poor, who, if religious, are almost invariably Dissenters," &c.

"In March, 1850," he writes, "I was called upon by two clergymen of the Church of England to ask me to sign a petition to have the Convocation restored. I asked, what was the object? They replied that the divided state of the Church of England had become scandalous, and that some remedy was necessary to bring people to one mind. I heard all they had

---

[1] In a letter from Exeter College, Oxford, September 25, 1843, he writes home : "I find a universal acquiescence [on the part of the Tractarians?] in the Council of Trent, as being the only basis upon which an ultimate reunion will be effected, *and a universal admission that the notion of independent national Churches is absurd,* and that the authority of a supreme patriarch is far, very far preferable to the slavery of the Church to an almost heathen State." "It seems strange," he says, December 8, 1843, to W. Ford, "that there should be in the Christian world a number of independent absolute authorities, deciding in opposite ways." He adds on the question of obedience : "If it is our duty to acquiesce in and obey the decisions of our national Church because it is such, it seems to be equally the duty of a Spaniard to obey in like manner *his* national Church, and of a Frenchman *his,* and so it becomes a duty to obey error."

to say, and then asked them this question : ' If you can get a
Convocation assembled in such a manner as to satisfy you, will
you abide by any decision they may come to on the various
questions on which we now differ,—for example, baptism ?'
They looked at one another, and at first gave no answer, but
after a time one of them said : ' Let us hope that the assembly
would be guided by the Holy Spirit to a right decison.' I
answered : ' But suppose they come to a conclusion of which
you do not approve?' They would not say they would submit,
and so I declined to sign the petition, saying that an authority
that we were not prepared to obey was not such an authority
as I was looking for ; upon which they took their leave."

"Docility, humility, and childlike submissiveness," the
Serjeant writes to his step-father, October, 1850. "are plainly
the qualities demanded in Holy Scripture of all those who
would enter the Kingdom of Heaven ; the difficulty in these
times is to know what is the object towards which these
qualities are to be exercised. Many had imagined it was the
Church of England, and clung to that hope in the face of no
ordinary discouragements ; that hope, however, has been cut
from beneath our feet, as her highest authorities declare that
she does not claim to be our guide, nor, indeed, are there any
to be found, high or low, Bishop, priest, or layman, who would
submit to her teaching, unless it should chance to be in
accordance with their own preconceptions of what it ought
to be."

It was the incident above related that led him at once to
address a letter to one of the two clergymen, entitled, *The
Judicial Committee of the Privy Council and the Petition for a
Church Tribunal in lieu of it : by an Anglican Layman,* wherein
he says : " Before we talk of independent Church courts, let us
know what the authority in the English Church is, to which *the
clergy themselves* are willing to submit, and in obedience to
which they are willing to teach.

"Do not suppose I would have you do nothing, do something, but do something effectual, and do it at once. Patience,
patience, I hear on all sides, but it is not a matter to be patient
about ; we have a voyage to make, time presses, for the summer
is passing away, the ship we are in is leaky, unseaworthy, and
with a mutinous crew ; it is to little purpose to tell us that in
some future season the vessel will be refitted, and the mutineers
reduced or ejected, our voyage must be made *now.*"

As this vigorous little pamphlet was passing through Pickering's Press, the Gorham decision came out, and in a second pamphlet of similar length, in April, called, *Convocations and Synods; are they the remedies for existing evils?* after a careful review of the question as matters then stood, he answers it in the negative, declaring the proposed remedies to be "either hopeless, useless, or of doubtful propriety,"[1] especially if Synod or Convocation were to bind no one.[2]

And in December, 1850, in a third pamphlet, entitled, *The Archbishop of Westminster: a Remonstrance with the Clergy of Westminster, from a Westminster Magistrate,* to which further reference will be made later on, he meets their outcry at the establishment of the Catholic Hierarchy by a complaint that they tamely submitted to much greater evils than any schismatical intrusion.

"Attacks upon the faith, even what you deemed to be such, have not so disturbed your tranquillity; but so soon as a trifling question arises about the taking of certain local names and designations by certain schismatical Bishops, as you deem them, and which you conceive to involve a slight upon your own personal rights and dignity, the whole kingdom is to be roused into indignation. . . . It can signify little to us, or to any one, what names people may think fit to call themselves by, but matters of faith are vital to us, and upon these we had a right to expect protests on your part at least as vigorous as those which are now called forth by your own peculiar grievance. I have said that the clergy seem unable to understand the position of the laity; I do not believe that they can realize the difficulties pressing upon fathers of families like myself. Our difficulty is doubt, our besetting danger is indifference, arising from constantly hearing an uncertain sound. You claim our allegiance, you call it schism to leave you; then teach us; tell me plainly what I am to teach my children. Is there grace in the Sacraments? Is there a Real Presence in the Eucharist?

[1] For his views and statements about the Court of Delegates, Judicial Committee, &c., see Appendix C.

[2] "If in what I have said," he adds, "I seem to have assumed a dogmatical tone, not warranted by my position as a layman, or to have urged my difficulties in an apparently hostile shape, I regret it, though I feel at the same time that I should almost be entitled to justify it," *i.e.,* "when I think of the gradual estrangement of friends, induced too obviously by our growing divisions; . . . when I see our children growing up, without the possibility of imbuing them with a docile, confiding spirit towards their religious instructors, becoming of necessity critical rather than reverential," &c.

Is it a true Sacrifice? Are we justified by Faith only, to the exclusion of works? Have you the power of forgiving and retaining sin? If you were all assembled and could be asked these questions, and many others like them, you must either hold down your heads in confusion, or if you spoke, your answer would be Babel."

"The great question to be solved is," he repeats once more, "*what is the authority to which as Christians we are bound to submit ourselves.*' This is the great controversy; God Almighty has given us a revelation, on that we are all agreed; but to whom or to what are we to look for it? Some of you would say, ' To the Bible, and the Bible only,' but the majority of you would at once repudiate that solution; you would tell us that unlearned persons would wrest the Holy Scriptures to their own destruction, as a sick man might misuse the Pharmacopœia if he attempted to read it and cure himself. Where then must we look for our guide? 'To the Church; you are bound to hear the Church.' 'But which Church?' 'The Church of England,' you reply, 'the Church hath authority in controversies of faith, and you, being an Englishman, must adhere to the English Church, to refuse to do so is schism.' Plainly answered; now answer me another question as plainly; there is a subject now much agitated amongst us, 'regeneration in baptism,' one half of you say that to deny it is to deny an article of the Creed, the other half say that to teach it is to teach a 'soul-destroying heresy;' what am I, a layman, to teach my children? You cannot answer me, but you desire a convocation, a synod, to 'settle the point.' Now, mark my farther question, should you succeed in obtaining the most perfect assembly you can devise representing the Church of England, and should it determine the question one way or other, will you submit to the decision? It is said you would not, and that there is not a single individual, from the Archbishop of Canterbury downwards, who would submit to the decision, unless it was in accordance with his own prepossessions. If this be so, as it undoubtedly is, what is the meaning of 'Church authority,' and what the meaning of 'schism' in your vocabulary? I might add, what is the meaning of 'faith'?"

"At this time," the Serjeant says, "my misgivings about the Anglican Church were such that I hesitated when I came to the baptism of my son, and it was put off for several weeks in a kind of vague hope that I might see my way to having him baptized by a Catholic priest; however, he was ultimately baptized at the parish church, and on that occasion I signed the following declaration:

"'I, Edward Bellasis, Serjeant-at-Law, being about to present my son for baptism at the district church of Christ Church, Marylebone, by the name of Richard Garnett, hereby declare that I present him for such baptism, not as an admission into the Anglican Church exclusively, but into the Catholic Church, which alone I deem to be the Church of his baptism.

"'EDWARD BELLASIS.

"'Feast of the Purification, 1850.'"

The first Catholic book he appears to have read was Moehler's *Symbolik*, begun in or before 1843. He followed this up with Walsingham's *Search into matters of Religion*, in which the writings and spirit of Protestants and Catholics were contrasted. This was in 1845, and in 1849 he continued his reading with Bossuet's *Exposition* and his *Variations of Protestantism*, De Maistre's *Du Pape*, and in 1850, Balmez's *Catholicism and Protestantism compared*, and Audin's *Life of Luther*, of whom he had written to a friend as early as 1843: "I have a strong opinion about him myself, but I am by no means bent upon forcing that opinion down the throats of other people; it is very unimportant to the Church of England whether he was a holy man raised up by the Almighty to reform His Church, or whether he was what I think him; we have nothing to do with him, and his character does not affect us; nevertheless, I cannot help thinking that if any one rose up in these days to teach forgotten religious truths, or to promulgate new views of Christianity, we should not listen to him for a moment if he habitually used profane and blasphemous language."[1]

[1] To C. Blundy he writes, March 31, 1843: "Have you seen a little book of Ward's, *Questions for self-examination*, published by Toovey, St. James' Street? I would send you a copy, but I have not one by me. By the by, would you like to read Audin's *Life of Luther*? if you would, I will send it to you. I think you ought to read it." Apropos of the *British Critic's* demise, he wrote to W. J. Garnett, January 8, 1844: "There is not much news stirring here, though Morris and Ward are both in town; the only important matters I hear in ecclesiastical matters are that the *British Critic* is finally concluded, and that a new quarterly Review is coming out, to be edited by William Palmer, of Worcester, and all the articles are to be submitted to Dr. Spry and Dr. Jelf for their approval. I think this a good thing; it is desirable that that school should be placed in the situation of being obliged to fix and determine their own principles, a much more difficult task than objecting to

Then there were the Oxford *Lives of the Saints*, and here he wrote to Mr. Newman, March 6, 1844: "We expected to be interested, but we had no notion that the Lives would be so very attractive." Speaking of the number containing "St. Stephen Harding," he adds, "it was impossible to put the book down. . . . I hear it has been written by Dalgairns, will you remember me to him and tell him how much we have been pleased; I think the mode in which the story is told beautiful." "Your letter," wrote Newman, the 12th of July, "was the first opinion I had had upon it, and very acceptable it was. The second edition is now almost running out, and there is appearance of a third being probable." [1]

It should be mentioned that the Serjeant had attended in May, 1849, a course of lectures given by Father Newman at the Oratory, then opened in King William Street, Strand. In this year, too, he had removed from Bedford Square to North-wood House, St. John's Wood, and made the acquaintance of Father O'Neal, the priest of the district, afterwards Vicar-General of the Westminster diocese, and from time to time he stole into a Catholic church for Benediction. The late Father Moore, of Southend, used to relate that one day being in need of alms for a charity, he was advised to call on the Serjeant, "a kind Protestant gentleman." He did so, was courteously received, and given £5, while he was not allowed to go away till he had given his blessing to some of the Bellasis children who happened to be within reach.

Hope-Scott and the Serjeant had, a friend states, never discussed religious topics together until one winter day in February, 1850, when, as they were walking home together from

those of others; moreover, it will oblige them to make use of Catholic weapons, in the contest they will have to undergo with the Evangelicals, who will, no doubt, have as much to say against the new Review as they had against the *British Critic*."

[1] On March 15, 1848, Oakeley wrote from St. Edmund's College to the Serjeant: "Newman's new book, *Loss and Gain, or the Story of a Convert*, will give you a great deal of pleasure. I am not certain whether he has ever written anything more showing the versatility of his genius and his knowledge of human nature. By those who did not know him it will be called 'satirical,' however, it is Newman all over." On August 20, 1843, the Serjeant writes about a pleasant meeting at Upton Richards' house with literary people, who were all converts and Catholic writers later on. "We had," he says, "a very pleasant party at dinner yesterday at Mr. Richards', Badeley, Thompson, Wingfield, Goldsmid, Aubrey de Vere, and a Mr. Rhodes (formerly at Bird's). Mr. Bird seems, Protestant as he is, to produce most Catholic people, but I can tell you more about Rhodes when I see you." This is the late Mr. M. J. Rhodes, author of a valuable work on the *Visible Unity of the Catholic Church*.

Westminster, Hope-Scott said: "Bellasis, you know if I were
dying I should send for a Catholic priest." "Whom would
you send for?" asked the Serjeant. They came under the
light of a gas-lamp, and Hope-Scott stopped and took out
a pocket-book and turned over to a leaf with a name and
address. These the Serjeant jotted down; they then walked on.
Walks and talks with Hope-Scott, Robert Williams, and
William Dodsworth ensued.

"July 6, 1850: I walked home with James Hope from
Westminster. He asked me what I felt as to the present
state of religious matters in England. I said, I had myself
lost all confidence in the Church of England, and thought
there was but one course for us to take; we had been for
the last ten or twelve years setting up the authority of the
Church, and objecting to private judgment, and now, if we were
to remain, it must be by repudiating authority and exercising our
private judgment, a degree of inconsistency I could not reconcile
myself to. Hope said that Newman in his lectures at the
Oratory laid great stress upon that point . . . he thought these
lectures as perfect as anything he had ever read, and that was
the opinion of persons not concurring in his opinions, for
instance, his father-in-law, Lockhart, who had quoted passages
to him which he said were, as compositions, perfect. I asked
him if he ever saw Newman; he said he had not for some
years, but he had some thought of writing to him to ask him
to introduce him to some priest in London, with whom he
might have a little conversation. . . . He had thought of going
to see Dr. Döllinger, for whom he had a great regard. I said
I had heard Father Brownbill spoken of as a very excellent
person, an elderly man. . . . Hope asked whether he was
not a Jesuit and at the chapel in Farm Street. I said he
was. He said he had a great partiality for the Jesuits, . . . they
could better understand the position of a layman. Did I know
Father Brownbill? I said no, but my friend Hood[1] had been
received into the Catholic Church by him, and spoke in high
terms of him.

" I said, most persons hesitated at the worship of the Virgin
Mary, and could not reconcile themselves to that, whereas that
formed no obstacle to me. I thought, too, if intercessory prayer
was admitted by the Almighty by living men, why not by
departed saints, and if by departed saints, why not chiefly

---

[1] The late Rev. Theophilus Hood, S.J., of Wardour.

by the Virgin Mary? Hope saw no difficulty whatever in that, certainly nothing repulsive in it.

"I said, that many persons had to make their change in the face of pecuniary difficulties, that neither he nor I had that difficulty to encounter. He said, no, that in our case our position and standing in society would not be in the least affected by it.

"Hope further said he strongly suspected that if we were once Catholics, we should be astonished that we ever could have held on to the Anglican Church, and should look back with wonder at what we had left ;[1] he did not believe that the writer of *From Oxford to Rome* represented in her own case a probable state of mind, or that there were many, if any, who had misgivings after the change. I said that the bringing up of children was the great difficulty in the English Church ; that I had no belief in the efficacy of teaching children religion in general, but to be useful it must be *specific*, and that in the Church of England it was impossible to teach children anything specific on many most important subjects. That I had always taught my children as much as possible of Catholic rules and principles, but if they remained Protestants, they would experience hereafter nothing but impediments and hindrances from their Church in carrying them out.[2] Hope said that in practice there was no difficulty in children becoming Catholics ; that there was something that accommodated itself wonderfully to their innocent minds ; Mrs. Bowden's children lapped it up at once like milk."

"July 7, 1850. Called on Robert Williams after dinner, at his house in the Regent's Park ; I had not seen him for some months, and did not know how he might have been affected by the occurrences of the last few months. He thought there was no Divine authority save the Bible . . . the disturbance now making about Mr. Gorham's opinions was absurd. What did it signify what the clergyman of Bampford Speke might think ? . . . if the Bishops and Church propounded doctrines he did not approve of, he should reject them. . . . This is what the Prussians and Germans generally did at the Reformation. . . . That was the period of the emancipation of

---

[1] "As in fairy tales, the magic castle vanishes when the spell is broken, and nothing is seen but the wild heath, the barren rock, and the forlorn sheep-walk, so is it with us as regards the Church of England, when we look in amazement on that we thought so unearthly, and find so commonplace or worthless." (Cardinal Newman's *Anglican Difficulties*, vol. i. p. 6, Edit. 1876.)

[2] "Tempora mutantur et nos mutamur in illis." (1893.)

the human mind. . . . There was no doctrine absolutely necessary to be believed, in his opinion, but the Trinity and the Incarnation, all the rest was matter of opinion. People might entertain different views of the sacraments, some might think them simple forms, others might think them mysteries. . . . The Roman Catholic Church, he was convinced, was coming to an end, it must fall, it was clearly foreshown in the Revelations. He had been reading a work on Prophecy by Mr. Elliott, which was in his judgment irresistible, it was in four volumes. . . . In answer to an observation from me, that if the Catholic system was corrupt it was very early corrupted, for the system of Athanasius and Ambrose and Augustine was essentially the same as the present Catholic system, and as plainly not the Anglican, he said he did not consider that period (so late as the fourth century) early, and he thought the Church was corrupt at that time.

"July 26, 1850. I called upon Mr. Dodsworth, and found him at home, alone. After some general conversation, he asked me whether we were going abroad this autumn? I said, we had really hardly made up our minds what to do, that I had thought of a tour in Ireland, having long had a wish to see something of the Irish people for myself.[1] He had long had a wish to visit Ireland himself; however, at present they were going down to the Isle of Wight for a few weeks, to a quiet place, Freshwater, where he might have time to think carefully over the present position of affairs. . . . He then spoke of Manning, and said he was very deliberate and one of the most earnest and sincere persons he had ever known. He had the greatest respect and admiration for him. None could have worked harder or more faithfully for the Church of England than he had, but Manning felt it was failing him. . . . He himself thought the theory of the independence of each individual Bishop a much more tenable one than that of National Churches, but the possibility of that theory was negatived by facts. Bishops do disagree, and that in essentials, therefore it cannot be a duty for all persons to submit to the Bishop they may chance to be under. Then, said I, what must we think of the National Church of England? It cannot be

---

[1] In the autumns of 1862 and 1865 he visited Ireland with some of his daughters, and was received with great kindness and distinction by Cardinal Cullen, Mr. (afterwards Lord) O'Hagan, Sir Bernard Burke, Sir John Ennis, Mr. More O'Ferrall, and Mr. Valentine O'Connor.

supported, it has no authority, we all admit that now. Well, but, said I, is there such a thing then as 'authority' in the Church at all, and if so, where are we to look for it? There is no authority in the Church at all, he said, unless it be—in Rome. If we seek *authority* elsewhere it cannot be found. . . . I see no result clearly, but one. What is that? Submission to the Catholic Church sooner or later. . . . Had he ever conversed with Catholic priests on the subject? No, never—he had never been at the service of a Catholic chapel in England, he thought he owed it to his position not to give unnecessary cause for observation or anxiety. . . . There was a Mr. Hunt at Spanish Place, whom he had heard highly spoken of. I said, we had heard him preach. He then said that there was one convert for whom he entertained the highest reverence, he might call it, Mr. Spencer, no one could speak to him without loving him; he had a place in the Edgware Road, towards Edgware. 'It is a matter that cannot be put aside, it must be met with calmness, with deliberation, and with firmness, for neither you nor I can plead invincible ignorance.'"

"At the end of November" (1850), the Serjeant writes, "my wife and I went on a visit to Mr. and Mrs. Hope-Scott, at Abbotsford. Mr. Hope-Scott was at that time in much the same state of mind as myself on the subject of religion, and being joined by the Hon. Gilbert Talbot (now Mgr. Talbot), we had much conversation on the subject, and of such a character, that a Miss Louisa Hope, a Presbyterian sister, after listening for a day or two, informed Mrs. Hope-Scott, that in her opinion we were three black Papists together.

"On one of the Sundays we spent at Abbotsford there was Holy Communion at Melrose, and it was proposed that we should all go over. This was an important incident, as I had made up my mind some time before, that whilst I did not believe in the Protestant Communion, I could not partake of it. I finally determined that I would not go, and my wife and I stayed away. I went, however, to the Morning Prayers, and that was the last time that I ever went to a Protestant church. I arrived in London on the 6th of December."

Two memoranda, referring to his first meetings with Cardinal Manning, are subjoined :

"December 7, 1850. Met Mr. (late Archdeacon) Manning, at Badeley's. He had just given up his archdeaconry and his living, compelled thereto by late events in the Church of

England. I asked him whether, if the state of the Church was such as not to be fit for him to teach in, it could be fit for me to learn in? He replied, 'I am prepared to answer the question—where I cannot *consecrate*, I cannot *communicate.*' . . . I asked him, if it was not possible that something might happen to resuscitate the Church of England? He said, the question did not depend upon the future, but upon the past. He did not think that any particular event had, as it were, killed the Church of England, but a succession of events of late had, conjointly with the past history of the Church, shown that it never had been a living portion of the Church since it separated itself at the Reformation.

"December 9, 1850. Met Mr. Manning by appointment at Pickering's, in Piccadilly. Drove with him to Notting Hill, and then to his house in Cadogan Place. Talked with him on his probable quitting of the English Church.

"He said, when he first took Orders, he believed the doctrine of the Trinity, and the Incarnation, and his theological views were those of D'Oyly and Mant.

"When he began to work in his parish, he commenced to reflect upon the grounds on which he claimed the right of instructing his parishioners, and of asking their attention, and this led him on to the doctrine of the Apostolical Succession.

"But he soon began to see that every priest having the Apostolical Succession, could not by that alone have authority to teach, each his own opinion, which would be absurd, so this led him to the doctrine of the traditional teaching of the Church, and he endeavoured to ascertain what that was, and to teach it.

"But again, he saw that priests differed as to what was the traditional teaching of the Church, and that, indeed, it was impossible but that they must differ when each endeavoured to ascertain for himself what was meant or implied by acts or writings fifteen hundred years old; and this led him to see that for a continuing tradition there must be a continuing traditive body, an existing exponent of the tradition of the Church.

"Then, if there must be such continuing authoritative expounder, where is it? Is it the Anglican Church? It neither claims to be so, nor does it exercise the office. What other can it be but the Roman Church, which has always claimed and exercised the office; and the Church of Rome interpenetrates all nations, whereas none of the other Churches even pretend to do so."

How carefully the Serjeant had weighed everything before taking any step to be received into the Church, is seen by his having noted down, in April, 1847, all the motives, good, bad, and mixed, that might be influencing him :

" In the aspirations I feel, and have felt, towards the Roman Catholic Church," he writes, " I am quite conscious that my motives may not be altogether religious motives, and further, that my life and conduct are not such as to make it certain that such aspirations come from God. I wish, therefore, to have clearly before me *all the motives* which *may by possibility* be acting upon me (perhaps unknown to myself), whether they be good or bad, that I may not imagine that I am swayed by one set of motives, whilst perhaps all the time motives of a very different character are really acting upon me :

" First. Motives (good) which are urging me towards the Roman Catholic Church.

" 1. Conviction historically and doctrinally that the Church of England is only one of the sects, and clearly wrong.

" 2. Fear that my opinion of the Anglican Church may, if I remain in the latter, make me altogether indifferent.

" 3. Fear that if I should die in the Church of England, and with my present feeling towards her and her ordinances, I could not be saved.

" 4. Fear that so long as I remain in the Church of England, I shall necessarily be occupying myself with doubting, hesitating, arguing, and determining for myself, amongst the various systems now current in her—that is, occupying myself with theology instead of religion.

" 5. Inability to teach my children with confidence any complete and specific religious system.

" 6. Hesitation as to leaving my children to practise the little I have taught them, without the support of the authorities to which they ought to look up, and in defiance of them.

" 7. Personal desire of the aid of confession, to induce a more salutary repentance than I am at present conscious of.

" Second. Other motives (bad) which *may be* operating upon me without my being aware of it.

" 1. Character of friends who are already gone, and confidence in their judgment.

" 2. Shame in exhibiting to them my want of courage to follow them, after committing myself so far.

" 3. Vexation at the opposition I have met with.

" 4. Shame at exhibiting to those who have opposed me my want of firmness.

" 5. Desire of novelty.

" 6. Desire of being introduced to a new class of friends, who would think more of me than my present friends now do.

" 7. Fear that if I stay in the Church of England I shall form no intimacies, and so leave my children when I die without real friends."

He adds to the above motives *for* moving, the following *against* :

" Third. Motives (good and bad) which are *holding me where I am.*

" 1. Fear that my conclusions *may be* wrong, and that I may be leading those who are dependent upon me into error.

" 2. Distaste at taking so important a step unless in concurrence with my dear wife.

" 3. Fear of the consequences to our children if they see their parents differing.

" 4. Hesitation at giving pain to my other friends.

" 5. Want of courage to meet the contempt or pity of the world.

" 6. Hesitation at separating myself from every relative I have.

" There may be other motives acting upon me which I do not discern, but the above are sufficient to make me very careful and thoughtful as to what my real motives may be."

Later on, under the heading of " Considerations," as to whether he ought not to move, and at once, he first asks :

" 1. Is it probable that the Church of England—that is to say, the independent Anglican system—will ever again obtain a hold upon my confidence and affection ?

" The origin of the Church of England, the characters and motives of its founders, its history, its general policy, its sympathy with Protestant and heretical bodies, the double aspect of its formularies, the untenableness of its theory as regards unity, and, as it now appears, the entire absence in it of any authority on matters of faith, have impressed me so strongly, and so unfavourably, that I cannot think it possible I can ever again admire it, or love, or even respect it, as I ought to do that Church to which I entrust myself and all that are dear to me.

" 2. Assuming that there is no probability that the Church of England will regain my confidence, what course do I propose to myself?

" It is plain I shall either fall into indifference, or sooner or later I shall detach myself from the Church of England for some other Church—that other, of course, the Catholic Church.

" 3. If it is plain that, sooner or later, that step will be taken, then *when* shall it be taken, and how is it to be brought about?

" First, 'when.' There have been times heretofore when such a step on my part would have created surprise; it would create none now; my opinions and prepossessions are well known, in a great degree, to all my friends and associates, and to many, to their full extent, so that the surprise now is that I remain. . . . All know from my own lips that I am restrained solely by family considerations, whilst my two pamphlets have shown to all who know me to be the author, that I am vividly impressed with the defects of the English Church, and think them irremediable. As regards myself, then, and my character for honour and consistency, the answer to the question ' when,' ought to be ' now.' Further, I think I should be ashamed, as I ought to be, to commence another season of business, mixing with the world, without having acted upon those convictions I have so openly expressed; for either I should have talked less, or I should act more," &c.

" In truth, other motives than those of our religious convictions," he adds in his Autobiography, " were holding us both back, and those not altogether unworthy ones, such as sorrow at breaking with our friends, and displeasing kind and affectionate relatives, and disinclination to the taking of an irrevocable step which would cause them so much pain. My convictions being stronger than my wife's, were naturally the first to outweigh these motives, and when I felt myself irresistibly compelled to act upon them, she was not as yet prepared to do so."

" At last," he says, " I felt thoroughly convinced that if I were to die in my then position, I could not be saved; knowing what I did, I was acting against my conscience." On Sunday, the 8th of December, 1850, he visited Spanish Place Chapel. On the next two Sundays, the 15th and 22nd, he went with his wife and three elder children, Margaret, Katharine, and Mary, to St. George's Cathedral, and heard Cardinal Wiseman on the Hierarchy. On the 23rd, after a walk with Mr. Manning, who

had also dined with him on the 14th, he told Mrs. Bellasis that
he intended to call upon Cardinal Wiseman. His Eminence
received him very kindly at York Place, on the 26th. " I found
him," writes the Serjeant, " in his study, with a scarlet skull-cap,
a long black cassock, and tippet with little scarlet buttons, and
under a canopy on one side of him was a crucifix. I had not
much to say to him. I was already convinced, but wished to
know what it would become my duty to do (should I be
received into the Catholic Church) in regard to my family.
Must I forthwith withdraw my children from the Protestant
Church ? Must I discontinue prayers with my family as accustomed ? Lastly, would he give me a letter to some good priest
who might receive my confession ? He replied that I must not
press either my wife or children, my present duty was to secure
my own soul ; that family prayers might be continued, omitting
any prayers not suitable for Catholics ; and he concluded by
giving me his blessing and a letter to the Rev. James Brownbill,
a Jesuit priest, in Hill Street. I proceeded straightway to
Hill Street, found Father Brownbill at home, talked with him
for two hours, and arranged to come to him to confession, and
to be received on the following day. which I was ; and on the
next day, Saturday, the 28th, I was confirmed by the Cardinal
in his private chapel, Mr. Allies being my godfather."

When the news of the conversion reached Quernmore Park,
the residence of Mr. Garnett, Mrs. Bellasis' aunt, Miss Carson.
as a sincere Evangelical, was naturally much distressed, and the
old family cook, Mrs. Thornton, seeing her mistress in tears
inquired the cause ? Mr. Bellasis had "gone over to Rome."
" Ah," replied cook, " 'tis a pity. Isn't it very cold there ?
Hard nigh upon Russhee, I've heard tell."

CHAPTER V.

LETTERS ON HIS CONVERSION. HIS FAMILY RECEIVED INTO THE CHURCH. DEFENCE OF THE NEW HIERARCHY.

AMONG the first to congratulate Serjeant Bellasis upon his conversion was Father Newman. "It is with the greatest joy and thankfulness," he writes, December 30, 1850, three days after the event, "that I have just heard from Oakeley of your reception. Such events are continually recurring proofs of God's love to England, and the Catholics who are in it ; and witnesses to the truth of Catholicism, considering how carefully and anxiously you have sought the truth." Mr. Manning, too, still an Anglican, wrote to the Serjeant, on the 27th : "My dear friend,—Though we have seldom met, we have long known of each other, and we have had fellowship in a deep trial—this will, I trust, give me right so to call you. The prayer I have said for years, day by day, at the name of some very near to me, now in the Church of Rome is : 'If they are wrong, open their eyes; if they are right, open mine!' And this sums up all I felt in reading your kind note. May God ever keep you for Himself."

An old legal pupil of the Serjeant, Edward Hood, who had preceded him into the Church and joined the Society of Jesus, wrote from St. Beuno's on New Year's Day, 1851 : "The tidings your letter brought me yesterday have given general joy and satisfaction to our house, and called forth the warm congratu-

lations of all my friends. I said a *Te Deum* as soon as I had read your note, and this morning I offered the Holy Sacrifice in thanksgiving to our Heavenly Father for His great mercy and goodness. . . . It gives me additional pleasure that you should have had recourse on this occasion to my revered friend, Father Brownbill,

REV. J. BROWNBILL, S.J.   whose kind heart and good sound sense will, I think, recommend themselves to

G

you. He has done the same good office, as he did for you, for
a considerable number of persons during the last few years,
and when he was with us here some time since for a day or
two, he told me he had always several persons under instruction.
Indeed, it is becoming more and more manifest that men's minds
are set upon inquiry all over the kingdom, and the opponents
of Catholicity are but unwittingly lending themselves to its
propagation. . . . Oakeley speaks confidently of Dodsworth,
Manning, and Bennett, and has expectations about Badeley and
Hope, but I would rather trust your report of these last."

"What are Hope and Badeley doing?" inquires Mr. David
Lewis, on the 31st, in a letter of congratulation on the new
reception, "we hear that they are more than uneasy, and not
unlikely to be preparing for a similar step. If the Whigs win
and pass a penal law, which it is supposed they will, we shall
get plenty of converts."

"Any news of Scribes, Pharisees, or lawyers coming into
the Church will be acceptable to me." wrote also the erudite
Father J. Brande Morris, in his characteristic way. No one
had been more immediately concerned than he in helping on
the Serjeant's conversion, so much so that Mrs. Bellasis relates
that she had positively got to dislike the very sight of him
whenever he came round the corner into Bedford Square. When
she herself "came over," however, he could write to the Serjeant
to "congratulate Mrs. B. on her having now got rid of all
farther need of long faces at me."

Some of the most sympathetic letters at this time came from
Protestants. Thus, a sister-in-law wrote, December 31, 1850, to
Mrs. Bellasis: "Instead of offering you pity and condolence, I
do rejoice with you that your dear husband has found peace of
mind, and I am quite sure you are a happier woman now than
you have been for a long time, and as he thinks he has done
right in taking this step (awful though it appears to me), I, for
one, respect him for it, as it is no light thing to brave the world
'for conscience sake' . . . it is not by acting honestly and
conscientiously that a man should lose the esteem of his friends."

And in answer to his step-father, the Rev. J. Maude, he
wrote: "Your letter exhibits so temperate and Christian a
spirit, and is so kind and affectionate towards myself that I
cannot but thank you for it, although by some inexplicable
dispensation of the Almighty we are led to such opposite
conclusions. . . . I am not disposed to enter into theological

arguments; the advice which has been given me again and again since I became a Catholic, as well by the Cardinal Archbishop as by the good Jesuit priest who received me into the Church, is, 'do not argue, but pray,' and this I do constantly, and almost in your own words, that God by His Spirit may direct both of us, and all belonging to us, and that we may have a right judgment in all things.

"I perceive you throw aside all confidence in any visible Church. I cannot do this because I believe that Jesus Christ founded a visible Church in which, by His Holy Spirit, He dwells, and which He will preserve. . . . There must be some authority to which we are to submit ourselves, and towards which we are to exercise that docility, humility, and submissiveness, that childlike obedience, without which no one can enter into the Kingdom of God, and that authority I believe to be the Catholic Church.

"I have no manner of doubt that I have done an act pleasing to God, at some cost certainly, but at a cost infinitely less than that incurred by men far my superiors, many of whom have forsaken all, family, friends, honourable station, even the means of livelihood, to meet, in place of them, obloquy and contempt, and all for the purpose of buying the field in which their true treasure, Christ, is, as they believe, alone contained.

"I quite agree with you that it is . . . absolutely necessary to 'take our side.' . . . Are the fruits of the Spirit to be found on the Protestant side? Do their writings and speeches and lectures exhibit love, joy, peace, long-suffering, gentleness, goodness, meekness?[1] . . .

"I do not say this by way of criticism on yourself, for sure I am that the kind of spirit exhibited is utterly alien to your own gentleness and kindness, and that you could not and do not sympathize with it, but to show that if people are forced to

---

[1] In March, 1848, he had observed upon the different way that conversions to the "other side" affected Catholics and Protestants respectively: "If a Roman Catholic becomes a Protestant, the feeling excited in the minds of those he has left is sorrow and pity; this arises from their thorough conviction that it is a great privilege to belong to the Roman Catholic Church, and that by leaving it he has sustained a great loss. If an Anglican becomes a Roman Catholic, the feeling excited in the minds of those he has left is that of vexation and anger; this arises from the idea that their party has been injured by his secession. The Roman Catholic has a thorough conviction that the society of which he forms a part can never fail; he has no fear, therefore, of injury to the Church by the secession of individuals. The Anglican has no such conviction as to the Church of England; he feels that secessions weaken it, injure it, and may tend to its downfall."

take their side by regarding the present contending parties alone, no good Christian could take the Protestant side.

" Pray believe that I reciprocate all your affectionate regard, and feeling, as I do most sensibly, how far superior your personal character has always been to anything to which I ever attained, I can only wonder and thank God for His mercy in having brought my shattered bark into a haven of safety, whilst others are still left exposed to be tossed about the stormy and unprotected waters."

One very intimate friend, still an Anglican, wrote the 29th of December : " I received with deep emotion yesterday evening your letter announcing the solution of all your doubts and perplexities in your submission to the Church of Rome, and most earnestly do I pray God that you may abidingly derive from this most important step all the comfort and peace which can be desired. In any case, such a step must be accompanied by much anxiety and many painful trials, and especially when they have to be encountered apart from the concurrence (though not in your case without the sympathy) of wife and children, and they can only be alleviated by the entire conviction, which I know you have long felt, of its absolute necessity.

" How far we have travelled along this painful road together, through many a year of mutual interest and friendship, you well know—where I have stopped short of your definite conclusions against the Church of England on the one hand, or been unable to realize some of the doctrines and observances of the Church of Rome, on the other. You are also not ignorant of the manifold subjects of doubt and anxiety which press upon many members of the Church of England, my unworthy self included, at the present time, and I can only say that as I shall not cease to pray for your present peace and eternal warfare, I hope that you will still remember me and those most dear to me in your prayers, and especially at the Blessed Sacrament of the Altar."

In answer to a letter of less pleasing tenor from one relative, the Serjeant replied, January 14, 1851 : " My wife, who read your letter in conjunction with J.'s, was not prepared for that degree of assumption which they both, in her eyes, involved, and which enabled you to speak of my ' course of deviation from the Gospel truth,' of my having ' cast away the truth and left the pure faith of (my) fathers for the idolatries and abominations of an apostate Church,' and of her having to choose between her husband and her Saviour, as if all these were indubitable and admitted facts, instead of being, as they are, merely your own private opinion, which is, of course, liable to error. . . . If you really hold private judgment to be a sacred right, you ought to be tolerant in your tone towards those who exercise it ; and bear in mind that it is possible you may be wrong. You say it is 'better to be deemed uncharitable than to be chargeable before God with speaking smooth things and prophesying deceits ;' this is a motive which should actuate an Apostle or an authorized teacher, but it is scarcely one to be alleged by you ; if I, on my part, were to adopt your principle of plain speaking, and say what I think of the Protestant system, it would only tend to the interchange of opprobrious epithets regarding what each of us holds to be sacred truth, a mode of treating religious differences which, though it may be honest, I cannot praise either for its good taste or Christian discretion.

" You remark, indeed, that I myself say that the Church of England forms no part of the Catholic Church ; what I said was that that was my conviction, and it was said merely in my own defence, and in making that observation I was merely alleging that which, and which only, would justify the step I had taken. . . . God bless you, and all of you. . . . To act up to your principles such as they are (as I do not doubt you do) is the surest way to obtain God's grace to lead you into farther truth."

"Though not as yet participating in my final conclusions," writes the Serjeant, " my dear wife sympathized with me, and, when opportunity offered, defended me."

" My sufferings," says Mrs. Bellasis, " were too great to dwell upon. I was torn hither and thither by love for my husband, and for my dear old father, . . . who had in the autumn told me that he would rather follow any child of his to the grave than that he should embrace Popery. Against the unanswerable arguments of the Serjeant, stood my prejudices, fostered from my birth in the depths of a rigid Protestantism and backed by a strong feeling that anything that might be good in me was the fruit of the system in which I had been brought up. Added to this were ridiculous notions that if I ever did join my husband, I should have to give up my Bible, get re-married, and regard so many that I loved as everything that was bad in the category of heretics."

Describing the above interview with Mr. Garnett, Mrs. Bellasis wrote to her husband in November, 1850: "He was sure you were quite an altered man since you had imbibed new doctrines; you used to be so buoyant and cheerful, whereas the reverse now was the case. . . . Then he wished to know what my sentiments were; I said I was not prepared to become a Roman Catholic, and that you did not wish to make me one unless upon conviction; and that you had repeatedly told me so. . . . I said . . . the events of the last few years in the English Church had done more than anything else to detach you from it; he admitted this, and that things were quite shocking, unjustifiable, &c. I thought that at fifty you must judge for yourself, that you had no wrong motive, nothing to gain; that it was the uncertainty of your position which made you grave and unhappy, and that if settled, one way or the other, you would probably be far happier; that considering the importance of the subject, it must affect the cheerfulness of any man in earnest. Then he talked about the Pope, and begged me to read Dr. Hook's sermon,[1] I said I had no respect for Dr. Hook, but would read his sermon. . . . I don't know whether I did right or wrong. My great object was to keep calm, and to say nothing to wound or irritate him and to stand up for you, and in doing this I said many things which I cannot now remember."

With respect to temporal prospects, it seemed as likely as not that on the Serjeant's conversion, Scotch clients would leave him *en masse*. At any rate this possibility distinctly presented itself to him. His reputation, on the other hand, was made, and, as it turned out, his business suffered in no way. Doubtless the Scotch, for one thing, shrewdly guessed that becoming a "Romanist," albeit a terrible thing, could scarcely suffice of itself to turn a competent advocate all of a sudden into a blundering one.

Meanwhile time wore on, and Mrs. Bellasis' position after the "event" will be best explained by an extract from a letter of March 24, 1851, to her father:

"It is now three months since the Serjeant became a Roman Catholic, and I have had time to feel my way, both as regards the children and myself, . . . my varying health and the Serjeant's talent for teaching had led him in the past gradually

---

[1] This may be the sermon of Dean Hook to which the Serjeant refers in a letter of August 18, 1843: "Hook's sermon is truly melancholy. I thank you for it. I thought Dr. Hook would at least have avoided harsh language, however strongly he might feel, against Popery."

to become their sole instructor in religious matters, and of course that instruction has taken the phase of the eventful religious times of the last fifteen years we found ourselves involved in ever since the death of little Fanny, when distress of mind first led us to daily attendance at Divine Service at Margaret Street Chapel. The Serjeant has tried to make his children good *Church of England* Catholics, and now it is pretty plain, from a long series of events, that the Church of England has no longer any principles of Catholicity in her beyond her formularies, which the children themselves are sharp enough to see are quite at variance with the doctrines taught from the pulpit and held by the great mass of her members. . . . Their father, true to his promise of non-interference, no longer teaches them, for, as he truly says, if I teach now, it must be a greater extent of Catholic doctrine than I have hitherto taught; and the children are dissatisfied, they go to church with reluctance. Katty cried all the way yesterday, and I see pouting looks when an entreaty like 'Do, dear papa, take me with you to Vespers,' meets with a decided 'No,' from him. In short, I cannot shut my eyes to the fact that they feel themselves forced to remain in a system for which they have no love, and in which they know there are two *contradictory* views on every doctrine, both taught as *true*: they feel they must go to church *to please mamma.* Margaret said to me very lately: 'How can I like a Church that thinks papa a child of Satan, and has turned out Mr. Bennett?' Now mark what must be the result; they will grow up between papa and mamma attached to neither system, and having only a *total indifference* to both. . . . Had I returned, as you advised me, to the old state of things (in church) at Christmas, I should have had open rebellion at once; the children told me as much; my only chance of retaining them was the attraction of the counterbalancing beautiful services of the much-abused St. Andrew's, Wells Street. . . . I know they would jump for joy did I give them leave to join papa. . . . The children, sooner or later, will, I am sure, join their father; such a father must have unbounded weight. When they are gone, where will be my influence? I shall be like the hen looking after the duckling in the pond, and have about as much influence."

The Serjeant's briefer narrative says: "I did not at first put our children under regular instruction, but the elder ones, Margaret, Katharine, and Mary, went sometimes with me to

Catholic churches, and indeed, so did my dear wife, but the
children, who knew a good deal, tended more and more to
the Catholic religion, till my wife seeing their disposition, said
to me, ' I see their hearts are with us, and if you wish to put
them under instruction I shall make no opposition.' Accordingly on the 3rd of April, I took my three elder girls[1] to
Hill Street, and introduced them to Father Brownbill, and
they went regularly to see him every other day until Maundy
Thursday, the 17th, when they were all received into the
Church, and made their first Communion at Farm Street on
Easter Sunday."

On the 8th, Mr. Manning wrote about himself to the
Serjeant : " By God's mercy, my time of waiting cleared my
mind of every shade of doubt and fear. And when it expired
I felt the decision to be complete. It is too soon to speak :
lest I should say I know not what, but you have known and
do know all I would say. My whole reason, conscience, and
will, seem by God's grace to have found their rest and more.
Pray for me that I may be kept in the grace of God. It is a
thought of unspeakable joy to me that any word of mine should
have come to your help in that time of common suffering.
I am sure that you have more than repaid me by helping me
hither by your prayers. I had heard that your children were
under instruction, and I trust that soon you will be all one
again, never to be parted again for ever."

And when this happy event was realized he wrote to
Mrs. Bellasis, May 9, 1851 : " Your name comes always once
a day. I wish it were better commended to our Master. Let
me ask you both to give me a special remembrance for the
next six weeks that I may have the grace needful for the state
and work before me."

Meanwhile, on Palm Sunday, the Serjeant was present in
Cardinal Wiseman's private chapel, at the Confirmation both
of Mr. Manning, and of Mr. Hope-Scott, and stood god-father
to the latter. On the same day Mrs. Bellasis narrates of
herself : " I went out for a walk, I cared not whither, and
I walked on and across the river, my good angel, I think,
guiding me to the door of St. George's Catholic Cathedral,
Southwark. Anyway, I found myself there, and I sat down
inside the building, feeling, if not quite dead, to every religious
impression, decidedly sulky and stupid. A little bit of palm

---

[1] The eldest was nearly fourteen, the other two, eleven and nine respectively.

was given me, or I took it, and I put it into my muff. The service over, I walked all the way home again ; it must have been three miles at least. The rest were at luncheon. The little children quickly detected the smell of incense and palm about me, and with their faces all smiling and curious, came a chorus, 'Oh Mama, where have you been?' I could not resist their winsome ways and had a good cry, and from that day my mind was in an altered attitude."[1] "On the 21st of April, Easter Monday," the Serjeant writes, "my dear wife of her own accord went out alone, and called upon Mr. Manning, and after a long conference with him, he sent her to Father Brownbill," "whose kindness," Mrs. Bellasis continues, "I can never forget, and who on April 22nd, 1851, at my urgent request, baptized me and heard my recantation ; the waters of baptism seemed to clear away in a very strange way any doubts that might linger. I rose calm and collected, feeling I possessed a something I had never possessed before. Many, I believe, have felt the same at receiving on conversion conditional baptism ; for, indeed, baptism, as it used to be too often performed in the Protestant churches, with a tip of the finger barely moistened, and no water running, could be no baptism at all." Making her first Communion the next day, she and her three girls were confirmed together by Cardinal Wiseman on the 30th, Mr. Manning at the same time receiving minor orders.

Monsignor Searle, in arranging for this, wrote, April 24, 1851 : "I need not write with what real pleasure I fulfil Cardinal Wiseman's instructions to convey to you and Mrs. Bellasis his most sincere and cordial congratulations on the happy event that was alone wanting to complete all that you could desire of bliss on this earth. Though prayed for, and consequently in some way anticipated, it has not been less a source of comfort and joy.

"On Wednesday next, at 8.30 a.m., his Eminence will say Mass, and confer the four minor orders on Mr. Manning. Would this day suit for Mrs. Bellasis' Confirmation ? If so,

---

[1] The late Dr. Grant, Bishop of Southwark, thus refers to this incident in a letter from Rome to the Serjeant on St. George's day, 1870 : "Through your kind calculation, your generous gift comes on St. George's day, and therefore I accept it very gratefully as your tithe for the last stroke given to Mrs. Bellasis on Palm Sunday at St. George's, when her children detected a piece of palm in her muff, and the scent of incense which betrayed her secret. May our dear Lord be praised for gaining you all to His Church.'

will you kindly let me know, and his Eminence will ask Mrs. Scott-Murray to assist as sponsor at the function.

"The Cardinal sends his blessing to you and yours, and begs me to assure you of his fervent prayers for a continued increase of all heavenly graces."

"We do, indeed, rejoice with you," wrote Mrs. Allies, "on your soul having escaped as a bird out of the snare of the fowler; the snare is now broken, and you are delivered. What a blessed, happy day for you all! a whole family united." Hope-Scott wrote to the Serjeant, April 24th, 1851: "I give Mrs. Bellasis and yourself my hearty congratulations on the event which has occurred. You are now again an united family, and under the shadow of the united Church. To have been separated in order thus to meet again must add joy to joy." Badeley, too, although not yet a Catholic, could write on the 23rd: "I fully expected to hear of Mrs. Bellasis following your example, and I am quite prepared to give my 'approbation' as well as my 'congratulations,' if her mind is fully satisfied upon all her points of doubt. I shall congratulate Manning upon these first-fruits of his ministerial labours. . . . Assure her of my best wishes, and of my earnest hope, that if *faith* in any degree severs us, *charity* will at all events unite us, for even if in the former of these good gifts we were much further apart than I really believe we are, the latter would never allow me to be otherwise towards you and all yours than your most sincere friend and well-wisher."

From Miss Gladstone also on May 6, 1851, Mrs. Bellasis received a very kindly note: "The Cardinal," she writes, "has informed me that you are so happy as to have been received into the Church, and I embrace this occasion of renewing my very early acquaintance with you in offering you warm and sincere congratulations. Those may, indeed, rejoice who have followed the inspiration of God's grace. . . . The untold consolations of a Catholic are lightly won by what even the world can inflict. . . . As we believe that the first prayers of converts are swift-winged, let me beg you to pray for my brother William."

Lastly may be cited Dr. Arnott, the cultivated man of science, known to the Serjeant from early days, who thus expressed himself to Mrs. Bellasis, April 27, 1851: "While reading that note of yours, reasons for gladness crowded into my mind, and gave me the persuasion that happy as your family has been in past time, it will be happier still in the time to come. Your

husband has ever been held by me one of the best men I have
met in the world, and recent occurrences will prove his worth.
. . . Conscientious belief as to what is right is to him under any
trial or difficulty the paramount rule of action. In all he
resembles you as you resemble him. You are true partners.
That blessings from above may be showered on you and your
dear children is my hope and prayer."

The Serjeant's Anglican life had now ended and his Catholic
life begun, but they close and open respectively with one final
bit of controversy, amusing and interesting enough in itself, to
dwell upon before entering upon the calm of his later years.
"The whole storm of the Hierarchy and Liararchy," wrote
Father Brande Morris, in December, 1850, "has burst upon
us." Two brief but trenchant *Letters* at this time contain all
the Serjeant's say about the "Papal Aggression."

The first Anglican *Letter* written in the closing days of the
year 1850, and entitled, *The Archbishop of Westminster. A
Remonstrance with the Clergy of Westminster from a Westminster
Magistrate*, began by animadverting on their address to the
Bishop of London about this new Hierarchy. "I need not
particularly detail," he says, "the actual occurrence which has
called forth your ill-timed protest, farther than to say, that
whereas, until lately, England had been 'parcelled out' into
certain divisions, for the religious purposes of our Roman
Catholic countrymen, . . . these districts have been, by the
only authority acknowledged by Roman Catholics for such a
purpose, namely, by the Pope, re-arranged, increased in number,
and called by the name of some English town or city within
their respective limits. I may also say that the determination
to take this course was not arrived at hastily, suddenly, or
secretly, but, on the contrary, deliberately and openly, the
intention of making the new arrangement having been stated
and alluded to for years past, in the ordinary channels of public
intelligence, without exciting any but a formal protest on your
part unnoticed by any one else.

" As soon, however, as the arrangement has been made and
concluded, you, being, as you say, 'Bound by your ordination
vows to maintain peace and quietness in Church and State,'
proceed to address the Bishop with the view of rousing the
Protestant feeling of England upon the subject. Whether the
example *set by you* has tended or will tend to peace and
quietness, you have, by this time, ample means of judging ;

there is such a thing as raising a storm you cannot quell, and there is such a thing as calling in allies whom you cannot afterwards shake off. . . .

"Your first ground in justification of your attempt to agitate, in a country of religious liberty, against our conscientious Roman Catholic countrymen is, that it is an act of *schism*, inasmuch as there can be 'but one Metropolitan in a province, and one Bishop in a diocese;' no one will dispute your general proposition; but the act of schism, if it be one, was, as you very well know, consummated centuries ago: in 1623, Gregory XV. sent a Bishop here; in 1688, Innocent XI. sent four; so that your indignation comes somewhat late: you add, however, that Dr. Wiseman has now assumed the title of an English city;— this as regards the charge of schism, is trifling, it is the *thing* which makes the schism, not the *name*, and if the name of every single diocese in England had been assumed by newly appointed Roman Catholic Bishops, it would not have increased the schism, if schism it be, incurred by sending Bishops here at all. But . . . it is not for the Church of England to complain, for she has, again and again, encouraged similar acts, both in our colonies and elsewhere, wholly ignoring the rights of existing Bishops, as well of the Roman Catholic as of the Greek Church.

"If your complaint is that the Pope has sent Bishops to dioceses where an episcopate already existed, we have done the same thing in Jerusalem, to which, on your principles, we schismatically sent Drs. Alexander and Gobat. . . . Did we get the consent of the *then existing Bishop* of Jerusalem? you know we did not, and so, upon your own principles, our schism was complete . . . and it is notorious that the Bishop of Gibraltar, by the authority of the Queen and the Church of England, assumes Episcopal jurisdiction in France and Italy, and that, not to govern our own people only, but to convert the natives, as the Protestant College at Malta fully testifies.

"If your complaint is, that the names of particular towns and cities are assumed, the Church of England has, to name one instance only, assumed that of Quebec, previously occupied by a Catholic Bishop; in this case too, assuming the very name of the existing see.

"If your complaint is that England is, for Roman Catholic purposes, parcelled out into dioceses, *without Her Majesty's leave*, Scotland has been in like manner parcelled out for Anglican or Episcopalian purposes, equally without such leave.

"Your excuse, no doubt, for sending Bishops into Roman Catholic dioceses, would be, that you do not acknowledge the Roman Catholic Bishops, or rather, it would be the excuse of some of you ; the justification of the Roman Catholic Church is that she does not acknowledge the Protestant Bishops ; one or other, unquestionably is, in such cases, schismatical, the question is, which ? but it is absurd to assume the late Catholic arrangements to be an admitted act of schism, when, as every one knows, the question of schism or no schism depends upon much more important considerations than who was the first comer.

"The world, unfortunately, has too much reason to know, that there are two separate and distinct theories respecting the visible Church ; one, that all Christians were intended to be united in one body, whatever their race, nation, or language, and that they are all bound to submit themselves to the authority of that body, speaking by its head, or chief Bishop, without reference to the varying distinctions of States or civil governments ; the other, that all Christians, within each nation or State, form separate, distinct, and independent bodies, and that all are bound to attach themselves to that of their own nation, and submit to its authority, speaking by its head, the monarch, or other governing power ; the former is the Catholic system, the latter the National system, of which the English Church is an example. I am not now discussing which is right, but so long as this country professes to be one of religious liberty, those who conscientiously adhere to the former system must be allowed such rights as their religion requires, one of which is, that of living under the spiritual jurisdiction of pastors appointed by that authority which alone they recognize in spiritual matters. You speak, however, as if you altogether ignored the existence of such a system, or as if you thought it was to be trampled out by violence. Pursue your intolerant task, if you have the heart, but cease to boast any more of religious liberty, and hide your heads among the persecuting tyrants of Protestant Switzerland.

"Another ground of complaint alleged is, that the recent arrangements are a denial of the validity of Anglican Orders ; no doubt the Roman Catholics do deny the validity of our Orders, but they have not waited till now to proclaim it ; since the time of Archbishop Parker they have always denied them, and, as is well known, Anglican clergymen, who have conformed to Rome, have always been re-ordained ; it is therefore, in this

respect as in the last, the merest trifling to talk of these arrangements as a *present* denial of the validity of Orders hitherto
admitted. The Roman Catholics may be right or may be
wrong in not acknowledging our Orders, but it is scarcely fair
to endeavour to hound on a mixed multitude, of partially
informed persons, by representing this as a present insult,
newly offered, in order to excite a present enmity. . . .

"But there is another ground suggested in justification of
the present attempt at excitement, which, from the stress you
lay upon it, is obviously the chief. You say, in your address,
that Roman Catholics are 'guilty of invading Her Majesty's
constitutional prerogative, which is to be the sole dispenser of
titles in the realm, and so are justly chargeable with an outrage
upon the British constitution, and with indignity to the British
crown.' You call attention to the fact that you have 'solemnly
declared your assent to the principle embodied in the articles
and canons of our Church, that the Queen's majesty under God
is the only supreme governor of this realm, as well in all
spiritual or ecclesiastical causes as in temporal;' the Bishop of
London says, in his reply, that 'the appointment of bishops to
preside over new dioceses in England, is virtually a denial of
the legitimate authority of the British Sovereign:' again, he
calls the new arrangement 'an encroachment upon the rights
and honour of the Crown. . . .'

". . . If I do not mistake, there are many amongst you, who
have heretofore openly expressed your dissatisfaction at what
you then considered the undue interference of the State, in the
appointment of Bishops, in the abolition of bishoprics, in
the reconstruction of dioceses, and otherwise; you have said,
'The Church is enslaved by the State;' 'She is in chains;'
'These are infringements of her unalienable rights;' 'The
royal supremacy is a usurpation,' and so on; and we have
listened to you, we have allowed ourselves to be pacified by
you, we have thought it possible that there might prove to be
a spirit within the Church and amongst yourselves, which would
disentangle us from secular bonds, and enable the Church to
speak a plainer language, and show herself a true member of
the Catholic body; . . . now you are doing your best to cut our
only hope from beneath our feet, you set up and insist upon
'royal rights' and 'constitutional prerogatives,' and reassert
your solemn assent to the principle, that the Queen is the
'supreme ruler, under God,' of our spiritual as well as temporal
concerns. . . .

" Either you have been using unreal language to us regarding the domination of the State, to serve the purpose of quieting such of us as were offended at it, or you are using language now which does not accord with your real sentiments, in order to get the support of the State in your agitation. Pilate and Herod are made friends together over what they deem their common foe, but in your anxiety to effect this, you have flung to the winds all thought of the difficulties, of the distresses, which you knew were pressing upon us. . . . Nothing, positively nothing, has occurred, of late, more calculated to shake the small remaining confidence of many of us in the Church of England than this almost unanimous burst of Erastianism. . . . And what are the remedies suggested for the 'insult' which has been put upon you? First, to petition the legislature to re-enact in part the penal laws! noble suggestion, from 'the most tolerant Church in the world!' . . . The other remedy is 'controversial preaching.'

" Now, if you are to adopt controversial preaching, allow me to make a suggestion to you; do not, I intreat you, imagine that all you have to do is to take some doctrine of the Roman Catholic Church, and hold it up to reprobation singly and apart from the system to which it belongs; the truth or falsehood of these doctrines does not depend upon their abstract probability or improbability, but upon the *authority* on which they are received ; Protestant doctrines will not bear such treatment any more than Catholic doctrines, and if you set the example of exciting simple minds against prayers for the dead, for instance, or the invocation of saints, on the score of their being, in your judgment, inconsistent with the justice or the honour of God, or with common sense, or for such like reasons, you set an example, which infidels will not be slow to follow, and they on their part will allege the same objections against the Incarnation and the Trinity. . . .

" And what shall I say of the allies whom you have roused, and with whom you are now associated? Have you no misgivings as to the language your new friends use on your behalf? When they talk with scorn of the 'Italian Priest,' did it ever occur to you to observe upon which word they lay the emphasis?"

He ends with a warning and a prophecy: " You may, as you have done, exhibit yourselves to the world as agitators ; you may, as you have done, avail yourself of the aid of your natural enemies, the Dissenter, the latitudinarian, the sceptic,

the infidel, the Jew; you may, for a time, parade your hetero-
geneous army as an exhibition of Protestant strength and
unity; but your present allies have no intention that *you*
should profit by the contest; they will not be contented with
the lean and meagre game which you have marked for them,
but will, and that soon, turn upon the stronger scent of your
own rich preserves; upon your luxurious foundations, upon
your colleges and universities, in the soft retirement of which,
having shared with you the labours of the fight, they will feel
themselves entitled to share also your repose. The first, the
immediate result of your present movement will be the opening
of the Universities. . . . And now I take my leave of you; the
storm you have raised, *for you did raise it*, will, sooner or later,
cease, the waters will subside, and then you will be at leisure,
like the inhabitants of a mountain valley overwhelmed by an
inundation, to survey the *débris*, to reconstruct your landmarks,
and seek your scattered flock; but be sure of this, your fences
will never again stand where they did, nor will all your sheep
be found."

The second (Catholic) *Letter* was dated April 4, 1851, and
entitled, *The Anglican Bishops, versus the Catholic Hierarchy: a
demurrer to further proceedings,* and thus probably came out
before, at or very latest, simultaneously with Dr. Newman's
famous Lecture, entitled, *Tradition the sustaining power of the
Protestant View.* Both publications treated of the same strange
phenomenon which the Serjeant had observed and commented
upon at Manchester as early as 1840, and apropos of which
Dr. Newman now wrote of the Establishment in a well-known
passage aptly termed "The Peal of Bells:"[1] "Unitarians,

---

[1] "Neither the words nor the idea occur," wrote Cardinal Newman, October 10,
1882, "in (the Serjeant's) pamphlet, and I am sure that I did not take it from him.
My idea is the *monotonous* repetition in *changed* order of a *few* words, 'atrocious,
insolent,' &c., and I got these words, not from him, but from Episcopal charges, as
he did. . . . *My* lecture was *delivered*, July 5, 1851, and the writing took me some
time, especially to get information about bell-ringers. I ought still to have the MS.
information from the person whom I got to make inquiries through Birmingham."
And on the 13th, his Eminence wrote: "When a new edition of my volume comes
out, I will gladly make a reference to (the Serjeant's) forcible pamphlet, nay, I
would put the whole of it in my Appendix. . . . His pamphlet is dated . . .
when he *wrote* it. I do not know when it was *published*, which is often a
later act, and especially in the case of a collection of spicy bits from Episcopal
charges." On the 19th he wrote: "I have changed my mind on reading (the
Serjeant's) pamphlets; they are too good, and run to too many pages, not to claim
a reprint handsomely carried out. . . . I think I should spoil a good job, if I
reprinted in my 'Lectures' *one* out of so many which ought to be preserved. This
would not hinder my referring in a note to Anglican vituperations."

Sabellians, Utilitarians, Wesleyans, Calvinists, Swedenborgians, Irvingites, Freethinkers, all these it can tolerate in its very bosom; no form of opinion comes amiss; but Rome it cannot abide. It agrees to differ with its children on a thousand points, one is sacred—that Her Majesty the Queen is 'the Mother and Mistress of all Churches;' on one dogma it is infallible, on one it may securely insist without fear of being unreasonable or excessive—that 'the Bishop of Rome hath no jurisdiction in this realm.' Here is sunshine amid the darkness, sense amid confusion, an intelligible strain amid a Babel of sounds; whatever befalls, here is sure footing; it is, 'No peace with Rome,' 'Down with the Pope,' and 'The Church in danger.' Never has the Establishment failed in the use of these important and effective watchwords; many are its shortcomings, but it is without reproach in the execution of this, its special charge. Heresy and scepticism and infidelity and fanaticism may challenge it in vain; but fling upon the gale the faintest whisper of Catholicism, and it recognizes by instinct the presence of its connatural foe. Forthwith, as during the last year, the atmosphere is tremulous with agitations, and discharges its vibrations far and wide. A movement is in birth which has no natural crisis or resolution. Spontaneously the bells of the steeples begin to sound. Not by any act of volition, but by a sort of mechanical impulse, bishop and dean, archdeacon and canon, rector and curate, one after another, each on his high tower, off they set, swinging and booming, tolling and chiming, with nervous intenseness and thickening emotion, and deepening volume, the old ding-dong which has scared town and country this weary time; tolling and chiming away, jingling and clamouring, and ringing the changes on their poor half-dozen notes all about the 'Popish aggression,' 'insolent and insidious,'" &c., "bobs (I think the ringers call them), bobs, and bobs-royal, and triple bob-majors and grandsires, to the extent of their compass, and the full ring of their metal, in honour of Queen Bess and to the confusion of the Holy Father and the Princes of the Church." Such was the great Oratorian's powerful figure descriptive of the Protestant clerical outcry at the re-establishment of the Catholic Hierarchy in this country. The Serjeant likened the hubbub to a wind band out of tune.

"In the month of October last," he writes, "the Bishop of London, in his reply to an address from the clergy of the city of Westminster on the subject of the Catholic Hierarchy,

H

first raised the cry of 'insult' to the Queen and to the
Established Church, . . . the charge . . . has formed the key-
note to the inharmonious concert, which has continued from
that time to this.

"Four months have, however, elapsed, the tramp of the
motley band is dying away in the distance, and a solitary beat
of the drum, or an insulated blast on the ophicleide, is all that
is audible: surely at last the time is come when the drum-
major may cease his exaggerated flourishes, and when a
performance which has resolved itself into such intricate and
unmanageable cadences, may cease and recommence no more.
. . . The remedy unhesitatingly recommended by (the Bishop)
was a recurrence to penal laws; but at the same time (as indeed
became a Bishop) the advice to his clerical flock was this:
'The conduct to be pursued by you, ought, in my opinion, to be
temperate and charitable.'

"Of the efficiency of his lordship's advice I will speak
presently, but his opinion and his remedy were eagerly acquiesced in, and it is now plain that by endeavouring to act upon
them, the people of England have been led into an imprac-
ticable dilemma.

"To proceed with the proposed legislation, regarding the
Catholic Hierarchy, is impossible, consistently with the peace of
the United Kingdom; to withdraw from it with dignity seems,
at first sight, equally impossible. . . . An opportunity is now
afforded for a graceful cessation of hostilities on the part of
the nation and the legislature. . . . After the full explanations
which have been given, who is there who is not entirely
convinced . . . that intentional insult to the Queen never in
the most remote degree entered into the brain of any human
being.

"But the Bishop had also alleged that the erection of the
Hierarchy was *intended as an insult to the Established Church.*
There was as little real truth in this charge as in the former,
but there was more colour for it. No doubt the Church of
England was ignored (in regard, that is, to its spiritual character,
for no one does ignore it, or can ignore it as a temporal Establishment), and it is said that whether any affront was intended
or not, insult to the Church of England was inherent in the
very setting up of a rival hierarchy. Let us assume that this
is so, and farther, that the tone of the Papal documents was
unpleasing to the Anglican Bishops, and then let us see whether

the Church of England is under the circumstances in a condition
to pursue the matter further.

"There is a common and well-known rule that where a man
takes the law into his own hands, he forfeits his right to invoke
the law in the same matter for redress; this is obviously a just
rule, and one that can be shown to be strictly applicable in the
present case. Has, or has not, the Church of England taken
the law into her own hands? Has her conduct been ' temperate
and charitable'? . . . Now I am not going to rake up *all* the
harsh and bitter things that have been hastily said of the
Catholic Church by sincere but mistaken persons. . . . Let
bygones be bygones. . . . I put aside, also, all that has been
spoken and written by deans, archdeacons, canons, rectors, and
others of the Anglican clergy, . . . and I confine myself to that
language, and that only, which has been deliberately adopted by
Bishops of the Established Church, in their communications
with their clergy and people, and I ask whether the Church of
England, thus speaking by these her highest accredited organs,
has not taken the law into her own hands, and *avenged
herself?* . . .

"My neighbour accidentally jostles me in the street, I collar
him, kick him, knock off his hat and trample it under my feet,
spit upon him, roll him in the kennel, spatter him with mud, set
the boys to hoot at him and pelt him, and then, out of breath
with my exertions, I magnanimously shout for the police and
charge him with an assault. Is not this precisely the mode in
which the Church of England has acted and is acting towards
the Catholic Church? Has her language been ' temperate and
charitable'? Let the following extracts (to which every Bishop
in England, without exception, has contributed his share) furnish
the answer, and let it be remembered that the real question in
dispute is loudly affirmed to be *temporal and not spiritual ;* that
therefore abuse of the doctrines of the Catholic Church could
have had nothing to do with its solution."

Then follow in tabulated form " expressions extracted from
the addresses, replies, and speeches of Anglican Bishops since
October last, as reported in the *Times* newspaper." They
are scheduled under four heads: (1) The Catholic Church ;
(2) Catholic doctrines and practices ; (3) Catholic Bishops and
clergy ; (4) The erection of the Catholic Hierarchy ; with forty,
fifty-one, nineteen, and seventy-one appalling specimens of
vituperations under each head respectively, with the Bishops

responsible for the several examples duly recorded opposite each. The Serjeant then concludes: "Such is the 'temperate and charitable' language which Anglican Bishops have allowed themselves to use against those upon whom they were also calling down the aid of the law; now the remonstrance of the negro who was obliged to listen to a sermon whilst he was under the lash, has never been considered unreasonable: 'If you preachee, preachee, and if you floggee, floggee, but no preachee, floggee too!' Why, then, should a harder measure be dealt out to Catholics? The Anglican Church has chosen its part, namely, preaching, of which the above are specimens, why should it be allowed to insist on flogging too? Insult! Is it no insult to hear ourselves and our most sacred convictions called anti-Christian, blasphemous, unclean, apostate, arrogant, profane, pestilent, satanic, degraded, dishonest, false, tyrannical, offensive, selfish, contemptible, artful, blind, shameless, scandalous, disgusting, ignorant, cunning, audacious, ungrateful, defiled, domineering, gross, cursed, insidious, revolting, pagan, malignant, infatuated, corrupt in doctrine, and idolatrous in practice? And this not by an ignorant mob led by demagogues, but by Bishops instructing and advising their flocks? If this be 'temperate and charitable,' what is it to be *intemperate and uncharitable?*

"Here I am sorely tempted to single out one of the episcopal band [1] for a special remonstrance, who, having deliberately prepared a solemn document for the assent of his assembled clergy, was induced to add to its bitterness at the behest of those whom he had called together to advise. There are those who grieve for the hand that crowned the vocabulary with the term 'idolatrous.' Such a charge, if made at all, should not be merely an accidental afterthought; but my object is not personal.

"To conclude: the ground, then, on which I demur to farther proceedings, and urge upon Englishmen that they should now generously withdraw from the conflict, is that even assuming that the Catholics have, by the erection of their own Hierarchy, insulted the Established Church, the Hierarchy of the Church of England has taken its own revenge, and that so fully and unreservedly as to render all farther retaliation alike unnecessary, ungenerous, and unjust."

Thus ends the last of Mr. Serjeant Bellasis' four small, but not

---

[1] He referred to Samuel Wilberforce, then Bishop of Oxford.

ineffective public contributions to the controversies of a memor-
able epoch : "The pamphlets are all valuable," Cardinal Newman
wrote, October 19, 1882. "The *Vituperations* have an historical
value. . . . The *Judicial Committee*, &c., deals with the great
question still alive and vigorous, the present issue of which is
the imprisonment of Mr. Green in Lancaster (shame on you[1])
Gaol." The pamphlets have a certain sharpness of tone, partly
engendered by irritation at the insecure theological position
their writer found himself in, through no fault of his own ;
and in the case of the fourth, the *Demurrer* Letter, owing
to a sense of the injustice displayed by those who really
ought to have set the best example of "charitable" language
towards a small minority of their Christian fellow-countrymen.

Apart from occasional outbreaks, the generally tolerant spirit
of the present age is indeed far removed from the bigoted tone
of forty years ago, but at the period in question there can be
no doubt that there were many innocent sufferers from the
language complained of by the Serjeant.[2]

In a letter to a friend, of January 9, 1853, he gives some
specific instances that it may not be without interest to recall,
albeit illustrating a state of feeling that has now happily passed
away, and, as we may hope, for ever, making room for that
spirit of fair-play which is one of John Bull's most honourable
characteristics.

He writes to say that the Catholics are "discouraged by
a persevering opposition, and I will give you some instances :

"A generous lady built a school in Little Albany Street for
Catholic girls. I am a trustee of that school, and it cost her
£1,500, but it stands vacant and unused to this hour, because it
is Government property, and the consent of the Government is
required to its being used as a school, and that consent is with-
held.[3]

---

[1] An allusion to his correspondent's official title, *i.e.*, that of "Lancaster" herald.

[2] "The storm of abuse and calumny against Catholicity on pretext of Papal
aggression is still far from being subsided." (Letter of Father Pagani, General of
the Institute of Charity, dated from Ratcliffe College, November 3, 1851.)

[3] "Can you give me any information about the school in Little Albany Street?"
wrote Cardinal Wiseman to the Serjeant, August 4, 1853. "All matters with the
Sylvan department of Her Majesty's Government are, I hope, come to an end, so
that I hope we may see no trace of Woods and Forests there, except the Tree of
Knowledge, and all the requisite school plant, in the shape of forms and desks,
which I hear are growing in the place. At this moment," his Eminence continues,
"Somers Town is widowed of its chief pastor, Mr. Rolfe, and before making a new
appointment, it is worthy of consideration whether a new district could be formed
having the Albany School for its seat of government. I should, therefore, be glad

"A lady took a lease of a house at Kensington for Catholic educational purposes, large sums of money were laid out upon it, and at the instance of the Protestant clergy, the landlord took advantage of a technical breach of covenant by a former occupier, and ejected them with the loss of all their outlay.

"I myself applied for the lease of a house which has stood vacant twenty years, but when the bargain was on the point of completion, we were told there should be a covenant not to use it for Catholic purposes. The house is still vacant.

"I send you an article from a newspaper giving an account of the absolute failure to obtain a site for a church at Westminster; the article is mine, barring certain rude expressions which are not mine. The building which should be schools is obliged to be used for the church, whilst £10,000, chiefly the offer of one individual, has been refused for a site which is now a mere rubbish heap, for no other reason but to prevent Catholic accommodation. Such instances are innumerable, and in some degree account, over and above the want of means, for Catholic affairs being no better than they are."

Let us continue his letter: "As to the bribery of Catholics to send their children to Protestant schools, which I allege to be so prevalent, but which you seem to doubt and are convinced would be punished if known, of course all depends upon what is bribery.

"I call it bribery to send messengers into a Catholic district in a time of famine, and to hold out to starving parents food for themselves and their children on condition of their coming to the Protestant church, and sending their children to the Protestant schools.

"I call it bribery (there are cases in London), to set up a Protestant school near a Catholic school, and to tempt the children away by offering breakfast and dinner as well as instruction, an example which it is notorious that Catholics are too poor to follow.

"The extent to which this system is carried both in Ireland

to receive any information respecting the condition, architectural, political, legal, sanitary, and general, of the schools in question, and their adjoining premises. We are enjoying some summer at last, and St. Swithin, I trust, has broken with Aquarius, or this gentleman has broken his urn." On March 31, 1857, the Serjeant wrote to his second daughter: "We are preparing to celebrate our first Mass at St. Ann's School on Friday next, so I beg that all of you will join your prayers with ours for the prosperity of the school, and the protection of Our Blessed Lady of Dolours, to whom the altar is to be dedicated."

and in London is immense, and so the poor children are induced by present bribes to leave their home of safety, and take up their abode in an empty house, a very Babel of confusion in itself, without shelter from the blasts of heresy and infidelity, and tottering to its fall.

"My complaint is that the Reformation Society in Ireland, and the Scripture readers in London, are undermining the Catholic Faith in the minds of the poor, their chief weapon being ridicule, and the object of their ridicule, confession and the Blessed Sacrament, and that no one, Bishop or clergy, condemns or protests against it in any open or effectual manner.

"This it is that grieves me, that you and others should continue, by your adhesion to it, to fortify and uphold a system which is day by day making infidels by thousands, teaching doctrines that you abhor from the bottom of your hearts, and denying truths which you hold as you would your life, whilst you are powerless to prevent either the one or the other. . . ."

He continues : "Relieve yourself from the fear that I can be hurt by the deportment of any one towards me in regard to my being a Catholic. It is very rare : I do, however, sometimes meet an averted eye or a cold and distant recognition, but such things only serve to remind me of my own happy advantage in being in the Catholic Church, and affect me no more than a nobleman would be affected if he heard that some Radical sneered at his coronet.

"There is another passage in your letter which rejoices me as indicating your real sentiments ; you say, speaking of Mr. Ringrose, 'I have every feeling of respect towards him as a priest of the Catholic Church ;' allow me, however, to say that the truly Catholic disposition you show in speaking thus of a priest of the Roman Catholic Church would hardly be participated in by the Anglican Episcopate. I send you a pamphlet published by me more than a year ago, you may have seen it before, but, if you have, it will recall the contents to your memory, and you will there find in unmistakeable clearness the sentiments entertained by the whole Anglican Episcopate regarding the Roman Catholic Church, doctrines, and clergy, which must, I should think, show you how out of place you are with spiritual fathers who use such language as is there to be found, and to which every one of them, without exception, contributed his share.

"I appreciate, my dear B., that constancy of friendship

on your part which enabled you to hold me in your affectionate regard, notwithstanding the coolness of your 'old and valued friend;' he may be old, but allow me to doubt the value of a friendship which was only to be retained by the sacrifice of one who had ever regarded you with the most constant and unvarying affection; let me confess to you, if you had withdrawn yourself I think I should have grieved as much as for any relative, however dear, a feeling I am not conscious of towards any of my former associates to the same extent.

"One word more, and I have finished this long letter; you look forward to the time which will 'bring us to see eye to eye, when there shall be no room for doubt and all will be made clear.' That time will undoubtedly come, but you may find yourself among the number of those who refused to believe without *proof*, who wished to put their fingers into the print of the nails before they would commit themselves by acquiescence. It will be a terrible thing at the great day, when the Truth is plain, to say, 'Lord, Lord, all is now clear, now I see eye to eye, my doubts are at an end, I believe,' and to hear the mournful but certain answer of our Blessed Lord, 'Son, it is too late, the time for faith is past.'

"My entire belief is that God destines you and your good wife for better things, that He has not brought your earnest minds thus far towards His Church except for the purpose of landing you safely in it, and my anxiety is that your part of the work should not remain undone, that your will should correspond with His grace, and that you should dedicate your-selves to Him and His Church whilst you have energy and health to serve Him in it, and not delay till you are driven into it by necessity, and your submission will have lost all its gracefulness as well as all its merit."

Gratitude to God for his own and his family's reception into the Church finds frequent expression in the Serjeant's correspondence. To his daughters, Katharine and Mary, he writes, April 11, 1857: "I hope you will get this on the anni-versary of your first Communion, a happy day for me as well as for yourselves, and that you will believe how permanent has been the gratification I experienced on that day, when, of your own free-will, you stepped into the boat in which your dear papa had embarked so shortly before. I never cease to thank God for this, as well as for the perseverance He has granted to us all, and it makes me quite happy to feel sure that you are so firmly established in our holy religion that neither prosperity nor adversity are likely to shake you." [1]

To his second son, about to make his first Communion, he says, December 5, 1862: "I am rejoiced at it from the bottom of my heart, as the one great object of my life is to see all my dear children firmly planted and steadily growing in the Catholic Church, and as you, one by one, arrive at the important period of your first Communion, I feel an additional security that the great blessing God has given us will not be withdrawn from us, but that we shall, one and all, remain true and faithful members of His Church all our lives, and *in æternum. . . .* It cost me much to become a Catholic, it is for you and your dear brothers and sisters to preserve the blessing, and I hope you will do so as the most valuable possession you can ever have."

"If I have succeeded in this," he writes in March, 1870, to a daughter (*i.e.* in making you "good Catholics"), "it is the great work, the only work in which I can rest with satisfaction." Lastly, he speaks, December 23, 1870, to Mrs. Bellasis of the "gratitude we owe to Almighty God . . . for the very many blessings with which He has surrounded us, . . . trials must come to us some day, but in the meantime let us appreciate the blessings and acknowledge them, and that they are due to no deserts of our own," [2] and foremost among them he places the fact of all his children being "safe in the ark of God's Church, to which I trust they will all cling as to the greatest blessing their parents have provided for them. This is my Christmas salutation to you all."

And he was prepared to defend his religion. It chanced to be violently attacked in his presence by some of his brother-magistrates at the Clerkenwell April Sessions in 1864, whereupon he got up and said that "he did not believe it to be the

---

[1] He writes to his cousin, A. F. Bellasis, November 13, 1861: "You probably heard that my sister and four of her sons had become Catholics; this, I dare say, you will not break your heart about, especially as it is only a return to the ancient religion of our family. However, seriously speaking, they have done what they have done, conscientiously, and are as happy a group as could be found anywhere. The Doctor had a great run made against him at first, but latterly he has regained and far surpassed his former professional position, notwithstanding his religion."

[2] In the same spirit of humble thankfulness he wrote to his mother, November 28, 1836, of the blessings he was then enjoying as being "the result of many years of anxiety on your part. I try to hold all these blessings at arm's length, knowing how fragile they are and how little to be depended upon, and feel grateful in the highest degree at times to be allowed to possess them. Why these blessings are showered upon me I cannot tell. God only knows; possibly to reward some good unrequited on earth in generations back."

desire of the Justices to make that court the arena for theological discussion, and at all events he would be no party to it. . . . He might, however, take leave to remind the court that the religion so maligned was the religion of their forefathers for a thousand years, that it was the religion of two hundred millions of Christians, and that in our own country it was the religion of men quite as honourable, and quite as estimable, as any of the members of the court around him, and of men quite as able, intellectually, to understand and appreciate their religion. Further he might be allowed to say, mixing as he had done for years in Catholic society, and being well able to speak upon the subject, that there was every desire on the part of Catholics to stand well with their Protestant fellow-countrymen, that they were ready to join in any benevolent or social work for the general benefit, and in particular that he had never heard in Catholic society any disrespectful word of Protestants or of the Protestant clergy as such; Catholics differ from them, essentially differ, but such unjust language about Protestants, and uncharitable imputations of motives, as had been heard that day about Catholics were, he undertook to say, never heard in Catholic society. More than that, there was every disposition to acknowledge the generous services formerly rendered by Protestants to Catholics in times of difficulty ; and traditions remain of many an estate, which would otherwise have been lost through the penal laws, having been preserved to the Catholic family by the generosity of their Protestant neighbours."

CHAPTER VI.

"THERE are amongst you," the Serjeant observed at the
wedding of his eldest daughter in 1864, "two distinct classes
of friends—the one consisting of friends of my earlier days,
whose regard for me has stood the test of half a century's
lapse, as well as of certain disturbing causes that have wafted
others away like leaves in autumn, . . . on the other hand,
there is another class, the friends of my maturer years, whose
regard and affection, as if to compensate us for what we have
lost, have budded forth towards us like flowers in spring." Such
was his own happy experience on becoming a Catholic.

The first among the Catholic laity whom he got to know
are mentioned in his *MS. Autobiography*. "At this time"
(1851), he writes, "I made the acquaintance of Lord Arundel
and Surrey, Mr. Scott-Murray, Mr. George Weld of Leagram,
and Lady Lothian. . . . At the beginning of August we betook
ourselves with all the children to Scarborough for the autumn ;
here we got to know more Catholics . . . and were most
kindly received by them." A near neighbour in London, Lady
Doughty, who was ever affectionate towards his family, was
also one of his earliest Catholic friends. "He and his," writes
his wife of this time, "met with great hospitality ; happy
days of *Auld lang syne*, of which all the actors have long since
passed on to their eternal home!" [1]

"I have said," the Serjeant continues, "I was kindly received
by the Catholics to whom I had been introduced ; but more
than this, I was highly edified by the habits of the Catholic
households. I was particularly struck with the unobtrusive and
natural manner in which religion was mixed up with the

[1] In 1854, she describes Llanarth as "one of those charming houses where
English hospitality is dispensed without ceremoniousness."

ordinary affairs and even amusements of life." [1]   And he gives
the following instances of his meaning :

"Whilst we were staying at Everingham, the hounds were
on the lawn, and the horses of the guests parading in front, and
groups of gentry preparing to start, when I went into the
chapel; there was no one there but Mr. William Maxwell
(afterwards Lord Herries), and he was on his knees making
his morning meditation in a scarlet coat and top boots. This
looked to me, at first, like an incongruity. I soon saw,
however, that it was not so. . . . On another occasion, whilst
we were staying at Holme, I was up early on a Sunday
morning, and had gone into the tribune of the chapel, which
was a gallery opening from the staircase, and where I was
not visible to any one in the chapel below ; at first there was
no one, but after some time the sacristy door opened and the
young lady of the house entered, who during the previous
evening had been foremost in making merriment amongst a
young party. She was not conscious of my presence, and
proceeded to prepare the altar for Mass, doing this with
such reverence and devotion that I could hardly believe her
to be the same person who the night before had been acting
charades and playing forfeits with such a merry countenance.
Everything now was done with deliberation ; she never passed
in front of the altar without kneeling, and everything was
touched and handled so gently and so devotionally that she
might have been serving in the presence of some great monarch ;
she finally knelt, and prayed, and retired. I had not yet learned
the effect produced upon Catholics by the consciousness of the
Presence of the Blessed Sacrament. This sight was most
impressive to me. . . . Again, whilst we were staying at
Broughton Hall, I saw nothing in Sir Charles Tempest but a
cheerful, courteous, good-humoured country gentleman, with
strong political feelings ; he was not at all the man whom I
should have expected to find at early morning alone, in his
chapel, and staying there during two Masses with unmistakable
devotion. He practised his religion, but I do not think I ever
heard him talk about it. Once more, Mr. Charles Waterton, a
vigorous old man, the well-known naturalist, full of cheerful
anecdote, with whom we spent some weeks at Walton Hall,

---

[1] He had noticed the same thing in Bohemia when staying with Count Thun at Tetschen. His wife mentions, for one thing, children running to kiss Count Thun's hand, when he was out walking, and saying, "Gelaubt sei Jesus Christus," to which he responded with another phrase.

was also a well-read theologian and liked to talk upon Catholic
subjects. . . . After his wife's death, a blanket, a log of
wood, and the bare floor, were all the appliances he had for
sleeping. Also at four in the morning, winter and summer, he
made a meditation bareheaded in the open air on the borders
of his lake. But these acts of mortification appeared to be
quite consistent in him with a joyful, not to say jovial, character.
All these things were new to me."[1]

The edification given to the Serjeant by these Catholic
families is referred to by his wife. "These old Catholic Yorkshire
houses are truly patriarchal," she writes, "and models of what
Christian households may and ought to be. The *Angelus*
awakes us in the morning, Mass comes before breakfast, at
noon *Angelus* and again at sunset, family prayers at night,
punctual to the minute, nobody absent from the church, and
throughout the day religion forming one of the topics of conversation in the most natural way." And in describing a
Christmas visit in 1859 to Wardour, after speaking of the
festivities, she adds : "With all this, religion came first and
foremost : daily Mass, always attended by the family and their
dependents, night prayers, and the *Angelus* bell."

What the Serjeant admired in Catholic houses in England
and on the Continent, he took care to carry out at home.
Believing himself to be a man without much sentiment or
feeling, he said that he relied greatly upon *externals* in religion,
and as in the Anglican Church, so as a Catholic, he continued
exact and punctual in outward observances. He disliked
availing himself even of dispensations that the Church allows.[2]

He had family prayers regularly, morning and evening, and
his manner in saying them was one of quiet reverence and
touching simplicity. On Sunday evenings he added the singing

---

[1] "The Walton visit," writes Mrs. Bellasis, "was most interesting. Although it
was November, the old gentleman never allowed the sitting-room window to be shut.
The fire, however, was a roaring one, and by carefully avoiding the line of direct
draught, we took no cold. Mass was said in the house in the 'upper room,' for such
it was, of the days of persecution, when during the Holy Sacrifice, a man was kept
on the watch to see if the scouts in search of Papists were coming, as all was so
contrived that in a few minutes everything about the altar could be secreted and
the priest hidden. Mr. Waterton's dress was like a gardener's, and it used to be his
pleasure to show people about Walton and hear their remarks about himself."

[2] As, for example, when upon a voyage, with respect to fasting and abstinence,
it was a difficulty to persuade him to eat meat on a Friday when age and ill-health
had liberated him from the obligation. He would in such cases endeavour to hide
his real motive by suggesting his preference for fish, and then subsequently declare
that his appetite was satisfied.

of the Litany, starting it himself ; and at Christmas there was
the *Adeste*, and during Lent he read the Gospel of the day to
the assembled household.   Prayers over, he would bury his head
at the foot of a large crucifix in the chapel, and then kiss it
devoutly ; and so at Hyères, he had a habit of stopping to
contemplate a picture of our Lady in the hall as he passed from
the dining-room.   He liked to get any of his family together of
an evening for the Rosary, but he seldom asked them, fearing to
trouble them.   When they responded to his invitation, he would
say at the close, "Thank you, my dears," in a voice full of
genuine pleasure, as though they had done him a great favour.
He expressed a dread of wearying people, and so avoided long
prayers before others.   On this account he gave up his practice
at family prayers of praying one by one for his absent children,
much as it pleased him to do so.   On going out to any evening
party, or on any other short journey of pleasure, he recited
in the carriage the Litany ; and prior to starting upon any
longer excursion he would assemble the household in the
chapel for the same object.   As the train moved off the
platform, he quietly made the sign of the Cross, and when
travelling, as well as at other times, he would recite the Little
Office of our Lady.   And Hope-Scott and himself, when in a
cab together, might sometimes be seen pulling out their rosaries
in the simplest way imaginable.[1]

  "In legal cases of more than ordinary difficulty, and where
considerable interests were involved," wrote Father Garside, "it
was his custom (and I write from personal knowledge), to
commend his own labours to God by special acts of prayer."

  Referring to a great thunder-storm at Rednal, when the
Oratory School were there, on occasion of the funeral of a
school-fellow, Archdale Pope, he wrote to a son in July, 1866 :
"It might have been the flock of boys around the Fathers,
instead of the flock of sheep, upon whom the bolt might have
fallen.   Thank God you were mercifully saved from this possibility ; it seems to me as if the thunder-storms of the last year
or two have been more violent and destructive than usual ;
however, if we keep ourselves in the favour of our good God by
thinking of Him, and loving Him, we may be sure He will
protect us, and if temporal misfortune comes upon us, even
death itself, we may be sure our Blessed Lady will be near us
to shield us or help us according to our necessity."

  [1] See *Memoirs of J. R. Hope-Scott*, vol. ii. pp. 192—195.

Whilst, too, it was a great pleasure to him to see his children devout and religious, he did not usually exhort them to be so, otherwise than by his example, which told more than any words. He never pressed religious practices upon his children. He was, however, anxious on this score, carefully observed all, and rejoiced when his silent teaching succeeded.

"Be careful," he tells a son at school, "in the observance of all such religious habits as your confessor may recommend to you, and treat him as your friend in every way. If it is Father Henry,[1] I have the greatest love and respect for him, but whoever it is, my advice to you would be the same, make a second father of him."

On December 5, 1862, he wrote to another, then about to make his first Communion: "You know how anxious I am that you should grow up a good and pious boy, and an example to your younger brothers and sister; this is a very, very important period of your life, and as, when you receive our Blessed Lord you will be more His than ever before, I look forward with the greatest anxiety, but with the greatest confidence also, that you will be one of the great joys of my life."

To a daughter he wrote in a similar strain: "I have only just heard . . . that you have been considered worthy to be received as a Child of Mary; this is a very great gratification to me, my dear child, and I thank God with all my heart for giving me this additional blessing. I have tried to do my best to make you good children, and these incidents are my rewards." . . .

To his second daughter, in 1866: "I send you my blessing, and I pray God to bless you in such manner as may most conduce to your real happiness, and that you may continue to be one of the chief joys of our lives. Moreover, I commend you to the patronage of our Blessed Lady and St. Katharine, and hope you will repay me by praying for your old father."

He liked to enter into the spirit of the ecclesiastical year as it unfolded itself. "On All-Saints' Day," his wife writes, "he would exclaim the first thing in the morning, *Vidi turbam magnam quam dinumerare nemo poterat;* and so with the other great festivals, his first thoughts and words were given to God. At Easter the greeting to all at home was, *Surrexit Dominus vere;* at Christmas, *Gloria in excelsis Deo.* Indeed, every

[1] The late Rev. H. Bittleston, of the Birmingham Oratory.

morning he sanctified his rising by some phrase or other, indicating his abiding sense of the presence of God;" and sometimes his children would awake to find a text in his writing, appropriate to the day, pinned to the bed-curtain.

In the same way he would follow each month's particular devotion. Thus, writing to a daughter in March, 1872, from Hyères, he says: "Monica has established an altar to St. Joseph in the dining-room, the statue of St. Joseph stands in the niche at the end, surrounded by lilies, and there is a table in front of it quite brilliant with flowers, and all from our own garden, and we have a little service to St. Joseph every day after dinner."

In 1851, the Serjeant made his first spiritual retreat at Hodder under Father Clarke, S.J., the first of many yearly retreats either at Beaumont Lodge, Windsor, or at Manresa House, Roehampton, and on one of these occasions, after returning home, he said to a daughter : "I have learnt a grand lesson in this retreat. I must not leave the painful work of separation from all I love to be done for me by my good God at the moment of death. I must give Him all long before by the daily *fiat*, said in Faith, Hope, and Charity. This will take away in that hour all the bitterness of my separation from you."

He was also Treasurer of St. Anselm's Society, for the diffusion of good books, and a member of the Sodality of the Immaculate Conception at Farm Street, London, attending the Saturday afternoon instructions in Hill Street, and the Communion on the first Thursday of the month as often as he could.

It was his invariable custom to hear Mass every morning ; and when travelling, he would make it his first care on arriving at a place to ascertain overnight, often at no little trouble, where and at what time he could satisfy his devotion.

Abroad, in place of criticizing, he looked to the pious spirit that prompted, devotional habits and practices, so that homely customs were in his eyes neither irreverent, "gaudy," nor in "bad taste," but rather the objects of his admiration, even more so than the decorum and artistic beauty to be met with in many of our own churches. In such matters his heart rose to the simple piety that erected statues by the wayside, to sink again as these faded into mile-stones, and the cross on the steeple was replaced by the weather-cock.

He had once read in a notice of the *Times,* on some

published Essays, that "to fashion conduct according to the law
of God, to conform to the dictates of the pure conscience, to be
just and honest in all our dealings, not to fulfil a round of
devotional exercises and to be addicted to pious services—this
he (Mr. Froude) represents as the genuine mark of the real
Christian ; and the aim of each individual person, and of those
entrusted with the conduct of States ought, he teaches, rather
to be virtuous action than religious practices, creeds, and
ceremonies." And animadverting on the above to his sons,
he said : "It, in fact, inculcates that virtuous action, the
doing what is just and honest in our dealings and following
the dictates of our conscience are the *criteria* of true religion.
That is, it makes religion consist, so far as our duty to man
is concerned, in doing what each thinks to be right, and so
far as God is concerned, in doing nothing. It is very taking
to a person who has no disposition to religion to be told,
that his duty to men should be conformed to the dictates of
his own conscience, and that he need not trouble himself with
'devotional exercises and pious services.'

"This kind of teaching ignores the existence of a great
Maker and Governor of the world, to whom our homage and
love are due ; and it is indicative of a serious decay of religion
when such ideas can be promulgated by writers having the ear
of the multitude in this country. Religious practices, creeds,
and ceremonies are the mile-stones and direction-posts for
those who wish to live so as to please God, and the natural
personal conscience, without them, would soon degenerate into
a vicious wilfulness."

On devotion to the Mother of God, *à propos* of Dr. Newman's
Letter to Dr. Pusey, he wrote in 1866 to his eldest son
at school, at his correspondent's request : "At the Reformation,
in the time of Henry VIII., Edward VI., and Elizabeth, changes
were made by bad men, for evil purposes, in the faith and
practices of the people of England, the object being to detach
them from the Catholic Church, and to enlist their sympathies
with an independent national Church, and this for political and
sordid reasons. To do this it was necessary to attack and
hold up to opprobrium certain Catholic doctrines.

"One of the doctrines so attacked was the invocation of
saints, and their intercession for us, and as a part of this
doctrine, the position our Blessed Lady holds towards us. All
Catholics then held, and still hold, that, as the greatest of all

I

the Saints, our Lady is a most powerful intercessor for us with God, and that it is pleasing to our Blessed Lord that we should love and honour her, as He did Himself, and obtain from her, and by her intercession, blessings and favours we might little deserve on our own account.

" It has accordingly always appeared to good Catholics, that those who love and honour our dear Lady most are always to be found amongst those who love our Lord most, and, as a fact, prayers and addresses to Mary have for ages been spread over the whole Church, and have formed an important part of the devotions of every nation.

" These devotions to our Lady, and the honours paid to her, are amongst the things which the Protestants deliberately abolished, and they have since always been brought up to think them useless, and even wicked.

" It is plain, therefore, that when Protestants read in our books of devotion earnest, affectionate, and loving addresses to her, they are displeased and shocked because they never address her themselves at all.

" These devotions to our Lady vary in degree according to the nature of the persons using them, and even according to the country whence they originate, and the genius of the language. In some countries, such as our own, for example, the language of admiration and love is of a less ardent kind than in others, such, for example, as Italy. Again, some persons are of a warmer disposition, and express themselves more warmly, using expressions of affection that other colder persons would not readily appropriate. The warmth of language, however, is no true measure of the warmth of feeling, the former may exist where the feeling is but small, and the latter may exist where the language is what would appear to others cold and inadequate. You will remember that Cordelia, in *King Lear*, loved her father intensely, and yet her language seemed formal and cold. . . .

" As you may suppose, when Dr. Pusey has selected passages from writings extending back for centuries, and used by all manner of persons, some of authority, others of little or none, he has found many which cannot be justified for general use, and Dr. Newman has pointed out that he disapproves of some of these, and would have no taste for others, and shows that it is not necessary for all Catholics to approve of everything that enthusiastic persons may in their ecstatic devotions have used.

"This has been a difficult thing to do, because a casual observer might imagine that Dr. Newman loves our Lady less because he approves of the more moderate tone of expression towards her. . . . You will, however, comprehend that it is impossible to love our dear Lady too well, and yet it may be desirable to avoid exaggerated expressions, which offend others who are wholly unable to appropriate them.

"God bless you, dear Dick, and I pray your and my good Mother Mary to take us under her patronage, and keep us from all that is evil of every kind, and increase in us our love for her, and so our love for her Son, our dear Lord."

He thus begged a favour, in May, 1871, of the daughters in religion : "I have come to perceive that the real love of God is the key to everything else, and that if we have that, everything else follows, faith, contrition, perseverance, &c. You remember I used to doubt whether what I had was genuine, and I have my misgivings still. Now our Blessed Saviour says, when any two of you shall agree respecting anything they shall ask, it shall be done for them by My Father who is in Heaven, so I want you two to agree with me to ask for me the grace to have a *true genuine love of God, as much as I am capable of.* If dear C. will join, it must make our prayer the stronger ; so I propose you should join me in this little prayer with one ' Hail Mary ' for nine days, beginning Sunday, the 14th, and ending Monday, the 22nd."

And here it may not be uninteresting, to cite the reply of the younger to her father's request. "What a darling you are to write to us such a lovely long letter, I only wish you could have some idea of the happiness it gave us, but words fail to express our feelings. We rejoice to hear that you are so much better, free from pain and able to be downstairs again, *D.G.* How good our Lord is to us ! You ask us to join with you in a novena that you may obtain a genuine love of God ; indeed we will do so, and unite our prayers with yours to-night for that end ; but not only during the nine days you specially mention, but we will make it the end of our daily prayer, and ask our dear Lord to grant you this grace, especially when I receive Him in Holy Communion.

"Darling papa, if you think so little of your love for our Lord, what must mine be? nevertheless, I console myself with the thought that in order to love God it is not necessary to do so with the feelings but with our *will ;* hence it follows that the

ardent desire you have to love God is actually and in effect the
love of God working in your soul, only without any apparent
or sensible feeling. I will, indeed, pray that you may have this
sensible devotion, and I know you will pray for me that I in
like manner may partake of your love for our good God and
serve Him with greater fidelity. There is something very
wonderful in a religious life, quite beyond our comprehension,
so many graces and blessings given to us, everything to make
us good and to help us to Heaven, and day after day passes
with such rapidity, and we never seem to have enough time for
all we would wish to do. I am sure very few persons have the
least idea of the genuine and peaceful happiness that we enjoy,
something so solid; and to think that the same happiness,
only greatly increased, will last for all eternity if we are only
faithful, and do our best to live up to the end of our vocation!
And then I often think of you, through whose good prayers
I have been so greatly favoured, and of darling mamma
also, who has made so many sacrifices to bring us into the
Church, and how grateful I feel for the goodness of God
towards us all, each one in particular. To-day we begin the
six Sundays' devotion in preparation for the feast of my dear
patron, St. Aloysius. I shall ask him to intercede for you for
what you so ardently desire."

The Serjeant replied, in May, 1871 : "I thank both of
you for your very kind letter, and acquiescence in my request.
. . . It seems to me that love in its proper sense is not an
independent quality, but is always responsive—that is, your
love is excited by a consciousness of sympathy, by services
rendered, by sacrifices made, &c. All these things excite love
towards human objects, *a fortiori* should they towards God,
who exhibits Himself to us in all these various characters.

" But we perceive in the lives of the saints a degree of love,
as exemplified in their language, to which, as it seems to me,
others can hardly pretend, so that I thought, perhaps others
may not be capable of it, and that each of us may have an
amount of sensible love beyond which we cannot advance.
This it is that makes me desire to have that degree of genuine
love of which I am capable, and not to be disappointed if I
cannot rise to the exalted love of others."

To the same, later on : " I trust our little novena has
had its effect ; it has been a great satisfaction to me that you,
my darlings, have partaken in it, and helped me. Father Clare

says that there are different degrees of capacity for the love of
God, looking at it from the human side, and he instanced
St. Francis Xavier as possessing it in the enthusiastic degree,
and St. Francis of Sales in the gentle degree, so we have not
been asking for anything unsuitable. . . . God bless you, my
dear children, the main object of this letter is to thank you for
acquiescing in my request, which I do with as much love as I
am capable of."

"The fulness of his love for his Maker and Redeemer,"
writes Father R. Bellasis of the Serjeant, "none perhaps knew
here below," adding, that "the mainspring of all his actions,
and the guiding principle of his life, was Christian charity, a
virtue that shone forth in his piety and devotion, in the education of his children, in the management of his household, in his
intercourse with friends and reception of strangers, in the exercise of his duties, and the enjoyment of his pleasures; from
morning till night, by word and by deed, he first practised and
then taught it."

He was passionately fond of giving pleasure to other people,
as his letters indicate, and this became a very distinguishing
mark of character with him. He was never weary of inculcating
that the greatest of pleasures was giving pleasure. The next
best thing to cultivate was a pain in giving pain. Then came
two feelings to be suppressed, *i.e.*, the pleasure in giving pain,
and the pain in giving pleasure. "Take pleasure in giving
pleasure to your school-fellows," he wrote to a son in February,
1870. "Do kind things to them whenever you have an opportunity. It will soon become a habit. Some boys take pleasure
in being ill-natured. This is simply because they have never
practised giving pleasure." And what he preached, none practised better than he. "To please you," he wrote to a daughter in
June, 1862, "and because I love you very much, I have with my
own hand copied out the rules of the Sodality of Children of
Mary, leaving, as you wished, the headings to be done by yourself. It pleases me to think the book will be handed to your
successors as our joint work. It took me exactly twelve hours
to accomplish the job, but I was not at all tired with it, as I
was thinking all the time how much it would please you." To
his cousin, A. F. Bellasis, he wrote, May 13th, 1853: "Further,
should you want any advice or assistance that I can render you,
I should think you treated me ill if you did not write and ask
it with confidence that you would be giving pleasure by asking

it ; you may rely, also, upon my giving the same attention to your good mother, should she require it, as you would give yourself if you were here."

His desire to instil into his children an unselfish aim, led to rather an original institution in the family for birthdays. The child whose natal day approached received a liberal sum to spend in presents for every one in the house, from the Serjeant himself down to the little scullery-maid, with a balance for the poor. It was a grand success, a death-blow to selfishness, and proved out and out the value of his kind and generous teaching.

When young he would take compassion at parties on the plain ladies, or on those who seemed to know nobody, or to wear a disappointed look, and ask them to dance. Visitors he showed to their carriages in person, and this even at a time when his age might have excused the attention. He was fond of calling upon and of being attentive to old people. In March, 1828, a lady wrote to his mother : " I sometimes wonder whether there were in my younger days any young persons at all comparable with many of those whom we see here occasionally. I perceive this beautiful feature of humanity among their assemblage of graces, in their attention to us very old folks ; and I am sure that this is a shining quality in the mind of a certain young barrister, and it sits upon him so naturally that I call it *innate*, and am seldom better pleased than when he looks in upon us."

It will be believed then what his attention to his old mother was. "And now, my dear mother," he wrote, in November, 1836, "I hope you will be able to arrange about the visit I speak of, as I get dissatisfied at seeing you so seldom. I cannot see the time when I can be spared to leave, 'so as the mountain cannot come to Mahomet, Mahomet must come to the mountain.'" ".A chorus of voices all join in best love to grandmama," he tells her, in April, 1864, "hoping she will come to town, in which no one joins more heartily than her son ; and if you will come you shall have everything your own way ; do what you like, and go where you like, and have our little brougham to go in." And on Michaelmas Day, 1843, he sent her word : " I have just arrived at Stafford in time to send you a few lines by the post to convey my best love to you, my congratulations upon your completing your eightieth year, and still by God's blessing in health both of body and mind, and my hearty desire that you may be preserved to us many years,

L. C. Viell.
Leah C. Bellafis.
L. C. Maude.

There cannot be a mother who has done more for her children than you have done, and for myself I can truly say that I never could have been surrounded by the many blessings I have, but for the unwearied sacrifices you were ever ready to make on my account. Believe me, I neither forget you myself, nor allow you to be forgotten by my children in our prayers. May God Almighty bless you, my dearest mother, and make you happy here and hereafter, and may a sure and full reward be given you at the resurrection of the just."

"The remembrance of the dear Serjeant's grasp of hearty welcome will never pass," wrote one of his oldest friends. "I often think," the same wrote to his wife, in 1873, "of how you and your dear husband stood by me and my own blessed wife in our first great sorrow, when those two sweet boys lay side by side in their early death, and again, how your sympathy supported me in the greatest affliction of my life."

Again, when Count Thun came over to England, in 1851, the year of the great Exhibition, the Serjeant, who had been hospitably received by him in Bohemia, placed his own house and servants at his disposal, and the Count wrote, 25th of September, 1851, from London to his host : "I cannot leave England without thanking you for the kindness you and your whole family have shown us, and for the hospitable offer of your house for the time of our stay in London. *Tel maitre, tel valet*, is an old French proverb which has shown its truth in our case, for all your people were full of kindness and attention for us, and even Susan received us as old friends with all the amiability of conscious beauty. But had I thought beforehand of all the trouble we would give to your people, and could I have had an idea of the expense our stay in your house would occasion you—for the demand on our part for any bill, bill of fare, bill for carriage, is always returned with the standard answer of, 'Master has prohibited to give any'— I never would have been bold enough to accept your kind offer. Now, however, nothing remains for me but to reiterate my best thanks, adding the wish that you may soon give me the possibility of doing it verbally by coming and staying some time with us with your family to Tetschen."

Once more, Badeley and the Serjeant had been able to be of great assistance to a lady of rank who, on becoming a Catholic, had had to fly to the Continent with her children in order to avoid their being taken from her by the legal representatives of her husband, and she wrote to Mrs. Bellasis : "I must write you a few lines now lest you should think that I had forgotten you all and all your goodness to me, in union with your kind husband and family. It would be impossible for such kindness *ever* to be erased from my memory. Therefore, though I do not write you will believe that I love you all and never forget you."

To a son recounting some little kindly traits of the Serjeant, Dr. Newman replied, March 6th, 1873 : "It was very pleasant to read your letter. All the small items you give of dear papa are just like him. They are parts of a whole, a whole which it is impossible to mistake. He is *sui similis*, as much so as his painted portrait would be. Of course every one is *sui similis*, but I mean his character was brought out by his innumerable gentle, sweet, and affectionate acts, so that one looks at it as at a portrait." "You know your father better than I can," he wrote, April 18th, 1870, to the Serjeant's eldest daughter, "and know that I have not said a word too strong of him, or rather I could not speak too strongly, whatever I said, of the affectionateness, sweetness, gentleness, and kindheartedness of his character. No one, I know, can know him without loving him, and no one can come near him without receiving some kindness or other from him."

Nor did he tire of a good work once taken in hand; and efforts to compass the end, *Ad majorem Dei gloriam*, only redoubled under difficulty ; and an episode that extended over many years is worth recording as an illustration of his continued interest in people amidst their trials, while at the same time it throws a good deal of side-light upon his own religious character :

He was returning home from his chambers one day, when passing up Regent Street the sight of a jeweller's shop reminded him that he had a silver watch to buy for one of his daughters, who was about to enter a convent. He drew the check-string, and ordered the coachman to draw up. It was the season, and no easy matter to reach the shop, which the carriage had already passed. The coachman pleaded this difficulty, and asked if another jeweller, a little in advance, would not do as well. Contrary to the Serjeant's habitual course of action, which was to save others trouble, and lessen their difficulties, even at the expense of his own, he insisted on a return to the first shop. The sequel will show how Divine Providence

urged his decision. After inspecting several watches, always
with the same remark, " They are not good enough," he at
last added, " It's for my daughter, and I want the best I can
get." " Oh, sir," replied the person who was serving him, " you
could get a gold one for less than these." " You won't understand it," answered the Serjeant, " but it must be silver, because
she is going to be a nun." Mrs. A—— (it was the jeweller's
wife) was silent for a moment, and then she said with some
emotion, " Oh yes, sir, I do, I am a Catholic." A conversation
then ensued wherein the Serjeant learnt the old story of the
difficulties of a mixed marriage, and of the years of apparently
unanswered prayer for the conversion of a good and kind
husband. Here was an opportunity, and he never lost one, of
trying to impart to others what he looked upon as God's
greatest gift to himself, the knowledge of the true faith. The
watch was not purchased, but Mrs. A—— was directed to send
up her husband to Northwood House with a selection.

The following day Mr. A—— arrived, little dreaming that
he had been the object of prayer in the family during the intervening hours, and that his soul, far more than his watches, was
the interest of the moment.

The purchase was soon concluded, but not so soon did
Mr. A—— leave the house! Legal business could always wait
when there was question of consoling the afflicted, counselling
the doubtful, or instructing the ignorant. So the heavy briefs
were put on one side, and for over an hour a serious conversation followed, ending in Mr. A —— departing with some books
in his hand, conducted to the hall-door by one who trusted in
God that a seed had been sown that would bring forth fruit in
due season to His greater honour and glory.

The following spring, in passing up Regent Street, the
Serjeant remembered his friend, and thought he would go in and
see how matters were progressing. Making an excuse in the
purchase of a watch-key, he entered the shop, and found Mrs.
A—— in the greatest possible grief. Her husband was at the
point of death, and still a Protestant; but " So changed, sir, since
his conversation with you." " Should I be a welcome visitor?"
asked the Serjeant. " None more so," replied Mrs. A——, " do
come upstairs." It was evident death was at hand. What
passed in that short interview is not recorded, but that evening
Mr. A—— was received into the Church by the Rev. Father
William Eyre, S.J., and a *Te Deum* was said by the Serjeant

and his family for the conversion. With the resurrection of the soul to health Mr. A—— recovered.

Some months passed, and our convert presented himself again at Northwood House, not this time to sell a watch, but to seek advice. As a Catholic Mr. A—— felt that he could not conscientiously continue his business in Regent Street on the same lines as hitherto, yet not to do so meant ruin. Did God ask a great sacrifice of him? Grace had done its work, and it needed not the gentle persuasion of the conscientious lawyer to answer for him the question. He had but to agree with him and to remind him of the promise, "Seek first the kingdom of God and His justice, and all other things shall be added unto you." Mr. A—— sold up his business and made a fresh start in the country, which in diminishing his income on earth increased his treasure in Heaven.

Several years elapsed, the watch was ticking beneath a religious habit when the Sister was summoned to the parlour. The unknown visitor spoke of her husband's holy and happy death, and asked the prayers of the community for the repose of his soul. It was Mrs. A——. She was accompanied on the occasion by a boy whom she introduced as her adopted son. She spoke of her greatest friend and benefactor with tears, and before leaving the convent, whispered : " Pray that this boy may have a vocation for the priesthood."

Some years later, the Serjeant's eldest son, who had become a priest, was making his annual retreat at Roehampton, and the Father who gave it came one morning and asked him if he would have any objection to going through the rubrics of Holy Mass each day with a young deacon who was preparing for his ordination. It was an occupation quite according to Father Bellasis' taste, and he gladly acquiesced. On coming out of retreat he discovered that his pupil was no other than the adopted son of Mr. and Mrs. A——.

" There was something about him," writes his daughter Mary (in noting how Mrs. A——, at her first chance interview with him, a total stranger, in a shop, had thus openly spoken to him of her family sorrow), " a something or other that not only inspired confidence, but drew from others, whether old or young, and without any seeking on his part, the tale of their cares and troubles, of the hopes and interests of their lives. It might be the case of a coachman in marital difficulties at Hyères, or of a barber's assistant at Kensington asking of him a knotty point

of law across the counter ; that of a learned brother lawyer, or
of a simple servant girl ; that of a weather-beaten cabdriver,
or of the fellow-traveller in a railway-carriage. He often said,
' I can't understand it ; I wonder if they take me for a priest ? ' "

In his intercourse, however, with his children, perhaps more
than anywhere else, was his remarkable gift of Christian charity
best exemplified. And here he appeared to aim at modelling
his domestic life on that of Sir Thomas More, whom, long
before that Chancellor's beatification, the Serjeant was wont to
call his patron Saint.

" If," said he in a memorandum of October, 1848, on the
father's influence in a home, " mistrust or want of confidence
exist in a family, if it does not exhibit the affectionate harmony
that should prevail, the father must not too hastily conclude
that the cause is necessarily to be found in the character or
disposition of his wife, children, or servants ; it is almost certain
that the fault is his own, and that he has failed so to comport
himself as to gain their confidence or to preserve his authority.

" In all these cases, it does not become the father to be angry
or vexed, or to complain of the dispositions of those whose
attention or confidence or respect he has failed to obtain ; the
fault is almost certainly his own, and this conviction should only
render him more careful and considerate, more gentle, if need
be, and more forbearing, and teach him that it is highly probable
that he must seek the true remedy in himself."

This memorandum, it may be observed, was probably
written after giving advice to the father of a family in difficulties. The Serjeant could not conscientiously have written
it from realization of personal deficiencies. However, he
certainly seemed better pleased to find himself at fault than
another. He would encourage his children to use such little
sentences as " It was my fault ;" " I was in the wrong ;" " I was
mistaken ;" and if the positive acknowledgment was too difficult
to extract, he would playfully draw from them the possibility
of error.

There were two ways of ruling and teaching, he was wont to
tell his children, one by exciting fear, the other by inspiring
affection. He had essayed the latter way with them, and if it
failed it would be the great failure of his life. He laid stress
on love being demonstrative between parent and child, since
if the outward signs of affection were neglected, especially by
the young, there was danger of love itself evaporating. And,

doubtless to secure their confidence, he put himself on an equality, so to speak, with his children, and made them his familiars. They must not be afraid of him. His daughter Mary makes reference to "the power that he had of teaching us through stories graphically told, and with a wonderful power of illustration. He was never tired of getting us together to tell us tales, evidently carefully put together, and always with the view of instilling and strengthening some great principle of virtue. When we were children he was never too fatigued of an evening to amuse us and entertain us and teach us. His unselfishness showed itself in everything."

The Serjeant, therefore, had only to say, "Shall I tell you a story?" when the answer came promptly back in a general chorus of "Yes;" and then ensued a highly exciting narrative, listened to with rapt attention. Great favourites were Southey's popular ballads, parts of the *Devil's Walk* and the *Dragon of Wantley*, slain by More of More Hall, of whom it was said, to the wonderment of gaping little boys and girls—

> Had you but seen him in this dress,
> How fierce he look'd and how big,
> You would have thought him for to be
> Some Egyptian porcupig.

Later on he would recite the great poets, such as parts of *Paradise Lost, L'Allegro, Il Penseroso, Alexander's Feast, The Corsair, Lara,* and bits of Shakespeare. " I am much pleased," he wrote to the same in March, 1866, "to hear that you are learning parts of Shakespeare's plays by heart, they are full of imagery, and also of expressions which will remain firmly in the memory, and afford you much pleasure hereafter." Himself a versifier now and again, he encouraged some of his children to try their hands at verses also. An early specimen of his own composition, dated 1825, runs as follows :

ON SOME WILDFLOWERS.

> O'er hill and dale, thro' tangled copse,
> By hedge-row, heath, and rill,
> Whilst morning dew in silver drops
> Hung bright and sparkling still,
> At break of early dawn I sped,
> To gather these to deck thy head.
> No fostering art their favour'd lot,
> No pamper'd nurselings these,

Free native beauties, slight them not,
Nor let my gift displease ;
Sown by the winds, their bed the sod,
The world their garden, and the gardener God.

A letter of November, 1865, to a son at school, apparently written in prose, but really in rhyme, affords an example of his playful mood : " I hope the athletic sports are commenced satisfactorily, and that you have neither broken your head nor your nose, and that you have not come to blows, by treading on some one's toes, thus adding to your woes, further than that, I suppose, there is danger of tearing your clothes, making them fit for scare-crows, and then, goodness knows, how a small hole grows, you see how my rhyme flows, and if I don't stop you will doze, so here goes, to continue in prose, which less trouble bestows," &c.

" I have been much pleased," he wrote to the same in December, 1868, " by your account of your debate, in which you contrasted poetry and prose. I conclude, after such felicitous examples, the decision must have been with you.

" I need not tell you, however, that poetry is not in reality the opposite of prose, inasmuch as the highest poetical thoughts may be expressed in prose without the ornamental framing which is given to them by skilful versification. The real opposite to 'prose' is 'rhythm,' or 'metre.' Milton, in invoking his muse from ' Sion's hill,' speaks of his song, which is to soar

Above the Æonian mount while it pursues
Things unattempted yet in *prose* or *rhyme*,

not prose or poetry.

" Turning a poetical idea into rhyme or metre is doing that which a man does who has got a beautiful painting, viz., he encloses it in a beautiful frame ; or a rich gem, which he furnishes with a suitable setting. Moreover, as you say, rhyme perpetuates an idea which left merely in prose, would be lost like an unframed sketch."

Popular scientific experiments were another means brought into requisition to interest the children. At one time electricity, at another meteorology, or astronomy, or mechanics, or optics ; he got together quite a collection of instruments and appliances illustrating the scientific progress of the day. " Robert Wharton and my dear mother," he wrote, " gave me a taste for scientific matters, particularly geology, astronomy, and meteorology, which have been sources of

great amusement to me." "I quite find," he wrote to her
in 1831, "that my little knowledge in geology gives me
another object and affords me additional pleasure." A
memorandum of June, 1837, records his spending a whole
day with Faraday and other scientific men, and what they
said and did. Another note elaborately describes an aurora
observed at Scarborough, September 29, 1851. "My chief
relaxation during this year" (1837), he wrote, "was astronomy.
My neighbour, Dr. Scott, a *dilettante* astronomer, had lent me
some fine telescopes, one a very large one, a Cassegrain, the
other a dumpy reflector, I ultimately bought them both." [1]

The Serjeant impressed on his children the importance of an
observant spirit and intelligent interest in all they saw, and
star-gazing on the leads and nautical almanacks became all the
rage.[2] A favourite book was Foster's *On the Atmosphere.* Out
walking, he would bid them notice cloud formations, the
differences between *cirrus, cumulus, stratus, nimbus,* &c., and
bid them tell him the names of trees and plants that they
passed.

Other accomplishments were not neglected. We hear of
numismatics in a note from school : "Some of the coins you
gave me seem to be rather rare, some dating from 1500
and something."

Then he would have fishing with gentles essayed at Ted-
dington Weir, with good result, and at Putney Bridge, with
none, and *à propos* of cricket, he wrote, in June, 1862 : "Well,
I hope the grand match has come off to-day to the satisfaction
of all the school ; of course I think it is very likely that you
will be beaten, but never mind that. 'Rome was not built in
a day,' and even cricket takes a little time to learn. However,
either you or R. must write and tell me all about it."

Skill at billiards was also encouraged ; archery, too, as
being a manly and healthy pastime ; and one day as Bishop

---

[1] The large one he subsequently gave to the Jesuit Fathers at Stonyhurst. This
instrument did valuable service in the cause of science, in the hands of the late
Father Perry, S.J., the well-known astronomer, who was in the habit of using it on
the various expeditions which he was officially charged to conduct, for the purpose
of observing eclipses and transits.

[2] A son writes from Edgbaston in July, 1865, "I send you a little book of the
constellations, which I think is a very good one in its way. Mr. Pope has lent me
a beautiful book on astronomy called *The Heavens,* by Guillemin ; also his micro-
scope, which is a very fine one." The game-keeper at Bleasdale, being asked
whether he had seen any shooting stars, replied : "Can't say as I see'd any as yet,
tho' some looks as if they were a-goin' to."

Grant stood on the lawn at Putney and watched the shooting, he remarked : "This is a perfect home, the children have everything to keep them united." The Serjeant had been a well-known and proficient archer in North Wales as a young man. "In the autumn of 1826," he writes, "I attended a meeting of the Royal British Bowmen at Eaton Hall, Lord Grosvenor's, a large county gathering, where having been asked to write a song for the occasion, I did so, and sang it in the great hall at Eaton," the 6th of October, to the air, "Blue bonnets are over the border." It began :

> March, march, Acton and Gresford vale,
> Bowmen of Cymri march forward in order,
> March, march, Harden and Leasewood vale,
> Now your green bonnets are over the border.

The success of the song resulted next year in a new call upon him. "I was at two of the Bow meetings," he wrote to his mother in October, 1827, "one at the Hon. and Rev. Neville Grenville (who is brother to Lady Glynne), at Hawarden Rectory, and the other at Colonel Phillipps's, at Erbistock. At Hawarden, every one seemed to expect that I had, of course, got a new song for them, and after dinner there was a call upon me for one, but I replied to the President that I should have considered it a sort of presumption in me, a stranger, to come prepared with a song, and that, in fact, I was quite unprepared." He was not, however, to be let off, and a note from Lady Cunliffe, at Acton Park, resulted in a new song being sung at Erbistock Hall, on the 14th of September, to the tune of " Draw the sword, Scotland."[1]

The Serjeant, then, inherited some slight musical taste. In early days he used to sing glees with his cousins the Gwynnes, and there is an *Ave Maris Stella*, a simple and devout air, composed by him. In furthering the musical propensities of some of his children he had Dr. Newman on his side. The Serjeant was just afraid lest so absorbing an art might interfere with studies ; and because it was so absorbing, Dr. Newman was in favour of its cultivation, provided the other danger were avoided. "To my mind," he wrote in September, 1865, "music is an important part of education where boys have a turn for it. It is a great resource when they are thrown

---

[1] The Serjeant, no keen sportsman, once had some little shooting on the Lancashire Moors, but after accidentally killing two birds at one fire, he thought it as well to rest on the laurels of so unusual an achievement.

on the world, it is a social amusement perfectly innocent, and, what is so great a point, employs their thoughts. Drawing does not do this. It is often a great point for a boy to escape from himself, and music enables him. He cannot be playing difficult passages on the violin and thinking of anything else."[1] And so we learn from the Serjeant at Kensington in March, 1871, that "our evenings are very musical, as W. has taken to the violoncello, and E. to the tenor, so that with C.'s piano and R.'s violin, we have a regular concert." "I like to write and hear your name," wrote a cousin of the Serjeant to one of his sons, "it brings pleasant times of olden days back to my memory! How little your good father suspected that the wee child he used to fetch to her music-lessons would ever be writing to a son of his her thanks for a bit of music of his own composing."

"I am now occupied," the Serjeant wrote to his mother in Sept., 1847, "with superintending the removal of an organ (an old Snetzler), which formed part of my purchase (of Northwood House), to the organ-builders for repairs and improvements. I hope he won't steal a stop, as I remember some organ-builder did for Dr. Bellasis."[2] At Christmastide, the Serjeant's daughters used to sing in harmony along the many passages of Northwood House, the rise and fall of voices in harmony having a very pretty effect, and one of them used to play the organ before she left for the convent.

Providing, therefore, every kind of indoor and outdoor recreation for his children, the Serjeant skilfully contrived to make home exceedingly attractive to them. Then there were dogs, cats, birds, rabbits, parrots, and squirrels for those who liked

---

[1] A son of the Serjeant wrote from Edgbaston, January 31, 1864: "I am getting on all right with my fiddle. I can't think of anything else, so you must think of this letter till you get another." And again, March 12, 1865, "Every Sunday evening now, in Lent, as Father Ambrose [St. John] wishes us to pass them quietly at this time, we come in at 7.30, and we, the musicians, play some sacred or classical music, and then Father Ambrose tells us about the Life of St. Philip, and then we play some more, and then come night prayers as usual ; it is very nice." And in October he sends word, "Dr. Newman has just had a present of a violin. I suppose it is from Sir F. Rogers [Lord Blachford], whom we met on board the Folkestone boat."

[2] "Do you remember," wrote the Doctor's second son, Colonel George Bridges Bellasis, to Edmund Lodge (Norroy), January 19, 1800, "the King's arms falling into the organ in the church, and the Doctor sitting down very deliberately to play on it, to see if every pipe wasn't smashed ? Such a countenance of woe I never saw, and the exclamation, so very unusual to the Doctor, of 'damnation !' I thought would have been the death of you and me."

pets, and a farm-yard for such as still felt inclined to go in for cows and poultry, after the startling experience that at Putney cows gave double the amount of milk, and hens laid twice as many eggs, on Sundays as they did on week-days, all owing, so it was uncharitably averred, to the gardeners being away on those days.[1]

A tragic event in connection with one of the household pets should not go unrecorded.

A canary bird belonging to the Serjeant's eldest daughter was accidentally starved to death at Bedford Square, in 1845. The seed-vessel was a glass that hung outside the cage, its aperture corresponding to one at the side of the bars. By some accident the glass had got placed in such a way that the bird could not get at its seed, but this was not perceived, and every one, seeing the glass full, never thought anything was amiss. "The poor little bird," writes the Serjeant, "lived four days, trying every means in its power to attract notice, but in vain, and on the night of the fourth day I was up late, and went into the drawing-room, and I heard the bird chirp, and went and spoke to it, but like the rest did not perceive what was the matter. In the morning it was found dead, the seed-glass cracked, and the bird's beak bruised and sore. The following lines were written by me on the occasion : "

A canary dwelt in a gilded cage,
Tho' a slave he was happy and gay,
Skipping and jumping with nimble foot,
He carolled his hours away;
From earliest morning he swell'd his throat,
With his cheerful chirp and his brilliant note.

" Oh, mistress dear, I am glad you are come,
My glass has been plac'd awry,
I have peck'd and press'd, and to get at my seed
I have never ceas'd to try,
But I can't reach a grain, so pray put it right,
For I've got a most ravenous appetite."

Alas ! no one hears, and the day passes on,
And fast to the wires he clings,
'Tis in vain that his loudest chirp he tries,
And his sweetest song he sings ;
Dishearten'd at length, he sinks down on his breast,
To linger, to pine thro' the night, not to rest.

[1] On the other hand there was the head-gardener's explicit statement that the wind being unusually high on the nights in question, the loss of the fruit and other things was to be accounted for in this way.

J

The morning is come. " My dear mistress again,
You are kind, and you love me I know,
      Maria, dear Margaret, Katharine dear,
One thought on your songster bestow.
Ah ! you hear me, you mark me, you chirp in reply,
You love me, yet leave me of hunger to die."

" How sweetly you're singing, my beautiful bird,
I wish I could tell what you say.
No doubt you are telling how happy you are
When you warble so sweetly all day."
Thus noon passes o'er, and evening draws near,
And the poor fainting bird can find no one to hear.

Again dawns the morning. " Maria is come,
Oh, Maria, I've so wish'd for you,
The glass for my seed has slipp'd out of its place,
I have tried, and can't get my head thro' ;
I have broken the glass, and my beak's very sore,
And I've peck'd every grain I can find on the floor.

" You give me fresh water—ah ! give me some seed.
You do not know what I have suffer'd this night,
I knew you would come, and that made me hold up.
Don't leave me, pray put the glass right.
I have sung to you, talk'd to you, now hear my cry,
And pray do not leave me 'midst plenty to die."

Now four weary days have pass'd over, and still
No one sees that the glass is set wrong,
And midnight is come, and all voices are hush'd,
And hush'd is the dying bird's song.
" But hark ! here's a step ! 'tis my master, tho' late.
If I chirp he may come, he may put my glass straight.

" Dear master, my last hope, you know my soft call,
I am weak, but I hope you will hear,
Let me win you once more to look into my cage,
You may save me, tho' death is so near."
" My dear little bird, I can hear your soft cry.
What keeps you awake ? Go to roost, and good-bye."

Of what pass'd in the night, how he struggled to live,
How he flutter'd, how fainted, how fell,
How he linger'd in hope, how he sank in despair,
I cannot, I wish not to tell.
This only is known to be placed on my page,
That morn found young eyes weeping over his cage.

It was the Serjeant's aim to make home the centre of
affection and interest, and herein he succeeded thoroughly. His
love for his own early home, amidst Benedictine abbey ruins,
was great, and he once went a journey to Reading to see

whether it still stood, or no, but alas! it was no longer to be
found. "I looked in vain in the Forbury," he wrote to his
mother, April 22, 1833, "for even a trace of your old house, or
Mrs. Le Noir's, or the Scotch yard, or Mrs. Curtis' school ; as a
German would say, 'Alles ist weg,' it is all gone. I, however,
found the remains of the old mulberry-tree."[1]

Home, then, possessed all that could be desired except
facilities for smoking, a taste against which the Serjeant set
his face, all that he would allow for the practice being that it
was no sin ; and amusement outside home was rarely sought.
Occasionally, indeed, the Serjeant would take his children to
the play. He liked a natural, unaffected style of acting, and
this predilection led him to leave the Princess' Theatre with a
youthful party after patiently enduring for some time what
seemed to him a considerable amount of ranting on the part
of Charles Kean in *Henry VIII.*[2]

Home theatricals, however, flourished at Christmas-tide.
And here *Puss in Boots, Cinderella*, and other pieces found
favour, and went without mishap, save in one instance, where
a son, as a blackbird representing one of the traditional four
and twenty, declined to sing, and had to be carried out of the
pie to the nursery, uttering notes that were not musical.

While the Serjeant encouraged content with home, he was
at the same time a strong advocate of travelling in holiday
time as a means of education. Year after year he went touring
with his children, and the only mistake he made was in
beginning this once too soon with one of his sons, who was
found much more absorbed in watching a toy-boat attached
by a string to the steamer, than in admiring the beauties of the
River Meuse.

"Never was a father more appreciated," writes Mrs. Bellasis,
"I may almost say idolized, by his children." "When I'm

---

[1] His mother and her husband, Mr. Maude (as the incumbent), had finally settled
at Northwood and Carisbrooke, and he wrote to her October 9, 1827 : "I am very
much pleased to hear that you are gratified with the offer made to Mr. Maude in the
Isle of Wight, and that he has accepted it, although it will leave me without a single
relation in London."

[2] The Gallery of Illustration was, of course, a favourite place of amusement in holiday time. "Last night," writes a son, "mamma, E., and I, drove in to see Mr. and
Mrs. German Reed and Mr. Parry. . . . Mamma laughed so much that her throat was
quite sore this morning, and at the time she really thought she would be ill with
laughing. Mr. Parry gave us a sketch of a wedding breakfast, which was most
amusing. First came the wedding, then the quarter of an hour that comes between
the wedding and breakfast, in which Miss Fluenza sang a song, then came the
breakfast and speeches, which were most ludicrous but very natural."

dead and gone," he was fond of saying to them, "you'll perhaps say, 'Well, that old Serjeant wasn't such a bad fellow after all.' No one will ever care for you more than I do." On the other hand, let any praise of himself reach his ears, and he would say at once, "Ah! they'll *find me out* some of these days." "Nothing pained him more," writes his daughter Mary, "than to be praised; it would bring tears to his eyes, and such speeches were rejected immediately, with a generous remark about others, or, in the case of his children, with a playful retort."

There was an oft-recurring dispute between the Serjeant and one of his daughters in a convent as to which of the two loved the other the most : "As I think I have now got a leisure morning," he wrote, in May, 1869, "I must have a little talk with you, lest you should be confirmed in your foolish notion that I don't love you more than you love me." And in October, 1868 : "You know how I love you, because you know how much you love me, and you have nothing to do but to multiply that by two, which gives the required result." And again : "You say you hope I shall soon love you *as much* as you love me ; well, I am happy to inform you that your hopes are already accomplished and surpassed. Ah! you see I have got you there. You do, indeed, say that you believe that to be impossible, but is not that rather inconsistent? How can you really hope for what you believe to be impossible, eh? The mistress of novices, I suppose, does not teach logic. But I beg pardon for being so presumptuous as to joke with a religious. . . . Assure yourself, my darling C., that I appreciate the great affection always shown for me by my dear children, and, as you very well know, by yourself, and I thank God for it, as for one of the greatest blessings He has given me."

In correcting faults he waited days for a quiet opportunity in private, so as to avoid giving any offence, and here he rather suggested and advised, and with such tact too, that it hardly seemed correction. He rarely used a harsh word, and then only when it seemed necessary for the children's good ; and but two things found him severe, disrespect to their religion or to their mother. "It is well," he said, "to praise in people any signs of those virtues that you wish them to possess." He shrank from the ungrateful task of mere fault-finding, and, as has been said, cautioned his children against a critical or sceptical spirit.

He was careful to give good advice to his children as they grew up and went out into the world.

"Do not form opinions of people or things hastily," he wrote to a daughter in 1853, "but reserve your thoughts to talk them over with those you love; it will delight them, and save you from misconception.

"2. Do not be too ready to believe anything you hear to another's disadvantage. Of such stories the greater part are wholly untrue, or greatly exaggerated, therefore *mistrust* them all.

"3. Never express your opinion in a positive manner, especially to those older than yourself. The habit of doing so is called 'forwardness,' and is most unpleasing. If you have occasion to express your opinion, do it modestly, and as if you were not quite sure of it.

"4. Do not be too ready to make objections to the opinions you may hear expressed. This habit is called captiousness, and is always offensive. It may be, you are obliged to disagree, if so, do it with gentleness, and if possible in the form of a question.

"5. Avoid a critical spirit; in other words, do not find fault with individuals or things. There are few things which will not admit of criticism, but remember, a critical spirit is often ill-natured, and indicative of a common-place understanding.

"6. Never trust yourself to criticize Catholic religious practices or habits, at home or abroad; most likely you misapprehend them, but to find fault with them, is, in truth, to act a Protestant spirit.

"7. Ask the opinion of others as often as you please, but give your own as seldom as possible, unless you are asked; and then give it diffidently.

"8. Beware of the pleasure of differing from others in matters of opinion; on the contrary, learn to take a pleasure in acquiescing when the subject is indifferent. It is a sure way of pleasing, whilst a habit of disagreeing is very objectionable."

If he differed from any speaker he would say, "I have no doubt there is a great deal in what you say, but don't you think so and so?" and thus gently suggest his own view. His principle was rather to extract his own opinion from, than to force it upon others. His discretion in conversation ensured him universal popularity. He never interrupted, heard everybody out, and by his manner showed that his whole attention was being given to what was being said. When himself interrupted, he quietly held his peace, and when even children had been interrupted, he took the first opportunity of giving them the lead again, with "You were saying so and so." He paid great deference to any speaker of distinction at table, and discouraged miscellaneous conversation independently of him. He would listen with undiminished attention to familiar anecdotes, applauding them, and concealing his acquaintance with them, and if discovered herein, he would express his wish to hear the story once again, on the plea that he did not remember it well; and lastly, he never corrected mistakes in the telling, however badly the tale might be told. In thus making a point of listening to what everybody else had to say, he secured a willing audience for himself.

He used to sit silent and ill at ease as ill-managed conversation on indifferent topics degenerated into warmth or altercation. "Gently, gently," he would murmur; while any thoughtless or ill-judged remark, especially in the presence of servants, would draw from him an exclamation of pain. He sometimes at the end of an unsuccessful conversation amongst his children, pointed out the mistakes committed both in tone and expression, substituting a more charitable and judicious rendering of the subject under discussion.

In December, 1839, he had written down for his own guidance some "Rules for Conversation." "I find myself," he says, "frequently engaged in an argument which does not end in agreement, and where both parties would without doubt have been of the same opinion if the discussion had been commenced without prejudice, prejudice, too, not pre-existing, but excited at the time, *e.g.*, a new proposition positively stated, is apt to be felt as an assumption on the part of the proposer, and is at once met by objections occurring only at the moment, and prompted by our self love : our ingenuity is then taxed to support our objections, and as most persons pay more attention to their own arguments than to those of their opponent, our sudden and casual objections are converted into strong impressions, and possibly permanent ones.

"Again—a proposition is not always the expression of an opinion, it is frequently but a passing thought of the speaker ; if it is met by a sudden denial, the proposer is driven to defend it, and thus, as in the former case, a passing thought is converted into a strong or permanent impression.

"The manner, therefore, of our conversation may have a most important effect upon our opinions, and so upon our whole lives, as well as upon the opinions of those with whom we converse, indeed it is highly probable that many, perhaps most, of our wrong opinions have no other origin than this, viz., the defence of them forced upon us by positively stated opinions or objections coming from those conversing with us.

"In discussing religious matters how serious this consideration becomes! we may, by obtruding too suddenly or too positively an undoubted truth, drive those with whom we converse into a denial of it, and possibly into a lasting impression against it, and we may also by an incautious vehemence against error, fix it in a mind where, but for us, it might have had no permanent place.

"I am myself guilty of both these serious faults, which may be called 'dogmatizing' and 'captiousness,'[1] and this may be the reason why I do not convince when I feel that I ought; I write down my confession of them in order to bring them more clearly before me and to help me to be upon my guard in future.

"I resolve therefore to endeavour as follows:

"1. However clear I may be in any opinion I am about to express, to do so modestly, and as if I were not clear about it; to suggest it as perhaps tenable, or to use some other device to get the opinion upon the carpet for discussion without claiming it as my own exclusive property.

"2. However erroneous an opinion expressed in my opinion may be, not to deny it flatly, or say 'I don't agree,' but as gently as may be, to suggest the other opinion. Query. Would it be wrong in a case where the matter was not one of principle, to appear to acquiesce at first and then to throw out doubts gently?

"3. Not to be betrayed into disputing an expressed opinion, or into defending an unconsidered one of my own merely by the manner in which the opinion or objection may be made."

He thus counselled his eldest daughter, about to go on a

---

[1] This self-accusation may be put down to the Serjeant's humility; at least it would not be endorsed by those who knew him. Although "a man is never a hero to his own valet," yet Mr. John O. Dunn, Mr. Hope-Scott's trusted confidential clerk, who had so near a view of the Serjeant hour by hour, observes: "It is something to say that I who knew him so long in daily intercourse, and in the turmoil of business, never once saw him ruffled or disturbed, and never heard him utter an unkind or harsh word, even when it was deserved." He adds his opinion, "that this did not arise from any lightness or weakness of character, but from a fine balanced and superior Christian attitude of mind."

visit in 1861 : "Do not joke upon any religious subject, nor
introduce one save with great care ; you may do a great deal
of good, but be sure you never omit to cross yourself, and
remember, amongst Protestants, all you say and do is observed,
and is, for good or for ill, attributed to your religion. Avoid
all stories about Catholics which might be repeated and mis-
apprehended ; for instance, say nothing against Catholic schools,
although we know they may have some faults.[1] Do not talk or
act as if you were a *liberal* Catholic, and thought little of the
differences in religion."

His second daughter, when engaged to be married, received
the following, in June, 1867 : "Well, you are going to leave us,
and I do not contemplate it with sorrow—on the contrary, with
joy ! I have had the blessing of your dear society for a longer
period indeed than I had any right to expect, and during the
whole time I know that it has been your delight to please me,
and make me happy, as you know you have done. To one not
worthy of you I could not have borne to give you up. . . . You
must be to him, I will not say what you have been, but what
you are, and always will continue to be to me, for it will be no
transfer of affection, nor any partition of love, you will merely
have a new object and a new home to shine upon, without

---

[1] To a friend observing about poor Catholic children in London, and asking :
"How is it that they are so neglected?" and alluding to the Catholic Church's
system and to the Christian Brothers "working for love," and remarking that
the "state of the children ought to be very different from what you describe,"
the Serjeant wrote, January 9, 1852 : "Now, although, as you say, you do not
accuse the Catholic clergy of supineness, your observations imply this, 'with the
alleged superior means possessed by the Catholic Church, the condition of her
children ought to be better than it is.' To go into the whole question, including
former spoliations, would be tedious, but I reply :

"1. The main body of the Catholics actually resident in London are very poor,
there are probably not five in a thousand who can afford to contribute more than
pence to religious or charitable purposes, and but for the support afforded by Catholics
throughout the country, all of whom have pressing claims at home, Catholic schools
and other charities could not be supported at all.

"2. Even Christian Brothers who 'work for love,' must be clothed and fed, and
more than that, they must be brought up and educated to teach, all of which, as you
know, must cost money.

"3. Our very priests are in most cases dependent upon the offerings of their
flocks, and live in great measure upon the pence of the poor, who have little to spare
from their poverty for normal schools and education.

"If you really knew the life led by Catholic priests and schoolmasters in London,
how hard they lie, how poorly they are clad, and how scantily they eat ; and again,
if you knew the extent to which Catholics who have the means habitually contribute
to their unaided charities and schools, you would not require an answer to your
question, 'How is it the children are so neglected?'"

withdrawing one ray of your affectionate heart from those you leave. And now for my sermon which I promised you.

"Your husband's friends are your friends, and they must come first on any occasion you may have of showing respect and attention.

"Avoid continuing intimacies, or too frequent correspondence with persons unknown to your husband.

"Remember, what I have often taught you in other words, that the act of pleasing is a higher and nobler gratification than the passive condition of being pleased.

"Never cease from seeking opportunities of pleasing, especially your husband ; it is wholly immaterial how trifling they may be, the consciousness that they have been planned and sought on purpose to please is an irresistible attraction.

"You have hitherto talked with freedom without the necessity of heeding what you said, being certain of a loving reception of anything you might say ; as mistress of a house, and amongst strangers, you must be more reserved. Especially, never speak of your husband's affairs.

"Be courteous to everybody, and forward to do any act of kindness.

"Never imagine slights, and if such should occur, persist in putting a good construction upon them, or ignore them.

"Never state your opinions positively, or differ abruptly. You will find the interrogative attitude most useful and inoffensive.

"Be an attentive listener ; no compliment is greater.

"In all you do, have it constantly in your mind, will this tend to the credit of my religion ?

"Act up to your principles, and never fear offending any one by doing so."

To the same, he added another line in a more religious strain in July, 1867 : "I am much pleased at the opportunity you are having of a little recollection before you commence your new voyage, and pray that it may confirm in you a constant love of our dear Lord and His dear Mother, to whose charge I entrust you. I have no kind of fear that your new mode of life will dim your remembrance of home ; however different it may be, there will be one tie which will never change, our common religion and all its observances. You know you have been the delight of my life, and you may be sure you will continue to be so, for absence will be no separation, and I

shall never fail to have my dear child in my mind, especially
when occupied with any religious observance. I send you my
blessing, and all the best wishes my heart can imagine."

To another daughter, about to become a religious, he wrote
in August, 1869 : "I acquiesce willingly in what seems to
be your continuing wishes, and you shall at all events begin
your novitiate with your father's blessing. At the same time, if
you have any hesitation, and turn your thoughts at all towards
home, it is only my duty to tell you that the same corner of the
nest is ready for you, and the same affectionate welcome you
ever had. Further, I should be ungrateful to the good God
who gave me such a treasure as you have been to me, and as
you will still continue to be wherever you are, if I was not
ready to give you up to Him if that is His holy will, and your
determination : indeed, I shall do so with confidence, having
before me the example of dear Mary Francis [her sister], of
whose happiness I never entertain a doubt.

"Further still, I am not unmindful of the affectionate love I
have ever received from you ; few parents have received, or had
the opportunity of receiving from their children such devoted
service as, for so many years, I received from you, during which
your innocent cheerfulness was like a constant sunshine to me.
So I send you my thanks, my darling, and only hope that your
novitiate may have the effect of increasing your humility, and
of eradicating from your mind the (may I call it the) silly idea
that your love for me can equal that which is felt for you by
your ever affectionate father."

To the same he wrote, in August, 1871 : "I have the greatest
confidence that I am doing God's will in acceding to your wish,
and in giving you to Him, being quite certain that if she had
any kind of misgiving, my affectionate daughter would not
withhold it from her affectionate father." And again, September 13th, on her "profession" : "I pray that you may
have health and strength to do the service of your Master, and
to be a worthy associate of the kind and good religious whom
I have almost learnt to look upon as my own sisters." [1]

Though he was thus "willing," to quote from Bishop Grant's
testimony about him in September, 1868, "to give to our Lord

---

[1] His third, fifth, and sixth daughters all joined the "Society of the Holy Child
Jesus," the Mother-house being at the "Old Palace, Mayfield," with branches in
London, St. Leonard's, Blackpool, Preston, Bletchingley, and in France and
America.

the gifts that He claims, however hard the sacrifice of them
may be to their devoted parents," he was cautious in testing the
genuineness of a religious vocation, as is shown in a letter
of November, 1861, to A. F. Bellasis, referring to his third
daughter, the first to enter religion : " I first heard of her
wishes two years and a half ago, and then told her that it
was my duty to test her vocation, and that she must come
home, visit with her father's friends, associate with her sisters,
go into society with them, and see what kind of a home she
had, before I could even consider the subject. She did this,
went to balls and parties like the rest, visited amongst our
friends, accompanied us into Switzerland last year, and was
as bright and merry as the best of them, and during two years
the subject was never mentioned. At the end of that time . . .
I talked to her, and found her heart set upon it, and so, after
taking the best and most skilful advice I could get, I consented,
and she has been now four months in the convent, and her
letters are full of expressions of the 'intense happiness' she
feels. Happily it is an Order which is not shut up, but occupied
in teaching and in visiting the poor, so that we can see her and
hear of her as often as we like."

It may be added that the Serjeant was a generous
man, although, with his large family, not a rich one. His
children knew that he would refuse them nothing in reason,
and so became at last almost chary of asking anything of
him at all. But they were his first consideration. Let
them only come into his study for anything, and then, no
matter how busy he might be, he would at once put down
his pen and meet them with, "Well, my dear, what can I
do for you ?"

" Is there anything that you want," he inquires in January,
1872, of a daughter in religion, " or that I might have the
pleasure of sending you ? if there is, and you don't tell me,
I shall treat you very disrespectfully." He did not grudge
strangers' servants remuneration for extra trouble or incon-
venience, but it was given on that understanding. On principle
he objected to promiscuous liberality, or to anything out of
the ordinary.[1] " If you want any contributions to your altar,"

<hr>

[1] His dealings with his servants were in keeping with what has been said as to
his intercourse with relatives and friends. He had a distaste for troubling them, and
even shrank from ringing a bell, if he could get what he wanted for himself. In the
first place he asked anything of them kindly, and subsequently thanked them for any

he wrote in September, 1859, to a son at school, "let me know, but I do not wish you to make yourself conspicuous by contributing more than others do." There was an exception made here in cases where he was going in a cab along with a priest, or to a religious house; an extra sixpence was then inevitable, because "this poor cabman, if I give him more than his fare, may perhaps have a prejudice lessened against Catholics, and go away saying to himself, 'They're not such a bad lot.'"

In dress he advocated a judicious economy, as being compatible with the neatness and tidiness practised by himself, suitable to his children's station, and in principle right and meritorious. There was nothing slipshod about him; his handwriting alone would show that he was order itself. Henry Wilberforce told his children that it was the Serjeant who taught him a methodical system of accounts. With respect to handwriting, he took great pains with his own, and like many of his generation, deplored the gradual disappearance of the goose-quill before the serried ranks of the metal-nib.[1] He observed in reason the *convenances* of society, but here again he disliked "overdoing it" in such matters. Thus he spoke against excessive display of mourning, and advised discretion in rounds of visiting. To descend to smaller matters, he had a way of putting imperfections of manner in a ridiculous light without wounding, endeavouring to joke his children out of them. A lady wrote to his wife: "I always look back to my tour with you, in 1836, as the most improving three months in my life, he used to correct me of silly habits and expressions so playfully and kindly."

He would lay stress on accuracy in expression and distinctness of utterance. Himself a fluent and pleasing, if not a

personal service done him, however small. He rarely found fault with them, and was as careful of their feelings as those of his equals. He had no sympathy with those who lord it over their servants, and find fault with them even before the company. "No master," writes his daughter Mary, "was ever more loved by his dependents. Years after his death, old servants would turn up, and tell of his countless little and even great acts of kindness, still fresh in their memory."

[1] "I have a pen," wrote Dr. Newman apologetically to the Serjeant, March 12, 1871, "which writes so badly that it re-acts upon my composition and my spelling. How odd this is! but it is true. I think best when I write. I cannot in the same way think while I speak. Some men are brilliant in conversation, others in public speaking, others find their minds act best when they have a pen in their hands. But then, if it is a bad pen? a steel pen? That is my case just now, and thus I find my brain won't work, much as I wish it. Therefore you must take pity on me, and send me a better answer than I a question."

brilliant speaker, he was careful to know beforehand what he meant to say, knew how to say it well, and quoted approvingly Punch's witticism, "If you have nothing to say, say it, and sit down." "It is a fortunate thing for me," he once remarked, "that I have had to speak to numbers of people in large rooms, because it has been absolutely necessary for me, in order to arrest their attention, that I should be distinct in my utterance, the great secret of which is, never to omit pronouncing a consonant : and I carry that out now, in ordinary conversation, without effort."

Nor was he without a sense of humour in public speaking that could serve him well on an occasion ; and his children remember his telling them how once at a municipal luncheon given in Great Yarmouth, the Serjeant, suddenly called upon to make a speech, belauded that town at the expense of an Essex port, citing, to the satisfaction of a Norfolk company, an old metrical description beginning, "Old Harwich stands upon two strands : "

> From filthy slips we saw the ships,
> And counted just thirteen,
> Two on the mud, five on the flood,
> And six in quarantine.
> The harbour view is fine 'tis true,
> If you knew but where it lay,
> But the houses are placed with such exquisite taste,
> They all look the other way.

CHAPTER VII

MR. SERJEANT BELLASIS' relations with the Catholic clergy
were not an unfitting complement to such as have been
indicated in connection with the Catholic laity.   Once a
Catholic, so some people had told him, he would be overrun
with priests.   "So far from that," he said, "I see far too little
of them."   If he chanced to meet a priest out of doors he
invariably saluted him, if only out of respect for his office ;
whenever he stayed at a place, even for a night, if there
happened to be a mission there, a call at the presbytery was
never willingly omitted.   In fact, he lost no opportunity of
doing anything for the priest that lay in his power.

Thus writing to a Protestant cousin, A. F. Bellasis, a
member of Council at Bombay, in May, 1852, the Serjeant
concludes : " I have only one favour to ask, and that is that if
any of our poor priests should come in your way in India, you
will say a kind word to them for my sake."   And he wrote to
the same, in July, 1855 : " I cannot tell you how much pleasure
you have given me by telling me of the opportunity you have
had of showing kindness to Dr. Harttman.   I am sure he would
appreciate it as much as I do, and I beg you will accept my most
affectionate thanks for this act of thoughtfulness on your part,
and recollection of me and my request.   To have procured a
friend for the good Bishop in those distant parts of his diocese,
and one so able as well as willing to serve him, is a source
of great satisfaction to me."   And in November, 1861, he
wrote : " There is a very intimate friend of mine now at
Bombay, at the Fort Chapel, Father Bridges, a Jesuit priest.
If you should by chance come across him, or if you could with
propriety show him any civility, I am sure you will be kind to
him for my sake.   I think he is now the priest of the Catholic
sailors in the port."

Writing in May and June, 1869, he thus gives an account

of a visit to a priest of the old school : "I went into
Worcestershire to take possession of the property which we
have recovered from Lord Shrewsbury for little Lord Edmund
Howard. It has been a long contest, but we have succeeded at
last, and I took Lord Edmund over with me from Edgbaston, in
order to present him to the Rev. Mr. Campbell, the old priest at
Grafton ; he is eighty-seven years of age, and has been the
priest there for fifty-five years, and I thought it would be a
pleasure to him that he had lived to see a Catholic owner back
again. For the last twelve years he has not been happily
placed, as the chapel at which he serves is part of the Manor
House, which is occupied by a Protestant, who does not behave
well to him. The old man was wheeled into his library to see
us, a very polished old gentleman, with hair very white. When
we came away, Lord Edmund went down on his knees to
ask his blessing, which quite overcame the dear old man." "I
paid him his arrears of £10 a year for twelve years (£120).
You [Hope-Scott] and the Duchess will think it was right that
the first payment made, after our first independent audit,
should be that to the old failing priest. He squeezed my
hand, and said, 'My dear sir, this makes me happy, it enables
me to pay all my debts.'"

He was generous in the priest's regard. "*Bis dat qui cito dat,*"
with a cheque towards repairs of the Farm Street Church organ,
was his prompt reply to a letter from Father William Maher,
S.J., asking for a contribution. So again, when Canon Smith,
of Marlow, sent, as the Serjeant considered, too moderate an
account for a son's four or five weeks' board and tuition there,
he added considerably to the amount put down. His liberality
to priests in their financial troubles was but a continuation
of the same charitable spirit displayed in the old Anglican
days. "When I came to Margaret Street, in 1839," wrote
Canon Oakeley, in February, 1873, to a son of the Serjeant,
"the first offering I received was from your father, then
a total stranger to me. . . . The next week he brought a
second offering of equally large amount, telling me that they
consisted of two fees he had received in a case he had lately
conducted." In the autumn of 1872, a few months before his
death, he sent £100 to Dr. Newman towards the expenses of a
new chapel and other improvements at his school at Edgbaston.
"I submit," wrote the latter, September 9, "to your peremptory
munificence." A letter from Father James Brownbill, S.J., not

long after the Serjeant's conversion, speaks for itself: "I hardly
know what I may say in answer to your kind letter and its
enclosure, which I received this morning. I cannot but feel,
however, that your generosity has carried you beyond all
bounds of moderation. I had been more than sufficiently
rewarded already by the great comfort and happiness which the
fulfilment of a duty had afforded me. . . . You would not have
been, therefore, at all irregular had you left me to the enjoyment
of this one blessing. Your having done more makes me, of
course, more grateful. . . . I propose using your more than
liberal offering for the direct service and glory of Almighty
God, and shall pray that He would accept it from you, and
bestow every best blessing and comfort on the donor."

The Serjeant seconded, in 1863, at the November Sessions
of the Middlesex magistrates, held at Clerkenwell, Mr. Richard
Swift's motion that priests be duly appointed and salaried at
Coldbath Fields and Westminster Houses of Correction, at £250
a year each, and that an annual £100 be paid to the priest
visiting the Clerkenwell House of Detention ; and Lord Enfield
(the Chairman) said that had he heard, before the passing of
the "Prison Ministers' Act," the Serjeant's speech on this
occasion in favour of the priest's influence, he would have
voted "aye" in the lobbies for the Bill, instead of "no"
against it. "I am told," said the Serjeant, "that a Catholic
prisoner can be visited by a priest if he request his presence.
But spontaneous repentance is not the natural frame of mind
with a thief. The kind words from a minister of his own
religion may awaken early sentiments which have long slum-
bered in an atmosphere of sin, and many a criminal may prove
that he has still a heart if you only approach him in the right
way. But to do so with effect, you must know the tone of his
feelings. As well might you try to wind a clock with a key
that did not fit as seek to arouse the conscience of a prisoner
with an appeal lacking sympathy. . . . Now when a Protestant
clergyman approaches a Catholic prisoner with religious instruction, he must begin by proselytizing. He must attempt to overthrow what remains of one religion, and seek to found another
in its place. The result may be hypocrisy or infidelity. . . .
You do not neglect the body of the Catholic prisoner. Why do
you feed him ? Because for his fault you take from him by law
the opportunity of earning bread. Why do you clothe him?
Because for the same reason you take from him the power of

earning means to buy raiment. Surely, then, when it is his sin
that places him in your power, . . . you will be generous to his
soul's weal, and let that priest freely approach him, whom he
recognizes, and who may win him to the paths of repentance.
. . . We ought not to delay one single week. In a week
souls may be lost. Do not put us off by any procrastinating
course. Do not leave the prisoners for whom we plead to-day
to the chance of spontaneous repentance. Do not encourage
them to a course akin to hypocrisy; give them the blessings
of spiritual aid unsought, and tarry not till those whose souls
are dark shall of themselves perchance ask for the light." And
in supporting Mr. Laurie's similar motion at the April Sessions,
1864, he took occasion to testify "from his own knowledge"
of Catholic priests, "that a more honourable, upright, hard-
working body of clergy were nowhere to be found, dedicating
themselves day and night to the service of the poor." He elsewhere notes a priest as being an "apostle," not a "policeman;"
as "a man who has made a sacrifice to God," not "a man
with a good place." As an Anglican, too, he had observed,
in August, 1847: "There have always been found in the
Church a sufficient number of men who have been willing to
dedicate themselves wholly to the priesthood, foregoing the
solace of wife and children; eager, earnest, enthusiastic persons,
and again, sober and quiet persons, so that, except such
unworthy persons as will intrude themselves into the sacred
office under any system, priests as a body are composed of
persons best suited to serve God in that capacity."[1]

His kindness to nuns was in keeping with his conduct
towards priests. "Last week," he writes, in March, 1857,
"I was in Staffordshire, and this week I am going there again
for an election to vote against a man who votes against the
nuns, an unpardonable offence." His charity in their regard
was often, as it appeared to him, rewarded by the unexpected
arrival of a big brief, so that he would say: "Really I have

---

[1] He goes on to deplore, as an Anglican, that after the Reformation there was no
longer a celibate clergy. "The consequence has been," he observes, "that the
class of persons who become clergymen in England is altogether changed, and it
now consists chiefly of the younger branches of the richer classes, and of the
children of clergymen, too many of whom make the office subservient to enabling
them to marry, so that there are more married persons amongst the clergy than in
any other class of society." In a letter to H. Tritton, of January 15, 1844, about "a
house for curates," he seems to discuss the question of a sort of "brotherhood" in
embryo, since vainly essayed by the Protestant Establishment.

K

no merit in such almsgiving, as it is continually being returned
to me fivefold."

A Superioress-General, writing from Nazareth House,
Hammersmith, observes that "when the foundation was made
at Aberdeen, in 1862, the Sisters underwent a regular persecution every time they went into the streets to collect alms, and
the Serjeant, hearing of this, wrote to the Lord Provost (Sir
Alexander Anderson), asking him to protect them. Whereupon
the Provost effectually inquired into the matter, and gave the
Sisters a donation towards their institution. Henceforward they
went about unmolested, and are treated to this day with the
greatest courtesy by persons of all denominations.

"The Serjeant was a great benefactor from the first to the
Home in Hammersmith, and would try to induce his friends to
become subscribers to it, taking them himself to visit the Home.
He would also give letters of introduction to the Sisters, and
tell them when they were out collecting, 'Now, when you have
a bad day for the poor, come to me, and I will make up the
deficiency.' When he saw any of them coming towards his
house, he would run to open the door for them in person.
Sometimes in giving his subscriptions he would add something
more to the amount, saying, 'This is for a private intention, for
a petition I want granted. I find there is no better way for
getting your prayers answered than by giving alms to our Lord
in the person of His poor;' adding, 'You must go all the
same to Mrs. Bellasis.'

"Once a Sister called, looking pale and ill. 'I am sorry to
see you so poorly, Sister,' he said. 'Now, about how much
would you be collecting to-day?' On being told, he immediately
gave the sum, called a cab, paid the cabman, sent both Sisters
home, and told them to take a good day's rest."

In the *Life of Mother Margaret* (O'Halloran), is a pleasing
incident of his giving the community at Stone a picture from
Alton Towers that they desired, on condition of their praying,
which they did with good result, for an adjournment in the
Shrewsbury case.[1]

[1] It may be mentioned here that it was the Serjeant's good offices in the first
instance that enabled the late Mr. Scott-Murray to obtain the hand of St. James the
Apostle for the beautiful domestic chapel at Danesfield. The Serjeant informed him
that the hand was to be seen in the Museum of the Reading Athenæum, and in
consequence of this intimation Mr. and the Hon. Mrs. Scott-Murray, in April, 1853,
went over to Reading with Mr. Lewis Mackenzie and Canon Morris (now S.J.).
They saw the relic, labelled by Protestants "the hand of St. James," upon a mantel-

Shortly after his conversion he made the acquaintance of two eminent priests in the Catholic Church, Père de Ravignan, S.J., and Dr. Döllinger ; the former was at that time giving a course of lectures at the Hanover Square Rooms. "On the 17th of June, 1851," he also tells us, "I assisted at Mr. Manning's first Mass, at Farm Street, London, Père de Ravignan accompanying him."

Accidental circumstances made the Serjeant's intimacy with Canon Oakeley less in the Catholic days than it had been as an Anglican ; but their mutual regard continued undiminished.

The Canon was for some years away from London at St. Edmund's, Ware. "I am still here," he wrote from the College, in March, 1848, "very quietly and happily preaching to the students. I suppose I cannot hope for these golden days much longer. On Passion Sunday, and thence till the middle of Holy Week, I am to preach in London. Newman, &c., are also to come up at that time to preach."

Of all the clergy, however, the Serjeant was perhaps most intimate in later years with the Rev. Charles Brierley Garside,

Hulme's Exhibitioner at Brazenose College, the scholarly author of *Discourses on some Parables of the New Testament*, the *Prophet of Carmel*, and one or two other volumes. The former work, indeed, was dedicated to the Serjeant "in remembrance of a friendship which grows more precious with the advance of years, and which, however long may be the duration of life, will always seem to have been too brief."

With Cardinal Wiseman the Serjeant was for many years,

piece between two specimens of dried fish. A correspondence ensued with the Board of Management discussing the possibility of the purchase of the relic, and £50 was named by the authorities as "an offer that would be entertained." The letters in Mr. Scott-Murray's behalf, wherein amongst other things the Museum people were asked whether they would not prefer an electrical machine to the possession of the hand, were signed by Mr. Mackenzie, but written entirely by the Serjeant. The offer of £50 was then refused, as the Board came to the conclusion that it was not in their power to part with the relic, but some years afterwards the Museum was broken up, and the relic, along with the letters that had passed, came into the possession of the daughter of the late Dr. Hooper, by whom the hand had been originally given to the Museum. (See *The Month* for February, 1882, giving the whole account of the ancient history of this relic, and how it eventually came into Mr. Scott-Murray's hands, Art. by Father Morris, S.J., Chaplain, in 1853, at Danesfield.)

and until his Eminence's death in 1865, on very friendly terms. The acquaintance probably began with an introduction from Oakeley. "You may possibly like to know," wrote Oakeley from St. Edmund's to the Serjeant, as early as March 15, 1848, "that Dr. Wiseman is *at home* (without invitation) to distinguished and undistinguished Catholics and Protestants, especially those fond of literature and the fine arts, every Tuesday evening from eight to ten, at 35, Golden Square. If you would like to go, I can answer for it you would be very welcome; and it might, perhaps, occasionally give me the opportunity of meeting you. He talks of sacred music, too, during Lent. You might meet interesting people; and you might like to know Dr. Wiseman, who is himself an interesting person. But I have not told him that I have told you, so if you never go, he will not be disappointed, because he will not know his loss." Later on the Cardinal would invite the Serjeant's children to a juvenile Christmas party at York Place, or he would come himself to dine *en famille* at Northwood House. He performed the marriage rite at the wedding of the Serjeant's eldest daughter to Dr. Charlton, in April, 1864, as Ordinary of the diocese, giving an affectionate address, and subsequently attending, *in cappa magna*, the nuptial Mass said by his Vicar-General.

A glimpse is afforded of the attention aroused by the Cardinal's appearance in this country after the re-establishment of the Hierarchy, in a letter of the Serjeant's, dating from Mr. Grimshaw's, at Errwood Hall, in July, 1852: "We drove to Chatsworth. Our party occupied four carriages, the Cardinal in a carriage and four, with smart postilions, the others following. . . . The most amusing part of to-day's proceedings has been the sensation caused by the Cardinal; neither water-works nor fountains had any attraction while he was by."

"In October, 1852," writes the Serjeant, "I accompanied Cardinal Wiseman to the centenary of Notre Dame de Grace, at Cambrai, and made the acquaintance of the Archbishop there, as well as of the Bishops of Nevers, Angers, Ghent, Soissons, Angoulême, Bruges, and Frejus, and spent some days there, and walked in the procession, which was of a very interesting, not to say magnificent, character. One morning, after breakfast, I found myself in an amusing position. I was walking in the Archbishop's garden with the above-named Bishops, Archbishop, and Cardinal, when we came to a pear-tree laden with beautiful fruit, but out of reach. None of the party were in costume fitted for climbing trees except myself, so I offered to do so, mounted the tree, plucked the fruit, and threw it down to the dignitaries below. Whilst on the tree, and so occupied, it struck me how improbable a situation it would have seemed to me if I could have foreseen it a few years before, viz., up in a pear-tree, throwing down fruit to Cardinal, Archbishop, and Bishops, all in grand costume on the grass beneath me."

Amongst the English prelates the Serjeant was most intimate with Dr. Grant, first Bishop of Southwark, and for some years (1865—1870) his own Ordinary: "I cannot name Dr. Grant," he writes, "now departed to his rest, without expressing my sense of the advantage his friendship was to my family. He was a learned man, deeply versed as well in theology as in canon law, clear and distinct in expressing himself, always ready to afford advice, and prompt in giving it. His manner was more than cheerful, it was playful, and he was full of stories for the amusement of children. His modest demeanour was extraordinary, so that strangers accidentally in his company could never discover the rank he held. Of all the people I ever knew he gave me the nearest impression of a saint, and yet this was not derived from any sanctified manner, but from his conduct in all matters in which I had anything to do with him." "He was small in person," writes Mrs. Bellasis, "with eyes cast down, and a not infrequent expression of suffering, yet always cheery, and never happier than when with children." Every Christmas the Serjeant called with his sons at St. George's Cathedral. "It is no little comfort to me," the Bishop wrote in September, 1868, "amidst the changes of seventeen years to feel that your kindness is still the same, and that your children are willing to continue it to me." When Hope-Scott and the Serjeant contributed to the Bishop's expenses in attending the Vatican Council, Dr. Grant wrote to the latter in November, 1869: "May God bless you and your gift to your own complete recovery, and may it draw down a thousand blessings on your wife and children and sister, here and at a distance." And again from Rome in December: "The *Tablet* received yesterday shows that just at the moment when by your patient suffering and your generous alms for my journey you were earning blessings for your family, your prayers for your daughter in India were heard. May God and His Immaculate Mother and St. Joseph watch over your grandson and his parents, and gain every grace and happiness for them." His affection for the

Serjeant was very great. When near to dying himself, he wrote from Rome on St. George's day, 1870, on hearing of the Serjeant's convalescence (following upon a dangerous illness) : "May our dear Lord be praised now for His goodness in hearing our prayers for your speedy recovery."

An incident that occurred in 1852 was especially instrumental in bringing about this close friendship between the Bishop and the Serjeant. "A son of his," as his wife writes, "lay sick unto death, when Dr. Grant called and said to me, 'You have a little child very ill, haven't you?' I replied, 'Yes,' and the Bishop said, 'Where is he?' and followed me up to the bed-room where the poor infant lay white and motionless. Dr. Grant knelt down, took off his pectoral cross, which contained a relic of the true Cross, and touched baby's forehead and breast. He opened his eyes, as if electrified, and began to cry. Dr. Grant then put a small phial of St. Walburga's oil on the table, telling me to give him some of it should he not improve, and made a hasty departure.[1] He almost ran downstairs, and was out of the door before I could collect my wits. The child then fell into a sleep of forty-five minutes, his little hands, previously clenched for many hours, were now soft and open, and his arms were flung out in the form of a cross. He did not look behind him, but got better and better, to the surprise of Dr. West, who expected to find him gone." "And it was observed that for a long time afterwards," writes the

---

[1] On June 25, 1855, Lord Shrewsbury wrote to Vienna to the Serjeant an account of Eichstadt and St. Walburga's oil. "We left Munich," he says, "on the 16th inst., and arrived that evening at Eichstadt, a small town prettily situated in a fertile valley. The next morning we heard Mr. Garside's Mass at the Shrine of St. Walburga —during the day we returned to see it, being most obligingly accompanied by the Chaplain of the Benedictine convent, Father Schmid, a Jesuit ; the bones are encased above the altar, and rest upon a stone, through which flows that wonderful liquid called St. Walburga's oil. It falls into a silver vase and is carried away by the nuns once a week. It only flows between October and May. We were allowed to taste the oil, but it really has no taste, only it feels like water in the mouth and like oil in the throat. Once a great professor of chemistry attempted to analyze it, but came to the conclusion that it was a futile attempt, as he could not discern what were its component parts. In the convent they showed us a bottle of the oil which had been collected in 1834, and has never since been opened. It seems as fresh as if it had only been taken the day before. The good nuns allowed us to take a large number of St. Walburga's ribbons, which have touched the shrine. I enclose two for you and Mrs. Bellasis. I also obtained one hundred small bottles of the oil. Over the shrine is the following inscription : 'Non hunc dant lapides, sed virginis ossa liquorem, et fluit ex virea virginitate latex.' An extraordinary number of miracles take place every year at St. Walburga's shrine."

Serjeant, "whenever he went to sleep, he lay with his arms extended in the form of a cross." [1]

Referring to this anxiety a letter of Father Brownbill may be added. On the 8th of July he wrote to Mrs. Bellasis : "I shall hear, no doubt, during the day if the happy news you were so very kind as to send me last evening be confirmed, and if so, how little shall I heed the horrid rattling of cabs and omnibuses in Farm Street. . . . Your dear husband was so good as to call yesterday, and told me of the change which had taken place, but he himself looked so worn and no wonder. . . . He told me also of the *prayings* that were going on in Northwood House. After he left I had a good cry ; for how could I help it, when thinking of the simplicity of the confidence with which the dear children were appealing to Almighty God as if He could not, or would not, take their little brother from them. One might even think it a very nice thing that the prayers of those dear innocents should prevail over those of the Angels in Heaven, who would, no doubt, be glad of another companion in glory."

When this child had grown up to the age of nine, Dr. Grant wished him to be trained directly for the religious state without going to a public school, and in some uncertainty what course to take, whether he should send him to Edgbaston or not, the Serjeant wrote to Dr. Newman asking for his opinion, and received from him the following interesting reply : "Well, as to your boy, you see my mind runs so much its own way, that I do not know how to trust it. If I spoke it, it would be this, viz., I have little belief in true vocations being destroyed by contact with the world—I don't mean contact with sin and evil—but that contact with the world which consists of such intercourse as is natural and necessary. Many boys seem to have vocations, in whom it is but appearance. They go to school, and the appearance fades away—and then people may say, ' They have lost their vocation,' when they never had one.

---

[1] Two curious incidents are also mentioned by Mrs. Bellasis about Dr. Grant when visiting the Serjeant. One of her daughters had tried to get a new stamp off an envelope, but not succeeding, had thrown the whole impatiently into the fire. The Bishop, shortly after, came upstairs from the dining-room, and said at once to the child: "Do you know how to get a stamp off an envelope? You should always breathe upon it ; it will then come off easily." On another occasion he said to another daughter : "I think you have had a tumble over the coal-box, haven't you?" It was so, and as it arose from a little act of disobedience, she had concealed the mishap, and had borne in silence an unseen but sore cut of the lip caused through her fall. How the Bishop knew of either of these events nobody could tell.

In such cases, it is, on the other hand, rather a positive good that they and their parents were not deceived. What I shrink from with dread, as the more likely danger, is not the Church losing priests whom she ought to have had, but gaining priests whom she never should have been burdened with. The thought is awful, that boys should have had no trial of their heart, till at the end of some fourteen years, they go out into the world with the most solemn vows upon them, and then, perhaps for the first time, learn that the world is not a seminary;—when they exchange the atmosphere of the church, the lecture-room, and the study, the *horarium* of devotion, work, meals, and recreation, for this most bright, various, and seductive world.

"Moreover, I dread too early a separation from the world for another reason—for the spirit of formalism, affectation, and preciseness, which it is so very apt to occasion.

"That there are real vocations in the case of children I fully believe, we meet with them in the Lives of the Saints—and in the case of others too—but, if some of these were early introduced into the religious life, as St. Thomas or the Prophet Samuel, still, some of those most familiar to us, and who seem to have had their vocation, not in after-life (as St. Ignatius or St. Anselm) but from childhood, nevertheless cherished it and matured it, in the course of a secular training, as St. Carlo, St. Aloysius, St. Philip, and St. Alfonso.

"Under, then, the two opposite difficulties, of depriving our Lord of His priests, and of giving to Him unworthy ones, I myself, if left to myself, should be disposed to act with far greater sensitiveness of the latter. I think a true vocation in a boy is not lost by secular education—at most it is but merged for a time, and comes up again—whereas a false vocation may be fatally and irreversibly fostered in a seminary. Or at least, it is *more* common in this age for false vocations to be made by an early dedication to the religious or ecclesiastical state, than for true vocations to be lost by early secular education.

"I found Mrs. W—— take the same view, as far as she spoke upon it. She spoke from such experience as she had. I wish you would write to her.

"My conclusion is, as far as I have a right to an opinion, you should send your boy to us."

The above leads us to the Serjeant's interest in Catholic education, and especially his connection with the establishment of the Oratory School, in which he had become actively concerned by the beginning of 1858. "Several Catholics," he writes, "who had sons to educate, had heard that Dr. Newman was not unwilling to commence a classical school at the Oratory, Edgbaston, so meetings were held at my chambers upon the subject, and ultimately it was determined that Sir John Acton and I should go as a deputation to Dr. Newman to ascertain whether he was willing to undertake the task. Our interview was a successful one, and after it, communications were made with many of the principal Catholics on the subject. A prospectus of February 21, 1859, ran: "It is the intention of Father Newman, of the Birmingham Oratory, with the blessing of God, to commence on the 1st of May next, a school for the education of boys not destined to the ecclesiastical state, and not above twelve years of age on their admission. He takes this step at the instance of various friends, with the concurrence and countenance of a number of Catholic gentlemen whose names have been transmitted to him, and with the approbation and good-will of the Right Rev. the Bishop of the diocese."

In a memorandum in the Serjeant's handwriting, to proposed answers to some interrogatories of Cardinal Wiseman with reference to the projected school, we read: "Those who have occupied themselves in considering the mode in which a new Catholic lay-school might be best established, have been far from losing sight of the necessity, not only of providing proper religious instruction, but of ensuring such a Catholic training throughout as should at the same time lead the students to habitual piety, and produce a deep love and veneration for old Catholic usages and practices. It will be seen that many of the promoters of the scheme are converts, which has tended to make the above consideration a prominent one from the first, as being (if that be possible) more essential for them than to those who have been all their lives subject to Catholic influences."[1]

"We thought," observes the Serjeant in his MS. *Autobiography*,

[1] The following were amongst those who expressed their concurrence in the proposal for a new Catholic school in England: The Duke of Norfolk, Viscount Campden, Lord Feilding, Lord C. Thynne, Lord H. Kerr, Sir R. Throckmorton, Sir J. (now Lord) Acton, Sir J. Simeon, R. Berkeley, E. Badeley, J. A. Herbert, R. Monteith, J. R. Hope-Scott, C. R. Scott-Murray, R. Biddulph Phillips, W. Dodsworth, W. Jones, H. W. Wilberforce, W. H. Bagshawe, F. R. Wegg-Prosser, W. G. Ward, F. R. Ward, S. Nasmyth Stokes, Sir R. Gerard, Rt. Hon. W. Monsell (now Lord Emly), S. de Vere, M.P., E. Jerningham, T. W. Allies, H. Bowden, T. W. Marshall, T. Gaisford, and Mr. Serjeant Bellasis.

"that the existing Catholic colleges were at that time in some respects deficient. So far as the kindness with which the boys in them were treated, and so far as the religious element was concerned, there was nothing to be desired, but we thought (1) that the classical instruction might be improved and made more conformable in degree to that of the highest Protestant schools; (2) that in the existing schools there was too great an admixture of classes, many of the scholars coming from homely dwellings, bringing with them provincialisms, not to say vulgarities, which were, perhaps, in great measure, got rid of by associating with their school-fellows, but at the cost of leaving a portion of them behind; (3) that the charge for education was not sufficient to ensure really competent masters, who were, in general, divines, themselves in course of education, and only temporarily occupied as teachers, having in many cases, no taste for teaching, and, if possessed of any talent, certain to be carried off to more important duties; (4) that it was desirable that a little more attention should be paid to the *personnel* of the boys, and it was also thought that lay-brothers were hardly adequate to the charge of little boys just come from home. Many partook of these opinions, and during the year (1858) much discussion took place on the subject. Some talked of a proprietary school, others thought that some individual Catholic should be selected as the head of such a school: I was, however, myself of opinion that the school would be a failure unless it were firmly united to some religious body; that there would be no security for proper religious training if the school depended in the first instance upon such unoccupied priests as the Bishop might be able to spare from amongst his own clergy. These reasons prevailed, and the Fathers of the Oratory undertook to commence the school." It was opened on May 2, 1859, the feast of St. Athanasius, the first boy to arrive being the Serjeant's eldest son, now a priest at the Birmingham Oratory.

In 1864-5 the Serjeant was likewise interested in the project of the Birmingham Oratory taking over the Oxford mission. He could not, indeed, be indifferent to any scheme that enlisted Dr. Newman's services in the Catholic cause. "I think Dr. Newman's going to Oxford," he writes, "of the greatest importance, religious matters there have got into such a state that they are ripe for the sickle."

This question, however, was intimately connected with another question, viz., whether Catholic young men should, or

should not be allowed to frequent the Universities of Oxford
and Cambridge. The Serjeant chanced to be wintering in
Rome in 1864-5, when the matter was under discussion there,
and having four sons of his own growing up, he felt himself
personally concerned in the result. He, therefore, actively
interested himself in the matter on his own account, and on
behalf of others similarly situated, by correspondence and
interviews with the authorities. Sympathizing with the views
of those who desired no interference with the discretion up till
that time exercised by parents, he spared no pains to delay, if
not to hinder, anything in the nature of a positive prohibition
being issued. In the event when the highest authority determined to discourage, without forbidding, recourse to Oxford and
Cambridge, he, with characteristic loyalty, deemed such an
intimation to be for him equivalent to a command to keep
away from those Universities. As he expressed it to his
eldest son, when his school course was over, and the question
of his subsequent training had to be determined : " I have not
come into the Catholic Church to take my own line in such
matters independently of my ecclesiastical superiors." The
result was that the advantages of an University education in
any true sense of the term, the value of which he fully understood, were cheerfully sacrificed, and recourse was had for
degrees to the Examining Board of the London University.[1]

[1] It was a sequel to this renunciation of an Oxford course for the Serjeant's
sons, that Dr. Newman, in "coaching" the eldest of them and Dr. W. J. Sparrow
for the London matriculation, had very seriously to find fault with some of the text-
books, which he did in a long and powerful letter of remonstrance, dated 25th
January, 1868, addressed to the Serjeant. Bishop Grant, too, wrote to the
Serjeant : "I have seen to-night one of the Senate (I think) of the London
University and found him quite willing to enter my complaint about Plautus and the
French books. It still strikes me that if you, as the father of a family, and not
supposed to be prejudiced by merely ecclesiastical views, would write a letter
mourning over the evil which your son is asked to learn, your letter would do real
good, and would put our complaint into a practical shape. My friend would then
argue the subject with his colleagues." A draft letter from the Serjeant for the *Pall
Mall Gazette*, runs as follows : " I am a father with sons educating at a public school,
the oldest of whom has already matriculated at the University of London, and is
preparing to proceed to his B.A. examination. My attention, however, was some
time since called by the Superior of the school to the character . . . of the classical
works which are selected as of necessity to be mastered by the candidates [*i.e.*, the
Adelphi of Terence, and the *Menæchmi*, and *Miles Gloriosus*, of Plautus], and I
requested him, an ecclesiastic of known scholarship, to specify his objections in
writing. He did so and I enclose his letter. . . . I am told that similar objections
apply to the class of French novels selected for the examination of the students. I
will name but one, *La Tulipe Noire*, by A. Dumas. . . . I think it possible that the
publication of the accompanying letter may strengthen the hands of those among the
authorities of the University who would willingly remedy the evil.

The Serjeant was anxious as a Catholic to visit Rome, and previous to wintering abroad in 1864-5, Cardinal Wiseman gave him a passport of introduction that recommended him everywhere to prelates and clergy.[1] The summer holidays of 1864 had been spent at Lucerne, and Einsiedeln monastery had been visited for the feast of the Assumption. "The concourse of people," he wrote, "was immense, and the great church was filled from morning till night, and as the custom is for all to say their prayers out loud, without reference to the rest, the roar was something extraordinary. R—— and I said the Rosary together aloud amidst a perfect din of prayers."[2]

From Florence he wrote to a son at school, in October, 1864: "I send you, within, a picture, which represents the state of things in the new kingdom of Italy. Whilst we were at Bologna (a city which formerly belonged to the Pope, but of which he was robbed by Victor Emmanuel, the King of Piedmont), there was a trial going on of one hundred and twenty villains, robbers, and assassins, and they were of so violent a character (Garibaldians in fact), that they were afraid

[1] The full text of the document, somewhat of a curiosity, and ornamented with the Wiseman arms and seal in black and white, with Cardinal's hat, and patriarchal cross, and two supporting angels, runs: " Nicolaus, Miseratione Divinâ Tit. Sanctae Pudentianae S.R.E. Presbyter Cardinalis Wiseman Archiepiscopus Westmonasteriensis etc., Dnum Eduardum Bellasis, nobilem Anglum Magistraturam Londini exercentem, unâ cum uxore atque familiâ suâ per varias regiones peregrinaturum, virum Catholicum, optimi exempli et de Ecclesia benemerentem, Illmis et Rmis Unis et Fratribus Archiepiscopis et Episcopis, locorum Ordinariis, cœterisque de Clero libenter commendamus, enixe rogantes ut in omnibus præsertim quæ ad pietatem fovendam conferunt, ei præsto sint et adjuvent, pro quibus humanitatis officiis utpote Nobismetipsis exhibitis grates Nostras rependimus. Datum Westmonasterii die 3 Augusti, 1864, N. Card. Wiseman, De mandato Emi et Rmi Dni Card. Archiepi, Joan. Can. Morris, a Secr. Vic."

[2] In September he had moved on to the Italian lakes, and notes: "One evening, walking on the shore of the Lago Maggiore, at Pallanza, I fell in with a priest and got into conversation with him ; a house was building on the hill-side and I asked whose it was, he answered that it was being built by a countryman of mine. 'What is his name?' I asked; he replied, 'Broveney.' I said, 'That does not sound like an English name, how do you spell it?' to which he answered, 'B-r-o doppio v-n-e,' under which disguise I recognized the not unfamiliar English name of Brown." "Broveney" was, perhaps, an improvement on Brown. The Serjeant's own name was seldom improved upon. On one occasion, he took the pains to collate from tradesmen's bills and other documents the various renderings, to the number of eighty, of his own surname, his legal title introducing a fresh element of confusion into the shop-keeping brain. The result was endless varieties ranging from General Pegasus to Corporal Bellows ; and once when examining a witness in humble life as to his calling, the seemingly innocent reply came, to the merriment of the Court, "Well, we makes pots and pans and mends old bellowses." "You've got it now, Brother Bellasis," said the Judge.

to try them loose, so they had them all put into a large cage made on purpose to hold them, in the Court itself; the picture I send represents the cage and the prisoners in it, you will see also in front of the cage a body of soldiers with guns ready to fire upon them if they offered to make any resistance, . . . such a set of vagabonds I never saw before."

He had, of course, no sympathy with the methods of the Italian Revolution, and says in October, 1867: "We are rejoiced at the failure of the scheme concerted between Garibaldi and M. Rattazzi, by which the former was to make an inroad upon the Holy Father and the latter was to pretend to try and prevent him; the consequence is they are both in the ditch, and the bitter newspapers are obliged to admit that the Roman people, whom they represent as eager to rebel, have refused to sympathize with the invaders, on the contrary have joined with the regular troops in giving the revolutionists a thorough licking."

"There is a great conspiracy," he writes again, "on the part of the revolution all over Europe to destroy the Christian religion, and, so far, our Protestant fellow-countrymen, not seeing that the conspiracy is aimed at themselves as well as at us, take part with the revolution in the hope of doing some damage to the Catholic Church, and then stemming the tide. You will see a good deal said about the abolition of the Austrian Concordat, the real object being the depriving the Church of all hand in education, and secularizing the Sacrament of Marriage; the result of this must be the heathenizing of the rising generation, so far as this object can be achieved. Yet, strange to say, our countrymen are carried away, and make common cause with the foreign revolutionaries;" and on 4th December he says, "It is astonishing that our Protestant countrymen cannot see that in aiding and praising Garibaldi and his volunteers, they preclude themselves from condemning the Fenians and their American volunteers; in truth we have been encouraging revolution in every part of the globe for the last forty years, and now we are surprised to find that our own crop is beginning to sprout among ourselves." And on the 24th: "We are thoroughly frightened here (in England) by the revolutionaries. Fenianism is merely an incident in a movement which has its roots quite as much abroad as in Ireland, and we hear the Government knows much more than we do of its extent. Our countrymen have

now got to solve the problem how 'revolution' is right in
other countries and wrong here."

Lastly, in a letter of April, 1868, to Hope-Scott : " Your
view of our political condition is enough to make serious
men thoughtful, we seem to be cut away from our moorings,
and where is the man who can anchor us safely again ? The
Irish Church Question is one of justice, and therefore important,
but it seems a small question in comparison with the revolutionary ideas which seem to be cropping up among ourselves
while we thought we were only sowing the seeds in our
neighbour's field."

Arriving in Rome at the end of October, 1864, he thus
observes upon his stay there : " We spent our time in the usual
occupation of Roman visitors, in religious services and ceremo-
nials, and in visiting holy places ; I cannot enumerate them, it
would become a diary ; we also diligently inspected the
antiquities sacred and profane. We were, of course, frequently
at St. Peter's, and were present at the beatification of Peter
Canisius, and also at the Christmas services, being in St. Peter's
long before it was light, and remaining to hear the Holy Father
sing High Mass on Christmas Day. We were present at the
Te Deum at the Gesù at the end of the year. Of course we
visited the catacombs, and we heard Masses, said for us by the
Rev. Mr. Dolman and by Dr. Smith, in the crypt of St. Peter's,
upon the tomb of the Apostles."   " The beatification of the
Jesuit Father Canisius was very grand," his wife adds. " St.
Peter's was lighted up by three thousand wax candles in
splendid chandeliers, and when the decree was read, the cannons
of the Castle fired, and the *Te Deum* was sung by all the people
and by two choirs.   It was magnificent."

In a letter of November to his eldest daughter, he gives the
following account of an audience with Pope Pius IX. : " I need
not tell you that you are always in our thoughts, and we find
no end of opportunities of praying for you and your welfare
in all respects, whether we go to the tomb of the Apostles or
to the *Quarant' Ore* at this or that church, or when we say
our Rosary together. You may suppose, therefore, that you
were foremost, when we had our interview with the Holy
Father yesterday. We got notice on Saturday evening (by
an official letter brought to us by a mounted *chasseur*), that
we were to have an audience on Sunday at half-past three, and
forthwith a complete *razzia* was made upon the piety shops

for rosaries, medals, &c., which, however, had been nearly
cleared out before we arrived; nevertheless we supplied
ourselves pretty well, and at the appointed time we presented
ourselves in the anti-camera, where we found about a dozen
persons assembled, who were summoned into the Pope's
presence, each party separately. When our turn came we were
called by Mgr. Talbot, and at once introduced into a long room,
where stood His Holiness at a little table at the end, and then
Mgr. Talbot, having mentioned who we were, left us alone. We
knelt at the door on entering, again in the middle of the room,
and again when we were close to him; he put out his hand and
tried to prevent us from kissing his foot, but we persisted and
he permitted it. The Pope at once commenced in a cheerful
and familiar tone. Mamma talked French, and got out what
she wanted to say well. I then chimed in in Italian, and asked
his blessing for my own family and for that of my sister, and
amongst others for my three boys at school under Dr. Newman
at the Oratory, and for Dr. N. and his school. This he gave,
quoting a passage out of Ecclesiasticus.[1] He then talked about
Dr. Newman, as the first English convert he had ever seen, and
of his first coming to Rome; then about Father St. John, and
Dr. Faber. Our interview lasted about ten minutes, during
which we got all our rosaries blest. He looked well and in good
health, his eye was bright, his voice clear, and we all came
away charmed."

In November, again, the Serjeant wrote to his sons:
"On All Saints' Day I went to the Sistine chapel for High
Mass, where I saw the Pope and more than twenty Cardinals,
and was glad to see the Holy Father looking so well. . . .
This, the 4th, is the festival of St. Carlo Borromeo, and the
Pope has been in procession with the Cardinals to the Church
of St. Carlo, and we went to see him go; it was a very beautiful
sight; there were a great many Cardinals with very handsomely
ornamented carriages, and last of all came the Holy Father and
his attendants. He was preceded by the cross-bearer riding
on a white mule and carrying a cross. The Pope himself was in
a carriage with glass panels, so we could see him perfectly.
Every one went down on their knees as he passed, to receive
his blessing."

---

[1] In his MS. *Autobiography* the Serjeant says he also asked a particular blessing
upon the convent school at St. Leonard's. The Holy Father, he adds, "asked many
questions, talked freely, and put us quite at our ease. I think I remember most his
bright eye as he looked from one to the other of us."

In December the Serjeant writes from his residence, 14, Trinità di Monti, Rome,[1] to Hope-Scott: "We find no day long enough, and amidst all our sight-seeing, Pagan, Christian, and artistic, the visiting comes to occupy every scrap of time.[2] Of course we have seen the Father General (S.J.), and Father Secchi in his Observatory, and Father Kirby at the Irish College, and Dr. Neave at the English College, and Dr. M'Closkey at the American College, and Gibson the sculptor, and Overbeck the painter,[3] and Liszt the musician, and Louis Veuillot the journalist, and other celebrities. As far as I can judge, everything, religiously speaking, is most flourishing here ; it is a sight to see the Gesù at any time, and the various Colleges are full, and in good working order. Among other things which have struck me in this latter respect, nothing has pleased me more than the American College. I dined there last Sunday, and there were sixty people at table, a mixture of students (ecclesiastical) from both Federal and Confederate States ; they live here together in perfect harmony, the bond of the Catholic Church binding and holding them together in the face of disturbing causes which create a bitter antagonism everywhere else ; I asked Dr. M'Closkey if the subject of American difficulties was forbidden, and he said he knew his countrymen too well to attempt to enforce any rule to that effect, but that as a matter of fact they did live in harmony. . . .

"As to politics, everything seems very quiet, there have been no disturbances of any kind since we have been here, and it amuses us to hear from the English newspapers of the insecurity of Rome, and how that no one can stir out after dark without danger of brigands ; it is all nonsense, the streets are all well lighted, and I walk in them after dark with as great a feeling of security, at least, as I should in London.

"We went a few days since to see one of the pictures which has the reputation of moving its eyes ; it is a head of our Blessed Lord, called *Il Nazareno*, and is in the Church of Sta. Maria in Monticelli : it had some time since attracted great crowds so great that the Pope had it removed to some other

---

[1] "The house of the Tempietto," Mrs. Bellasis writes, "a quaint, curious habitation having a glorious view," now, 1893, somewhat curtailed.

[2] Also, he says elsewhere, "we paid our respects, by permission, to the ex-King and Queen of Naples" (conveyed to the Serjeant from the Farnese Palace, Rome, November 24, 1864).

[3] "With whose appearance and manners," he says elsewhere, "we were charmed."

place for a time, but Monsignor Talbot having told us that it
had been lately sent back, we went to see it. Now I will tell
what we saw. The picture is in clear light and can be distinctly
seen, the eyes are, not shut, but looking downward, in such
a manner as to appear to be shut. We knelt down at the
faldstool in front of the picture, and the sacristan was telling
us that the eyes did not move now, and, in answer to my
question, that he had never seen them move. . . . All this time
I saw nothing, but on looking again I saw the prodigy, if
prodigy it be; what I saw was this, the dark lines forming
the downcast eyes seemed to me to fade away like a dissolving
view, and the ovals forming the eyelids seemed to become eyes
somewhat turned up. The effect produced on my sight was
no mistake, but after an instant or two, I saw the downcast
eyes again, and then again the eyes looking up. I changed
my position, but still I saw the same changing expression.
All this time the sacristan saw nothing. Now I do not pretend
to define how all this was caused, but I came to this conclusion,
that the instances from time to time alleged of pictures appear-
ing to move their eyes have at least not been frauds or silly
fancies, but appearances really existing. Whether there is
any natural explanation of the phenomenon, or whether the
Almighty permits such impressions to be made, I cannot
determine, but as I saw it. I describe it, since I think it may
interest you."

In January, 1865, he wrote to his eldest daughter : " I
have been overwhelmed with business till the last, and the
last piece was one of the most important of the whole. A
proposal was made to present an address, on the part of the
Catholic foreigners in Rome, to the Holy Father, and a meeting
was held for the purpose at Lord Stafford's. . . . There were
present in all twelve, Belgians, French, Germans, and English ;
these formed a committee, of which I was one. A. B. came prepared with an address ready cut and dried, well expressed and
unexceptionable in all but one respect, and that was that there
was no mention whatever made of the late Encyclical [that of
1864]. This I and others objected to, saying that to omit mention
of so important an act of the Holy Father, and one so abused,
vilified, and misrepresented, would cause it to be supposed that
we did not approve of it, and we should be claimed as allies
by his enemies. Duke Scotti of Milan, Count Gozzi, M. de
Beaulieu, and ultimately all, concurred in this view save A. B.

L

and Count d'Arco, who the next day sent in their resignations.
I was the more determined to stand out as I had carefully
studied this much abused document, and was and am of opinion
that every word of it was just and true, and more than that,
necessary to be expressed at this time. So much do I believe
it to be founded upon natural justice and right, independently
of the doctrines of the Catholic Church, that I do not doubt
that, when it comes to be canvassed, right-thinking Protestants,
free from the bias of party, will concur in the principles it lays
down." [1]

" His devotedness to the Holy Father, always strong," wrote
the late Rev. C. B. Garside about the Serjeant in 1873, "grew more
intense with his own advancing years and the increasing trials
of Pius IX. If there was one thing more than another that
moved his whole nature, usually so gentle and tolerant, it was
any remark or insinuation written, or spoken in conversation,
hostile to the Holy See. He, who was never known to say
an unkind word against any human being, felt an instinctive
repugnance to the lukewarmness and indifference of so-called
Liberal Catholics." "His devotion to the Holy Father was unbounded," says Father R. Bellasis. " He loved him, prayed for
him, and could not abide the slightest indifference or want of
thorough loyalty to his person and office ; and in proportion to
his affection he denounced the violence and injustice of all the
enemies of the Holy Father, and one of his last acts, less than
a month before his death, was to depute his eldest son to
represent him as a member of a deputation proposed to be sent
to Rome on occasion of a Bill passing the Italian Parliament
to suppress the heads of religious orders in that city. " I am
rejoiced," he writes from Hyères, in December, 1872, "that a
deputation is to go to the Holy Father, as proposed by the
Duke. I wish I could go myself, but as that is not possible, I

[1] Of another "Encyclical," he writes to his eldest son, at school, in October,
1867 : "'We have no defence, but please to abuse the plaintiff's attorney.' This
was the endorsement upon a brief for a defendant, when the case came on to be
heard ; and if you have chanced to see the Encyclical of the Protestant Bishops, you
will see that it is just the course they have taken in addressing their flocks. In the
Anglican Church the doctrines held by various sections of it are of the most
antagonistic kind, many being not only heretical in the eye of the Catholic Church,
but fundamentally erroneous even from their own point of view, infidelity of
various degrees becoming more and more prevalent every year ; at a meeting,
however, of the United Protestant Episcopate, not one word is said to point out and
correct the errors prevailing amongst themselves, in fact nothing is said except to
abuse the authority of the Pope, and the invocation of the Blessed Virgin. In fact
they dare not find fault with their own people, who would assuredly disobey them."

am delighted that you should have an opportunity of supplying my place. I cannot doubt that you will be equally pleased to do so.

"Let me know, as soon as you yourself know, when it is proposed to start, that I may send you the wherewithal in good time. You will get to know who is going, and perhaps find an agreeable companion. You will write to the Duke, saying that you have heard from me, and that I say that you must by no means omit going. God bless you all."

His visit to Rome in 1864-5 was drawing to a close. "In order to be in time for the opening of Parliament," as the Serjeant tells us in his *Autobiography*, "I was obliged to leave Rome at the end of January,[1] 1865, and I applied through Mgr. Talbot to be allowed to receive Holy Communion at the hands of the Holy Father, which was granted, and on the 26th of January I went to the Vatican at seven o'clock, and after waiting for a short time in an ante-room, I was shown into the Pope's private chapel, where he says his daily Mass. It was a room of considerable size, consisting, in fact, of two rooms divided by an arch, the altar being in a further room, at the end. In the archway was a seat and a *prie-dieu*, looking, of course, towards the altar. When I entered, which I did with an officer in full uniform, who was also come for the same purpose as myself, there was no one in the chapel but ourselves, but after a few minutes the Holy Father entered in his usual dress, accompanied by two chaplains acting as acolyths; he knelt for a few minutes at the *prie-dieu* I have mentioned, and then proceeded to vest at the altar, where the vestments were ready arranged. There was no difference in the vestments that he wore from those used by other priests at an ordinary Low Mass. The Mass proceeded as usual, the Holy Father being very distinct and deliberate, and at the proper time I went forward to the altar and received Communion, kissing the ring on the Pope's hand,

---

[1] He wrote, January 28, 1865, "I am leaving home an hour hence for Civita Vecchia, in the hope of finding the sea favourable for a voyage to Marseilles. I am making my way to Hope-Scott at Hyères, where I shall spend a few days." He ultimately went round by the Corniche and Riviera, the sea being too rough. Since more people were coming into Italy at this time of the year than leaving it, it was easy to get an empty carriage going into France to bring back voyagers coming eastward. Thus the Serjeant sent a letter to his children in England in which he drew a sketch of himself, seated in solitary state in a carriage and four, driving along the Mediterranean shore. People then inquired who it was passing by. "C'est un sergeant Anglais," volunteered one, whereupon followed the comment, "Si les sergeants voyagent ainsi, comment vont les généraux."

which he presented to me for that purpose, returning to my place immediately behind the *prie-dieu.* The Holy Father having unvested, returned to his place in the archway, and another Mass commenced. By the side of the Pope's *prie-dieu* was a little table, upon which were two or three books, that he used from time to time. I was so immediately behind him, that as he held up the book he was reading, I could have read it at the same time, especially as he held it a little to the right in order to get the light, which came from behind.

" As the second Mass proceeded, I became conscious that the room was gradually filling behind me, and after a while a chaplain came in, knelt under the arch by the side of the Pope, and said family prayers for the household and attendants. These finished, the Pope retired from the chapel as he had come, and I retired also, having arrived at the highest privilege of my Catholic life, viz., that of receiving our Blessed Lord from the hands of His Vicar upon earth."

CHAPTER VIII.

AFTER he had been forty years at the Bar, Mr. Serjeant Bellasis, as has been stated, retired from practice in 1866, although this did not mean with him any cessation of activity in work of a more private character. In December, Hope-Scott called upon him at his residence, the Lawn, Putney, and persuaded him to recruit his somewhat indifferent health by following himself and family to Hyères, in Provence, for the winter months. This was the first of a series of winterings abroad, interrupted but once, *i.e.*, in 1870–1, by the Franco-German War. Hope-Scott had bought a property on a hill with a southern aspect at Hyères, and on the 23rd of March, 1869, the Serjeant purchased a smaller *terrain* adjoining it. To the west lay the town of Hyères, the birth-place of Massillon, with its ancient ruined chateau crowning the height, and in the further distance extended vast ranges of higher hills, covered with pine-forests, while in the foreground the Church of Notre Dame de la Consolation stood out in picturesque contrast, dominating the plain that stretched some two or three miles to the Mediterranean. It was a lovely place with dry, sunny air, and pleasant French society. A picture of the Serjeant's life at this time, and of his enjoyment of this quiet retreat, as Hyères then was, may be gathered from his letters home.

To a son, December 17, 1866 : " We have all arrived safely at Hyères, and have got excellent apartments close to Hope-Scott, and also near the church, and I feel myself already better, and am able to walk about. The change of climate was not perceived until we got to Marseilles, and in sight of the Mediterranean. But on our road the foliage gradually changed, first vines, then mulberry-trees, then, as we got further south, olive-trees and cypresses, and as we drove from the station to the town of Hyères the hedges were covered with roses, and we finished up with palm-trees, ilexes, and oranges,

which are hanging quite ripe opposite my window. As to the
temperature, the difficulty we shall have will be to keep
ourselves sufficiently cool. I am now writing in a room, the
south windows of which I have closed with shutters, . . . and
the window which looks to the west is wide open, and C. is
sitting at it at work, and E. is at the table drawing a map
of the country. We were out this morning at Mass, and before
eight o'clock, the sun was hot, and the general feeling was as if
it were an early hour on a brilliant morning in June in England.
Mr. Hope-Scott has a very nice villa close by, and has bought
an adjacent estate, which he is preparing for building himself a
house. I walked out with him yesterday, and beneath our feet
were thyme, rue, lavender, and other sweet-smelling herbs, and
the hedges he has planted are made of cactuses and aloes,
similar to that which we have on our lawn in a tub. . . .
E. and I have just come in from a stroll upon the hill-
side ; the clearness of the atmosphere is extreme ; we look
hence over a flat plain covered with olives, terminated by the
sea at a distance of two miles or so, then, beyond that, the sea,
with French vessels of war and others, and in the distance the
Isles of Hyères. The sun is now setting, and the outline of
the distant hills is sharp as if it were cut out of paper. At
night the stars are far clearer than in England, and Jupiter, and
Mars, and Orion, and Sirius, are magnificent. We have not yet
tried our telescope upon them, but mean to do so, as our
windows look south, and east, and west."

To a daughter, December 20 : "To-day, E. and I, on
mules, in company with some French ladies and gentlemen,
made the ascent of the mountain Fenouillet. It took us two
hours to ascend, and two to return. The views of Hyères,
Toulon, the Islands, were magnificent, and there was not a
cloud in the sky. It was as hot as summer, and butterflies
were chasing one another at the top. Our road lay through
woods of cork-trees and pines, but lavender, myrtle, and
arbutus formed the underwood. We passed two parties
picnicing on the mountain-side, just as you would in the
height of summer."

To his wife, January 12, 1867 : "We have just come in
from a drive to Carqueiranne, a small village on the coast.
The drive is *à la corniche*, and most beautiful, on the land side
hills rising to a great height, covered with pines and olives ;
we got out and stood upon the shore watching the waves

breaking, as it was rather rough. The coast is rocky, and the rocks are a deep red, and the dark green of the maritime pine, which grows close down to the sea, contrasted most beautifully with the red rocks.

"There was a little rocky bay bordered by a copse of pine, most beautiful and picturesque, the perfection of a place for a

pic-nic. I can't draw it—but something like this. All this close to the water, and as I have said before, bright red and green. I enclose you some flowers which formed the carpet close to the sea."

To a daughter, January 1: "We had a very nice service at the church last night, the *Miserere*, followed by a sermon from the Curé, and then a *Te Deum*. The sermon was beautiful, just like a father talking to his children; he addressed all classes in turn, and amongst others, the visitors, to whom, he said, the town owed so much temporally by the prosperity they brought with them, and further, morally, by the good example they set by their attention to the duties of their religion. This was very complimentary, but I am sure we may return it, as the conduct of the people at Mass is most exemplary. There is an old gentleman, a Pole, constant in his attendance, and he always stretches out his arms, and holds them out during the Elevation. I can't say much for the organ music, the instrument is grand, but the music is sometimes in the style of 'Polly, put the kettle on.'"

Secular music, too, seems to have been on a precarious footing in those days at Hyères, judging from an account given by one of the party of a concert at the Casino.

January 21: "I went for a musical entertainment to be given by a M. Levasseur, a great performer from Paris. Well, we waited two hours, and no one arrived, but the French people didn't seem to mind. I had nearly lost patience, when in rushed a person saying M. Levasseur was taking his dinner at one of the hotels, and would not be long. Then another person said, M. Levasseur was at Nice, eighty miles off, but the French people sat chattering away. Then another person rushed in, saying he really *was* coming, so we waited and waited on. At last three people came in altogether, and said M. Levasseur was at Monaco, one hundred miles away, and hadn't the slightest notion of coming to Hyères. You see, I saw a farce instead of a musical entertainment."

The Serjeant to his wife, January 29: "Yesterday, Hope-Scott, Lady Victoria, Miss McKenzie, and Mary Monica [Hope-Scott] breakfasted with us at twelve o'clock, it being E.'s birth-day. On Sunday I attended a weekly conference of St. Vincent of Paul's Society. A dozen gentlemen—French, of course—prayers, reports of poor wanting relief, prayers again, and separation. When these French are good, they are very good. I was told that one gentleman, M. Castueil, dedicates every farthing he can earn to the poor. Cecy, too, has found a society of ladies who meet once a week at the Sœurs de la Charité to work for the poor."

To a daughter, February 5: "Yesterday E. and I went to see the drawing for the conscription, which took place with great formality at the town-hall, before the Préfet, the Mayor, &c. There were eighty young men of eighteen years of age, and twenty-five of them were to be drawn by lot, to serve seven years in the army. They were all present, and came up one at a time as their names were called out, and then, with their own hands, drew a number out of a glass vessel; the lowest numbers, that is, from one to twenty-five, were those whose fate it was to become soldiers, the higher numbers escaped.

"This was the process. The youth, having drawn a little packet out of the glass, handed it to the Préfet, who opened it, called out the number, and showed it to the assembled people. The anxiety both in the room and in the square adjoining was extreme, and when a lad had drawn his number, and was waiting to hear it declared, his look was sometimes most distressing, and when an unsuccessful number was announced, the disappointed countenance showed that the army is not a popular occupation; but by far the most affecting part was where a high number was drawn. The kissing and hugging of brothers and fathers and friends, which seemed as if it would never end, and the flushed face of the lad who had escaped, and then the rush through the crowd to get home to tell their families, were affecting in the extreme ; it was impossible to keep a dry eye. The grief of the unsuccessful was not so obvious ; that took place at home. The brother of our maid was one of them, and she says her mother has been crying ever since."

To a son, March 21 : "My dearest E., otherwise, you old rascal, you can take whichever epithet you please, especially as they mean the same thing. I miss you very much now that the weather has become so fine. Here is the *Louis Quatorze* steaming about the bay, and blazing away with her great guns by hours together, every shot as it touches the water throwing the water aloft in a pyramidal form as white as snow, and as each shot rebounds eight or ten times, it makes the great ship look as if it was surrounded by a fleet of little vessels and white sails, and whilst all this thundering is going on on the sea-side, Mr. Hope-Scott's Piedmontese are blasting away on land, so that you might imagine it was the Battle of Lissa and Custozza all in one. Then with the fine weather all the butter-flies have come out ; and now I dare say you phlegmatic people, who live in fog and snow, think I mean certain small insects with coloured wings which flit about the air sometimes in England. Well, I don't mean anything of the kind, quite the reverse. I mean creatures equally *papillonaceous*, but who confine themselves to the *terra firma*, and who walk about in a dignified manner with their wings, if they are wings, trailing after them on the ground, at the same time, especially as to their heads, they exhibit very beautiful and varied colours— all the colours of the rainbow in fact, and a great many more besides.

"Well, wonders will never cease. All yesterday workmen were engaged in pulling down a large bit of the wall of M. Denis' garden opposite our windows. We could not think what was going to happen. Well, you have heard of Birnam Wood coming to Dunsinane ? Here the stately palm-trees in M. Denis' garden, which used to wave their slim branches before the mistral, all at once begin to move : like giants they are making their way towards (not Dunsinane, but) the hole in the wall. The Emperor desired their presence at Paris to ornament the Great Exhibition, and all the skill of Hyères, including M. Boyer's, is engaged in trying to make them march.

"Haven't we had a jolly morning at Madame de Prailly's? Madame most politely invited me to walk to the *top* of the hill behind the house! I pleaded gout, and so chatted away with Madame de Beauregard in the house."

To his wife, 22 March: "The French gentry are coming out with the fine weather, and are disposed to be very kind to us. On Thursday I went to Mme. de Prailly's (at Costabelle), a jewel of a house, about three miles from Hyères. . . M. de Prailly is a retired judge, . . . they have a nice little chapel with the Blessed Sacrament; the views from the *terrasses* in the garden are magnificent, and the dresses of the company, which were undeniable, made the whole scene look like a picture of Watteau."

To the same, 14 April: "You and dear K. are, no doubt, getting on very happily in your Retreat. C. has been more or less in Retreat all Lent, as she spends a large part of her time in church, whilst I have been able to do little or nothing. On Friday, however, Miss McKenzie, Mary Monica, and little Minna, with C. in one carriage, and the Curé and I in another, drove out to the Hermitage to have Mass on the feast of the Seven Dolours of our Lady; Hope-Scott and Lady Victoria were not able to accompany us; however, we had a beautiful drive, and I served M. le Curé's Mass. After Mass he wished to call on Madame de Prailly, so I drove him there; we found her, scissors in hand, cutting flowers in her garden; she was, in fact, decorating the altar of her chapel, a small detached building in the garden. The French gentry here are very good religious people, and very agreeable; they receive certain days, in the afternoon, and then you meet everybody. As Catholics, and especially as friends of Hope-Scott, we are welcome everywhere."[1]

To a daughter, 13 February, 1868: "Our life here is a very quiet one. Mamma, who expected nothing, is enchanted with the place, and says this is really enjoying life. We are about half a mile from the church, but it is a beautiful walk. The first person moving in the house is C., she is up and out by herself at an early Mass, say seven o'clock; at eight a donkey and a little boy appear at our gate, and papa mounts in his light grey

---

[1] The French society included at one time or another the Duc de Luynes, Bishop Dupanloup, de Belcastel the Deputy, the brothers Télasne, the well-known scientists, MM. de Beauregard, de Gutchen, de Chambray, de Bonstettin, de Rocheplatte, de Bouiny, Chateaubriand, Mme. de Semainville, &c.

coat, a wide-awake hat, and a large white parasol, and wends
his way after C., whom he finds doing her meditation after
Mass. After papa has heard his Mass, he and C. accompany
one another home to breakfast, and on the way they meet first
E., and at some distance behind them mamma and C., who
prefer having their breakfast before their walk. Then papa
mounts his donkey again, and ascends to the heights behind
the villa to see the works proceeding in Mr. Hope-Scott's
'terrain,' and after an hour's loitering in the fresh air and hot
sun, returns to the villa to find mamma at a little table with
her colours, completing a sketch. At one o'clock we dine.
Then in comes Miss McKenzie, and dear Mary Monica, or C.
and C. are off again to pay a visit at the church. All this time
our windows are open, and the sun is pouring in upon us,
accompanied, however, by a cool, refreshing wind. Papa
generally stays at home in the afternoon, as does E., and there
he may be seen stooping over a map which he is laboriously
completing, while papa gets through his multitudinous correspondence. At five we begin to shut our windows, and as it gets
dark a wood fire is not disagreeable ; then we read and work
and say our Rosary, and at seven we have our supper, and soon
after nine we begin to prepare for rest."

To J. R. Hope-Scott, 19 March : " Your hill-side has lost its
liveliness since the tall grey figure with the white parasol is no
longer visible as I ride to Mass in the morning."

E. Badeley to the Serjeant, 19 February : " I was ex-
tremely glad to receive your letter and to hear also from
Hope that you were so much better. By this time I hope you
have shaken off all the traces of your ailments, and thrown
physic and the gout to the winds. . . . Alas! poor Justice Shee
is gone! He expired this morning, as I understand, about
half-past eight. . . . All persons who knew him must lament
his loss, and I most bitterly deplore it for his family as well as
for his friends and the public. . . . It was very kind in Mrs.
Bellasis to call upon me before she went, but I dread to think
how long it may be before I see her or you again. You are
lucky in having such excellent neighbours at Hyères, and I
suppose you will stay there till the warm weather thaws you
apart."

The Serjeant to a daughter, 25 April: "Dear Badeley's death
some one would have told you of. He was about my own age, we
had been friends for thirty years, and he was very fond of us ;

when mamma left England to come here, she went to see him ;
he kissed her hand, and said he should never see her again.
He had successive fits of paralysis without pain, during about a
fortnight, and then died whilst Hope-Scott was sitting by his
side talking to him."

To the same, 3 May : "The whole town were up at the
Hermitage yesterday to bring down in procession the statue
of our Lady to St. Louis. The day was brilliant and every one
went, and it was a very pretty sight, and the statue, beautifully
dressed, and with a crown on, was carried on the shoulders of
young girls, and is placed aloft behind the altar."

To another daughter, 16 January, 1869 : "Now you must
fancy me sitting by your bed-side in the chair of your angel
guardian, whilst I report the progress we have made. . . . At
half-past two we got to the Hyères station. . . . Then we drove
along the lower road, turned sharp round up by the Villa Favart,
and then as usual galloped up the hill between the rose hedges.
. . . We had not been in long before I saw a slight figure in blue
coming up the road, running up, I should say. The first question
was, 'How is dear C.?' I was rejoiced to give a good account of
you. Then we must come down to tea immediately, and
dine with them [the Hope-Scotts] afterwards, which we did.
. . . This morning we saw Dr. Laur and the little lame
priest ; the sacristan shook me by both hands, and was greatly
pleased to hear that you were better, and I made him put up
two candles, one for our safe arrival, and one for your complete
recovery. . . . Whilst I am writing in comes M. Bernard. . . .
He means to say Mass for you on the Purification (as I understood him), at the Hermitage. . . . The sea is shining brightly
and we have been sitting with our windows open, the almond-
trees are in full bloom, and everything looks fresh, for we have
had plenty of rain. I have been up into your room, and the
view from the balcony is as beautiful as ever. Pompey is
waiting for the letters, so adieu, dearest C. I think of you
all day long. . . . God bless you, and may our Lady protect
you.

To the same, March 2 : "For the last three days we
have had one of our Hyères hurricanes, but the villa stood
firm, and even your lofty cabin (now R.'s) withstood it ; the sea
was white with foam, and we saw the spray dashing over the
isthmus of Giens and sweeping all across the Pesquier, until it
was finally lost among the pine-trees of the Pinède.

"The day before the wind began, we had a most successful expedition to Fenouillet, the party were mamma, Lady Henry Kerr, Hon. Mrs. Hope (a widow, sister-in-law of Mr. Hope-Scott), in a carriage, with myself, and two Miss Hopes on mules, and Lord Henry, Commander Hope, and Clara on foot ; the air was mild, and it was not too hot. We had our picnic in the usual snug corner, and, afterwards, the more enterprising of the party, of whom I was one, mounted to the top, whilst mamma and Miss Hope sketched below. The view was very beautiful, and the weather so mild that butterflies and lady-birds by the score were sporting themselves on the summit. We have begun the month of St. Joseph as usual. . . . On Sunday last we had a sermon and a *quête* by the Bishop of Constantine, for his orphanages of poor Arab children left destitute by the death of their parents from the famine in Algiers. It was a fine sermon and a successful collection, and the Bishop himself was very like the prints of St. Ignatius. We still have Archbishop Errington here, and next Sunday we are expecting Archbishop Manning for a day or two. Every one is interested about you, and all ask after you, and we are told over and over again that they miss you sadly in the church. . . . We have had one or two visits from M. le Curé, the last time bringing with him the Prédicateur, who seems a very earnest man as well as a good preacher ; he spares himself no trouble, and has even proposed to come to our meetings of the Conference of St. Vincent of Paul. . . . I hope this will find you still improving, . . . but I know you are in good hands, as well as in the hands of God, and under the protection of our Lady and St. Joseph, so I am very happy about you.

To the same, March 12 : "The weather has been rather cold, and we have had a violent storm of wind, such as we had last year, only on the present occasion it has lasted for ten days, and the tiles and chimney-pots were flying about in every direction. . . . We are down at Mass always as usual, that is to the half-past nine Mass after our breakfast, unless when we go to Communion, and then we generally breakfast at Lord Henry Kerr's. . . . When we return home we have our little service to St. Joseph. . . . Clara has set up a little altar in the window of our dining-room over the fire-place. . . . Archbishop Manning has been here, and Mr. Hope-Scott gave an entertainment, a grand breakfast, in fact, at the Hôtel d'Orient, and I give you below the places of the guests.

One of the Vicaires was absent, Abbé Arnaud, giving a retreat in the Presqu'île. Everything went off remarkably well, and Archbishop Manning went off the next day for England. . . . We are going to be very grand indeed. Queen Christina of Spain is here, at M. Denis' house in the Place de la Rade, and the Queen of Prussia has been here for the last two days, and, it is supposed, is going to take the Duc de Luynes' house."

To the same, October 15: "Continue to pray for me as I will for you, and so we may continue to shake hands over the intervening space, as I trust, most effectually. God bless you, my darling. Have you read the *Life of the Curé d'Ars?* His character is very attractive to me, especially his imperturbable modesty and slight opinion of himself."

To the same, January 26, 1870: "This week we have had Mr. Garside on his way from Rome . . . and have had from him, as you may suppose, a full account of his stay in the Holy City and of the magnificent assemblies he witnessed. He goes back charmed with everything. . . . Our villa is really becoming very pretty, we occupy the new dining-room and it is very comfortable, and the entrance-hall (formerly the wood-house and hay-loft), with its glass doors and steps down into the garden, is a great success; the principal ornament of it is the painting of our Blessed Lady and the Infant Jesus, which we had at the Lawn, and which gives a Catholic character to the house, and greatly pleases the priests. Of course you heard that we had the house regularly blest by M. le Curé, accompanied by M. Gasquet and M. Bernard."

"Shortly after our arrival at Hyères," the Serjeant writes, "I began to be incommoded by a small wound in the foot caused by cutting the nail; it got rapidly worse, and I was soon unable to put my foot to the ground for four months. . . . I no sooner began to go out after so long a confinement, than I was seized with an attack of bronchitis, which once more laid me

up, and detained me at Hyères up to the 31st of May, 1870.
I got safely to Paris, and thence to Boulogne, where, however, I
was reduced to great extremities, so much so that I received
Extreme Unction from the hands of Father Forbes." He had
sufficiently recovered by the 30th of June to cross the Channel,
and reach home safely.

The following extracts from letters refer to this time of
sickness.

J. R. Hope-Scott to the Serjeant, November 2, 1869: "Yours
of the 30th disappoints me. I was in hopes from your previous
letters that you were rallying quicker, and did not realize how
unwell you have been. . . . As to spirits, I know too well their
fluctuations to treat depression as more than a transient evil.
Gout has its special trials in this way, and during our great
Shrewsbury anxieties I made it a rule to think of them several
times a day, and by comparing my impressions in different
states of body and mind, to strike an average between cheerfulness and misery. There is a still higher method, no doubt,
but this you know better than myself."

Dr. Newman to J. R. Hope-Scott, March 3, 1870: "After
writing a conversational letter to Bellasis yesterday, I heard
at night so sad an account, which I had not anticipated, of
his pain and weakness and want of sleep, that I not only
was distressed that it had gone, and felt that it would harass
him to receive a second letter so soon, and, as he would
anticipate, as unreasonable as the former. Therefore I enclose
with this a few lines to him, which you can let him have when
you think right.

"I do not undervalue the seriousness of your first letter
about him, and have had him constantly in my mind, but I did
not contemplate his pain, or his sudden decline. I thought it
would be a long business, but now I find that the complaint is
making its way.

"What a severe blow it must be to you! but to me, in my
own way, it is very great too, though in a different way; for,
though I am not in his constant society as you are, he has long
been *pars magna* of this place, and he has, by his various acts
of friendship through a succession of years, created for himself
a presence in my thoughts, so that the thought of being without
him carries with it the sense of a void, to which it is difficult
to assign a limit. Three *æquales* I shall have lost—Badeley,
H. Bowden, and Bellasis; and such losses seem to say that

I have no business here myself. It is the penalty of living, to
lose the great props of life. . . . I shall, I trust, say two Masses
a week for him. He is on our prayer lists. What a vanity is
life! how it crumbles under one's touch. I hope you are
getting strong and that this does not weigh too heavily on you."

J. R. Hope-Scott to Dr. Newman, March 6th: "I received
yours yesterday, but withhold the enclosure for Bellasis, as
I think it might do him harm. . . . Masses and prayers
I am sure he has many, and I know how grateful he is
for your deep interest in him. . . . Should he be able to get
out, I hope for more progress; but, with slight exceptions, he
has now been confined to the house for weeks. However, his
patience helps him greatly, and when, as lately he has often
been, free from pain, his cheerfulness revives, and with it his
interest in the works he has undertaken, and the subjects
which have long interested him.

"I am sure that the dedication of your new work to him
affects him, as that of your poems did Badeley, in a very
soothing way. Few have such extensive means of testifying
to their friendship as you have." [1]

"Tell me your style and title," Dr. Newman had written to
the Serjeant, December 5, 1869, "you will still let me put your
name, won't you, to the beginning of my book? I suppose it
will be my last. I have not finished it. I have written in all
(good or bad) five constructive books. . . . This, I think, has
tried me most of all. I have written and re-written it more
times than I can count. I have now got up to my highest
point. I mean, I could not do better, did I spend a century on
it—but then, it may be 'bad is the best.'" [2]

---

[1] *Memoirs*, ii. pp. 236, 237. "What you tell me of his feeling about my
Dedication," Dr. Newman wrote, February 2, 1873, to Mrs. Bellasis, "is, as you
may suppose, very grateful to me, and most surprising. It does but show how true
and thorough a friend he was to me, and I bless God for putting it into my heart to
do a simple, natural act of gratitude towards him in memory of his many, many
services to me, which I little thought, when I did it, would receive from him so great
a reward as he has bestowed upon me in the words he used conversing with you."
This dedication (in the *Grammar of Assent*) runs: "To Edward Bellasis, Serjeant-at-
Law, in memory of a long, equable, sunny friendship, in gratitude for continual
kindnesses shown to me, for an unwearied zeal in my behalf, for a trust in me which
has never wavered, and for a prompt and effectual succour and support in times of
special trial, from his affectionate J. H. N."

[2] He wrote about it to the Serjeant, August 1, 1868: "I have my own subject,
one I have wished to do all my life, one which I fear would not interest you and
Hope-Scott at all, one which, if I did, I should, of course, think it the best thing I
had done, being, on the contrary, perhaps the worst. I have the same fidget about

The Serjeant to a daughter, March 7, 1870: "I must
send you a line to tell you how your dear, affectionate letter
cheered my heart. To have had such children, and to find
them clinging to me in my old age with such affection as
you display, is indeed a reward to me. I know my malady is
critical, and may take a bad turn, but I am surrounded by
everything that can be desired."

To another, March 21: "Although I am discouraged
from writing letters, how can I resist sending a line to you,
whom, whilst I think of, and of your never failing love for
me, the tears come into my eyes. I hear you have been
praying for me, and I thank you and your whole party for
your goodness, and I hope you will include in your prayers
that I may be brought into good dispositions for death, if
that be God's will; this, indeed, I am more anxious about
than about my recovery, pray that I may have a more perfect
love of God and truer contrition. . . . As I cannot go to church,
the Curé came up here to hear my confession, and yesterday
the Blessed Sacrament was brought to me, and my five children
and the party from the convent accompanied It. C. put up
a very pretty little altar, and the priest who brought our Lord
was the Pole who is like M. Plauchu. I do not remember
whether I told you that, fearing that I might be left with
none but French priests, I requested Mr. [now Monsignor]
Fenton before he left to hear my general confession, so as to
be as much prepared as possible. Dear C., I may not be able
to write much to you, but whether I do or not, remember
that my thoughts are always with you . . . and to see you
all, whether in the world or out of it, holding firm to the
Catholic Church is the greatest joy to me. . . . Now I must say
Adieu in its noblest sense."

After reaching England, he writes from the Lawn, Putney,
to his daughters in religion, on the 9th of July: "My
thoughts have never ceased to wander, even in the worst
periods of my illness, to my two darlings at Mayfield, and to
their prayers, and Communions, and watchings for me before
the Blessed Sacrament. That I am here shows how effectual
they must have been, and I beg you not only to accept my

it as a horseman might feel about a certain five feet stone wall which he passes by
means of a gate every day of his life, yet is resolved he must and will some day clear
—and at last breaks his neck in attempting. It is on 'Assent, Certitude, Proof.'
I have no right to look to having time to do anything, but if I have, it must be this."

M

affectionate thanks, but to give them to all your community, who, I know, have joined with you in anxiety for me. The great difficulty in getting home from Boulogne lay in the risk of crossing, as sickness in my then state, would have been hazardous, but it so fell out that we had a perfectly fair passage, the only calm day for some time before and since, and this I attribute to you. . . . I have been once or twice into the garden ; however, I keep myself as quiet as possible, seeing almost no one. Father Gallwey came to see me, and I had a very nice talk with him, tending to give me that confidence, which you remember, dear M., I was deficient in at Hyères.

"Mr. M'Enery said Mass for us on Thursday and Saturday ; it was five months since I had heard Mass. . . . We shall now get Mass regularly twice a week. Now my dear, good, loving children, Adieu, I send you both my blessing. I don't think of you as absent, you are always present to the mind and heart of your loving father."

Dr. Newman wrote to him the same day : "I congratulate you with all my heart, and all yours, and so do we all, at your having, through God's mercy, arrived at length at your own calm and green home. I am too much of a John Bull to like Hyères, or any foreign place, except in the light of a medicinal necessity. In that light I will not be ungrateful to it."

The winter of 1870–1 was spent by the Serjeant at Torquay, and at his new house in Prince of Wales' Terrace, Kensington, since Paris was at this time besieged by the Prussians, and the road to the south of France was not available, the railways being in many places taken up, and the country occupied by the enemy.

To a daughter March 18, 1871 : "I think it would have been a disadvantage that I should have been absent from home at the time when your brothers are starting on their several courses. I like to hear when they come home at night what they have been doing, and give them my advice, which I could not so well have given them at a distance. They are very regular and punctual ; after nine in the morning the house is quite quiet until six, when it becomes noisy enough again. . . . We like our house very much, it is very warm, very comfortable, and very quiet, and with a church (that of the Carmelites) close by, and Kensington Gardens at hand, it suits all of us."

At the beginning of April he was again attacked by

bronchitis and sciatica, which lasted till the 30th of May. On April 21st, he wrote to Rev. Mother Connelly, at St. Leonard's : "I hope you will pray for me, not that I may be relieved from pain, for I willingly suffer that, but that I may be confirmed in the love of God, so as to use that as my motive in obtaining true contrition and perseverance. Mamma makes a most excellent nurse, and persists that I am getting better, but I reserve my acquiescence till my pulse gets below 90. I lead a very quiet life. Father Clare visits me from time to time, and brings me the Blessed Sacrament at midnight." In September the Serjeant visited his son-in-law, Dr. Charlton, at Newcastle, and Hope-Scott, at Abbotsford, for the last time.

To Lady H. Kerr, October 17 : "I am about to depart for Hyères, but I cannot expect that it will be again to me what it has been, for I shall miss the kind faces of your family."

To a son, November 8, from Hyères : "After two or three days of exquisite weather, we have had three days of downfall of rain, to the great joy of every one. Our cistern is full and our garden thoroughly watered, but the rain has driven the flies in, they watch every opportunity of entering, and, when they do get in, they bite. I am sadly at a loss for such an expert *chasseur* as you to help me to exterminate them, however, there are no mosquitoes, that is a comfort. We are revelling in figs, fresh figs ; they peel beautifully, and C. is charged with having made the following slip in expressing her admiration :

> From a Tartar's skull they had stripp'd the flesh,
> As you *feel* a *pig* when the fruit is fresh."

To the same, December 7, at this time studying at the Heralds' College : "Genealogy seems to me to be greatly undervalued in England at this time, and it is no credit to us that it is so. All nations that have, or had, any pretence to civilization, have respected and preserved their family genealogies ; even at this time, in all Eastern countries, family pedigrees are preserved with far more care and accuracy than they are by us, and it is not creditable to us. The cause of this is, in part, that our society is now so mixed up with *nouveaux riches*, who have no pedigrees, and many of whom hardly know who their grandfathers were, that there is a large body of persons who profess to be wholly indifferent to them, and, as in the House of Commons, laugh at any allusion to genealogy, and its handmaid, heraldry. Nevertheless, the preservation of the records of families has a high moral object, it tends to preserve a respect for our forefathers, and to induce a disposition to avoid anything which could bring discredit upon an honourable race. Moreover, the known alliances of families keep up a friendly sentiment between them, sometimes for many generations; to abandon, therefore, or to neglect, such means as there are, of preserving these records, is a shameful barbarism. Do not suppose, therefore, that in entering, if you do enter, a College having charge of this important subject, that you are occupying yourself with a useless matter; properly attended to, it has a great moral effect upon a people, and the question is, how the busy, working world, engrossed in amassing wealth, can be brought to think so. I think it may be done, but it must be done by a body having authority, like the College of Arms, and it ought not to be left to the speculations of booksellers, many of whom, as is well known, will insert in their catalogues anything that is paid for.

"I say, the world must be let known by some means, that there is a place where their family trees can be accurately preserved according to established rules, and at trifling cost, and I wish Garter would do something to have it brought into notice, so as to avoid, however, the appearance of touting for business."

To a daughter, December 15, 1871: "I fancy I can see you with your magisterial finger up, and your grave tutorial face, and the little ones in front of you in great awe; I wish I was one of your class just for a little bit. . . . Mamma and C. have just gone out on to Mr. Hope-Scott's hill to choose shrubs and flowers for transplanting into our garden, which he has given us leave to do. . . . We have ordered a Mass on the 20th for Lady Victoria, the day of her death, and we mean to notify it to all who knew her. . . . We had the Curé and M. Bernard to dine with us, and since that, M. Planchu and M. Arnaud, and C. gave them very nice dinners, quite equal to those entertainments which you used to give on the Boulevard, when the cook kept her baby in the kitchen drawer. . . . I have got a puzzle for you: St. Alphonsus says in a passage I came upon a day or two since, that of all love, paternal love is the strongest; now I think I have checkmated you."

To a daughter, 21 January, 1872: "Mr. Demay, the artist here, is said to have made a good photograph of me, *un peu sévère*, M. le Curé says, but I send you a copy."

This was the last likeness taken of the Serjeant. Of the

various portraits of him, the two McClises, in pencil (1829) and in sepia respectively, come first in point of time. McClise took various pictures of the Serjeant's family, as has been already mentioned, and it is to the picture of the latter's mother that Edmund Lodge (Norroy) refers, August 28, 1828: "I shall be very glad to find, when you return, that McClise's masterly drawing is not yet despatched to Carisbrooke. M. L. is most anxious to see it, and we here had only a glance at it, but enough to convince me that Vandyke could have done but little more."

Of the 1846 portrait by Knight, the Serjeant wrote to his wife at the time it was taken: "I have had three long sittings to Mr. Knight, and he is obviously taking infinite pains. I have not myself seen it yet, but Robert (no great judge, perhaps) saw it when he went to fetch my wig away, and he says he never saw such a likeness. Mr. Knight, however, says that he is convinced he shall not please you with any likeness of me in a wig."[1] And he says to his mother, April 24, 1846: "You may have the opportunity of seeing the portrait of 'Mr. Serjeant Bellasis' in the Exhibition of the Royal Academy, which you know has been some time painting by J. P. Knight, R.A. All agree that it is an excellent likeness, and it is certainly a very beautiful picture." It did

1846.

not, however, with its display of robes, quite please the Serjeant's own preference for a quieter style of portraiture.

To a son, February 23, 1872: "I had a visit yesterday from M. de Bonstettin. He said he had been a *libre-penseur* all his life, but some time since saw that that *débouchait en rien*, that the Protestant clergy in Switzerland were them-

---

[1] In November, 1844, he wrote to his mother that he had had to go with the Judges, in full forensic costume, to dine at Goldit M. his clerk having to accompany him to hold up his train. "This is somewhat amusing." He adds, "I remember being with you at the Lord Mayor's feast some twenty years ago, and seeing the scarlet-robed lawyers with their long wigs, and expecting to have to take my place amongst them."

selves *libre-penseurs*, and yet they had raised a perfect storm against him and his wife for exercising what they all claim a right to exercise themselves, *libre examen.*

"Madame de Bonstettin was an active Protestant, at the head of the Protestant charities, &c., at Thun. They arrived at their conclusions quite independently of each other; the Baron by distaste at the want of logic and conclusiveness in the Protestant teachers, who disagreed among themselves, Madame by her own reading."

To a daughter, March 4th : "We have established a beautiful St. Joseph's altar in the dining-room, and we have 'Hail, holy Joseph' regularly after dinner, and before family prayers. . . . I know I have your prayers, particularly the Hail Mary at night you promised me, and to which I attribute the good health I have had for the last four months."

On occasion of a serious impending loss to him, especially now in his old age, in his eldest son's call to the religious state, his wife received the following sympathetic letter at Easter from Dr. Newman : "Thank you for your most kind and touching letter which has just come. I can believe (I have no right to say I can estimate) how much you and the Serjeant must suffer. It is the price you pay for your having brought up your children so religiously ; and be sure that He who makes you pay so dearly will repay it to you abundantly in His own blessed way, so that you yourself will acknowledge that it is good to have been so afflicted. . . . Oh, that I could say anything to comfort you and the dear Serjeant, but you need a comfort greater than human. I can only pray earnestly that He who, after a time of sorrow, gladdened His disciples with the sight of Him on Easter morning, may in like manner, even here below, give you the fulness of that heavenly consolation which alone can support you under your trial."

The party returned from Hyères in the May of 1872, the Serjeant going straight from Dover to St. Leonard's to see his two daughters, nuns there at the Convent of the Holy Child. In June he visited Dr. Newman, and St. Ignatius' day, at the close of July, saw him at the breakfast given by the Jesuit Fathers in Mount Street, London, where he met Archbishop Manning, Bishop Danell, Mr. Monsell (Lord Emly), Mr. Macmullen, Mr. Garside, Father Morris, S.J., and other friends. In August he visited his daughter, Mrs. Bowring, at Torquay.

To his daughter Clara, he wrote August 20: "So to-morrow is your birthday, and this comes with the most affectionate love and best wishes of dear papa. . . . How much I appreciate all your kindness and attention to me, and hope you may never be without similar affectionate regard when you get old and want it."

On the 13th of October, St. Edward's day, and the eve of his own birthday, he wrote to a daughter: "We are now really beginning to prepare for our southern journey. . . . I groan, however, over the absence of my dear Monica, and our diminished party at Hyères; we talk, indeed, of letting dear H. come out for six weeks at Christmas, but there are difficulties about it, as we doubt whether he could find his way by himself. . . . The boys are gone down to Westminster Abbey to visit the tomb of St. Edward and to pray for me thereat, if the authorities will allow it; fortunately, however, the Saint can be reached without their leave. I shall not be able to visit St. Leonard's again before we go, except in spirit; and that is a visit I often make, my darling daughter, and that with never failing affection. . . . Tell dear M. that I congratulate her on the progress she seems to be making in her studies, especially in the science of astronomy, for which I perceive the convent account contains a charge of 9d. for the half-year.

"Monday morning. The post has just brought me in a host of letters from my dear children. My grateful thanks for yours."

On the 19th of November he left for Hyères, and in January, 1873, his wife wrote to England: "Mr. S. gives papa *séances* of two or three hours at a time; he begins his pedigree with Noah and then *après moi le Déluge*. . . . Then Mr. Singer calls and asks Mr. S. to read the Bible with him twice a week to counterbalance the Popery. Papa is delight-fully well thus far, he goes out into the pretty garden, and is amused by the green waxy-looking frogs who disport them-selves on the aloe leaves; he makes calls, and is the general legal adviser of his compatriots and of the Beauregard trainer, who rejoices in the name of Benjamin Hutchins, and who wishes to marry a *Marseillaise* and become a good Catholic all at once! both (especially the former step) being unsmooth in their course, through red tapeism and the fatal lack of a baptismal register in a parish church of old England. Benjamin is a right good fellow, and says he quite understands how Protestantism *derailed* (his own expression for got off the rails) in the sixteenth century, and how entirely he quite intends to go to Heaven by the *regular train* or the *old family coach.* These last, his own words, are quite consistent with his calling as head-groom. Papa is immensely interested in poor Benjamin and his love affairs, and he hopes to weedle the Mayors of Marseilles and Hyères into a swift concurrence. C. is reading aloud a novel at my elbow, Miss B. is nodding, and Papa deep in the arms of Morpheus."

The Serjeant, however, one Sunday, with a hot sun and cold wind, stayed out in the garden too long, showing the frogs to a friend of his, Mr. Dénis, who had called; he took a severe chill and seemed to have a presentiment that it was *le commencement de la fin,* as he put it. On Wednesday, the 22nd, he recurred to his great desire to obtain a real, personal love for God as his Father and Benefactor, and expressed a fear that he had no such love. He spoke also to his wife about his prayers, how the first thing he did was to thank God for his preservation during the night, then he thanked Him for His great mercies, and prayed for his children that they might have such temporal blessings as were needed, and above all be preserved in the Faith and have the gift of perseverance. He had their likenesses brought to him, and kissed them one by one with an expression of affection for each. Then he said : "We have nothing further to say upon our worldly affairs. I hope dear R. will replace me." Father Harkin, an old Canadian priest, wintering in Hyères, called about 3 p.m. the same day, and said to the family that he had seen many deaths, and had no doubt about the Serjeant's approaching dissolution : with some misgiving he left him, but only to go and tell the Curé (*Doyen* Gabriel) that the Serjeant ought to receive the last Sacraments without delay.

Father Harkin returned at 8 a.m. next day, and heard his confession. At 10 a.m., the Curé came with a procession, headed by the cross, and gave him the Viaticum and Extreme Unction. "I am surprised I do not feel terrified," he said to the Curé, "not at all."[1] Thursday passed quietly, the Serjeant was

---

[1] In 1833 he had written : "We fear death, whilst perhaps those who love us, and are gone before, are hoping, probably praying, for our release and reunion with them ; they know the folly of our fears, and the amount and nature of the happiness from which we are hanging back, and would rejoice to see us in the act of death."

cheerful, and in submitting as a patient to orders from his daughter, he made use against her of an old joke about a Westminster magistrate's language, *i.e.*, "when she says what she says, that's what she always says."[1] Now and again he repeated some pious ejaculations. This was up till 1.30 on Friday morning. He "seemed to be without suffering," his daughter wrote, "and before he became unconscious he said he had no pain at all, he only felt very weak, and we hope this continued to the end, as he never complained. Once he said he felt an oppression at the heart, and that was all." Dr. Griffiths remained to the end. At 1.30 a.m. on the morning of Friday the 24th, his daughter, noticing that he kept looking towards the door, asked him if he wanted anything? and then he said, "Yes," his last word. So she somehow bethought her of the Apostolic blessing, and Father Harkin was sent for, but could not be roused, as there was no bell at the Pension du Louvre where he was staying. This was fortunate, as the Father had not the requisite faculties, so no further delay ensued in sending for M. le Curé, who arrived at 3.30 a.m. "We do not know whether he heard M. le Curé speaking to him," says the same eye-witness, "but mamma thinks he did. About 5 a.m., while his daughter was invoking the names of Jesus, Mary, and Joseph, and making the sign of the Cross over him with holy water, the Serjeant opened his eyes "with a look of joy and surprise," or, as his wife says elsewhere, he regarded a "corner of the room with an indescribable expression of awe and wonder. Then the eyelids closed, and the dark veil of death clouded the loved countenance." Two brief sighs, and he was gone. It was the 24th of January, the same date as his father's death seventy-one years before, at the age of seventy-one years, he himself being seventy-two years old.

"What a beautiful, happy death, just like his life," wrote Mrs. Allies, "that look when his soul seemed to see Heaven opening to him. . . . We never shall have such another true, kind, affectionate friend as he was." "Yes, dear E., as you say, 'a great soul is gone,'" wrote Miss McKenzie, "and oh, what a sweet soul it was! so gentle, so loving, so true and

---

[1] "What a privilege for you, dear, above all the others," wrote Miss McKenzie. "to assist at his last moments, and well you deserved it. You have been a faithful daughter, and how he loved and admired you! how thankful you must feel to have added to the happiness and comfort of such a father."

faithful, so persuasive and powerful. I never knew any one like him."

"To me," Father Bittleston said, "the withdrawal of that visible light, that sweet face, . . . the very soul of charity . . is a joy the less in the darkening shadows of this poor life." "A countenance," wrote Lady Henry Kerr, "that always brought sunshine, and a voice that confirmed it. . . . I cannot quite bear to think that I shall never enjoy both again—but yes, please God, we shall in our heavenly home. . . . It would have pleased you to have heard what our two S.J.'s wrote to us, showing how fully they, and all around them at St. Beuno's, appreciated both the blessedness and the loss."

"He presented a type of character," Father Garside said in the columns of the *Tablet*, "of which the value can hardly be over-estimated. He had all the freshness of youth, tempered with the mellow wisdom of age. It would be difficult, however, to describe him to strangers on account of the balance and harmonious proportions of those qualities which constituted his excellence. Salient angles and features are easy to reproduce, but not symmetry. They who knew him intimately will understand me when I say that the recollection will long remain vivid and precious of his spotless integrity, his transparent openness, his cheerful humility, his charity of word and deed, and that refined geniality of manner which was the artless outcome of what may be truly called, a 'delicate' soul."

"He died at Hyères," wrote Hope-Scott, during his own last illness, and in the *Golden Manual* that the Serjeant had given him as his godfather in Confirmation, "leaving an example to us all." That is a note struck by two testimonies to the Serjeant's worth, the last to be cited out of some hundred and fifty received after his death. "His uprightness and goodness and simplicity were wonderful, and an example to us all," wrote Archbishop Manning, from York Place. "In him I have lost a dear friend, whom I shall ever affectionately remember, and especially at the altar. . . . May God console you all!"

"I have just got your letter," said Dr. Newman, "so very sad, yet so very joyful. For is it not joyful to know that a soul so dear to God is at length in His glorious presence, and in His eternal embrace? He has now the reward of His long faithfulness to God's service, and assuredly not one of his many good deeds, not any day of his lifelong devotion, not any one of the many services he has done to religion, not any part of his care for his family, of his kindness to his friends, of his dutifulness to the Church, of his zeal for the faith, no aspect of his bright and beautiful example, but is now having its full reward.

"I know my pain is nothing to yours, and those about you, but I feel deeply I have lost one of my best, my most constant, dearest friends. Still it is a great consolation, beyond words, to think that I have such a friend with God, who, I am sure, still loves me (though he is now cleansed from all sin and infirmity, and I am still encompassed by both), that I have such an intimate friend so near to my Saviour and my Judge. You, my dear Mrs. Bellasis, must feel the bitter and the sweet a hundred times more intensely than I. You have an irreparable loss, but you have an inestimable gain. You have a memory which will cheer and support you through life, and will gladden you in that hour, whenever it shall be, when Divine Mercy shall call you hence. As for me, I can only trust and pray that when my own time comes, I may be found as ready to leave the world as he has been."

"God has been very good to us all," he wrote the same day to the Serjeant's youngest daughter at school, "in letting so good, so devout, so loving a soul . . . remain so long here, when his place was prepared in Heaven. He was one of the best men I ever knew. His loss is irreparable, but I bless and praise God, and you, my dear child, must do so too, that he has been allowed to live so long. It is your great consolation that he has lived long enough for you to know him. You have a thought for your whole life, a beautiful, soothing thought. The sorrow is for a time, but the consolation will be lasting.

"Praise God, my dear child, for all things. All He does is good and loving. He will give you abundant grace and comfort for all your affliction. He will never leave you, nor forsake you." "God can make up for every loss," he wrote again, "and can be more to us than all friends." "For myself," he wrote on

Candlemas day, " though I have felt greater pain than I have
felt ever since we lost Father Joseph Gordon, in 1853, still I
could not really grieve, and though I have said Mass for the dear
Serjeant's soul, and hope to say more Masses, yet I cannot say
them as really believing in my heart that he needs them, any
more than I could say them from my heart for dear Mary Anne
Bowden, whom I had known from a child, and who died a few
years ago, a nun at Westbury. Father Ambrose feels the same,
and I am sure it is the feeling of all of us, so deeply impressed
is our imagination with the conviction of his fitness for the
heavenly Paradise.

" In like manner, when I wrote to Mamo, fearing her father
[Mr. Hope-Scott] might be thrown back by the tidings of his
great loss, she answers to the same effect, that the Serjeant's
beautiful death has overcome all his natural grief and dejection
at his bereavement."

Dr. Newman then repeats, even more feelingly, the prayer of
his letter of the 27th of January : " May God's mercy grant
that I may be prepared to go, when my time comes, at least
with some measure of the hope, love, and peace which have so
remarkably shone forth in him."

On Monday, January 27, the coffin was carried in procession
to the church. It was a calm, sunny day, and the building was
full of friends, praying for him. The procession was headed
by the cross, carried by M. l'Abbé Bernard (now Curé of
Hyères), the Serjeant's three elder sons following as chief
mourners.[1] The *cortège* proceeded to St. Louis, the grand old
church of the Cordeliers. Here the obsequies took place, the
remains being subsequently placed in the vault of the Bona Mors
chapel, awaiting decision as to their final resting-place. On the
21st of February, the interment took place at Hyères cemetery.
Mrs. Maxwell-Scott wrote, January 31, 1873, that her father,
Mr. Hope-Scott, " is much pleased at the thought that the dear

---

[1] Of the Serjeant's youngest son, at this time away at school, a friend wrote :
" Poor dear fellow, he did after the first blow feel so sad and lonely, but Dr. Newman
took him near to himself quite paternally, and the dear boy amiably accepted the
consolations afforded, and was made quite happy by all the Fathers at the Oratory."
" He is in our house," one of the latter wrote, " in the room opposite the tribune
over St. Philip's chapel." He wrote himself on the day of the funeral : " Father
Newman is so kind to me. I was in his room all the morning on Monday. He told
me that what God does is always for the best, and that papa will do us a great deal
more good by pleading our cause in Heaven than he could ever have done on earth.
He and all the Fathers say Mass for papa every day. He has given me R.'s room in
the Oratory, and I dine with them every day."

Serjeant should be buried at Hyères. . . . He says his brightest recollections, of late years, of our dear Serjeant have been connected with Hyères. It is a happy thought that he should lie in a Catholic country, and in a place where he was so much beloved."

In 1888, the tomb, with many others, had to be transferred to the new cemetery, a little further east of the town than the old one, in a quiet valley with a south-eastern prospect out to seawards. Round the plinth a brief epitaph is inscribed :

ORA PRO ANIMA

EDUARDI BELLASIS,

SERVIENTIS AD LEGEM,

QUI, EXIMIE ERGA DEUM HOMINESQUE CHARITATIS

NOBIS IN EXEMPLUM DATUS,

A SPE LONGA ET DESIDERIO

AD IPSA IMMORTALITATIS PRÆMIA,

DIE JAN. 24, 1873, ÆTAT. 73,

SINE DOLORE AC LÆTUS TRANSIVIT.

THE END.

APPENDIX A. (pp. 1, 2.)

THE earliest deeds in the Serjeant's possession relative to his own family (of which he became the head upon his brother George's death in 1825), are dated 12 April, 23 Eliz. (1580), and 28 April, 40 Eliz. (1598), respectively, and make mention of Stephen, Lancelot, and George Bellasies, otherwise Bellesses, of Marton, Westmorland, as being admitted to Woodhill and Mill Alley, there held of Philip, Lord Wharton, for a term of years. The name of Bellasis is also found in Northumberland, and Durham ; and later on in Yorkshire, through Anthony and Richard Bellasis receiving, as Commissioners of Henry VIII., church lands therein. Their descendants became extinct in the male line on the death, in 1815, of the last Lord Fauconberg, a Catholic priest of that Church which had been despoiled by his ancestors in the sixteenth century.

George Bellasis of Longmarton, Westmorland, married, in 1655. He and his son George (born in 1656), were both holding Marton Low Moor of another Philip, Lord Wharton, in 1681.[1] The son, whose initials still appear on a house dated 1715, married, in 1683, Elizabeth, daughter of John Furnas of Dufton, Westmorland (two of whose nephews, John and Thomas Furnas, graduated at Queen's College, Oxford, in 1706—1712), and they had an only son Joseph, born in 1691, who married in 1727 Margaret, daughter of Hugh Hill of Crackenthorpe, Westmorland, niece of the Rev. Dr. John Hill, and sister of the Rev. Dr. Benjamin Hill, both of Queen's (1693, 1720), and Fellows of their College, the former being nicknamed "the Major," because of his connection with the Oxford University Volunteers at the earlier Rebellion of 1715.[2] Joseph and

---

[1] The father's will was proved at Carlisle in 1703-4. and is endorsed, "Testamentum George Bellases, Longmarton." He describes himself as being "sounde in mind and memory, praised be God for it," and adds : "I bequeath my soule into ye hands of Almighty God my Maker, hopeing for salvation through ye merits of Jesus Christ my onely Savior and Redeemer."

[2] By Joseph's will, proved at Carlisle in 1767, wherein he describes himself as "of Longmarton, gentleman," he divides his estate into three parts, for his wife Margaret, his daughter Margaret, and his son Hugh, respectively.

Margaret had three sons, Dr. Bellasis (the Serjeant's father), Hugh Bellasis, born in 1740, whose male descendants are extinct, and General John Bellasis, born in 1743, of whose sons, by Anne Martha Hutchins, only child of the historian of Dorset, may be mentioned General Edward, born in 1781, and Colonel Daniel, who received a gold medal for the Egyptian campaign of 1801. The late General John Bellasis, born in 1806, was their nephew.

Dr. Bellasis had also four sisters: Elizabeth, born in 1728, and wife of the Rev. William Kilner, Rector of Dufton; Emma, born in 1732, and wife of the Rev. Nathaniel Springett, B.A., of Brasenose College, Oxford; Hannah, born in 1735, and wife of Thomas Crosby, of Kirkby Thore, Westmorland; and Margaret, born in 1738, who married her first cousin, John Hill, of Crackenthorpe.

About the two half-brothers of the Serjeant, the following extracts from the *Bengal Telegraph*, February 1, 1800, and from the *Bombay Courier*, October 22, 1825, respectively, ought possibly to be relegated to the "Curiosities of Literature."

Of General J. H. Bellasis: "His courage bordered on temerity, his integrity was irreproachable, his generosity unbounded, and his liberal mode of thinking rare and honourable. He was a fine Greek and Latin scholar; a man of letters. . . . In music he was perfect, and in painting much above mediocrity. He was an excellent engineer, uncommonly skilled in military tactics. In his manners he was not only affable, open, and conciliating, but enchanting. . . . His memory will be cherished and respected by every person acquainted with his many amiable, useful, and dignified qualities. His person was tall and handsome, and there was something very engaging in his countenance. He was a man of uncommon ingenuity and elegant taste, and we may justly mourn his loss in the language of Horace:

> Quis desiderio sic pudor aut modus,
> Tam cari capitis."

Of Colonel G. B. Bellasis: "Death has deprived us of Colonel Bellasis, the life of every party:

> Bellasis, the brilliant and the gay,
> The boon companion of the social day,
> The war-tried warrior and the time-tried friend,
> Whose spirit Fate could neither break nor bend.

The board that spread such welcome with its fare,
That strangers felt themselves no strangers there.
His was the voice whose laugh-inspiring sound
Flung the bright halo of enjoyment round,
The song whose melody each list'ner won,
The jest that glanc'd at all and wounded none.
The genuine tale inimitably told,
The mirth whose influence like enchantment roll'd,
And charm'd the young, and more than cheer'd the old."

APPENDIX B. (p. 49.

DRAFT OF PROPOSED ADDRESS FROM LAWYERS TO THE PRIMATE, 1842.

"We, the undersigned members of the profession of the Law, have been informed that an Address has lately been presented to your Grace from certain lay inhabitants of Cheltenham, stating that they regard with dismay the recent development of the views inculcated by the authors of the *Tracts for the Times*, and are persuaded that many of their writings are utterly repugnant to the Word of God, at variance with the plain meaning of the Articles, Liturgy, and Homilies of the Church of England, and contain the essence of many of the most fatal errors of the Church of Rome, and entreating your Grace to take such measures as to your Grace may seem most advisable for the Episcopal Bench to declare, authoritatively, their united disapprobation of those opinions ; and we have been further informed that your Grace has returned an answer to the parties who signed the Address, assuring them that in compliance with their wish, you will give your grave consideration to it.

"We do not presume as laymen to approach your Grace with any expression of our own opinions upon the writings alluded to, or the doctrines contained therein, but we trust we may without impropriety represent to your Grace that we have reason to believe that there are many members of the Church of England who hold the opinions apparently sought to be condemned, and who honestly believe them to be in accordance with her teaching, and we fear that any authoritative condemnation of such opinions by the Episcopal body at the present time might cause the estrangement from our communion of

N

many good and earnest persons who are sincerely desirous of remaining in it from conscientious motives.

"We believe also that there are many others whose minds are at present in an unsettled and excited state, and who would be much distressed and probably driven to hasty and ill-considered conclusions if they were compelled to make up their minds suddenly upon the points in question, we, therefore, trust that even if your Grace should think fit to take any steps towards such a decision, it will at least be delayed until the conflicting opinions are better understood, and a quieter spirit prevails.

"But we especially entreat your Grace that you will not countenance any attempt to alter the formularies of our Church, or to rule their sense by any exclusive interpretation, or to obtain any formal decision condemning any doctrine or practice not now condemned therein, by any authority less than that upon which we now receive them, namely, the Convocation of Archbishops, Bishops, and Clergy, the only Ecclesiastical body lawfully representing the English Church.

"We should not have addressed your Grace on the subject but for the unusual nature of the request made to you, and the tenor of your Grace's reply, and trusting that your Grace will now pardon any irregularity in our mode of addressing you, We are, &c."

APPENDIX C. (p. 68.)

Mr. Serjeant Bellasis' pamphlet, *The Judicial Committee of the Privy Council,* &c., begins with the following advertisement :

A Petition is in circulation, and proposed to be presented to Her Majesty, praying that the Church of England may have its own Courts for the determination of matters of doctrine; the writer, on being applied to, found himself unable to sign it, and the following letter contains his reasons. The prayer of the Petition is subjoined :

"Your Petitioners, therefore, humbly pray that, in order to the redress of the above grievance, your Majesty will be pleased to grant licence to the Church, in Convocation or Synod, to deliberate, for the special purpose of devising a proper tribunal for determining, with the authority of the Church, all questions of doctrine and other matters purely spiritual.

"That your Majesty will be pleased to give your royal permission for leave to bring a Bill into Parliament for enacting that the judgment of such tribunal shall be binding upon the temporal Courts of these realms.

"That so the English Church may enjoy full freedom to exercise its inherent and inalienable office of declaring and judging in all matters purely Spiritual, to the welfare of your Majesty and of these realms, the salvation of souls, and the glory of its Divine Head.

"And your Petitioners, as in duty bound, will ever pray, &c."

In the letter dated from London, March 4, 1850, that follows, he says:

"I am afraid I expressed myself but in a confused manner this morning, when you did me the favour to call with the Petition to the Queen, and as I was not able to acquiesce in your request to me to sign it, perhaps you will allow me, somewhat more at my leisure, to tell you why.

"Your Petition is, that the Church, in Convocation, may be allowed to devise a tribunal for determining all questions of doctrine; and, that the judgment of such tribunal shall be binding on the temporal Courts of the realm.

"That any civil court or authority should have power to determine what shall be the doctrine of the Church, is, of course, altogether inconsistent with her sacred character and office. Such a Court could, legitimately, neither legislate upon doctrine nor interpret doctrine, any assumption of such a power would be an insupportable tyranny, and any grant of such a power, by the Church, would be an abandonment of its mission, and an abdication of its high office.

"But, at the period of the Reformation, the Church of England, under stress of circumstances, and, as some think, incautiously, entered into an alliance with the Sovereign, and also with the realm or State of England, of a more intimate character than that which had previously existed, and an arrangement, or, to speak plainly, a compromise, was gradually accomplished between the parties, whereby the Church, in consideration of certain supposed advantages to be conferred upon, or preserved to her by the State, agreed to confine her teaching within certain limits, which were defined and mutually agreed upon by the contracting parties, and whereby she agreed to place her legislative power as a Church under restraint, and bound herself to make no alteration in her laws or formularies without the consent of the civil power.

"Now, wherever there are mutually contracting parties, it is always possible that doubts may arise as to the tenor or construction of the contract, and some authority is necessary to solve such doubts; so, in the present instance, a tribunal, a civil tribunal, was agreed upon, to decide finally all differences which might arise, in regard to the contract so made between the Church and the State, and, as involved in that contract, all questions which might arise as to doctrines alleged to be included or excluded by the limit, within which the Church had agreed to confine her teaching.

"This tribunal was that which, while it existed, was called the Court of Delegates (the members of which were to be nominated wholly by the Crown, and might be all laymen), and this court had the right to determine in the last resort, all questions, not of doctrine properly so speaking, nor of interpretation of doctrine, that is, not of the truth or falseness of doctrine, but questions, whether this or that doctrine, true or false, was or was not included within the limits agreed upon.

"The Judicial Committee of the Privy Council, which has succeeded to the Court of Delegates, are now engaged[1] upon a question of this kind, involving, it is true, the consideration and interpretation of doctrine, as many other civil proceedings do, but only so far as it is necessary to determine whether a particular doctrine, or the denial of a particular doctrine, is or is not in accordance with the contract.

"Now, it is made a matter of objection and complaint that it is a mere body of lawyers who are about to decide the pending question, whereas, in my judgment, lawyers are the very persons to decide it; they will decide it as they would decide upon the meaning of an Act of Parliament, that is, they will decide, by reference to the Church formularies (which in fact comprise the terms of the contract), whether the doctrine in question is or is not tenable in the English Church, and

[1] This letter was in type before the decision in the Gorham Case was given.

notwithstanding the outcry which is made against a decision by
'mere lawyers,' I am of opinion that their judgment ought to
be received as conclusive, and that it will be so received by the
laity of England, not as to the truth or otherwise of the
doctrine in question, but as to the *fact* of the doctrine, whether
true or false, being, or not being, within the limits to which the
Anglican Church is pledged. I go farther, I say that none but
laymen could decide such a question impartially; if the Court
had been a Court of Bishops, how could they do other than
decide according to what they might believe to be true doctrine,
seeing that every one of them, from their position, must long
ago have resolved the doctrinal question by adopting one or
other of those theories which now divide the Church, and at
the same time must have deemed their respective solutions
consistent with the Church formularies; whereas, on the other
hand, lawyers, such as those constituting the Judicial Committee, and whom all will admit to be amongst the acutest
and most distinguished of the English Judges, will, most
undoubtedly, apply their minds solely to the matter as it
comes judicially before them, with reference to the true construction of the Church formularies, and without reference to
their own theological opinions. For I repeat, *the question is not
whether what Mr. Gorham holds is heresy, but whether the
doctrine Mr. Gorham holds, heresy or not heresy, may be taught
in the Church of England,* according to her laws and formularies,
as they have been accepted and allowed by the State; and the
decision on this point will be considered to be that of competent
and impartial men, and will not only be entitled to weight, but
will have it.

"So long as the Church retained in her own hands the
power of laying down and defining her own doctrine, she alone
was the tribunal to determine whether any particular teaching
was or was not in conformity with it, but so soon as she
submitted, by agreement, to confine her teaching within certain
bounds, and to abstain from extending it without the consent
of the State, she necessarily admitted the principle of some
tribunal, *other than herself,* to determine disputed points; to
petition therefore, as you propose to do, that the Church herself
should be that tribunal, or have the control of it, would be to
claim the sole power of interpreting her contract with the
State, and to demand to act independently, although she has
submitted herself to control.

"But, it is said, the Church consented to the Court of Delegates, but she has never consented to the Judicial Committee. There are many answers to this; in the first place, as the Court of Delegates was entirely in the appointment of the Crown, so the Judicial Committee has had likewise, for its appointment, the consent of the Crown, the Crown in both cases no doubt acting under advice, so that there seems to be no great hardship in the exchange; if the Court of Delegates had subsisted till now, it might have consisted of the same or similar members, so that the objection is merely technical, if it be a valid objection at all.

"But, secondly, the Queen is the Supreme Head of the Church of England, and, as such, has, I suppose, the same power as that which was exercised by Henry VIII. and Queen Elizabeth, and other subsequent monarchs. Now let us take an instance of the exercise of this supremacy in former times by way of comparison; Queen Elizabeth, in her Commission to certain persons to consecrate Parker, dispensed, by her supreme Royal authority, with all Ecclesiastical laws whatever which were contravened or over-ridden by such Commission. Now, either she had this power or she had not, either she was right in this view of the extent of her supremacy, or she was wrong: if right, then the substitution of the Judicial Committee, a far less important act of supremacy, was right also; if wrong, the whole English hierarchy and priesthood, so far as Queen Elizabeth's dispensation was required, rises from an unsound foundation.

"But, thirdly, the Court of Delegates had been found inconvenient, a change was proposed, considered, and passed through Parliament without objection or protest on the part of the Bishops, and the present Judicial Committee was substituted; since that time, the new tribunal has been called into operation upon a point of doctrine, in the case of Escott *v.* Mastin, and judgment was given thereupon in the most open and public manner, and again no protest or objection was made; so that even if the substitution of the new tribunal has been a stretch of supremacy, it has been, with full knowledge, acquiesced in, both by the Bishops and by the Church in general.

"But there is a farther objection to your Petition, and one which deserves serious consideration: it prays that the decisions of the proposed Church Court should be binding upon the temporal Courts, that is, upon the State and realm of England,

and of course upon the Queen as the Head of it; it prays, in
fact, that the Church may be relieved from that control on the
part of the State, to which it deliberately consented at the
period of the Reformation; it proposes that the State should
submit absolutely to countenance such teachings as the proposed Church Court shall determine; but *are those clergymen
who sign this Petition prepared to submit to be themselves bound to
teach in accordance with the decision of such Church Court?*
Suppose, for instance, the new Church Court should determine
that Baptismal Regeneration is not held by the Church of
England, are you, and other High Churchmen, prepared to
submit to teach in accordance with such decision? because, if
you are not, how can you reasonably require *that the State shall
continue to submit to a teaching which you yourselves would
repudiate;* is not this like praying the State to allow itself to
be bound to what may be a sinking ship, reserving to yourselves
exclusively the right of escape? or, to change the figure, is it
not like decoying the elephant into a trap from which free
egress is reserved to yourselves?

"That the State should absolutely submit itself to the
judgment of the English Church, speaking by her own Courts,
would be a high claim to make, even if the Church herself, and
the various sections of it, were prepared unhesitatingly to
submit themselves to the judgment of the same tribunal; such
a claim would be consistent on the part of a body claiming
infallibility. But if no such claim is made on the part of the
Church of England, and if neither one nor other of the two
great parties in it, which are divided upon this question, would
so submit themselves, upon what principle is it that you demand
that the State should be bound to the car of the successful
competitor? Would you desire, in case of a decision against
Baptismal Regeneration, that the State should remain subject
to what you would deem erroneous teaching? And if not, by
what means do you propose that she should extricate herself,
after you have bound her to submit to the decision of the
Church Courts whatever they may be?

"I hear every one saying that we need not mind what the
decision of the Judicial Committee may be, that it has no
authority over our consciences: to this I quite agree, but,
depend upon it, it will not be a nullity on that account, *it will
inform us of a fact,* namely, what, in the judgment of honourable and impartial men, has been and is the true construction

of the Church of England formularies on the point in question;
and as to its having no authority, I do not understand that the
proposed Church Court, if formed, would be allowed by any
party to have *authority* over their consciences, should it decide
contrary to their convictions.

"These are the considerations which prevent me from
signing your Petition; you are beginning at the wrong end;
so long as there is a binding compact, between the Church and
State, that the Church shall confine her teaching within certain
specified limits, a demand for distinct Church Courts, which
shall have power to interpret the terms of the compact independently of the State, is, on the face of it, unreasonable; you must,
as a preliminary step, petition to be freed from the compact
which enslaves and controls you, and from the supremacy
which, even if reasonable when the Monarch was Monarch,
ceased to be so when other authorities were associated with
the Monarchy, if not substituted for it. Petition against the
'Act of Submission,' and the Royal Supremacy, or else
repudiate it, and then you may talk of independent Church
Courts.

"So long as the present compact subsists, there must be
some Court to interpret it, and, this admitted, you will not
easily obtain a more competent and impartial tribunal than the
present Judicial Committee of the Privy Council, and certainly
not by the introduction of an Ecclesiastical element; who is
there amongst your friends who would not have deemed the
tribunal before which the Gorham Case has been heard,
deteriorated in impartiality, if the Most Reverend and Right
Reverend Members of the Episcopal Bench, who were present
at the hearing, had been members of the Court instead of
assessors merely? The observation of the learned counsel for
the Bishop of Exeter, regarding the disadvantage he was under,
in having them in any way associated with the Court, only
expressed the general feeling."

APPENDIX D. (p. 22.)

"There is a very curious, and I think, interesting book," the Serjeant wrote to his mother, March 2, 1834, "about to be published by Mr. Forster, Dr. Jebb's chaplain, consisting of the correspondence of thirty years between Dr. J. and a Mr. [Alexander] Knox, a layman, upon all subjects, but chiefly on religious subjects, and the letters on both sides, many of which I have read, are exceedingly beautiful; some of them were written whilst the Bishop was a country clergyman in Ireland ; and speak of his pursuits and his prospects at that time, and the whole form a picture, and a very perfect one, of a mind believed by his friends to have been one of the purest and most chastened." He thus refers, we may as well add, to Jebb's death in a note to his mother, December 18, 1833: "You will, of course, have seen the account of the death of the excellent Bishop of Limerick. I certainly had been looking forward to spending many more pleasant hours in his gentle company, and quite look upon my acquaintance with him as a circumstance in my life, particularly as he rather seemed inclined to attach himself to me, and encouraged me to think that it was agreeable to him that I should come down whenever I pleased. He sent me a few days before his death, a present of Burnet's *Lives*, edited by himself, as a memorial."

APPENDIX E. (p. 29).

AN ANGLICAN'S PRAYER.

"Netley Abbey, August 1, 1840. *Pro defunctis.* O Lord, I beseech Thee, remember the souls of the Founders and Benefactors of Netley Abbey, and though the house they builded to Thy honour now lies desolate and in ruins, Thy sanctuary desecrated, Thy altar overthrown, grant that they may find a house not made with hands, eternal in the Heavens. Remember also all those who lived and worshipped in this place, holy bishops, reverent priests, and pious recluses, and especially all those who were driven from these walls with reproach and ignominy. Grant that they may be received into the same heavenly mansions, and a sure and full reward be given them of the Lord, at the resurrection of the just. Hear the solitary prayer of a stranger, who sees in these mouldering stones but the vestiges of an earnest faith in Thee; and though the names I pray for may never again be named in prayer to Thee, Thou knowest them, O Lord, for surely they are written in Thy book. Pardon aught amiss in this my prayer, and accept it through Jesus Christ. Amen."—E. B.

APPENDIX F. (p. 149.)

"In October, 1853," Mrs. Bellasis writes of another occasion whereat Cardinal Wiseman figured, "we were privileged to see one of the greatest functions of our religion in the translation of the relics of St. Theodosia, a martyr of Gaul, from the catacombs of Rome to Amiens, her supposed birth-place. It was a lovely day, and the procession, most beautifully organized, went out to the railway station to meet the remains. Banners and statues were carried, the old saints as it were going forth to meet their new companion. We saw all this with our friends the Scott-Murrays, outside the gates, and then, by a little manœuvering, managed to gain good places inside the Cathedral before St. Theodosia arrived. When the great gates were flung open, the organ pealed forth its strains, and all rising, rows upon rows of venerable curés and clergy were seen lining the nave. All round the choir, high up in the triforium, children waving palm branches had a beautiful effect and a poetic significance. Twenty-eight bishops assisted at the ceremonial, the vestments were a blaze of crimson and gold, the martyr's colours, and various choirs chanted. The sermon at the High Mass was preached in French by Cardinal Wiseman, who walked in the procession. In the afternoon the Bishop of Poitiers preached, a veritable *bouche d'or*. We were entranced, and I shall ever deem being permitted to see and hear the doings of *that* day one of the singular providences of our lives; for it confirmed our faith in the truth and inalienable grandeur and majesty of the Catholic Church."

APPENDIX G. (p. 13.)

A letter from Mr. Hope-Scott to the Serjeant, from Abbotsford, February 13, 1854, bears upon the Serjeant's diffidence and under-rating of his own abilities: "I am touched by his (the Earl of Shrewsbury's) confidence in me, though I can scarcely guess through whom, except Mr. Belaney, he can have heard of me. Of course I shall be ready to assist in all ways I can, but I say without the slightest intention to flatter that he is very fortunate to have placed himself so much in your hands. Do not shrink from anything he asks of you, as I know your powers, I think, better than you do yourself."

APPENDIX H. (p. 74.)

When Mr. (afterwards Lord) O'Hagan was nominated Chancellor of Ireland under Mr. Gladstone's Government, the Serjeant took occasion to write to him, December 18th, 1868, as follows: "Forgive the expression of my most sincere congratulations upon your arrival at so well deserved and distinguished a dignity. I pray that your country may long possess the advantage now secured to it in having a Lord Chancellor to whom it would be an impertinence in me to apply the adjectives which are ready to flow from my pen, and which I hear connected with your name wherever I go. I hope the good God will give you health and long life as well for the duties of your high station as to aid in the great social and political advancement of Ireland, now commencing, I believe, in earnest. I entreat you not to answer this note, but to take it as indicating the good-will and affectionate respect and admiration of yours, my dear O'Hagan, most truly, EDWARD BELLASIS." To which Mr. O'Hagan replied, December 25th: "I was in England when you wrote your most kind letter, and I can only now acknowledge and thank you for it. Most cordially I do thank you for the true friendship which breathes through every line; and which, I trust, I am capable of valuing at its high worth. God grant that I may even in a small degree

justify your good opinion, in sustaining responsibilities which
I have undertaken with a solemn and somewhat fearful sense
of their great gravity! . . . Praying that you may enjoy
abundantly the graces and blessings of this holy time, I am,
my dear Serjeant, your sincere and affectionate friend, THOMAS
O'HAGAN."

APPENDIX I. (p. 125.)

ON A CERTAIN WITTY LAWYER.

1

Of course you've all heard of the fam'd Killigrew,
A jester of ancient renown,
With a merry conceit, and a cunning one too,
As tradition has handed him down,
 His trade by report
 Was to joke with the Court,
 And with banter to tickle the Crown.

2.

With banter to tickle the Crown was his trade,
And a privileged jacket he wore,
And carried a sword, but of lath was the blade,
And he'd horns on his bonnet before.
 But 'twas thought that his light
 Was extinguish'd quite,
 That the day of such wittols was o'er.

3.

That the day of such wittols was o'er it was thought,
Then how favour'd, how fortunate we,
That the mantle of old Killigrew has been caught
By a lawyer of lofty degree,
 Whom the wits of the town
 Had proclaim'd as their clown,
 Such a masterly mimic was he.

4.

A masterly mimic was he whom the wits
Had compar'd with the motleys of old,
But the sceptre of lath the new jester omits,
Lo! chang'd to the mace of gold.
 And instead of a bonnet,
 With two horns upon it,
 A wig doth the visage enfold.

       E. B.

EARLY MORNING IN AN ALPINE PASS.

1.

Now rises Phœbus from his eastern bed.
His earliest beams like mighty arms outspread,
All else extinguish, even put to shame
Thee, fair precursor of the regal flame.
As yet the valleys sleep, and, clad in grey,
Await the thrilling touch of coming day,
Church, village, streamlet, struggling into sight.
Above, the bristling pines have caught the light,
Aloft again the snows of Alps arise,
Fit throne to grace the kingdom of the skies.
Thence seated may the mighty Jove look down,
The earth his footstool, and the light his crown.

2.

To earth again,— list how the village bell
Gives to the early dawn a saintly air,
And lines of peasants from all quarters tell
Religion is the foremost duty there.
This done we climb, but aye with slackening speed,
The mountain pasture, where the crickets sing,
And straggling herds, not without music feed,
Then, breathless, rest we by a limpid spring.
But see ! what change is this, those lurid clouds
Are rolling hitherward, their sharpen'd edge
Comes swiftly on, peak after peak it shrouds,
Whilst distant rumblings are the tempest's pledge.

ROSENLAUI.

Rocks upon rocks surround me, up they rise,
Topping the highest pines, and shooting far
Higher and higher in the azure sky,
Hiding it, but with hues so beautiful,
Distinct and clear they rise, but over all
Piercing the vault of heaven, higher still
The eternal snows look down,—what words can tell
Their beauty, or describe their purity.
Perchance above the throne of God may thus
To ravish'd eyes appear, for well I ween
No other forms on earth e'er met my eye
So white, so pure, so beautiful as these.   E. B.

INDEX.

O

www.ingramcontent.com/pod-product-compliance
Lightning Source LLC
Chambersburg PA
CBHW020100030726
47498CB00006B/1881